Spanish Scandals

Spanish Scandals: Risking It All

CAROL MARINELLI

CATHY WILLIAMS

TRISH MOREY

MIX
Paper from
responsible sources
FSC
FSC C007454

This book is produced from independently certified FSC™ paper
to ensure responsible forest management.

For more information visit: www.harpercollins.co.uk/green

Printed and bound in Spain
by CPI, Barcelona

MILLS & BOON

First Published in Great Britain 2020
By Mills & Boon, an imprint of HarperCollins*Publishers*
1 London Bridge Street, London, SE1 9GF

SPANISH SCANDALS: RISKING IT ALL © 2020 Harlequin
Books S.A.

The Playboy of Puerto Banús © 2013 Carol Marinelli
The Real Romero © 2015 Cathy Williams
A Price Worth Paying? © 2013 Trish Morey

ISBN: 978-0-263-28177-4

THE PLAYBOY OF
PUERTO BANÚS

CAROL MARINELLI

For Anne and Tony
Thank you for all your love and support.
It means so much.
cxxxx

CHAPTER ONE

'ESTELLE, I PROMISE, you wouldn't have to do anything except hold Gordon's hand and dance....'

'And?' Estelle pushed, pulling down the corner on the page she was reading and closing her book, hardly able to believe she was having this conversation, let alone considering going along with Ginny's plan.

'Maybe a small kiss on the cheek or lips...' As Estelle shook her head Ginny pushed on. 'You just have to look as if you're madly in love.'

'With a sixty-four-year-old?'

'Yes.' Ginny sighed, but before Estelle could argue further broke in, 'Everyone will think you're a gold-digger, that you're only with Gordon for his money. Which you will be...' Ginny stopped talking then, interrupted by a terrible coughing fit.

They were housemates rather than best friends, two students trying to get through university. At twenty-five, Estelle was a few years older than Ginny, and had long wondered how Ginny managed to run a car and dress so well, but now she had found out. Ginny worked for a very exclusive escort agency and had a long-term client— Gordon Edwards, a politician with a secret. Which was why, Ginny had assured her, nothing would happen or be expected from Estelle if she took Ginny's place as his date at a very grand wedding being held this evening.

'I'd have to share a room with him.'

Estelle had never shared a room with a man in her life. She wasn't especially shy or retiring but she certainly had none of Ginny's confidence or social ease. Ginny thought the weekends were designed for parties, clubs and pubs, whereas Estelle's idea of a perfect weekend was looking around old churches or ruins and then curling up on the sofa with a book.

Not playing escort!

'Gordon always takes the sofa when we share a room.'

'No.' Estelle pushed up her glasses and returned to her book. She tried to carry on reading about the mausoleum of the first Qin Emperor but it was terribly hard to do so when she was so worried about her brother and he *still* hadn't rung to let her know if he had got the job.

There was no mistaking the fact that the money would help.

It was late Saturday morning in London, and the wedding was being held that evening in a castle in Scotland. If Estelle was going to go then she would have to start getting ready now, for they would fly to Edinburgh and then take a helicopter to the castle and time was fast running out.

'Please,' Ginny said. 'The agency are freaking because they can't get anyone suitable at such short notice. He's coming to pick me up in an hour.'

'What will people think?' Estelle asked. 'If people are used to seeing him with you…'

'Gordon will take care of that. He'll say that we had an argument, that I was pushing for an engagement ring or something. We were going to be finishing soon anyway, now that I'm nearly through university. Honestly, Estelle, Gordon really is the loveliest man. There's so much pressure on him to appear straight—he simply cannot go to this wedding without a date. Just think of the money!'

Estelle couldn't stop thinking about the money.

Attending this wedding would mean that she could pay her brother's mortgage for an entire month, as well as a couple of his bills.

Okay, it wouldn't entirely solve their dilemma, but it would buy Andrew and his young family a little bit more time and, given all they had been through this past year, and all that was still to come, they could certainly use the reprieve.

Andrew had done so much for her—had put his own life on hold to make sure that Estelle's life carried on as normally as possible when their parents had died when Estelle was seventeen.

It was time for Estelle to step up, just as Andrew had.

'Okay.' Estelle took a deep breath and her decision was made. 'Ring and say that I'll come.'

'I've already told him that you've agreed,' Ginny admitted. 'Estelle, don't look at me like that. I know how badly you need the money and I simply couldn't bear to tell Gordon that I didn't have someone else lined up.'

Ginny looked more closely at Estelle. Her long black hair was pulled back in a ponytail, her very pale skin was without a blemish, and there was no last night's make-up smudged under Estelle's green eyes because Estelle rarely wore any. Ginny was trying not to show it but she was actually more than a little nervous as to what a made-up Estelle would look like and whether or not she could carry it off.

'You need to get ready. I'll help with your hair and things.'

'You're not coming near me with that cough,' Estelle said. 'I can manage.' She looked at Ginny's doubtful expression. 'We can all look like tarts if we have to.' She smiled and Ginny laughed. 'Though I don't actually have anything I can wear...would anyone notice if I wore something of yours?'

'I bought a new dress for the wedding.' Ginny headed to the wardrobe in her bedroom and Estelle followed.

Estelle's jaw dropped when she held the flimsy gold fabric up.

'Does that go under the dress?'

'It looks stunning on.'

'On *you*, perhaps...' Estelle said, because Ginny was a lot slimmer and had a tiny pert bust, whereas, though small, Estelle was curvy. 'I'm going to look like...'

'Which is the whole point.' Ginny grinned. 'Honestly, Estelle, if you just relax you'll have fun.'

'I doubt it,' Estelle said, wrapping her long dark hair in heated rollers at Ginny's dressing table, and setting to work on her face under her housemate's very watchful eye. Gordon was supposed to be a womanizer, and somehow Estelle had to get the balance right between looking as if she adored him while being far, far too young for him too.

'You need more foundation.'

'More?' Estelle already felt as if she had an inch on.

'And lashings of mascara.'

Ginny watched as Estelle took out the heated rollers and her long dark hair tumbled into ringlets. 'Okay, loads of hairspray...' Ginny said. 'Oh, and by the way, Gordon calls me Virginia, just in case anyone mentions me.'

Ginny blinked a few times when Estelle turned around. The smoky grey eyeshadow and layers of mascara brought out the emerald in her green eyes, and the make-up accentuated Estelle's full lips. Seeing the long black curls framing her friend's petite face, Ginny started to believe that Estelle could carry this off.

'You look amazing! Let's see you in the dress.'

'Won't I change there?'

'Gordon's schedule is too busy. Once you land I would imagine you'll be straight into the wedding.'

The dress was beautiful—sheer and gold, it clung everywhere. It was far too revealing but it was delicious too. Ginny gaped when Estelle wobbled on very high shoes.

'I think Gordon might dump me.'

'This,' Estelle said firmly, 'is a one-off.'

'That's what I said when I first started at the agency,' Ginny admitted. 'But if it goes well…'

'Don't even *think* it!' Estelle said as a car tooted in the street.

'You'll be fine,' Ginny said as Estelle nearly jumped out of her skin. 'You look stunning. I know you can do this.'

Estelle clung onto that as she stepped out of her cheap student accommodation home. Teetering on the unfamiliar high heels, she walked out of the drive and towards a sleek silver car, more than a little terrified to meet the politician.

'I have amazing taste!'

Gordon greeted her with a smile as his driver held open the door and Estelle climbed in. He was chubby, dressed in full Scottish regalia, and he made her smile even before she'd properly sat down.

'And you've got far better legs than me! I feel ridiculous in a kilt.'

Instantly he made her relax.

As the car headed for the airport he brought Estelle up to speed. 'We met two weeks ago…'

'Where?' Estelle asked.

'At Dario's…'

'Dario who?'

Gordon laughed. 'You really don't know anything, do you? It's a bar in Soho—sugar daddy heaven.'

'Oh, God...' she groaned.

'Do you work?' Gordon asked.

'Part-time at the library.'

'Maybe don't mention that. Just say you do a little bit of modelling,' Gordon suggested. 'Keep it all very vague, or say that right now keeping Gordon happy is a full-time job.' Estelle blushed and Gordon noticed. 'I know. Awful, isn't it? I seem to have created this terrible persona.'

'I'm worried that I shan't be able to pull it off.'

'You'll be fine,' Gordon said, and he went through everything with her again.

They practised their story over and over on the short flight to Edinburgh. He even asked after her brother and niece, and she was surprised that he knew about their plight.

'Virginia and I have become good friends this past year,' Gordon said. 'She was ever so upset for you when your brother had his accident and when the baby was born so unwell...' He gave her hand a squeeze. 'How is she now?'

'Waiting for surgery.'

'Just remember that you're helping them,' Gordon said as they transferred to the helicopter that would take them to the castle where the very exclusive wedding was being held.

As they walked across the immaculate lawn Gordon took her hand and she was grateful to hold onto it. He really was nice—if they had met under any other circumstances she would be looking forward to this evening.

'I can't wait to get inside the castle,' Estelle admitted. She'd already told Gordon she was studying ancient architecture.

'There won't be much time for exploring,' Gordon said. 'We'll be shown to our room and there will just be time

to freshen up and touch up your hair and make-up before
we head down for the wedding.'

'Okay.'

'And just remember,' Gordon said, 'this time tomorrow it will all be over and you'll never have to see any of
them again.'

CHAPTER TWO

THE SOUND OF seagulls and the distant throb of music didn't wake Raúl from his slumber; instead they were the sounds that soothed him when he was startled in his sleep. He lay there, heart pounding for a moment, telling himself it was just a dream, while knowing that it was a memory that had jolted him awake.

The gentle motion of his berthed yacht almost tempted him back to sleep, but then he remembered that he was supposed to be meeting with his father.

Raúl forced his eyes open and stared at the tousled blonde hair on his pillow.

'Buenos días,' she purred.

'Buenos días.' Raúl responded, but instead of moving towards her he turned onto his back.

'What time do we leave for the wedding?'

Raúl closed his eyes at her presumption. He had never actually asked Kelly to join him as his guest, but that was the trouble with dating your PA—she knew your diary. The wedding was to be held this evening in the Scottish Highlands. It was nothing for Raúl to fly from Spain to Scotland for a wedding, but Kelly clearly thought that a few weeks out of his office and in his bed meant she was automatically invited.

'I'll speak to you about that later,' Raúl said, glancing at the clock. 'Right now I have to meet with my father.'

'Raúl…' Kelly turned to him in a move that was suggestive.

'Later,' he said, and climbed out of bed. 'I am supposed to be meeting with him in ten minutes.'

'That wouldn't have stopped you before.'

He took the stairs and walked up onto the deck, picking his way through the debris and the evidence of another wild Raúl Sanchez Fuente party. A maid was already starting the mammoth clean up and she gave a cheery wave to Raúl.

'*Gracias,*' she said as he gave her a substantial cash bonus without apologising for the mess. She did not mind his excesses—Raúl paid and treated her well, unlike the owners of some of the yachts, who expected her to work without complaint for very little.

Raúl put on his shades and walked along the Puerto Banús marina, where his yacht was moored. Here, Raúl belonged. Here, despite his decadent ways, he fitted in—because he was not the wildest. Raúl could hear a party continuing on, the music throbbing, the sound of laughter and merriment carrying across the sparkling water, and it reminded Raúl why he loved this place. Rarely was it ever silent. The marina was full of luxurious yachts and had the heady scent of filthy money. Ludicrously expensive cars were casually parked, all the fruits of serious wealth were on display here, and Raúl—dishevelled, unshaven and terribly beautiful—blended in well.

A couple of tourists stumbling home from a club nudged each other as Raúl walked past, trying to place him. For he was as good-looking as any film star and clearly he was *someone*. People-watching was a regular activity in Puerto

Banús, for amongst the tourists and locals were the rich, the famous and the notorious too.

Raúl scored two out of three—though he *was* famous in the business world.

Enrique, his driver, was waiting for him, and Raúl climbed in and gave a brief greeting, and then sat silently as he was driven the short distance to the Marbella branch of De La Fuente Holdings. He had no doubt as to what his father wanted to discuss, but his mind was going over what Kelly had just said.

'That wouldn't have stopped you before.'

Before what? Raúl asked himself.

Before he lost interest?

Before the chase had ended?

Before she assumed that a Saturday night would be shared?

Raúl was an island.

An island with frequent visitors and world-renowned parties, an island of endless sun and unlimited luxury, but one who preferred guests not to outstay their welcome, only allowed the superficial. Yes, Raúl was an island, and he intended to keep it that way. He certainly didn't want permanent boarders and he chose not to let anyone get too close.

He would never be responsible again for another's heart.

'I shan't be long,' Raúl told Enrique as the car door was lifted and he climbed out.

Raúl was not looking forward to this conversation, but his father had insisted they meet this morning and Raúl just wanted it over and done with.

'Buenos días.' He greeted Angela, his father's PA. 'What are you doing here on a Saturday?' he asked, because Angela usually flew home to her family for the weekend.

'I am trying to track down a certain Spaniard who said he would be here at eight a.m.,' Angela scolded mildly. She was the one woman who could get away with telling Raúl how it was. In her late fifties, she had been employed by the company for as long as Raúl could remember. 'I've been trying to call you—don't you ever have your phone on?'

'The battery is flat.'

'Well, before you speak with your father I need to go through your diary.'

'Later.'

'No, Raúl. I'm flying home later this morning. This needs to be done now. We also need to sort out a new PA for you—preferably one you *don't* fancy!' Angela was less than impressed with Raúl's brief eye-roll. 'Raúl, you need to remember that I'm going on long service leave in a few weeks' time. If I'm going to train somebody up for you, then I need to get on to it now.'

'Choose someone, then,' Raúl said. 'And you're right; perhaps it would be better if it was someone that I did not fancy.'

'Finally!' Angela sighed.

Yes, after having it pointed out to him on numerous occasions, Raúl was finally accepting that mixing business with pleasure had consequences, and sleeping with his PA was perhaps not such a good idea.

What was it with women? Raúl wondered. Why, once they'd made it to his bed, did they decide that they could no longer both work *and* sleep with him? Raúl could set his watch by it. After a few weeks they would decide, just as Kelly now had, that frequent dates and sex weren't enough. They wanted exclusivity, wanted inclusion, wanted commitment—which Raúl simply refused to give. Kelly would be found another position—or paid off handsomely, if that was what she preferred.

'All your flights and transfers are arranged for this afternoon,' Angela said. 'I can't believe that you'll be wearing a kilt.'

'I look good in a kilt.' Raúl smiled. 'Donald has asked that all the male guests wear them. I'm an honorary Scotsman, you know!' He was. He had studied in Scotland for four years, perhaps the best four years of his life, and the friendships he had made there had long continued.

Bar one.

His face hardened as he thought of his ex, who would be there tonight. Perhaps he *should* take Kelly after all, or arrive alone and get off with one of his old flames just to annoy the hell out of Araminta.

'Right, let's get this done…'

He went to walk towards his father's office but Angela called him back. 'It might be an idea to have a coffee before you see him.'

'No need,' Raúl said. 'I will get this over with and then go to Sol's for breakfast.' He loved Saturday mornings at Sol's—a beautiful waterfront café that moved you out quickly if you weren't one of the most beautiful. For people like Raúl they didn't even bother with a bill. They wanted his patronage, wanted the energy he brought to the place. Yes, Raúl decided, he would head there next—except Angela was calling him back again.

'Go and freshen up and I will bring you in coffee and a clean shirt.'

Yes, Angela was the only woman who could get away with speaking to him like that.

Raúl went into his own huge office—which was more like a luxurious hotel suite. As well as the office there was a sumptuous bedroom, and both rooms were put to good use. Heading towards the bathroom, he glanced at the bed and was briefly tempted to lie down. He had had two, possibly three hours' sleep last night. But he forced himself on to the bathroom, grimacing when he saw himself in the mirror. He could see now why Angela had been so insistent that he freshened up before facing his father.

Raúl's black eyes were bloodshot. He had forgotten to shave yesterday, so now two days' worth of black growth lined his strong jaw. His usually immaculate jet-black hair was tousled and fell over his forehead, and the lipstick on his collar, Raúl was sure, *wasn't* the colour that Kelly had been wearing last night.

Yes, he looked every inch the debauched playboy that his father accused him of being.

Raúl took off his jacket and shirt and splashed water on his face, and then set about changing, calling out his thanks to Angela when he heard her tell him that she had put a coffee on his desk.

'Gracias!' he called, and walked out mid-shave. Angela was possibly the only woman who did not blush at the sight of him without a shirt—she had seen him in nappies, after all. 'And thanks for pointing me in this direction before I meet with my father.'

'No problem.' She smiled. 'There is a fresh shirt hanging on the chair in your office also.'

'Do you know what it is that he wants to see me about?' Raúl was fishing. He knew exactly what his father would want to discuss. 'Am I to be given another lecture about taming my ways and settling down?'

'I'm not sure.' Only now did Angela's cheeks turn pink. 'Raúl, please listen to what your father has to say, though. This is no time for arguments. Your father is sick…'

'Just because he is ill, it does not necessarily make him right.'

'No,' Angela said carefully. 'But he does care for you, Raúl, even if he does not easily show it. Please listen to him… He is worried about you facing things on your own…' Angela saw Raúl's frown and stopped.

'I think you *do* know what this is about.'

'Raúl, I just ask that you listen—I can't bear to hear you two fighting.'

'Stop worrying,' Raúl said kindly. He liked Angela; she was the closest thing to a mum he had. 'I have no intention of fighting. I just think that at thirty years of age I don't have to be told my bedtime, and certainly not who I'm going to bed *with*…'

Raúl got back to shaving. He had no intention of being dictated to, but his hand did pause. Would it be such a big deal to let his father think that maybe he was actually serious about someone? Would it hurt just to hint that maybe he was close to settling down? His father was dying, after all.

'Wish me luck.' Raúl's voice was wry as, clean-shaven and bit clearer in the head, he walked past Angela to face his father. He glanced over, saw the tension and strain on her features. 'It will be fine,' he reassured her. 'Look…' He knew Angela would never keep news from his father. 'I *am* seeing someone, but I don't want him getting carried away.'

'Who?' Angela's eyes were wide.

'Just an old flame. We ran into each other again. She lives in England but I'm seeing her at the wedding tonight…'

'Araminta!'

'Stop there…' Raúl smiled. That was all that was needed. He knew the seed had been sewn.

Raúl knocked on his father's door and stepped in.

There should have been flames, he thought afterwards.

Or the smell of sulphur. Actually, there should have been the smell of car fuel and the sound of thunder followed by silence. There should at least have been some warning, as he was walked through the door, that he was returning to hell.

CHAPTER THREE

ESTELLE FELT AS if everyone knew what a fraud she was.

She closed her heavily made-up eyes and dragged in a deep breath. They were standing in the castle grounds, waiting to be led to their seating, and some pre-wedding drinks and nibbles were being served.

Why they hell had she agreed to this?

You know why, Estelle told herself, her resolve hardening.

'Are you okay, darling?' Gordon asked. 'The wedding should start soon.'

He'd been nothing but kind, just as Ginny had promised he would be.

'I'm fine,' Estelle said, and held a little more tightly onto his arm, just as Gordon had told her to do.

'This is Estelle.'

Gordon introduced her to a couple and Estelle watched the slight rise of the woman's eyebrow.

'Estelle, this is Veronica and James.'

'Estelle.' Veronica gave a curt nod and soon moved James away.

'You're doing wonderfully,' Gordon said, squeezing her hand and drawing her away from the mingling wedding guests so that they could speak without being overheard. 'Maybe you just need to smile a bit more,' he suggested gently, 'and, I know it calls for brilliant acting, could you try and look just a little more besotted with me? I've got my terrible reputation with women to think of.'

'Of course,' Estelle said through chattering teeth.

'The gay man and the virgin,' Gordon whispered in her ear. 'If only they knew!'

Estelle's eyes widened in horror and Gordon quickly apologised. 'I was just trying to make you smile,' he said.

'I can't believe that she *told* you!'

Estelle was horrified that Ginny would share something as personal and as sensitive as that. Then again, she could believe it—Ginny found it endlessly amusing that Estelle had never slept with anyone. It wasn't by deliberate choice; it wasn't something she'd actively decided. More that she'd been so shell shocked by her parents' death that homework and books had been her escape. By the time she'd emerged from her grief Estelle had felt two steps behind her peers. Clubs and parties had seemed frivolous. It was ancient ruins and buildings that fascinated her, and when she did meet someone there was always a panic that her virgin status must mean she was looking for a husband. More and more it had become an issue.

Now it would seem it was a joke!

She'd be having strong words with Ginny.

'Virginia didn't say it in a malicious way.' Gordon seemed devastated to have upset her. 'We were just talking one night. I really should never have brought it up.'

'It's okay,' Estelle conceded. 'I guess I am a bit of a rarity.'

'We all have our secrets,' Gordon said. 'And for tonight we both have to cover them up.' He smiled at her strained expression. 'Estelle, I know how hard it was for you to agree to this, but I promise you have nothing to feel nervous about. I'm soon to be a happily married man.'

'I know,' Estelle said. Gordon had told her on the plane about his long-term boyfriend, Frank, and the plans they had made. 'I just can't stand the disapproving looks and that everyone thinks of me as a gold-digger,' she admitted. 'Even though that's the whole point of the night.'

'Stop caring what everyone thinks,' Gordon said.

It was the same as she said to Andrew, who was acutely embarrassed to be in a wheelchair. 'You're right.'

Gordon lifted her chin and she smiled into his eyes. 'That's better.' Gordon smiled back. 'We'll get through this together.'

So Estelle held onto his arm and did her best to look suitably besotted, ignoring the occasional disapproving stare from the other guests, and she was just starting to relax and get into things when *he* arrived.

Till that moment Estelle had thought it would be the bride who would make an entrance, and it wasn't the sight of a helicopter landing that had heads turning—helicopters had been landing regularly since Estelle had got there— no, it was the man who stepped out who held everyone's attention.

'Oh, my, the evening just got interesting,' Gordon said as the most stunning man ducked under the blades and then walked towards the gathering.

He was tall, his thick black hair brushed back and gleaming, and his mouth was sulky and unsmiling. His Mediterranean colouring should surely mean that he'd look out of place wearing a kilt, but instead he looked as if he'd been born to wear one. Lean-hipped and long-limbed, but muscular too, he could absolutely carry it off.

He could carry me off right now, Estelle thought wildly—and wild thoughts were rare for Estelle.

She watched as he accepted whisky from a waiter and then stood still. He seemed removed and remote from everyone else. Even the women who flocked to him were quickly dismissed, as if at any minute he might simply walk off.

Then he met her eyes.

Estelle tried to flick hers away, except she found that she couldn't.

His eyes drifted down over the gold dress, but not in the disapproving way that Veronica's had. Although they weren't approving either. They were merely assessing.

She felt herself burn as his eyes moved then to her sixty-four-year-old date, and she wanted to correct him—wanted to tell him that the rotund, red-faced man who was struggling with the heat in his heavy kilt and jacket was not her lover. Though of course she could not.

She wanted to, though.

'Eyes only for me, darling,' Gordon reminded her, perhaps picking up on the crackle of energy crossing the lawn. His glance followed Estelle's gaze. 'Though frankly no one would blame you a bit for looking. He's completely divine.'

'Who?' Estelle tried to pretend that she hadn't noticed the delicious stranger—Gordon was paying her good money to be here, after all—but she wasn't fooling anyone.

'Raúl Sanchez Fuente,' Gordon said in a low voice. 'Our paths cross now and then at various functions. He owns everything but morals. The bastard even looks good in a kilt. He has my heart—not that he wants it…'

Estelle couldn't help but laugh.

Raúl's eyes lazily worked over the guests. He was questioning now his decision to come alone. He needed distraction tonight, but when he had thought of the old flames that he might run into he had been thinking of the perky breasts and the narrow waists of yesteryear, as if the clock might have stopped on his university days. Instead the hands of time had moved on.

There was Shona. Her once long red hair was now cut too severely and she stood next to a chinless wonder. She caught his eye and then blushed unbecomingly and shot him a furious look, as if their once torrid times could be erased and forgotten by her wedding ring.

He knew, though, that she was remembering.

'Raúl...'

He frowned when he saw Araminta walking towards him. She was wearing that slightly needy smile that Raúl recognised only too well and it made his early warning system react—because temporary distraction was his requirement tonight, not desperation.

'How are you?'

'Not bad,' she said, and then proceeded to tell him about her hellish divorce, how she was now single, how she'd thought about him often since the break-up, how she'd been looking forward to seeing him tonight, how she regretted the way things had worked out for them...

'I told you that you would at the time.' Raúl did not do sentiment. 'You'll have to excuse me. I have to make a call.'

'We'll catch up later, though?'

He could hear the hope in her voice and it irked him.

Was he good enough for her father now? Rich enough? Established enough?

'There's nothing to catch up on.'

Just like that he dismissed her, his black eyes not even watching her as she gave a small sob and walked off.

What on earth was he doing here? Raúl wondered. He should be getting ready to party on his yacht, or to hit the clubs—should be losing himself instead of getting reacquainted with his past. More to the point, there was hardly a limitless choice of women in this castle in the Scottish

Highlands. And after what Raúl had found out this morning his own company wasn't one he wanted to keep.

His hand tightened on the whisky glass he held. The full impact of what his father had told him was only now starting to hit him.

So black were his thoughts, so sideswiped was he by the revelations, Raúl actually considered leaving—just summoning his pilot and walking out. But then a tumble of dark hair and incredibly pale skin caught his eye and held it. She looked nervous and awkward—which was unusual for Gordon's tarts. They were normally brash and confident. But not this one.

He held her gaze when she caught his and now there was only one woman he wanted to walk towards him—except she was holding tightly to Gordon's arm.

She offered far more than distraction—she offered oblivion. Because for the first time since his conversation with his father he forgot about it.

Perhaps he would stay. At least for the service…

A deep Scottish voice filled the air and the guests were informed that the wedding would soon commence and they were to make their way to their seats.

'Come on.' Gordon took Estelle's hand. 'I love a good wedding.'

'And me.' Estelle smiled.

They walked through the mild night. The grounds were lit by torches and there were chairs set out. With the castle as a backdrop the scene looked completely stunning, and Estelle let go of her guilt, determined to enjoy herself. She'd been on a plane and, for the first time in her life, a helicopter, she was staying the night in a beautiful castle in the Scottish Highlands, and Gordon was an absolute delight. Despite having dreaded it, she was enjoying herself, Estelle realised as they took their seats and she made more small talk with Gordon.

'Donald says that Victoria's so nervous,' he told her. 'She's such a perfectionist, apparently, and she's been stressing over the details for months.'

'Well, it all seems to have paid off,' Estelle said. 'I can't wait to see what she's wearing.'

Just as she'd finally started to relax as the music changed and they all stood for the bride, just as she'd decided simply to enjoy herself, she turned to get a first glimpse of the bride—only to realise that Raúl was sitting behind her.

Directly behind her.

It should make no difference, Estelle told herself. It was a simple coincidence. But even coincidence was too big a word—after all, he had to sit *somewhere*. Estelle was just acutely aware that he was there.

She tried to concentrate on the bride as she made her way to Donald. Victoria really did look stunning. She was wearing a very simple white dress and carried a small posy of heather. The smile on Donald's face as his bride walked towards him had Estelle smiling too—but not for long. She could feel Raúl's eyes burning into her shoulder, and a little while later her scalp felt as if it were on fire. She was sure his eyes lingered there.

She did her best to focus on the service. It was incredibly romantic. So much so that when they got to the 'in sickness and in health' part it actually brought tears to her eyes as she remembered her brother Andrew's wedding, just over a year ago.

Who could have known then the hard blows fate had in store for him and his pregnant bride, Amanda?

Ever the gentleman, Gordon pressed a tissue into her hand.

'Thank you.' Estelle gave a watery smile and Gordon gave her hand a squeeze.

* * *

Please! Raúl thought. *Spare me the crocodile tears.* It had been the same with Gordon's previous girlfriend—what was her name? Raúl smiled to himself, as he had the day they were introduced.

Virginia.

This one, though, even if she wasn't to Raúl's usual taste, was stunning. Raven-haired women were far from a rarity where Raúl came from, and for that reason he certainly preferred a blonde—for variety, two blondes!

He wanted raven tonight.

Turn around, Raúl thought, for he wanted to meet those eyes again.

Turn around, he willed her, watching her shoulders stiffen, watching the slight tilt of her neck as if she was aware of but resisting his silent demand.

How she was resisting.

Estelle sat rigid and then stood in the same way after the service was over, when the bride and groom were letting doves fly. They fluttered high into the sky and the crowd murmured and pointed and turned to watch them in flight.

Reluctantly she also turned, and she must look up, Estelle thought helplessly as two black liquid pools invited her to dive in. She should, like everyone else, move her gaze upwards and watch the doves fly off into the distance.

Instead she faced him.

What the hell are you doing with him? Raúl wanted to ask. *What the hell are you doing with a man perhaps three times your age?*

Of course he knew the answer.

Money.

And Raúl knew then what to do—knew the answer to the dilemma that had been force-fed to him at breakfast-time.

His mouth moved into a smile and he watched as her head jerked away—watched as she stared, too late, up into the sky. And he saw her pale throat as her neck arched and he wanted his mouth there.

A piper led them back to the castle. He walked in front of her and Gordon. Estelle's heels kept sinking into the grass, but it was nothing compared to the feeling of drowning in quicksand when she had been caught in Raúl's gaze.

His kilt was greys and lilacs, his jacket a dark purple velvet, his posture and his stride exact and sensual. She wanted to run up to him, to tap him on the shoulder and tell him to please leave her alone. Yet he had done nothing. He wasn't even looking over his shoulder. He was just chatting with a fellow guest as they made their way back to the castle.

Very deliberately Raúl ignored her. He turned his back and chatted with Donald, asked a favour from a friend, and then flirted a little with a couple of old flames—but at all times he knew that her eyes more than occasionally searched out his.

Raúl knew exactly what he was doing and he knew exactly why.

Mixing business with pleasure had caused a few problems for Raúl in the past.

Tonight it was suddenly the solution.

CHAPTER FOUR

'EXCUSE ME, SIR.'

A waiter halted Estelle and Gordon as they made their way into the Grand Hall and to their table.

'There's been a change to the seating plan. Donald and Victoria didn't realise that you were seated so far back. It's all been rectified now. Please accept our apologies for the mistake.'

'*Oooh,* we're getting an upgrade,' Gordon said as they were led nearer to the front.

Estelle flushed when she saw that the rather teary woman she had seen earlier speaking with Raúl was being quietly shuffled back to the bowels of the hall. Estelle knew even before they arrived at the new table which one it would be.

Raúl did not look up as they made their way over. Not until they were being shown into their seats.

She smiled a greeting to Veronica and James, but could not even attempt one for Raúl—both seats either side of him were empty.

He had done this.

Estelle tried to tell herself she was imagining things, or overreacting, but somehow she knew she was right. Knew that those long, lingering stares had led to this.

The chair next to him was being held out. She wanted

to turn to Gordon, to ask if they could swap seats but she knew that would look ridiculous.

It was a simple change of seating, Estelle told herself.

She acknowledged to herself that she lied.

'Gordon.' Raúl shook his hand.

'Raúl.'

Gordon smiled as he took the seat next to Estelle, so she was sandwiched between them, and she leant back a little as they chatted.

'I haven't seen you since…' Gordon laughed. 'Since last wedding season. This is Estelle.'

'Estelle.' He raised one eyebrow as she took her seat beside him. 'In Spain you would be Estela.'

'We're in England.' She was aware of her brittle response, but her defences were up—though she did try to soften it with a brief smile.

'Of course.' Raúl shrugged. 'Though I must speak with my pilot. He was most insistent, when we landed, that this was *Scotland.*'

She tried so hard not to, but Estelle twitched her lips into a slight smile.

'This is Shona and Henry…' Raúl introduced them as a waiter poured some wine.

Estelle took a sip and then asked for water—for a draughty castle, it felt terribly warm.

There was brief conversation and more introductions taking place, and all would have been fine if Raúl were not there. But Estelle was aware, despite his nonchalant appearance, that he was carefully listening to her responses.

She laughed just a little too loudly at one of Gordon's jokes.

As she'd been told to do.

Gordon was busy speaking with James, and for something to do Estelle looked through the menu, squinting because Ginny had suggested that she leave her glasses at home.

Raúl misconstrued it as a frown.

'Vichyssoise,' came his low, deep voice. 'It is a soup. It's delicious.'

'I don't need hand-holding for the menu.' Estelle stopped herself, aware she was coming across as terribly rude, but her nerves were prickling in defensiveness. 'And you failed to mention it's served cold.'

'No.' He smiled. 'I was just about to tell you that.'

Soup was a terribly hard ask with Raúl sitting next to her, but she worked her way through it, even though her conversation with Gordon kept getting interrupted by his phone.

'I can't even get a night off.' He sighed.

'Important?' Estelle checked.

'It could be soon. I'll have to keep it on silent.'

The main course was served and it was the most gorgeous beef Estelle had ever tasted. Yet it stuck in her throat—especially when Veronica asked her a question.

'Do you work, Estelle?'

She took a drink of water before answering. 'I do a bit of modeling.' Estelle gave a small smile, remembering how Gordon had told her to respond to such a question. She just hadn't expected to be inhaling testosterone when she answered. 'Though, of course, taking care of Gordon is a full-time job...'

Estelle saw the pausing of Raúl's fork and then heard Gordon's stab of laughter. She was locked in a lie and there was no way out. It was an act, Estelle told herself. Just one night and she would never have to see these people again—and what did she care if Raúl thought her cheap?

'Could you pass me the pepper?' came the silk of his voice.

Was it the fact that it had been asked with a Spanish accent that made the question sound sexy, or was it that she was going mad?

She passed it, holding the heavy silver pot and releasing it to him, feeling the brief warmth of his fingertips as he took it. He immediately noticed her error. 'That's the salt,' Raúl said, and she had to go through it again.

It was bizarre. He had said hardly two words to her, had made no suggestions. There were no knees pressing into hers under the table and his hands had not lingered when she'd passed him the pepper, yet the air between them was thick with tension.

He declined dessert and spread cheese onto Scottish oatcakes. 'I'd forgotten how good these taste.'

She turned and watched as he took a bite and then ran his tongue over his lip, capturing a small sliver of quince paste.

'Now I remember.'

There was no implication. He was only making small talk.

It was Estelle's mind that searched every word.

She spread cheese on an oatcake herself and added quince.

'Fantastic?' Raúl asked.

'Yes.'

She knew he meant sex.

'Now the speeches.' Gordon sighed.

They were long. Terribly long. Especially when you had no idea who the couple were. Especially when you were supposed to be paying attention to the man on your right but your mind was on the one to your left.

First it was Victoria's father, who rambled on just a touch too long. Then it was the groom Donald's turn, and he was thankfully a bit quicker—and funnier too. He moved through the formalities and, on behalf of himself and his new wife, especially thanked all who had travelled from afar.

'I was hoping Raúl wouldn't make it, of course,' Donald said, looking over to Raúl, as did the whole room. 'I'm just thankful Victoria didn't see him in a kilt until *after* my ring was on her finger. Trust a Spaniard to wear a kilt so well.'

The whole room laughed. Raúl's shoulders moved in a light, good-natured laugh too. He wasn't remotely embarrassed—no doubt more than used to the attention and to having his beauty confirmed.

Then it was the best man's turn.

'In Spain there are no speeches at a wedding,' Raúl said, leaning across her a little to speak to Gordon.

She could smell his expensive cologne, and his arm was leaning slightly on her. Estelle watched her fingers around the stem of her glass tighten.

'We just have the wedding, a party, and then bed,' Raúl said.

It was the first hint of suggestion, but even so she could merely be reading into things too much. Except as he leant over her to hear Gordon's response Estelle wanted to put her hand up, wanted to ask for the lights to come on, for this assault on her senses to stop, to tell the room the inappropriateness of the man sitting beside her. Only not a single thing had he done—not a word or hand had he put wrong.

So why was her left breast aching, so close to where his arm was? Why were her two front teeth biting down on her lip at the sight of his cheek, inches away?

'Really?' Gordon checked. 'I might just have to move to Spain! In actual fact I was—'

Gordon was interrupted by the buzz of his phone and

Raúl moved back in his seat. Estelle sat watching the newly wed couple dancing.

'Darling, I am so sorry,' Gordon said as he read a message on his phone. 'I am going to have to find somewhere I can make some calls and use a computer.'

'Good luck getting internet access,' drawled Raúl. 'I have to go outside just to make a call.'

'I might be some time.'

'Trouble?' Estelle asked

'Always.' Gordon rolled his eyes. 'Though this is unexpected. But I'll deal with it as quickly as I can. I hate to leave you on your own.'

'She won't be on her own,' Raúl said. 'I can keep an eye.'

She rather wished that he wouldn't.

'Thanks so much,' Gordon said. 'In that dress she deserves to dance.' He turned to Estelle. 'I really am sorry to leave you...' For appearances' sake, he kissed her on the cheek.

What a waste of her mouth, Raúl thought.

Once Gordon had gone she turned to James and Veronica, on her right, desperately trying to feed into their conversation. But they were certainly not interested in Gordon's new date. Over and over they politely dismissed her, and then followed the other couples at their table and got up to dance—leaving her alone with Raúl.

'From the back you could be Spanish...'

She turned to the sound of his voice.

'But from the front...'

His eyes ran over her creamy complexion and she felt heat sear her face as his eyes bored into hers. And though they did not wander—he was far too suave for that—somehow he undressed her. Somehow she sat there on her seat beside him at the wedding as if they were a couple. And when he looked at her, she felt, for a bizarre second, as if she was completely naked.

He was as potent as that.

CHAPTER FIVE

'IRISH?' HE CHECKED, and Estelle hesitated for a moment before nodding.

She did not want to give any information to this man—did not even want to partake in conversation.

'Yet your accent is English?'

'My parents moved to England before I was born.' She gave a tight swallow and hoped her stilted response would halt the conversation. It did not.

'Where in England are they?'

'They're not,' Estelle answered, terribly reluctant to reveal *anything* of herself.

Raúl did not push. Instead he moved the conversation on.

'So, where did you and Gordon meet?'

'We met at Dario's.' Estelle answered the question as Gordon had told her to, trying to tell herself he was just being polite, but every sense in her body seemed set to high alert. 'It's a bar—'

'In Soho,' Raúl broke in. 'I have heard a lot about Dario's.'

Beneath her make-up her cheeks were scalding.

'Not that I have been,' Raúl said. 'As a male, I would perhaps be too young to get in there.' His lips rose in a slight smile and he watched the colour flood darker in her neck and to her ears. 'Maybe I should give it a try…'

He looked more closely at Estelle. She had eyes that were a very dark green and rounded cheeks—she really was astonishingly attractive. There was something rather sweet about her despite the clothes, despite the make-up, and there was an awkwardness that was as rare as it was refreshing. Raúl was not used to awkwardness in the women he dated.

'So, we both find ourselves alone at a wedding…'

'I'm not alone,' Estelle said. 'Gordon will be back soon.' She did not want to ask, but she found herself doing just that as she glanced to the empty chair beside him. 'How come…?' Her voice faded out. There was no polite way to address it.

'We broke up this morning.'

'I'm sorry.'

'Please don't be.' He thought for a moment before continuing. 'Really to say we broke up is perhaps an exaggeration. To break something would mean you had to have something, and we were only going out for a few weeks.'

'Even so…' Still she attempted to be polite. 'Breakups are hard.'

'I've never found them to be,' Raúl said. 'It's the bit before that I struggle with.'

'When it starts to go wrong?'

'No,' Raúl said. 'When it starts to go right.'

His eyes were looking right into hers, his voice was deep and low, and his words interesting—because despite herself she *did* want to know more about this fascinating man. So much so that she found herself leaning in a little to hear.

'When she starts asking what we are doing next weekend. When you hear her saying "Raúl said…" or "Raúl thinks…"' He paused for a second. 'I don't like to be told what I'm thinking.'

'I'm sure you don't.'

'Do you know what I'm thinking now?'

'I wouldn't presume to.' She could hardly breathe, because she was surely thinking the same.

'Would you like to dance?'

'No, thank you,' Estelle said, because it was far safer to stay seated than to self-combust in his arms. He was sinfully good-looking and, more worryingly, she had a sinking feeling as she realised he was pulling her in deeper with each measured word. 'I'll just wait here for Gordon.'

'Of course,' Raúl said. 'Have you met the bride or groom?'

'No.' Estelle felt as if she were being interviewed. 'You're friends with the groom?'

'I went to university with him.'

'In Spain?'

'No, here in Scotland.'

'Oh!' She wasn't sure why, but that surprised her.

'I was here for four years,' Raúl said. 'Then I moved back to Marbella. I still like to come here. Scotland is a very beautiful country.'

'It is,' Estelle said. 'Well, from the little I've seen.'

'It's your first time?'

She nodded.

'Have you ever been to Spain?'

'Last year,' Estelle said. 'Though only for a few days. Then there was a family emergency and I had to go home.'

'Raúl?'

He barely looked up as a woman came over. It was the same woman who had been moved from the table earlier.

'I thought we could dance.'

'I'm busy.'

'Raúl…'

'Araminta.' Now he turned and looked at her. 'If I wanted to dance with you then I would have asked.'

Estelle blinked, because despite the velvet of his voice his words were brutal.

'That was a bit harsh,' Estelle said as Araminta stumbled off.

'Far better to be harsh than to give mixed messages.'

'Perhaps.'

'So…' Raúl chose his words carefully. 'If taking care of Gordon is a full-time job, what do you do in your time off?'

'My time off?'

'When you're not *working*.'

She didn't frown this time. There was no mistake as to what he meant. Her green eyes flashed as she turned to him. 'I don't appreciate the implication.'

He was surprised by her challenge, liked that she met him head-on—it was rare that anyone did.

'Excuse me,' he said. 'Sometimes my English is not so good…'

When it suited him.

Estelle took a deep breath, her hand still toying with the stem of her glass as she wondered how to play this, deciding she would do her best to be polite.

'What work do you do?' She looked at him. She had absolutely no idea about this man. 'Are you in politics too?'

'Please!'

He watched the slight reluctant smile on her lips.

'I am a director for De La Fuente Holdings, which means I buy, improve or build, and then maybe I sell.' Still he watched her. 'Take this castle; if I owned it I would not have it exclusively as a wedding venue but also as a hotel. It is under-utilised. Mind you, it would need a lot of refurbishment. I have not shared a bathroom since my university days.'

She was far from impressed and tried not to show it. Raúl, of course, could not know that she was studying ancient architecture and that buildings were a passion of hers. The castle renovations she had seen were modest, the rooms cold and the bathrooms sparse—as it should be. The thought of this place being modernised and filled to capacity, no matter how tastefully, left her cold.

Unfortunately *he* didn't.

Not once in her twenty-five years had Estelle even come close to the reaction she was having to Raúl.

If they were anywhere else she would get up and leave.

Or, she conceded, if they were anywhere else she would lean forward and accept his mouth.

'So it's your father's business?' Estelle asked, trying to find a fault in him—trying to tell herself that it was his father's money that had eased his luxurious path to perfection.

'No, it was my mother's family business. My father bought into it when he married.' He saw her tiny frown.

'Sorry, you said De La Fuente, and I thought Fuente was *your* surname…'

For an occasional model who picked up men at Dario's she was rather perceptive, Raúl thought. 'In Spain it is different. You take your father's surname first and then your mother's…'

'I didn't know that.' She tried to fathom it. 'How does it work?'

'My father is Antonio Sanchez. My mother was Gabriella De La Fuente.'

'Was?'

'She passed away in a car accident…'

Normally he could just say it. Every other time he revealed it he just glossed over it, moved swiftly on—tonight, with all he had learnt this morning, suddenly he could not.

Every man except Raúl had struggled in the summer heat with full Scottish regalia. Supremely fit, and used to the sun, Raúl had not even broken a sweat. But now, when the castle was cool, when a draught swirled around the floor, he broke into one—except his face drained of colour.

He tried to right himself, reached for water; he had trained his mind not to linger. Of course he had not quite mastered his mind at night, but even then he had trained himself to wake up before he shouted out.

'Was it recent?' Estelle saw him struggle briefly, knew surely better than anyone how he must feel—for she had lost her parents the same way. She watched as he drained a glass of water and then blinked when he turned and the suave Raúl returned.

'Years ago,' he dismissed. 'When I was a child.' He got back to their discussion, refusing to linger on a deeply buried past. 'My actual name is Raúl Sanchez De La Fuente, but it gets a bit long during introductions.'

He smiled, and so too did Estelle.

'I can imagine.'

'But I don't want to lose my mother's name, and of course my father expects me to keep his.'

'It's nice that the woman's name passes on.'

'It doesn't, though,' Raúl said. 'Well, it does for one generation—it is still weighted to the man.' He saw her frown.

'So, if you had a baby…?'

'That's never going to happen.'

'But if you did?'

'God forbid.' He let out a small sigh. 'I will try to explain.'

He was very patient.

He took the salt and pepper she had so nervously passed to him and, heads together, they sat at the table while he made her a small family tree.

'What is your surname?'

'Connolly.'

'Okay, we have a baby and call her Jane…'

How he made her burn. Not at the baby part, but at the thought of the part to get to that.

'Her name would be Jane Sanchez Connolly.'

'I see.'

'And when Jane marries…' he lifted a hand and grabbed a fork as he plucked a name from the ether '…Harry Potter, her daughter…' he added a spoon '…who shall also be called Jane, would be Jane Sanchez Potter. Connolly would be gone!' He looked at her as she worked it out. 'It is simple. At least the name part is simple. It is the fifty years of marriage that might prove hard.' He glanced over to today's happy couple. 'I can't imagine being tied down to another, and I certainly don't believe in love.'

He always made that clear up-front.

'How can you sit at a wedding and say that?' Estelle challenged. 'Did you not see the smile on Donald's face when he saw his bride?'

'Of course I did,' Raúl said. 'I recognised it well—it was the same smile he gave at the last wedding of his I attended.'

She laughed. There was no choice but to. 'Are you serious?'

'Completely,' Raúl said.

Yet he was smiling, and when he did that she felt as if she should scrabble in her bag for sunglasses, because the force of his smile blinded her to all faults—and she was quite positive a man like Raúl had many.

'You're wrong, Raúl.' She refused to play his cynical game. 'My brother got married last year and he and his wife are deeply in love.'

'A year.' He gave a light shrug. 'It is still the honeymoon phase.'

'They've been through more in this year than most have been through in a lifetime.' And she'd never meant to but she found herself opening up to him. 'Andrew, my brother, was in an accident on their honeymoon—a jet ski...'

'Serious?'

Estelle nodded. 'He's now in a wheelchair.'

'That must take a lot of getting used to.' He thought for a moment. 'Is that the family emergency you had to fly home from your own holiday for?'

Estelle nodded. She didn't tell him it had been a trip around churches. No doubt he assumed she'd been hauled out of a club to hear the news. 'I raced home, and, really, since then things have been tough on them. Amanda was already pregnant when they got married...'

She didn't know why she was telling him. Perhaps it was safer to talk than to dance. Maybe it was easier to talk about her brother and the truth than make up stories about Dario's and seedy clubs in Soho. Or perhaps it was the black liquid eyes that invited conversation, the way he moved his chair a little closer so that he could hear.

'Their daughter was born four months ago. The prospect of being a dad was the main thing that kept Andrew motivated during his rehabilitation. Just when we thought things were turning around...'

Raúl watched her green eyes fill with tears, saw her rapid blink as she tried to stem them.

'She has a heart condition. They're waiting till she's a little bit bigger so they can operate.'

He watched pale hands go to her bag and Estelle took out a photo. He looked at her brother, Andrew, and his wife, and a small frail baby with a slight blue tinge to her skin, and he realised that they hadn't been crocodile tears he had witnessed during the wedding ceremony. He looked back to Estelle.

'What's her name?'

'Cecelia.'

Raúl looked at her as she gazed at the photo and he knew then the reason she was here with Gordon. 'Your brother?' Raúl asked, just to confirm things in his mind. 'Does he work?'

'No.' Estelle shook her head. 'He was self-employed. He...' She put away the photo, dragged in a breath, could not stand to think of all the problems her brother faced.

Exactly at that moment Raúl lightened things.

'My legs are cold.'

Estelle laughed, and as she did she blinked as a photographer's camera flashed in her face.

'Nice natural shot,' the photographer said.

'We're not...' Oh, what did it matter?

'I need to move.' He stood. 'And Gordon asked that I take care of you.' Raúl held out his hand to her. This dance was more important than she could ever know. This dance must ensure that tonight she was thinking only of *him*—that by the time he approached her with his suggestion it would not seem so unthinkable. But first he had to set the tone. First he had to make her aware that he knew the sort of business she was in. 'Would you like to dance?'

Estelle didn't really have a choice. Walking towards the dance floor, she had the futile hope that the band would break into something more frivolous than sensuous, but all hope was gone as his arms wrapped loosely around her.

'You are nervous?'

'No.'

'I would have thought you would enjoy dancing, given that you two met at Dario's.'

'I do love to dance.' Estelle forced a bright smile, remembered who she was supposed to be. 'It's just a bit early for me.'

'And me,' Raul said as he took her in his arms. 'About now I would only just be getting ready to go out.'

She couldn't read this man. Not in the least. He held her, he was skilled and graceful, but the eyes that looked down at her were not smiling.

'Relax.'

She tried to—except he'd said it into her ear, causing the sensitive skin there to tingle.

'Can I ask something?'

'Of course,' Estelle said, though she would rather he didn't. She just wanted this duty dance to end.

'What are you doing with Gordon?'

'Excuse me?' She could not believe he would ask that— could not think of anyone else who would be so direct. It was as if all pretence had gone—all tiny implications, all conversation left behind—and the truth was being revealed in his arms.

'There is a huge age difference...'

'That's none of your business.' She felt as if she was being attacked in broad daylight and everyone else was just carrying on, oblivious.

'You are twenty, yes?'

'Twenty-five.'

'He was ten years older than I am now when you were born.'

'They're just numbers.'

'We both work in numbers.'

Estelle went to walk off mid-dance, but his grip merely tightened. 'Of course...' He held her so she could feel the lean outline of his body, inhale the terribly masculine scent of him. 'You want him only for his money.'

'You're incredibly rude.'

'I'm incredibly honest,' Raúl corrected. 'I am not criti-
cizing—there is nothing wrong with that.'

'*Vete al infierno!*' Estelle said, grateful for a Spanish
schoolfriend and lunchtimes being taught by her how to
curse. She watched his mouth curve as she told him in
his own language to go to hell. 'Excuse me,' Estelle said.
'Sometimes my Spanish is not so good. What I mean to
say is...'

He pressed a finger to her lips before she could tell
him, in her own language and rather more crudely, exactly where he could go.

The contact with her mouth, the sensual pressure, the
intimacy of the gesture, had the desired effect and silenced
her.

'One more dance,' Raúl said. 'Then I return you to Gordon.' He removed his finger. 'I'm sorry if you thought I
was being rude—believe me, that was not my intention.
Accept my apology, please.'

Estelle's eyes narrowed in suspicious assessment. She
was aware of the pulse in her lips from his mere touch.
Logic told her to remove herself from this situation, yet
the stir of first arousal won.

The music slowed and, ignoring brief resistance, he
pulled her in tighter. If she thought he was judging her,
she was right—only it was not harshly. Raúl admired a
woman who could separate emotion from sex.

Raúl needed exactly such a woman if he were to see
this through.

He did not think her cheap: on the contrary, he intended
to pay her very well.

She should have gone then—back to the table, to be ignored by the other guests. Should have left this man at a
safer point. But her naïve body was refusing to walk away;
instead it was awakening in his arms.

He held her so that her head was resting on his chest. She could feel the soft velvet of his jacket on her cheek. But she was more aware of his hand resting lightly on the base of her spine.

A couple dancing, each in a world of their own.

Raúl's motives were temporarily suspended. He enjoyed the soft weight that leant against him, the quiet of his mind as he focused only on her. The hand on her shoulder crept beneath her hair, his fingers lightly stroking the back of her neck, and again he wanted his mouth there, wanted to lift the raven curtain and taste her.

His fingers told her so—they stroked in a soft probing and they circled and teased as she swayed in time to the music. Estelle felt the stirring between them, and though her head denied what was happening her body shifted a little to allow for him. Her nipples hurt against his chest. His hand pressed her in just a little tighter as again he broke all boundaries. Again he voiced what perhaps others would not.

'I always thought a sporran was for decorative purposes only...'

She could feel the heat of its fur against her stomach.

'Yet it is the only thing keeping me decent.'

'You're *so* far from decent,' Estelle rasped.

'I know.'

They danced—not much, just swaying in time. Except she was on fire.

He could feel the heat of her skin on his fingers, could feel her breath so shallow that he wanted to lower his head and breathe into her mouth for her. He thought of her dark hair on his pillow, of her pink nipples in his mouth at the same time. He wanted her more than he had wanted any other, though Raúl was not comfortable with that thought.

This was business, Raúl reminded himself as motive returned. Tonight she would think of *his* lean, aroused body. When she was bedded by Gordon it would be *his* lithe body she ached for. He must now make sure of that. It was a business decision, and he made business decisions well.

His hand slid from beneath her hair down to the side of her ribs, to the bare skin there.

She ached. She ached for his hand to move, to cup her breast. And again he confirmed what was happening.

'Soon I return you to Gordon,' Raúl said, 'but first you come to *me*.'

It was foreplay. So much so she felt that as if his fingers were inside her. So much so that she could feel, despite the sporran, the thick outline beneath his kilt. It was the most dangerous dance of her life. She wanted to turn. She wanted to run. Except her body wanted the feel of his arms. Her burning cheeks rested against purple velvet and she could hear the steady thud of his heart as hers tripped and galloped. No one around them had a clue about the fire in his arms.

He smelt exquisite, and his cheek near hers had her head wanting to turn, to seek the relief of his mouth. She did not know the range of *la petit mort* or that he was giving her a mere taste. Estelle was far too innocent to know that she was building up to doing exactly as instructed and coming to him.

Raúl knew exactly when he felt the tension in his arms slowly abate, felt her slip a little down his chest as for a brief moment she relaxed against him.

'Thank you for the dance.' Breathless, stunned, she went to step back.

But still he held her as he lifted her chin and offered his verdict. 'You know, I would like to see you *really* cuss in Spanish.'

He let her go then, and Estelle headed to the safety of the ladies' room and ran her wrists under the tap to cool them.

Careful, she told herself. *Be careful here, Estelle.*

There was a blaze of attraction more intense than any she had known. What Estelle *did* know, though, was that a man like Raúl would crush her in the palm of his hand.

She looked up into the mirror and took out her lipstick; she could not fathom what had just taken place—nor that she had allowed it.

That she had partaken in it.

And willingly at that.

'There you are.'

Gordon smiled as she headed back to the table and she could not feel more guilty: she'd even failed as an escort.

'I'm so sorry to have left you—some foreign minister wanted to speak urgently with me, but we couldn't get him on the line and when we did…' Gordon gave a weary smile. 'He had no idea what he wanted to speak to me about. I've been going around in circles.' Gordon drained his drink. 'Let's dance.'

It felt very different dancing with Gordon. They laughed and chatted as she tried not to think about the dance with Raúl.

Yes, she danced with Gordon—but it was the black eyes still on her that held her mind. Raúl sat at the table drinking whisky.

'I think you've made quite an impression. Raúl can't keep his eyes off you.'

She started in his arms. 'It's okay, Estelle.' Gordon smiled. 'I'm flattered—or rather my persona is. To have Raúl as competition is a compliment indeed.'

He kissed her cheek and she rested her head on his shoulder, and then her eyes fell to Raúl's black eyes that still watched and there was heat in her body, and she tried to look away but she could not. She watched his mouth move in a slow smile till Gordon danced her so that Raúl was out of her line of vision. Then, a moment later, her eyes scanned the room for him and prayed that the dangerous part of her night was now over.

Raúl was gone.

CHAPTER SIX

'SORRY!'

Gordon apologised profusely for scaring her, after Estelle had walked into the guest room much later that night to find a monster!

He whipped the mask off. 'It's for my breathing. I have sleep apnoea.'

Estelle had changed in a tiny bathroom along the draughty hall and was now wearing some very old, very tatty pale pink pyjamas that she only put on when she was sick or reading for an entire weekend. It was all she'd had at short notice, but Estelle was quite sure Gordon wasn't expecting cleavage and sexy nightdresses.

She offered to take the sofa bed—he was paying her, after all—but true to his word he insisted that she have the bed.

'Thank you so much for tonight, Estelle.'

'It's been fine,' Estelle said as she rubbed cold cream into her face and took her make-up off. 'It must be so hard on you, though,' she mused, trying to get off the last of her mascara. 'Having to hide your real life.'

'It certainly hasn't been easy, but six months from now I'll be able to be myself.'

'Can't you now?'

'If it was just about me then I probably would have by

now,' Gordon explained. 'Frank is so private, though—it would be awful for him to have our relationship discussed on the news, which it would be. Still, six months from now we'll be sunning it in Spain.'

'Is that where you're going to live?'

'And marry,' Gordon said. 'Gay marriage is legal there.'

Estelle was really tired now; she slipped into bed and they chatted a little while more.

'You know that Virginia has nearly finished her studies…?'

'I know.' Estelle sighed—not only because she would miss her housemate, but also because she would need to find someone else to share if she continued with *her* course. But then she realised what Gordon was referring to.

'She's starting work next month. I don't want to offend you by suggesting anything, but if you did want to accompany me to things for a few months…'

He didn't push, and for that Estelle was grateful.

'Have a think about it,' Gordon said, and wished her goodnight.

Estelle was soon drifting off, thinking not about Gordon's offer but about Raúl and his pursuit.

And it *had* been a pursuit.

From the moment their eyes had locked he had barely left her thoughts or her side, whether standing behind her at the wedding or sitting beside her at dinner. She still could not comprehend what had taken place on the dance floor; she had been searching for the bells and whistles and sirens of an orgasm, but how delicious and gentle that had been—how much more was there to know?

She didn't dare think too much about it now. Exhausted from a long and tiring day, Estelle was just about to drift off to sleep when Gordon turned on his ventilation machine.

Ginny hadn't told her about this part.

She lay there, head under pillow, at two a.m., still listening to the CPAP machine whirring and hissing. In the end she gave in.

She padded through the castle, her bare feet making not a sound on the stone floor. She headed to the small bathroom and took a drink from the tap, willing the night to be over.

Then she looked at her surroundings and regretted willing it over.

She stepped out onto a huge stone balcony, stared out to the loch. It was incredibly light for this time of the morning. She breathed in the warm summer night air and now her thoughts *did* turn to Gordon and his offer.

Estelle had already been coming to a reluctant decision to defer her studies and work full-time. It was all so big and scary—a future that was unknown.

She turned as the door opened, her eyes widening as Raúl stepped out.

He was wearing only his kilt.

Estelle would have preferred him with clothes on. Not because there was anything to disappoint—far from it— but the sight of olive skin, the light fan of hair on his chest and the way the kilt hung gave her eyes just one place to linger. There was nothing safe about meeting his gaze.

It was only then that she realised he had not followed her out here—that instead he was speaking on the phone.

He must have come out to get better reception. She gave him a brief smile and went to brush past, to get away from him without incident, but his hand caught her wrist and she stood there as he spoke into the phone.

'You don't need to know what room I am in…' He rolled his eyes. 'Araminta, I suggest that you go to bed.' He let out an irritated hiss. 'Alone!'

He ended the call and only then dropped Estelle's wrist. She stood as he examined her face.

'You know, without all the make-up you slather on…' His eyes searched her unmade-up skin. Her hair was tied in a low ponytail and she was dressed in a way he would not expect Gordon to find pleasing.

Raúl did.

She looked young—so much younger without all the make-up—and her baggy pyjamas left it all to Raúl's imagination. Which he was using now.

And then came his verdict.

'You look stunning,' Raúl said. 'I'm surprised Gordon has let you out of his sight.'

'I just needed some air.'

'I am hiding,' Raúl admitted.

'From Araminta?'

'Someone must have given her my phone number. I am going to have to change it.'

'She'll give in soon.' Estelle smiled, feeling a little sorry for the other woman. If Araminta had had a fling with him a few years ago and had known he would be here to-night—well, Estelle could see why her hopes might have been raised.

His phone rang again and he rolled his eyes and chose not to answer. 'So, what are you doing out here at this time of morning?'

'Just thinking.'

'About what?'

'Things.' She gave a wry smile, didn't add that far too many of her thoughts had been about him.

'And me,' Raúl admitted. 'It has been an interesting day.'

He looked out to the still, silent loch and felt a world away from where he had woken this morning. He didn't even know how he was feeling. He looked over to Estelle, who was gazing out into the night too, a woman who was comfortable with silence.

It was Raúl who was not—Raúl who made sure his days and nights were always filled to capacity so that exhaustion could claim him each night.

Here, for the first time in the longest time, he found himself alone with his thoughts—and that was not pleasant. But he refused to pick up to Araminta, knowing the chaos that might create.

It was Raúl who broke the silence. He wanted to hear her voice.

'When do you go back?'

'Late morning.' Estelle stared out ahead. 'You?'

'I will leave early.'

He walked to lean over the balcony, gazed into the night, and Estelle saw the huge scar that ran from his shoulder to his waist. He glanced around and saw the slight shock on her face. Usually he refused to offer an explanation for the scar—he did not need sympathy. Tonight he chose to explain it.

'It's from the car accident…'

'That killed your mother?'

He gave a curt nod and turned back to look into the night, breathing in the cool air. He was glad that she was here. For no other reason, Raúl realised, than he was glad. It was two a.m. in the second longest night of his life, and for the first one he had been alone.

'Can I ask again?' He had to know. 'What are you doing with Gordon?'

'He's nice.'

'So are many people. It doesn't mean we go around…' He did not complete his sentence yet he'd made his rather crude point. 'Are you here tonight for your brother?'

Estelle could not answer. She had agreed to be here for Gordon, yet she knew they both knew the truth.

'Do you have siblings?' Estelle asked.

There was a long stretch of silence. His father had asked that he not reveal anything just yet, but it would all be out in the open soon. Estelle came and stood beside him as she awaited his answer. Perhaps she would go straight to the press in the morning. Raúl actually did not care right now. He could not think about tomorrow. It was taking all his control to get through the night.

'Had you asked me that yesterday the answer would have been no.' He turned his head, saw her frown at his answer and was grateful that she did not push for more detail. Instead she stayed silent as Raúl admitted a little of the truth. 'This morning my father told me that I have a brother—Luka.' It felt strange to say his name. 'Luka Sanchez Garcia.'

From their little lesson earlier, Estelle knew they did not share the same mother. 'Have you met him?'

'Unwittingly.'

'How old is he?'

She asked the same question that he had asked his father, though the relevance of the answer she could not know.

'Twenty-five,' Raúl said. 'I walked into my father's office this morning, expecting my usual lecture—he insists it is time for me to settle down.' He gave a small mirthless laugh. 'I had no idea what was coming. My father is dying and he wants his affairs put in order. My affairs too. And so he told me he has another son...'

'It must have been the most terrible shock.'

'Skeletons in the closet are not unique,' Raúl said. 'But this was not some long-ago affair that has suddenly come to light. My father has kept another life. He sees his mistress in the north of Spain. I thought he went there so regularly for work. We have a hotel in San Sebastian. It is his main interest. Now I know why.'

Estelle tried to imagine what it was like, finding out something like this, and Raúl stood trying to comprehend that he had actually told another—how readily he had opened up to her. Then he reminded himself why. For his solution to come to fruition of *course* Estelle had to be told.

Some of it, at least.

He would never reveal all.

'His PA—Angela—she has always been…'

He gave a tight shrug. Angela had not been so much like a mother, but she had been a constant—a woman he trusted. Raúl closed his eyes, remembered walking out of his father's office and the words he had hurled to the one woman he had believed did not have an agenda.

'We have always got on. It turns out the son she speaks of often is in fact my half-brother.' He gave a wry smile. 'A lot of my childhood was spent with my aunt or uncle. I assumed my father was working at the hotel in San Sebastian. It turns out he was with his mistress and his son.' Black was the hiss that came from his mouth. 'It's all sorry and excuses now. I always prided myself on knowing what goes on, on being astute. It turns out I knew nothing.'

He had said enough. More than enough for one night.

'So, in answer to your question—yes. I have a brother.'

He shrugged naked shoulders and her fingers balled into her palms in an effort not to rest her hand on them.

'Unlike you, I care nothing for mine.'

'You might if you knew him.'

'That's not going to happen.'

She felt a small shiver, put it down to the night air. But his voice was so black with loathing it could have been that. 'I'm going to go in.'

'Please don't.'

Estelle had to get back—back to the safety of Gordon—yet she did not want to walk away from him.

She had to.

'Goodnight, Raúl…'

'Stay.'

She shook her head, grateful for the ringing of his phone—for the diversion it offered. But as she went to open the door she heard a woman's frantic voice coming down the corridor.

'Pick up Raúl. Where the hell are you?'

He had lightning reflexes. Quickly Raúl turned his phone off and pulled Estelle into the shadows.

'I need a favour.'

Before she knew what was happening she was in his arms, his tongue prising her lips open, his hand at her pyjama top. Estelle struggled against him before realising what was happening. She could hear Araminta calling out to Raúl, and if she saw the balcony any moment now she would come out.

But Araminta didn't. She stumbled past the balcony, the couple on it unseen.

He could stop now, Estelle thought. Except her pyjama top was completely open, her breasts splayed against his naked chest.

We *should* stop now, she thought as his tongue chased hers.

He made a low moan into her mouth; it was the sexiest thing she had ever heard or felt. He slid one hand over her bottom and his tongue was hot and moist.

Suddenly sending a message to Araminta was the last thing on Raúl's mind.

Estelle wanted his kiss to end, and yet she yearned for it to go on—like a forbidden path she was running down, wanting to get to the end, to glimpse again the woman he made her. It was a kiss that should not be happening, but it was one she did not want to end.

'Don't go back to him…' Raúl's mouth barely left hers as he voiced his command.

He had intended to speak with her at a later point, perhaps get her phone number, but having tasted her, having kissed her, he could not stand the thought of her in Gordon's bed. He would reveal his plan right now.

He peeled his mouth off hers, his breath coming hard on her lips. 'Come now with me.'

It was then that she fully realised her predicament. Raúl assumed this was the norm for her, that she readily gave her body.

As he moved in to kiss her again she slapped him. It was the only way she knew how to end this.

'You pay more, do you?' She was disgusted with his thought processes.

'I did not mean it like that.' Raúl felt the sting on his cheek and knew that it was merited—knew how his suggestion must have come across. But business had been the last thing on his mind. He had simply not wanted her going back to another man. 'I meant—'

'I know exactly what you meant.'

'Bastard!'

They both turned at the sight of a tear-streaked Araminta. 'You said you were tired, that you were in bed.'

'Can I suggest that you go back to your bed?' Raúl snapped to Araminta, clearly not welcoming the intrusion.

Estelle saw again just how brutal this man could be when he chose.

'How much clearer can I make it that I have absolutely no interest in you?'

He turned and came to help a mortified Estelle with her buttons, but her hand slapped him off.

'Don't touch me!'

She flew from the balcony and back to her room, stepped quietly in and slipped into bed, listened to the whirring of Gordon's machine, trying to forget the feel of Raúl's hands, his mouth.

Trying to deny that she lay there for the first time truly wanting.

CHAPTER SEVEN

'ESTELLE…'

Gordon was lovely when she told him what had happened. Well, not all of it. She didn't tell him about her conversation with Raúl, just that he had been trying to avoid a woman and had kissed her…

It was a terribly awkward conversation, but Gordon was writing her a cheque, so as not to embarrass her in front of his driver, and Estelle simply couldn't accept it and had to tell him why.

'Frank and I have three free passes.'

Estelle blinked as Gordon smiled and held out the cheque.

'We have three people each who, should something happen, wouldn't be construed as cheating with.' He gave her a smile. 'It's just a game, of course, and it's mainly movie stars, but Raúl could very easily make it to my list. No one can resist him when he sets his sights on them—especially someone as darling and innocent as you.'

'I feel awful.'

'Don't.' Gordon closed her hand around the cheque. 'My being in competition with Raúl Sanchez Fuente could only do wonders for my reputation, if word were ever to get out. It might even be the reason for our breaking up and me realising just how much I care for Virginia.'

'I'm sorry.'

'Don't be,' Gordon said, and gave her a kiss on the cheek. 'Just be careful.'

'I'll never see him again,' Estelle said. 'He doesn't know anything about me.'

'Mere details to a man like Raúl—and he takes care of them easily.'

Estelle felt the hairs on her arms stand up as she remembered that she had given him her name.

'Just do your hair and put on a ton of make-up and we'll head down for breakfast,' Gordon told her. 'If anyone says anything about last night just laugh and shrug it off.'

It was a relief to hide her blushes behind thick make-up. Estelle put on a skirt that was too short and some high wedges, and tied her hair in a high ponytail and then teased it with a comb and sprayed it.

'I feel like a clown,' she said to Gordon as she checked her reflection in the mirror.

'Well, you make *me* smile.'

Raúl had gone, and all Estelle had to endure were some daggers being thrown in her direction by Araminta as they ate a full Scottish breakfast. She was relieved not to see him, yet there was a curious disappointment at his absence which Estelle chose not to examine.

Finally they were on their way, but it was late afternoon before Gordon dropped her at her home.

'Think about what I said,' Gordon reminded Estelle as she climbed out.

'I think I've had my excitement for the year,' Estelle admitted as she farewelled him.

She let herself step into familiar surrounds and released a breath before calling out to Ginny that she was home.

'How are you feeling?' Estelle asked as she walked into the lounge.

'Awful!'

Ginny certainly looked it.

'I'm going to go home for a couple of days. My dad's coming to pick me up—I need Mum, soup and sympathy.'

'Sounds good.'

'How was it?

'It was fine,' Estelle said, really not in the mood to tell Ginny all that had happened.

Ginny would no doubt find out from Gordon, given how much the two of them discussed. Estelle was still irritated that Ginny told Gordon about her virginity but, seeing how sick Ginny was, Estelle chose to save that for later.

'Gordon was lovely.'

'I told you there was nothing to worry about.'

'I'm exhausted,' Estelle admitted. 'You didn't tell me about Gordon's sleep apnoea. I got the fright of my life when I walked in and he was strapped to a machine.'

Ginny laughed. 'I honestly forgot. Your brother's been calling you. A few times, actually.'

The phone rang then, and Estelle's heart lurched in hope when she saw that it was her brother. 'Maybe he's got that job.'

He hadn't.

'I found out on Friday,' Andrew said. 'I just couldn't face telling you.'

'Something will come up.'

'I'm not qualified for anything.'

Estelle could hear the hopelessness in his voice.

'I don't know what to do, Estelle. I've asked Amanda's parents if they can help—'

His voice broke then. Estelle knew the hell that would have paid with his pride.

'They can't.'

She could feel his mounting despair.

'Something will come up,' Estelle said, but she was finding it harder and harder to sound convincing. 'You've just got to keep applying for work.'

'I know.' He blew out a long breath in an effort to compose himself. 'Anyway, enough about me,' Andrew said, 'Ginny said you were in Scotland. How come?'

'I was at a wedding.'

'Whose?'

'I'll tell you all about it tomorrow.'

'Tomorrow?'

'I want to speak to you about something.' As a car tooted outside, Ginny stood. 'Andrew, I've got to go,' Estelle said. 'I'll call in tomorrow.'

Estelle didn't know how to tell Andrew she had some money for him, but anyway she knew that one month's mortgage payment would only be a Band-Aid solution. She was relieved that Ginny would be out for a few days because she really wanted some time to go over what she was considering.

The library was offering her more hours. Perhaps she could defer her studies and move in with Andrew and Amanda for a year, pay them rent, help out with little Cecelia, maybe even take Gordon up on his offer… Yes, she was glad Ginny would be away, because she needed to think properly.

'Your dad's here,' Estelle said.

'Thanks so much for last night, Estelle,' Ginny said, grabbing her bag and heading out of the door, waving to her father, who had climbed back into the car when he saw her.

Ginny was too dosed up on flu medication even to notice the expensive car a little further down the road.

Raúl noticed *her*, though—and a frown appeared on his face as he saw Virginia, Gordon's regular date, disappearing into a car driven by another older male. After Raúl's father's revelations he was past being surprised by anything, but there was a curious feeling of disappointment as he thought of Estelle and Virginia together with Gordon.

No.

He did not like the images that conjured, so he settled for the slightly more palatable version—that Estelle hadn't picked him up at Dario's; instead Estelle and Virginia must both work for the same escort agency.

He needed someone tough, Raúl told himself. He needed a woman who could separate sex from emotion, who could see what he was about to propose as a financial opportunity rather than a romantic proposition.

Except his knuckles were white as he clutched the steering wheel. Since last night there had been an incessant gnawing in his stomach when he thought of Estelle with Gordon. Now that gnawing had upgraded to a burn in the lining of his gut.

Estelle would be far better with him.

Was he arrogant to think so? Raúl pondered briefly as he walked up her garden path.

Perhaps, he conceded, but he was also assured enough to know that he was right.

'What did you forget…?' Estelle's voice trailed off when she saw that it wasn't Ginny.

Raúl preferred the way she'd looked last night on the balcony, but her appearance now—the short skirt, the heavy make-up, the lacquered hair—actually made things easier.

'What do you want?'

'I wanted to apologise for what I said last night. I think it was misconstrued.'

'I think you made things perfectly clear.' She drew in

a breath and then gave a small nod. 'Apology accepted. Now, if you'll excuse me?'

Her hand was ready to close the door on him. There was just a moment and Raúl knew he had to use it wisely. There was no time for mixed messages. He knew he had better reveal the truth up-front.

'You were right—I didn't want you to go back to Gordon, but not just because…' The door was closing on him so Raúl told her exactly what he was here for. 'I wanted to ask you to marry me.'

Estelle laughed.

After the tension of the last twenty-four hours, then her brother's tears on the phone, and now Raúl, standing absolutely immaculate in black jeans and a shirt at her door with his ridiculous proposal, all she could do was throw her head back and laugh.

'I'm serious.'

'Of course you are,' Estelle answered. 'Just as you were serious last night when you told me just how much you don't want to marry—ever.'

'I don't want to marry for love,' Raúl said, 'but I do need a bride. One with a level head. One who knows what she wants and goes for it.'

There was that implication again, Estelle realised. She was about to close the door, but then she looked down to the cheque Raul was holding—one with her name on it—and she saw the ridiculous amount he was offering. He surely wasn't serious. She looked up at him and realised that possibly he was—that he could pay for her services. As Gordon had.

Estelle gave a nervous swallow, reminding herself that whatever happened, whatever Raúl thought, she must not betray Gordon's confidence.

'Look—whatever you think, Gordon and I…'

'Should that be, Gordon, *Virginia* and I?' He watched her flaming cheeks pale. 'I just saw her leave. Are you both dating him?'

'I don't have to explain anything to you.'

'You're right,' Raúl conceded.

'How did you know where I lived?'

'I checked your bag when you were dancing with Gordon.'

Estelle blinked. He was honest, brutally honest—and, yes, she couldn't help herself. She was curious.

'Are you going to ask me in or do I stand and speak here?'

'I don't think so.' Common sense told her to close the door on him, but as she stared into black eyes curiosity was starting to win. Things like this—conversations like this—simply didn't happen to Estelle. But, more than that, she wanted to find out more about this man who had been on her mind from the second their eyes had locked.

'I ask for ten minutes,' Raúl said. 'If you want me to leave then, I shall, and I will never bother you again.'

He spoke in such a matter-of-fact voice. This was business to him, Estelle realised, and he assumed it was the same for her. She chose to keep it that way.

'Ten minutes,' Estelle said, and opened the door.

He looked around the small house. It was typical student accommodation, yet she was not your typical student.

'You are studying?'

'Yes.'

'Can I ask what?'

Estelle hesitated, not keen on revealing anything to him, but surely it could do no harm. 'Ancient architecture.'

'Really?' Raul frowned. Her response was not the one he'd been expecting.

She offered him a seat and Raúl took it. Estelle chose a

chair on the opposite side of the room to him. He wasted no time getting to the point.

'I have told you that my father is sick?' Raúl said, and Estelle nodded. 'And that for a long time he has wanted to see me settled? Now, with his death nearing, more and more he wishes to see his wish fulfilled—he has convinced himself that a wife will tame my ways.'

Estelle said nothing. She just looked at this man she doubted would ever be tamed; she had tasted his passion, had heard about his appalling reputation. A ring on his finger certainly wouldn't have stopped what had taken place last night.

'You might remember I told you my father revealed he has another son?'

Again Estelle nodded.

'He has said that if I do not comply, if I do not settle down, then he will leave his share of the business to my...' He could not bring himself to call Luka his brother. 'I refuse to allow that to happen.'

She could see the determination in his eyes.

'Which is why I have come this evening to speak with you.'

'Why aren't you having this conversation with Araminta? I'm sure she'd be delighted to marry you.'

'I did briefly consider it,' Raúl admitted, 'but there are several reasons. The main one being she would not be able to reconcile the fact that this is a business transaction. She would agree, I think, but it would be with hope that love would grow, that perhaps a baby might change my mind. It will not,' Raúl said. His voice was definite. 'Which is why I come to speak with you. A woman who understands a certain business.'

'I really think you have the wrong idea about me.'

'I am not here to judge you. On the contrary, I admire a woman who can separate love from sex.'

He did not understand the wry smile on her face. If only he knew. It faded as he continued.

'We are attracted to each other.' Raúl said it as a fact. 'Surely for you that can only be a bonus?'

Estelle blew out a breath; he was practically calling her a hooker and yet she was in a poor position to deny it.

'We both like to party,' Raúl said. 'And we like to live life in the fast lane—even if we know how to take things seriously at times.'

He was wrong about the fast lane, and Estelle knew if she admitted the truth he'd be gone. But, yes, she *was* undeniably attracted to him. Her skin was tingling just from his presence. Her mind was still begging for a moment of peace just to process the dance and the kiss they had shared last night.

He interrupted her wandering thoughts.

'Estelle. I have spoken with my father's doctor; it is a matter of weeks rather than months. You would only be away for a short while.'

'Away?'

'I live in Marbella.'

Now she definitely shook her head. 'Raúl, I have a life here. My niece is sick. I am studying…'

'You can return to your studies a wealthy woman—and naturally you will have regular trips home.'

He looked at her, with her gaudy make-up and teased hair. He chose to remember her fresh-faced on the balcony, recalled the comfort she had given even before they had kissed. He should not care, but he did not like the life she was leading. Suddenly it was imperative for reasons other than appeasing his father that she take this chance.

'I do not judge you, Estelle, but you could come back

and start over. You can live the life you want to without ever having to worry about the rent.'

Estelle stood and walked to the window, not wanting him to see the tears that sprang in her eyes because for a moment there he had sounded as if he actually cared.

'You certainly won't have to host dinner parties or cook for me. I work hard all day. You can shop. We'll eat out every night. And there are many clubs to choose from, parties to attend. You would never be bored.'

He had no idea about her at all.

'After my father's death, after a suitable pause, we will admit our whirlwind marriage cannot deal with the grief—that with regret we are to part. No one will ever know you married for money. That would be written into the contract.'

'Contract?'

'Of course,' Raúl said. 'One that will protect both of us, that will lay down all the rules. I have asked my lawyer to fly in for a meeting at midday tomorrow. Naturally it will be a lengthy meeting. We will have to go over terms.'

'I won't be there.'

He didn't look in the least deterred.

'Raúl, my brother would never believe me.'

'I will come with you and speak to him.'

'Oh, and he'll believe *you*? He'll believe we met yester-day and fell madly in love? He'll have me certified insane before he lets me fly off with a stranger—'

'We met last year.' Raúl interrupted her tirade. It was clear he had thought it all through. 'When you were in Spain. It was then that we fell madly in love, but of course with your brother's accident it was not the time to say so, or to make plans to move, so we put it down to a holiday romance. We met again a few weeks ago and this time around I had no intention of letting you go.'

'I don't want to lie to him.'

'You are always truthful?' Raúl checked. 'Does he know about Gordon, then? Does he know—?'

'Okay,' she interrupted. Because of course there were things her brother didn't know. She was actually considering it—so much so that she turned to him with a question. 'Would *your* family believe it?'

'Before I found out about my father's other life I chose to let him think I was serious about someone I used to date. It was not you I had in mind, but they do not know that.'

It could work.

The frown that was on her brow was smoothed, the impossibility of it all was fading, and Raúl knew it was time to leave.

'Sleep on it,' Raúl said. 'Naturally there is more that I have to tell you, but I am not prepared to discuss certain things until after the marriage.'

'What sort of things?'

'Nothing that impacts on you now—just things that a loving wife would know all about. It is something I would not reveal to anyone I did not trust or love.'

'Or pay for?'

'Yes.' He placed the cheque on the coffee table and handed her two business cards.

'That is the hotel my lawyer will be staying at. I have booked an office there. The other card contains my contact details—for now.'

'For now?'

'I am changing my phone number tomorrow,' Raúl said. 'One other thing…' He ran a finger along her cheek, looked at the full mouth he had so enjoyed kissing last night. 'There will be no one else for the duration of our contract…'

'It's not going to happen.'

'Well, in case you change your mind—' he handed her an envelope '—you might need this.'

She opened it, stared at the photo that had been taken last night. His arm was on the chair behind her, she was laughing, and there was Raúl—smiling, absolutely beautiful, his eyes on her, staring at her as if he was entranced.

He must have known the photographer was on his way, Estelle realised. He had been considering this even last night.

Raúl *had* rearranged the seating—she was certain of it now.

She realised then the lengths he would go to to get his way.

'Did you arrange for Gordon to be called away?'

'Of course.'

'You don't even try to deny it?'

He heard her anger.

'You'd prefer that I lie?' Raúl checked.

She looked to the mantelpiece, to the photo of her brother and Amanda holding a tiny, frail Cecelia. She was so tired of struggling. But she could not believe that she was considering his offer. She had considered Gordon's, though, Estelle told herself. Tomorrow she had been going to tell her brother she was deferring her studies and moving in with them.

She had already made the decision to up-end her life.

This would certainly up-end it—but in a rather more spectacular way.

She went into the kitchen with the excuse of making coffee, but really it was to gather her thoughts.

Bought by Raúl.

Estelle closed her eyes. It was against everything she believed in, yet it wasn't just the money that tempted her. It was something more base than that.

A man as beautiful as Raúl, for her first lover. The thought of sharing his bed, his life—even for a little while—was as tempting as the cheque he had written. Estelle blew out a breath, her skin on fire, aroused just at the thought of lying beside him. Yet she knew that if Raúl knew she was a virgin the deal would be off.

'Not for me.'

He was standing at the kitchen door, watching as she spooned instant coffee into two mugs.

'I'll leave you to think about it. If you do not arrive at the appointment then I will accept your decision and stop the cheque. As I said, tomorrow my phone number will be changing. It will be too late to change your mind.'

It really was, Estelle knew, a once-in-a-lifetime offer.

CHAPTER EIGHT

'I WILL FLY your family out for the wedding...'

They were sitting in Raúl's lawyer's office, going over details that made Estelle burn, but it was all being dealt with in a cool, precise manner.

'I will speak with your parents and brother.'

'My parents are both deceased.' Estelle said it in a matter-of-fact way. She was not after sympathy from Raúl and this was not a tender conversation. 'And my brother and his wife won't be able to attend—Cecelia is too sick to travel.'

'You should have *someone* there for you.'

'Won't your family believe us otherwise?' There was a slight sneer to her voice, which she fought to check. She had chosen to be here, after all. It was just the mention of her parents, of Cecelia, that had her throat tightening— the realisation that everything in this marriage bar love would be real and she would be going through it all alone.

'It has nothing to do with that,' Raúl said. 'It is your wedding day. You might find it overwhelming to be alone.'

'Oh, please,' Estelle responded, determined not to let him see her fear. 'I'll be fine.'

'Very well.' Raúl nodded. 'It will be a small wedding, but traditional. The press will go wild—they have been waiting a long time for me to marry—but we will not let them know we are married till after.'

They had been talking for hours; every detail from wardrobe allowance to hair and make-up had been discussed.

Estelle had insisted she could choose her own clothes.

'I have a reputation to think of,' had been Raúl's tart response.

Estelle was entitled to one week every month to come back to the UK and visit her family for the duration of the contract.

'I am sure we will both need the space,' had been Raúl's explanation. 'I am not used to having someone permanently around.'

There was now an extremely uncomfortable conversation—for Estelle, in any case—about the regularity of sex, and also about birth control and health checks. Raúl didn't appear in the least bit fazed.

'In the event of a pregnancy—' the lawyer started.

Raúl was quick to interrupt. Only now did he seem concerned by the subject matter being discussed. 'There is to be no pregnancy.' There was a low menace to his voice. 'I don't think my bride-to-be would be foolish enough to try and trap me in *that* way.'

'It still needs to be addressed.' The lawyer was very calm.

'I have no intention of getting pregnant.' Estelle gave a small nervous laugh, truly horrified at the prospect. She had seen the stress Cecelia had placed on Andrew and Amanda, and they were head over heels in love.

'You might change your mind,' Raúl said, for he trusted no one. 'You might decide that you like the lifestyle and don't want to give it up.' He looked to his lawyer. 'We need to make contingency plans.'

'Absolutely,' the lawyer said.

It could not be made clearer that this was all business. Estelle sat as with clinical detachment he ensured that he would provide for any child they might have on the condition that the child resided in Spain.

If she moved back to England, Estelle would have to fight against his might just to make the rent.

'I think that covers it,' the lawyer said.

'Not quite.' Estelle cleared her throat. 'I'd like us to agree that we won't sleep with each other till after the wedding.'

'There's no need for quaint.'

'I've agreed to all your terms.' She looked coolly at him. It was the only way for this to work. If he knew she was a virgin this meeting would close now. 'You can surely agree to one of mine? I'd like some time off before I start *working*.' She watched his jaw tighten slightly as she made it clear that this *was* work.

'Very well.' Raúl did not like to be told that sleeping with him would be a chore. 'You may well change your mind.'

'I shan't.'

'You will be flown in a couple of days before the wedding. I will be on my yacht, partying as grooms do before their marriage. You shall have the apartment to yourself.' He had no intention of holding hands and playing coy for a week. He waited for her nod and then turned to his lawyer. 'Draft it.'

They waited in a sumptuous lounge as the lawyer got to work, but Estelle couldn't relax.

'You are tense.'

'It's not every day you get offered a million dollars.' She could at least be honest about that. 'Nor move to Marbella...'

'You will love it,' Raúl said. 'The night-life is fantastic…'

He just didn't know her at all, Estelle realised yet again.

'How did your parents die?' Raúl asked, watching as her shoulders stiffened. 'My family are bound to ask.'

'In a car accident,' Estelle said, turning to him. 'The same as your mother.'

He opened his mouth to speak and then changed his mind.

'I just hope everyone believes us,' Estelle said.

'Why wouldn't they? Even when we divorce we'll maintain the lie. You understand the confidentiality clause?' Raúl checked. 'No one is ever to know that this is a marriage of convenience only.'

'No one will ever hear it from me,' she assured him. The prospect of being found out was abhorrent to Estelle. 'Just a whirlwind romance and a marriage that didn't work out.'

'Good,' Raúl said. 'And, Estelle—even if we do get on…even if you do like—'

'Don't worry, Raúl,' she interrupted. 'I'm not going to be falling in love with you.' She gave him a tight smile. 'I'll be out of your life, as per the contract.'

CHAPTER NINE

RAÚL HAD BEEN RIGHT.

Estelle stood on the balcony of his luxurious apartment, looking out at the marina, on the morning of her wedding day, and was, as Raúl had predicted, utterly and completely overwhelmed.

She had arrived in Marbella two days ago and had barely stopped for air since. Stepping into this vast apartment, she had fully glimpsed his wealth. Every room bar the movie screening room was angled to take in the stunning view of the Mediterranean, and every whim was catered for from Jacuzzi to sauna. There was a whole new wardrobe waiting for her too. The only thing lacking was that the kitchen cupboards and fridge were empty.

'Call Sol's if you don't want to go out,' Raúl had said. 'They will bring whatever you want straight over.'

The only vaguely familiar thing had been the photo of them both, taken at Donald's wedding, beautifully framed and on a wall. But even that had been dealt with by Raúl. It had been manipulated so that her make-up was softer, her cleavage less revealing.

It had been a sharp reminder that he thought her a tart.

Raúl knew the woman he wanted to marry, and it wasn't the woman he had met, so there had been trips to a beauty salon for hair treatments and make-up lessons.

'I don't *need* make-up lessons,' Estelle had said.

'Oh, baby, you do,' had been his response. 'Subtle is best.'

Constantly she had to remind herself to be the woman he thought he had met. A woman who acted as if delighted by her new designer wardrobe, who didn't mind at all when he told her to wear factor fifty-plus because he liked her pale skin.

But it wasn't that which concerned Estelle this morning as she looked out at the glittering sea and the luxurious yachts, wondering which one was Raúl's.

Tonight she would be on his yacht.

This night they would be sharing a bed.

Estelle wasn't sure if she was more terrified of losing her virginity, or of him finding out that she had never slept with anyone before.

Maybe he wouldn't notice, she thought helplessly. But she knew she didn't have a hope of delivering to his bed the sexually experienced woman that Raúl was expecting. Last night, before heading off with his sponsors for his final night as a single man, Raúl had kissed her slowly and deeply. The message his tongue had delivered had been an explicit one.

'Why do you make me wait?'

Tonight he would find out why.

'You have a phone call.' Rosa, his housekeeper, brought the phone up to the balcony. It was Amanda on the line.

'How are you doing?' Amanda asked.

'I'm petrified.' It was nice to be honest.

'All brides are,' Amanda said. 'But Raúl will take good care of you.'

He had utterly and completely charmed Amanda, but had not quite won over Andrew.

'I am not letting her go again.' He had looked Andrew

straight in the eye as he said it. 'If I move Estelle to Spain I want to make a proper commitment. That is why she will come to be my wife.'

So easily he had lied.

Estelle knew she must remember that fact.

'How did the dress turn out?' Amanda asked.

'It's beautiful,' Estelle said. 'Even better than I imagined it would be.'

It was the only thing Estelle had been allowed to organise. It had all be done online and by phone, and the final adjustments made when she had arrived.

'How is Cecelia?' Estelle asked, desperate for news of her niece.

'She's still asleep.'

It was nine a.m. in Spain, which meant it was eight a.m. in the UK. Cecelia had always been an early riser. More and more she slept these days, though Amanda always did her best to be upbeat.

'I'm going to dress her up for the wedding and take a photo and send it. Even if we can't be there today, know that we're thinking of you.'

'I know.'

'And I'm not your sister, but I do think of you as one.'

'Thank you,' Estelle said, her eyes welling up. 'I think of you as a sister too.'

They weren't idle words; many hours had been spent in hospital waiting rooms this past year.

'Is that the door?' Amanda asked.

'Yes. Don't worry, someone else will get it.'

'Do you have a butler?'

'No!' Estelle laughed, swallowing down her tears. 'Just Raúl's housekeeper. Though it's going to start to get busy soon, with the hairdresser...' She turned around as she heard her name being called, and Estelle's jaw dropped as she saw her brother coming through the door.

'Andrew!'

'Is that where he's got to?' Amanda laughed, and then she was serious. 'I'm so sorry that I couldn't be with you today—I'd have given anything. But with Cecelia…'

'Thank you,' Estelle said, and promptly burst into tears, all her pent-up nerves released.

'I think she's pleased to see me,' Andrew said, taking the phone and chatting to Amanda briefly before hanging up.

'I can't believe you're here,' Estelle admitted.

'Raúl said he thought you might need someone today, and of course I wanted to give you away. If anything happens with Cecelia he's assured me I'll be able to get straight back.'

She couldn't believe that Raúl would do this for her. Until now she hadn't fully realised how terrifying today was, how real it felt.

Raúl had.

'When did you get in?'

'Last night,' Andrew said. 'We went to Sol's.'

'You were out with Raúl?'

'He certainly knows how to party.' Andrew smiled. 'I'd forgotten how.'

Even if she was doing all this for her brother and his wife, of the many benefits of marrying Raúl, this was one Estelle had not even considered—that her brother, who was still having trouble accepting the diagnosis that he would never walk again, who had, apart from job interviews and hospital appointments, become almost reclusive, would fly not just to Spain but so far out of his comfort zone.

It was a huge and important step, and it was thanks to Raúl that he was here.

'I've got something for you.'

Estelle bit her lip, hoping they hadn't spent money they didn't have on a gift for a wedding that wasn't real.

'Remember these?' Andrew said as she opened the box. 'These' were small diamond studs that had belonged to her mother. 'Dad bought them for her for their wedding day.'

She had never felt more of a fraud.

'Enough tears,' Andrew said. 'Let's get this wedding underway.'

Raúl was rarely nervous, but as he stood at the altar and waited for Estelle, to his own surprise, he was.

His father had almost bought their story, and Raul's future with the company was secure, but instead of a gloating satisfaction that his plans were falling into place today he thought only of the reasons he had had to go to these lengths.

His head turned briefly and he caught a glimpse of Angela in the middle of the church. She was seated with his father, as ever-present PA. His mother's family were still unaware of the real role she played in his father's life—and the role she had played in his mother's death.

He stared ahead, anger churning in his gut that Angela had the gall to be here. He wouldn't put it past her to bring her bastard son.

Then he heard the murmur of the congregation and Raúl turned around. The churning faded. Just one thought was now in his mind.

She looked beautiful.

He had wondered how Estelle might look—had worried that, left to her own devices, a powder-puff ball would be wobbling towards him on glittery platform shoes, smiling from ruby-red lips.

He had not—could not have—imagined this.

Her dress was cream and made of intricate Spanish lace. It was fitted, and showing her curves, but in the most elegant of ways. The neckline was a simple halter neck. She carried orange blossom, as was the tradition for Spanish brides, and her lipstick was a pale coral.

'*Te ves bella.*' He told her that she looked beautiful as she joined him, and he meant every word. Not one thing would he change, from her black hair, piled high up on her head, to the simple diamond earrings and elegant cream shoes. She was visibly shaking, and he made a small joke to relax her. 'Your sewing is terrible.'

She glanced at his shirt and they shared a smile. With so little history, still they found a piece now, at the altar—as per tradition, the bride-to-be must embroider her groom's shirt.

'I'm not marrying a billionaire to sit sewing!' she had said teasingly, and Raúl had laughed, explaining that most women did not embroider all of the front of the shirt these days. Only a small area would be left for her, and Estelle could put on it whatever she wanted.

He had half expected a € but had frowned this morning when he had put on his shirt to find a small pineapple. Raúl still couldn't work out what it meant, but it was nice to see her relax and smile as the service started.

They knelt together, and as the service moved along he explained things in his low, deep voice, heard only by her.

'*El lazo,*' he said as a loop of satin decorated with orange blossom was placed over his shoulders and then another loop from the same piece was placed over hers. The priest spoke then for a moment, in broken English, and Estelle's cheeks burnt red as he told them that the rope that bound them showed that they shared the responsibility for this marriage. It would remain for the rest of the ceremony.

But not for life.

She felt like a fraud. She *was* a fraud, Estelle thought, panic starting to build. But Raúl took her hand and she looked into his black eyes. He seemed to sense that she was suddenly struggling.

'He asks now that you hand him the Arras,' Raúl said and she handed over the small purse he had given her on arrival. It contained thirteen coins, he had explained, and it showed his financial commitment to her.

It was the only honest part of the service, Estelle thought as the priest blessed them and handed it back to her.

Except it felt real.

'It's okay,' he said to her. 'We are here in this together.'

It felt far safer than being in it alone.

The service ended and an attendant removed the satin rope and presented it to Estelle; then they walked out to cheers and petals and rice being thrown at them. Raúl's hand was hot on her waist, and he gripped her tighter when she nearly shot out of her dress at the sound of an explosion.

'It's firecrackers,' Raúl said. 'Sorry I forgot to warn you.'

And there would be firecrackers later too, Estelle thought, when they got to bed and she told him the truth! But it was far too late now to warn him.

It really was a wonderful wedding.

As Raúl had told her on the night they had met, there were no speeches; instead it was an endless feast, with dancing and celebration and congratulations from all.

She met Paola and Carlos, Raúl's aunt and uncle, and they spoke of Raúl's mother, Gabriella.

'She would be so proud to be here today,' Paola said. 'Wouldn't she, Antonio?'

Estelle saw how friendly they were with Raúl's father,

and also with Angela, who was naturally seated with them. No longer were they names, but faces, and a shiver went down her arms as she imagined their reaction when the truth came out.

'My son has excellent taste.' Antonio kissed her on the cheek.

Estelle had met him very briefly the day before, and Raúl had handled most of the questions—though both had seen the doubt in his eyes as to whether this union was real.

It was slowly fading.

'It is good to see my son looking so happy.'

He *did* look happy.

Raúl smiled at her as they danced their first dance as husband and wife, with the room watching on.

'Remember our first dance?' Raúl smiled.

'Well, we shan't be repeating *that* tonight.'

'Not till later.' Raúl gazed down, saw her burning cheeks, and mistook it for arousal.

He could never have guessed her fear.

'I ache to be inside you.'

Other couples had joined them. The music was low and sensual and it seemed to beat low in her stomach. His hand dusted her bare arm and she shivered at the thought of what was to come, wondered if those eyes, soft now with lust and affection, would darken in anger.

'Raúl…' Surely here was not the place to tell him, but it felt better with people around them rather than being alone. 'I'm nervous about tonight.'

'Why would you be nervous?' he asked. 'I will take good care of you.'

He would, Raúl decided. He was rarely excited at the thought of monogamy but he actually wanted to take care of her, could not stand to think of what she might have put her body through. There was a surge of protectiveness that shot through him then, and his arms tightened around her. He could feel her tension and nervousness and again he wanted to make her smile.

'Can I ask why,' he whispered into her ear as they danced, 'you embroidered a pineapple on my shirt?'

'It's a thistle!'

A smile spread on her lips and he felt her relax a little in his arms.

'For Scotland.'

Raúl found himself smiling too. 'All day I have been trying to work out the significance of a pineapple.'

She started to laugh and Raúl found himself laughing a little too.

He lowered his head and kissed her lightly.

It was expected, of course. What groom would *not* kiss his bride?

Many times since he had put his proposition to her Estelle had had doubts—the morality of it, the feasibility of it, the logistics—but as he kissed her, as she felt his warm lips and the soft caress of his hand near the base of her spine, true doubt as to her ability to go through with the deal surfaced. For once it had nothing to do with her hymen. She was suddenly more worried about her heart.

It was the music. It was the moment. It was having her brother here. It was Raúl's kiss. All these things, she told herself, were the reasons she felt as she did—as if this were real…as if this were love.

Estelle excused herself a little while later and went to the bathroom, just so she might collect herself, but brides could not easily hide on their wedding day.

'Estelle?' She turned at the sound of a woman's voice. 'I am Angela—Raúl's father's PA.'

'Raúl has spoken about you,' Estelle responded carefully.

'I'm sure what he had to say was not very flattering.' There were tears in the older woman's eyes. 'Estelle, I don't know what to believe…'

'Excuse me?'

'About this sudden marriage.' Angela was being as up-front with Estelle as she was with Raúl. 'I do know, though, that Raúl seems the happiest I have seen him. If you *do* love your husband…'

'If?'

'I apologise,' Angela said. 'Given that you surely love your husband, I ask this not for me, and not even for Antonio's sake. Whatever Raúl thinks of me, I care for him. I want him to come and visit us. I want us to be a family, even for a little while.'

'You could have had that years ago.' Estelle answered as she hoped Raúl would expect his loyal wife to.

'I want him to make peace with his father while there is still time. I don't want him to have any guilt when his father passes. I know how much guilt he has over his mother.'

Estelle blinked, unsure how to respond because there was so much she didn't know about Raúl. What did he have to feel guilty about? Raúl had been a child, after all. He had agreed to tell her more on their honeymoon—had said that he would be the one to deal with any questions tonight.

'I have always loved Raúl. I have always thought of him as a son.'

'So why did you leave it so late to tell him?' Perhaps it was the emotion of the day, but the tears that flashed in Estelle's eyes were real. 'If you cared so much for him—'

Estelle halted. It wasn't her place to ask, and Raúl certainly wouldn't thank her for delving. She was here to ensure his father left his share of the business to him, that was all. She would do well to remember that.

'I *do* care,' Angela responded. 'Whatever Raúl thinks of me, from a distance I have loved him as a son.'

'From a distance?' Estelle repeated, making the bitter point.

Turning on her heel, she walked out and straight into Raúl's arms.

'She wanted to speak about you,' Estelle told him. 'I don't know how well I handled it.'

'We'll discuss it later,' Raúl said, for he had seen Angela follow her in. 'Now we have to hand out the favours.'

It really was an amazing party, and for reasons of her own Estelle didn't particularly want it to end.

As per tradition, the bride and groom had to see off all their guests and be the last to leave. Antonio tired first, and she felt the grip of Raúl's hand tighten on hers as his father left with his loyal PA.

'It's been great,' Andrew said as he prepared to head back to the hotel he was staying in. 'Once Cecelia is well, and I'm working, I'm going to bring Amanda and Cecelia here for a holiday, to visit you.'

'You do that,' Estelle said, and bent down and gave her brother a cuddle, then stood as Raúl shook his hand.

'Look after my sister.'

'You do not have to worry about that.'

'Have a great honeymoon.'

A driver sorted out the wheelchair and they waved Andrew off and then headed back inside.

Apart from the staff it was just Raúl and Estelle now, and still the music went on as they danced their last dance of the night.

'It really helped having Andrew here.' Her hands were round the back of his neck, he held her hips, and she would give anything not to disappoint him tonight—anything to be the experienced lover he assumed she was.

'I thought it might.'

'It didn't just help me,' Estelle admitted, and started to tell him about how Andrew's confidence had been lacking.

But he dropped a kiss on her shoulder. 'Enough about others.'

Estelle swallowed. She could feel his fingers exploring the halter neck, his other hand running down the row of tiny buttons that ran to the base of her spine, and she knew he was planning his movements, undressing her slowly in his mind as they danced.

'Raúl...' His mouth was working over her bare shoulder, kissing it deeply; she could feel the soft suction, feel the heat of his tongue and his ardour building. 'I've never slept with anyone before.'

He moaned into her shoulder and pulled her tighter into him, so she could feel every inch of the turn-on he thought she was giving him.

'I mean it.' Her voice was shaking. 'You'll be my first.'

'Come on, then.' His mouth was now at her ear. 'Let's go and play virgins.'

CHAPTER TEN

THEY WERE DRIVEN the short distance to the marina, but for Estelle it just passed in a blur.

It was almost morning, yet despite the hour the celebrations continued.

Alberto, the skipper, welcomed them, and briefly introduced the staff—but Estelle barely took in the names, let alone her surroundings. All she could think of was what was soon to come as the crew toasted them and then Raúl dismissed them.

'Tomorrow I will show you around properly,' Raúl said, taking her champagne glass. 'But for now...'

There was no escaping. He pulled her towards him, his tongue back on her neck, at the crease between her neck and shoulder. He *had* been mentally undressing her before, for now his hands moved straight to the halter neck and expertly unravelled the carefully tied bow.

He had been expecting a basque, had anticipated another contraption to disable, but the dress had an inbuilt bra and he gave a low growl of approval as one of the breasts that had filled his private visions in recent days fell heavy and ripe into his palm.

'Raúl, someone might come...'

'That would be *you*,' he said, but she did not relax. 'No one will disturb us.'

Raúl lowered his head and licked around the pale are-ola, flicked a nipple that had been crushed all day by fab-ric back into rapid life, surprised that she was concerned that someone might come in. The staff on his yacht had seen many a decadent party—a husband and wife on their wedding night paled in comparison with what usually took place. He took the breast he craved in his mouth again, felt her hand try to push him back. He was at first surprised by her reticence—but then he remembered their game.

'Of course.' He smiled. 'You are nervous.'

He lifted her up and carried her down to the master stateroom, kissing her the entire way. He lowered her to the ground, turning her around so he could work on the tiny buttons from behind. It did not halt his mouth; his tongue kissed every inch of newly exposed flesh till her spine felt as if it were on fire.

He peeled off her dress, then her shoes and stockings. As his tongue licked and nibbled her sex through her silk panties the sensations his mouth delivered drove her wild. He only removed her panties when the moisture his mouth had made matched the dampening silk.

'Raúl…' Her hands were on his head—contrary hands that tried to halt him, while her moans of mounting de-sire urged him on.

'I want you so bad.' He peeled off her panties and, kneeling, parted her lips, his tongue darting to the swell-ing bud over and over as her hands knotted in his hair.

'Raúl…' she whimpered, lost between bliss and fear. 'I'm serious. I really haven't slept with anyone before.'

He simply didn't believe her. As she came under his mouth she had a hopeless thought that maybe he wouldn't guess, maybe he wouldn't know. Because despite her naïveté her body responded with ease. She throbbed against his mouth, more aroused than sated as he softly kissed the lingering orgasm.

He relished her taste, was assured she was moist. He was desperate now to take her.

He rose to his full height then, and shrugged his jacket off.

Breathless, aroused, moving on instinct, her hands shaking with want, she undid the buttons of his shirt. He was so dark and sultry, and he wore it well. His lips parted as her hands roamed his chest and she licked at his nipples as she undid his belt.

Raúl wanted her fingers at his zipper, and he wished she would hurry, but she lingered instead, feeling his thick heat through the fabric, her fingers lightly exploring. His already aching erection hardened further beneath her fingers. 'Estelle...' He could barely get the word out, but thankfully she read the urgency and slid the zipper down, and he let out a breath as she freed him.

He was delicious to her hands. She ran her fingers along his length, felt the soft skin that belied the strength beneath. She was petrified at the thought of him inside her, but wanting him just the same. She could see a trickle of silver and caught it with her finger, then swirled it around the head, entranced by its beauty.

Raúl closed his eyes in a mixture of frustration and bliss, for he wanted her hand to grip him tight, yet conversely he liked the tentative tease and exploration, liked the feel of her other hand gently weighing him.

Deeply they kissed, his tongue urging her to move faster, his erection twitching at the pleasure of her teasing, till he could take it no more.

'Te quiero.'

He told her he wanted her in Spanish as he pushed her

onto the bed. *'Tengo que usted tiene.'* He told her he had to have her as he parted her legs.

'Be gentle.' She was writhing and hot beneath him, her words contrary to the wanton woman in his arms. Her sex was slippery and warm and engorged as his hand stroked her there. She was as close to coming as Raúl, and his answer to her final plea was delivered as he nudged her entrance.

'It's way too late for gentle, baby.'

How he regretted those words as he seared and tore into her.

Raúl heard her sob, heard her bite back a scream.

Estelle knew then she had been a fool to think he might somehow not notice. He tore through her barrier but the pain did not end there. His fierce erection drove through tight muscles full of resistance. Too late to halt, too late to be tender, he froze—just not quickly enough. He leant on his elbows above her as she tried to work out how to breathe with Raúl inside her.

He attempted slow withdrawal. She begged that he did not. She lay there, trying to accommodate him, waiting for the heat and pain to subside, her muscles clamped around him.

'I take it out slowly,' Raúl said. He felt sick—appalled by his own brutality—and guilty too at the pleasure of her, hot and tight around him. He was so close to coming and trying to hold on. 'I'll just—'

'Don't.'

Her eyes were screwed tight as he moved a fraction backwards, but when he halted, when he stilled, her body relaxed a little. Estelle tried to release herself. She moved to slide away from him. Yet the pain was subsiding to a throbbing heat so she moved again, warming to the sensation of him inside her.

It was a different type of command she gave next. 'Don't stop.'

'Estelle?' He did not want to stop, and yet he did not want to hurt her; he moved slowly a little within her, his breath shallow, panting as if he had already come.

Her hands moved to his buttocks and she felt them tauten beneath her fingers. It was Estelle who pressed and dictated the tempo and, rarely for Raúl, he let her. Rarely for Raúl, he was humbled. He did not think of the questions he must ask her, just focused on the tight grip and the heat of her on his unsheathed skin, and all he could do was kiss her. Every inch of him held back, resisting the beckoning of oiled muscles that gripped as he slid past them, that urged him now to move faster, to take her deeper.

Estelle's breath was quickening. He felt the somewhat impatient rise of her groin, the press of her hands in his buttocks, and he could hold back no more.

Still he had not taken her fully, but now he thrust in. Estelle's neck arched as he probed and located fresh virgin flesh with each deepening thrust, and when he had filled her, when every part of her was consumed, he moved out and did it again, angling his hips, hitting her deep inside till she was moaning.

He was moving fast now, and she wrapped her legs around him, could not believe how her body had just taken over. For she lifted to him, was building to him, working with him, both heading to the same mutual goal.

No longer naïve, her body shattered in an orgasm like nothing she had ever given herself—for there she could stop, there she could halt. And it was nothing like the teasing he had given her either, for here in Raúl's bed he urged her on further, broke all limits, ensured that she screamed.

She pulsed around the head of him. He was stroking her deep inside—one spot that had her sobbing, one tender spot that he hit over and over—till she sobbed, and then he released himself into her. Her thighs were in spasm as a fresh wave of orgasm crashed through her body—and, yes, just as he had warned her, she cussed him in Spanish till he kissed her, till she was lying beneath him no longer a virgin.

She looked up at him, expecting a barrage of questions, a demand for an explanation, but instead he moved onto his side and put his arm around her, pulling her into him.

'I should have known' was his reprimand.

'I tried to tell you.'

'Estelle…' he warned.

She gave a small nod, conceding that tonight might have been rather too late.

'We will speak about it in the morning.'

For now, they held each other, lay in each other's arms, tired and sated and both in a place they had never thought they might be.

Estelle a bought bride; Raúl a man who had married and made love to a virgin.

CHAPTER ELEVEN

ESTELLE WOKE AND had no idea where she was for a moment.

Her body was bruised and sore. She could hear a shower.

She rolled over in bed and saw the evidence of their union, and moved the top sheet to cover it.

'Hiding the evidence?'

Estelle turned and was shocked at the sight of him. There was a towel round his hips, but his chest was covered in the bruises she now remembered her mouth making. He turned and took a drink from the breakfast table that had presumably been delivered and she saw the scratches on his back, remembered the wanton place he had taken her to.

'I need to have a shower.'

'We need to talk.' But then he conceded, 'Have some lunch and a shower. Then we will talk.'

'Lunch?'

'Late lunch,' Raúl said. 'It is nearly two.'

Estelle quickly gulped down some grapefruit juice and then headed to the bathroom. When she had found out they would be honeymooning on a yacht she had expected basic bathroom facilities; instead it was like a five-star hotel. The bathroom was marble, the taps and lighting incredible, yet she barely noticed. Her only thought was getting to her make-up bag.

The doctor had told her how important it was to take her pill on time every day. She was still getting used to it. Her breasts felt sore and tender, as if she were getting her period, and she still felt a little bit queasy from the new medication.

Estelle swallowed down the pill, making a mental note to change the alarm on her phone to two p.m.—or should she take it at seven tomorrow?

Her mind felt dizzy. She had seen that Raúl was less than impressed with her this morning and no doubt he would want a thorough explanation. She still hadn't worked out what to say.

Estelle showered and put on the factor fifty he insisted on, then sorted out her hair and make-up, relieved when she headed back into the bedroom and Raúl wasn't there. She selected a bikini from the many he had bought her, and also a pale lilac sarong. Her head was splitting from too much champagne and too much Raúl. She sat on the bed and put on espadrilles. Then, dressed—or rather barely dressed, as Raúl would want her to be—she stood. But her eyes did not go to the mirror—instead they went to the bed.

Mortified at the thought of a maid seeing the stained sheets, Estelle started to strip the bed.

'What are you doing?'

'I'm just making up the bed.'

'If I had a thing for maids then it would have been stipulated in the contract,' Raúl said. 'And if I had a thing for virgins,' he added, 'that would have been stipulated too.'

Estelle said nothing.

'Just leave it.' His voice was dark. 'The crew will take care of that. I will show you around.'

'I'll just wander…' She went to walk past.

'You can't hide from me here,' he warned, taking her wrist. 'But we will discuss it later. I don't want the staff getting even a hint that this is anything but a normal honeymoon.'

'Don't you trust your staff?' It was meant as a small dig—because surely a man in his position could easily pay for his privacy?

'I don't trust anyone,' Raúl said, watching the fire mount on her cheeks as his words sank in. 'And with good reason.'

She followed him up onto the deck. The sun blinded her for a moment.

'Where are your sunglasses?'

'I forgot to bring them.' She turned to head back down, but Raúl halted her, calling out to one of the crew. 'I can get them myself.'

'Why would you?'

Sometimes she forgot just how rich and spoilt he was. This was not one of those times. Despite the fact there were some of the crew around, he pulled her into his arms and very slowly kissed her.

'Raúl....' She was embarrassed by his passion. She looked into his black eyes and knew he was making a point.

'We are here for two days, darling. The plan is for us to fully enjoy them.'

His words were soft, the message not.

'I'll show you around now.'

A maid handed her her sunglasses and then Raúl showed her their abode for the next few days. The lounge that she had barely noticed last night was huge, littered with low sofas; another maid was plumping the cushions. There was a huge screen and, though nervous around him, Estelle did her best to be enthusiastic. 'This will be lovely for watching a movie.'

Raúl swallowed and caught the maid's eyes, and as Estelle went over to look at his DVD collection he quickly led her away.

'Here is the gym.' He opened a door and they stepped in. 'Not that you'll need it. I will ensure that you get plenty of exercise.'

Only there, with the door safely closed, did he let his true frustration slip out. He closed the door and gave her a glimpse of what was to come.

'If you think we are going to be sitting around watching movies and holding hands—'

'I know what I'm here for.'

'Make sure that you do.'

Raúl had woken at lunchtime from his first decent sleep in days, from his first night without nightmares. For a moment he had glimpsed peace—but then she had stirred in his arms and he had looked down to a curtain of raven hair and felt the weight of her breast on his chest. The sheet had tumbled from them; he'd seen her soft pale stomach and the evidence of their coupling on her inner thigh.

He had gone to move the sheet to cover them, but the movement had disturbed her a little and he had lain still, willing her back to sleep, fighting the urge to roll over and kiss her awake, make love to her again. He had felt the heat from her palm on his stomach and had physically ached for that hand to move down. His erection had been uncomfortable.

He'd fought the bliss of the memories of last night as his hand had moved down—and then halted when he'd realised his own thought-processes.

Sex Raúl could manage—and often.

Making love—no.

Last night had been but one concession, and he reminded himself she had lied.

He had removed her hand from him then and spent a

full ten minutes examining her face—from the freckles dusting her nose to the full lips that had deceived him.

He stood in the well-equipped gym and looked at them now. Absolutely he would make things clear.

'We have several weeks of this,' Raúl said. 'I wanted a woman who could handle my life, who knew how to have fun.' He did not mince words. 'Who was good in bed.'

He watched her cheeks burn.

'I'm sure I'll soon learn. I'll keep up my end of the deal—I don't need hand-holding.'

'There will be no holding hands.' He took her hand and placed it exactly where it had been agreed it would visit regularly. 'You knew what you were signing up for...'

He had to hold her back; he had to be at his poisonous worst. He could not simply dump her, as he usually did when a woman fell too hard. They had weeks of this and he could not risk her heart.

Instead he would put her to work.

'Let's have a spa.'

She saw the challenge in his eyes, knew that he was testing her, and smiled sweetly. 'Let's!'

She followed him up onto the deck, trying to ignore the fact that he had fully stripped off as she took off her espadrilles and dropped her sarong.

'Take off your top.'

'In a moment...'

He could sense rather than see that she was upset, and it made him furious. He was actually wishing his father dead, just so this might end.

'Take off your top,' he said again. Because if she thought she was here to discuss the passing scenery, or for them to get to know each other better, then she was about to find out she was wrong.

Estelle might have taken him for a fool.

He wasn't one.

Her face was one burning blush as her shaking hands undid the clasp, and she sank beneath the water as she removed it and placed the bikini top on the edge.

'Good morning!' The skipper made his way over. Naked breasts were commonplace on the Costa Del Sol—and especially on Raúl Sanchez Fuante's boat. He had no trouble at all looking Estelle in the eye as he greeted her. She, though, Raúl noted, was close to tears as she attempted to smile back.

'We are heading towards Acantilados de Maro-Cerro Gordo,' Alberto said, and then turned to Raúl. 'Would you like us to stop there tonight? The chef is looking forward to preparing your dinner and he wondered if you would like us to set up for you to eat on the bay?'

'We'll eat on the boat,' Raúl said. 'We might take a couple of jet skis out a little later and take a walk.'

'Of course,' Alberto said, then turned to Estelle.

'Do you have any preferences for dinner? Any food choices you would like the chef to know about?'

'Anything.'

Raul heard her try to squeeze the word out through breathless lips.

'It's a beautiful bay we are stopping at.' Albert happily chatted on. 'It's not far at all from the more built-up areas, but soon we will start to come into the most stunning virgin terrain.'

He wished them a pleasant afternoon and headed off.

'I've already explored the virgin terrain...' Raúl drawled, once he was out of earshot.

Estelle said nothing.

'Here.' Annoyed with himself for giving in, but hating her discomfort, he threw her the bikini top. 'Put it on if you want.'

She really was shaken, Raúl thought with a stab of guilt as he watched her trembling hands trying to put the damp garment on. Going topless was nothing here—nothing at all—but then he remembered last night: her shaking, her asking him to be gentle. Pleas he had ignored.

He strode through the water and turned her around, helping her with the clasp of her bikini top. Then, and he didn't know why, he pulled her into his arms and held her till she had stopped shaking—held her till the blush had seeped from her skin.

And then he made her burn again as he dropped a kiss on her shoulder and admitted a truth to her about that virgin terrain.

'...and it was stunning.'

CHAPTER TWELVE

NORMALLY RAÚL'S YACHT sailed into the busiest port, often with a party underway.

This early evening, though, they sailed slowly into Acantilados de Maro-Cerro Gordo. The sky was an amazing pink, the cliffs sparkling as they dropped anchor near a secluded bay.

'The beaches are stunning here,' Alberto said, 'and the tourists know it. But this one has no road access.' He turned to Raúl. 'The jet skis are ready for you both.'

Only as they were about to be launched did Raúl remember. He turned and saw her pale face, saw that she was biting on her lip as she went to climb on the machine, and his apology was genuine.

'Estelle, I'm sorry. I forgot about your brother's accident.'

'It's fine,' she said through chattering teeth. 'He was showing off…mucking around…' She was trying to pretend that the machine she was about to climb on *didn't* petrify her. 'I know we'll be sensible.'

Raúl had had no intention of being sensible. He loved the exhilaration of being on a jet ski and had wanted to share it with her—had wanted to race and to chase.

Instead he was taking her hand. 'It's not fine. You don't have to pretend.'

Oh, but she did. At every turn she had to pretend, if she was to be the temporary woman he wanted.

'Come on this one with me,' Raúl said. 'Alberto, take her hand and help her on.'

They rode towards the bay in a rather more subdued fashion than Raúl was used to.

The maid who was setting up the dinner table caught Alberto's eye when he came to check on her progress and they shared a brief smile.

His bride and the effect she was having on Raúl was certainly not one they had been expecting.

'I think I might go and reorganise his DVD collection,' the maid suggested and Alberto nodded.

'I think that might be wise.'

Estelle held tightly onto Raul's waist as the jet ski chopped through the waves, and because her head kept knocking into his back in the end she gave in and rested it there, not sure if her rapid heart-rate was because she was scared by the vehicle, by the questions she would no doubt soon be facing, or just by the exhilaration.

Making love with Raúl had been amazing. She was sore and tender but now, feeling his skin beneath her cheek, feeling the ocean water sting her and the wind whip her hair, she could not regret a moment. Even her lie. Feeling his passion as he had seared into her was a memory she would be frequently revisiting. For now, though, Estelle knew she had to play it tough—had to convince him better than she had so far that she was up to the job he had paid her for.

He skidded into the shallows and she unpeeled herself from him and stepped down.

'It's amazing…' She looked up at the cliffs, shielding her eyes. 'Look how high it is.'

He did, but only briefly. Estelle was too busy admiring the stunning view to notice his pallor.

'What did Angela say to you at the wedding?' Raúl asked.

She had been expecting a barrage of questions about her lack of experience, and was momentarily sideswiped at his choice of topic for conversation, but then she reminded herself his interest in her was limited.

'She wasn't sure whether or not we were a true couple,' Estelle said.

'You corrected her?'

'Of course,' Estelle said. 'She seems to think that *if* I love my husband, then I should encourage you to make peace with your father while there is still time.' She glanced over to him as they walked. 'She wants us to go there and visit.'

'It is too late to play happy families.'

'Angela said that she doesn't want you to suffer any guilt, as you did over your mother's death…'

'Misplaced guilt,' Raúl said, but didn't elaborate any more.

He stopped and they sat on the beach, looking out to the yacht. She could see the lights were on, the staff on deck were preparing their meal. It was hard to believe such luxury even existed, let alone that for now it was hers to experience. It was the luxury of *him* she wanted, though; there was more about Raúl that she needed to know.

'I didn't know how to answer her,' Estelle admitted. 'You said there was more you would tell me. I have no real idea about your family, nor about you.'

'So I will tell you what you need to know.' He pondered for a moment on how best to explain it. 'My grandfather—my mother's father—ran a small hotel. It did well and he built another, and then he purchased some land in the north,' Raúl explained.

'In San Sebastian?' Estelle asked.

He nodded. 'On his death the business was left to his three children—De La Fuente Holdings. My father and mother married, and my father started to work in the family business. But he was always an outsider—or felt that he was, even though he oversaw the building of the San Sebastian hotel. When I was born my mother became unwell. In hindsight I would say she was depressed. It was then he started to sleep with Angela. Apparently Angela felt too much guilt and left work, moved back to her family, but they started seeing each other again...'

'How do you know all this?'

'My father told me the morning I met you.'

It was only then that Estelle fully realised this was almost as new to him as it was to her.

'Angela got pregnant, the guilt ate away at him, and he told my mother the truth. He wanted to know if she could forgive him. She cried and wailed and screamed. She told him to get out and he went to Angela—the baby was almost due. He assumed my mother would tell her family, that she would turn to them. Except she did not. When she had the car accident and died my father returned and soon realised no one knew he had another son. Instead they welcomed him back into the company.' He was silent for a moment. 'Soon they will find out the truth.'

'Angela said that you blamed yourself for your mother's death?'

'That is all you need to know.' He looked over to her. 'Your turn.'

'I don't know what to tell you.'

'Why you lied?'

'I didn't lie.'

'The same way my father didn't lie when he didn't tell me had another son? The same way Angela didn't lie when she failed to tell mention her son, Luka, was my brother?' He did not want to think about that. 'Okay, if you didn't outright lie, you *did* deceive.'

He watched her swallow, watched as her face jerked away to look out to the ocean.

'I wanted an experienced woman.'

'Sorry I don't know enough tricks—'

'I wasn't talking about *sex*!' Raúl hurled. 'I wanted a woman who could handle things. Who could keep to a deal. Who wasn't going to fall in love…'

'Again you assume!' Estelle flared. 'Why would I fall in love with some cold bastard who thinks only in money—who has no desire for true affection? A man who tells me what to wear and whether or not I can tan.'

Her eyes flashed as she let out some of the anger she had suppressed over the past few days while every decision apart from her wedding dress had been made by him.

'Raúl, I would not have a man choose my clothes or dictate to the hairdresser the style of my hair, or the beautician the colour of my nails. You're getting what you paid for—what you wanted—what you demanded. Consider my virginity a bonus!'

She dug her heels deep into the sand and almost believed her own words. Tried to ignore that last night, as she'd been falling asleep in his arms, foolish thoughts had invaded. Raúl's doubts about her ability to see this through perhaps had merit, for he would be terribly easy to love…

She turned around and faced him.

'I'm here for the money, Raúl.' And not for a single second more would she allow herself to forget it. 'I'm here with you for the same reason I was with Gordon.'

He could not stand the thought of her in bed with him—

could not bear to think about it. But when he did, Raúl frowned.

'If you were with Gordon for money, how come you were trying to change the sheets before the maid got in.'

'I was never with Gordon in that way. I just stood in for Ginny.'

'You shared his bed,' Raúl said. 'And we all know his reputation…'

'Unlike you, Gordon didn't feel comfortable going to a wedding alone,' Estelle said carefully.

'So he paid you to look like his tart?' Raúl checked. 'What about Dario's…?' His voice trailed off and he frowned as he realised the lengths Gordon had gone to, then frowned a little more as realisation hit. 'Is Gordon…?' He didn't finish the question—knew it was none of his business. 'You needed the money to help out your brother?'

She conceded with a nod.

'Estelle, it is not for me to question your reasons—'

'Then don't.'

Her warning did not stop him.

'Andrew would not want it.'

'Which is why he will never find out.'

'I know that if I had a sister I would not want her—'

'Don't compare yourself to my brother. You don't even have a sister, and the brother you *do* have you don't want to know.'

'What's that got to do with it?'

'We're two very different people, Raúl. If I discovered that I had a brother or sister somewhere I'd be doing everything I could to find out about them, to meet them—not plotting to bring them down.'

'I'm not plotting anything. I just don't want him taking what is rightfully mine. Neither do I want to end up working alongside him.'

She looked at the seductive eyes that invited you only to bed, at the mouth that kissed so easily but insisted you did not get close.

'You miss out on so much, Raúl.'

'I miss out on nothing,' Raúl said. 'I have everything I want.'

'You have everything money can buy,' Estelle said, remembering the reason she was here. 'Including me.'

When he kissed her it tasted of nothing. It tasted empty. It was a pale comparison to the kiss he had been the recipient of last night. And when he took her top off he knew she was faking it, knew she was thinking of the boat and of people watching, knew she was trying not to cry.

'Not here,' Raúl said for her.

'Please, Raúl…'

Her mouth sought his. She was still playing the part, too inexperienced to understand that he knew her body lied.

He wanted it back, the intimacy of last night, which meant taking care of her.

For now.

Surely for a couple of days he could take care of her. They could just enjoy each other and break her in properly. The last thing he wanted was her tense and teary, feeling exposed.

He had glimpsed her toughness, admired the lengths she would go to for her family, and he believed her now— she did not want his love

'Later.' Raúl pulled his head back from her mouth. 'I'm starving.'

He helped her with her bikini, used his chest as a shield as he did up the clasp, just in case any passing fish were having a peek, or telescopes were trained on them. But rather than making him feel irritated, her coyness now made him smile.

Especially when he thought of her unleashed.

'Come on,' Raúl said, despite the ache in his groin. 'Let's head back.'

CHAPTER THIRTEEN

'WE WILL GO and shower and get dressed for dinner,' Raúl said as they boarded and Alberto took the jet ski. 'Do you want me to ask Rita to come down and do your hair?'

'Rita?'

'She is a masseuse and a beautician. If you want her to come and help just ask Alberto,' Raúl said, heading off to the stateroom.

Estelle called him back. She could smell the food and was honestly starving. 'Why do we have to get dressed for dinner?' Estelle did not notice the twitch of his lips, though Alberto did. 'It's only us.'

'On a yacht such as this one, when the chef…' Raúl began. But he was torn, because etiquette often had no place on board and it seemed petty to put her right. 'Very well.' He turned to Alberto, who was already on to it.

'I'll let the chef know.'

They rinsed off under the shower on deck and then took their seats.

Raúl was rather more used to a well-made-up blonde in a revealing dress sitting opposite him, but there was something incredibly appealing about sitting for dinner half-naked and scooping up the delicacies the waiters were bringing.

'I could get far too used to this,' Estelle started, and

then stopped herself, remembering his words at the lawyer's. 'I meant…'

'I know what you meant.'

She was relieved to see he was smiling.

'The food really is amazing,' Raúl agreed. 'They chef is marvellous. Chefs on yachts generally are—that is why we keep coming back for more.'

They chatted as they ate, far more naturally than they had before, and it wasn't just for the benefit of the staff.

It was simply a blissful night.

They danced.

On the deck of his yacht they danced when the music came on.

'I understand now why we should have changed for dinner,' Estelle admitted. 'Do you think I've offended anyone?'

'I don't think you could if you tried.'

The sky was darkening and Raúl looked out to the cliffs, and rather than remembering hell he buried his face in her hair. It took only the smell of the ocean in her hair for him to escape.

'And for the record,' Raúl said, 'although you accuse me being a controlling bastard, I was worried about you burning. I have never seen paler skin.'

'I think I *am* a bit sunburnt.'

'I know.'

They moved down to the lounge room. Estelle was starting to relax—so much so that she didn't spring from his arms when some dessert wine was brought through to them.

'Let's go to bed…' His hand was in her bikini top, trying to free her breast.

'Not yet,' she breathed into his mouth. 'I'll never sleep.'

'I have no intention of letting you sleep.'

'Let's watch a movie,' Estelle said, unwrapping herself from him and heading over to his collection.

'Estelle—no!'

'Oh, sorry.' She'd forgotten what he'd told her in the gym, about no hand-holding and movies, and she turned and attempted a smile. 'Sure—let's go to bed.'

'I didn't mean that,' Raúl said through gritted teeth, wondering how he'd ended up with the one hooker to whom he'd have to apologise for his DVDs. 'I just don't think there will be anything there to your taste.'

He braced himself for the rapid demise of a pleasant night as Estelle flicked through his collection.

'I love this one.'

'Really?' Raúl was very pleasantly surprised.

'Actually...' She skimmed through a couple more. 'This one's my favourite.' She held up the cover to him and didn't understand his smile.

'Of course it is,' Raúl said, pulling her down beside him, smiling into her hair. One day he would tell her how funny that was—one day when it wouldn't offend, when she knew him better. He would laugh about it with her.

But there would not *be* that day, he reminded himself.

This was just for now.

He had not lain on a sofa and watched a movie—not one with a plot, anyway—since he couldn't remember when.

Estelle shivered. The doors were open and the air was cooling. He pulled down a rug from the back of the sofa and covered them, felt her bottom curving into him.

'Sore?' He kissed her pink shoulders as he made light work of her bikini top.

'A bit.'

Estelle concentrated on the movie as Raúl concentrated on Estelle. He kissed her neck and shoulders for ages, then played with her breasts, massaging them with his palms, taking her nipples between thumb and fingers. Then slowly, when he knew there would be no qualms from Estelle, moved one hand down and untied her bikini bottoms.

His question, when repeated, was a far more personal one as his fingers crept in.

'Sore?'

'A bit,' she said again, but he was so gentle, and it felt so sublime.

She could feel the motion of the boat, and him huge and hard behind her; she could feel the urging of his mouth to turn to him and growing insistence from behind.

'Turn around, Estelle.' His breathing was ragged.

'In a minute.' She wasn't even watching the film. Her eyes were closed. She was just loving the feel of him playing with her and longing for it to go on. 'It's coming to the best bit.'

He pulled her up a little further, so that her naked bum was against his stomach, and he angled her perfectly. She felt the long, slow slide of him where he had stabbed into her last night. She was still bruised and swollen and hot down below, and yet she closed around him in relief.

'*This* is the best bit,' Raúl's low voice corrected her.

He pressed slowly into her, his fingers playing with her clitoris, slid slowly and deeply, with none of the haste of last night, and it was Estelle who was fighting to hold back.

'I'm going to come.'

'Not yet,' he told her, teasing her harder with his fingers, thrusting himself deeper inside.

'I am.' She was trembling and trying to hold on.

'Not yet.'

He stroked her somewhere so deep, the feeling so intense that she let out a small squeal.

'There?' he asked.

Estelle didn't know what he meant, but then he stroked her there again and she sobbed. 'There!' She was begging as over and over he massaged her deep, hitting her somewhere she hadn't even known existed. 'There…'

She was starting to cry, but with intense pleasure, and then she could no longer hold it. There was no point even trying.

There was a flood of release as she pulsed around him, and Raúl moaned as she tightened over and over around his thick length. He felt the rush of her orgasm flowing into him and he shot back in instant response, spilling deep into her, loving her abandon, loving the Estelle his body revealed.

Loving too the tinge of embarrassment that crept in as she struggled to get her breath back.

'What was that?'

'Us,' he said, still inside her. And it was not the cliffs he feared now, but the perfume of the ocean in her hair as he inhaled it—a fear that was almost overwhelming as he realised how much he had enjoyed this night.

Not just the sex, not just the talking, not just dinner.

But *now*.

'We should head back.'

They had been snorkelling. It had all started off innocently, but had turned into a slightly more grown-up activity. Raúl did not know if it was her laughter, or the feel of her legs wrapped around him, or just that he was simply enjoying her too much, but he kissed her cheek and unwrapped her legs from his waist.

'Is it dinner-time?'

'I meant we should head back for Marbella…'

It had been two nights and two amazing days, and more of a honeymoon than Raúl had ever intended for it to be.

They *were* dressing for dinner tonight, because they wouldn't be dawdling on their return. Which meant this would be their last night on the yacht.

She missed it already.

Even as Rita did her hair and make-up she missed the yacht, because it had been the most magical time. As if they had suspended the rules of the contract, their time had been spent talking, laughing, eating, making love— but Raúl had made it clear that things would be different when they returned to Marbella.

She felt as if they were approaching that already as Rita pushed the last pin into Estelle's hair. Raúl's expression was tense as he picked up his ringing phone.

'I will tell the chef you will be up soon,' Rita said, and Estelle thanked her and started to put on her dress.

She didn't understand what was being said on the phone, but given the terse words, she guessed it wasn't pleasant.

'They are getting married.' Raúl hung up and was silent.

By the time he told her what the call had been about he was doing up his tie, but kept getting the knot wrong.

'Oh.' She didn't know what else to say, just went on struggling with her zip.

'Come here.' He found the side zipper. 'It's stuck.'

She stood still as he tried to undo it.

'My father says he wants to do the right thing by Angela—wants to give her the dignity of being his wife and his widow. He wants her to have a say in decisions by the medical staff.'

'What did you say?'

'That it was the first decent thing I had heard on the subject.'

'Are you going to attend?'

He didn't answer her question; instead he hurried her

along. 'Come on. They will be serving up soon. It is not fair to keep the chef waiting.'

Since when was Raúl thoughtful about his staff? Estelle thought, but said nothing.

It was an amazing dinner. The chef had made his own paella, and even Raúl agreed, it was the best he had tasted.

Yet he barely touched it.

He looked at Estelle; she looked exquisite. Her hair was up, as it had been on their wedding day, her black dress looked stunning, and he told himself he could do it—that it wasn't a problem after all.

'What would you think if we did not turn around for Marbella?'

Estelle swallowed the food she was relishing and took a drink of water, nervous for the same reasons as Raúl.

'We could head to the islands, extend our trip...'

'So that you miss your father's wedding?'

'He has chosen to marry when I am on my honeymoon. He doesn't know we were to be on our way back.'

'You'll have to face him at some point.'

'You don't tell me what I have to do!' he snapped, and then righted himself, trying to explain things a little better. 'He wants a wedding—one happy memory with his wife. I doubt that will be manageable with me there. Especially if Luka attends.' He took a breath. 'So how about a few more days?' He made it sound so simple. 'I have not had a proper holiday in years...'

'I thought your life was one big holiday?'

'No,' Raúl said. 'My life is one big party. We will return to that in a few days.' He issued it as a warning, telling her without saying as much that what happened at sea stayed at sea.

He was waiting for her decision. But then Raúl remembered the decision was entirely his. He was paying for her company—not her say in their location.

'I will let the staff know.'

'Now?'

'They have to plot the route, inform…'

He didn't finish, just headed off to let the crew know, and Estelle sat there, suddenly nervous.

She wanted to be back on safe water—because living with Raúl like this, seeing this side of him, she was struggling to remember the rules.

Their 'couple of days' turned into two weeks.

They sailed around Menorca and took their time exploring its many bays. Estelle's skin turned from pale to pink, from freckles to brown. He watched her get bolder, loved seeing her stretch out on a lounger wearing only bikini bottoms, not even a little embarrassed now. Her sexuality was blossoming to his touch, before his eyes.

Finally they sailed back into Marbella. Normally the sight of it was the one he loved best in the world, yet there was a moment when he wanted to tell the skipper to keep sailing, to bypass Marbella and head to Gibraltar, take the yacht to Morocco, just to prolong their time. Except he was growing far too fond of her.

She put a hand on his shoulder, joined him to watch the splendid sight, but she felt his shoulder tense beneath her touch.

Raúl turned. She was wearing espadrilles and bikini bottoms, his own wedding shirt knotted beneath her now rosy bust, her cheeks flushed and her lips still swollen from their recent lovemaking.

'You'd better get dressed.'

Usually Raúl was telling her she was *over*dressed.

'The press may be there. The cream dress,' he told her. 'And have Rita do your make-up.'

As easily at that he demoted her, reminded her of her place.

Back on dry land he took her hand. But it was just for the cameras that he put his shoulders around his new wife.

It was in case of a long lens that he picked up her and carried her into his apartment, back to the reality of his life.

CHAPTER FOURTEEN

IT WAS A life she could never have imagined.

Raúl worked harder than anyone she knew.

His punishing day started at six, but rather than coming in drained at the end of it he would have a quick swim in the pool, or they'd make love—or rather they'd have sex. Because the Raúl from the yacht was gone now. A quick shower after that and then they'd get changed for dinner. Meals were always eaten out, and then they would hit the pulsing nightlife, dancing and partying into the early hours.

Estelle couldn't believe this was the toned-down version of Raúl.

'I can cook,' Estelle said, and smiled one night as they sat at Sol's and waited for their dishes to be served. 'It might be a novelty...'

'Why would you cook when a few steps away you can have whatever you choose?'

It was how he lived: life was a smorgasbord of pleasure. But six weeks married to Raúl, even with a week off to visit her family, was proving exhausting for Estelle—and she wasn't the one working. Or rather, she corrected herself as the waiter brought her a drink, she *was* working, twenty-four-seven, because no way would she be dining out every night, no way would she be wandering along streets that still pumped with music well after midnight on a Tuesday.

It had been Cecelia's cardiology appointment today, and Estelle was worried sick and doing her best not to show it. But she kept glancing at her phone, willing it to ring, wondering when she'd hear.

'How's your new PA?' Estelle asked as she bit into the most gorgeous braised beef, which had been cooked over an open fire.

'Okay.' Raúl shrugged. 'Angela trained her well…'

He looked down at her plate, stabbed a piece of beef with a fork and helped himself. Estelle was getting used to the way they shared their meals; it was the norm here.

'It *is* much more difficult without Angela,' Raúl admitted. 'Only now she is gone are we seeing how much she did around the place.'

'When will she be back?'

'She won't,' Raúl said. 'She is taking long service leave to nurse my father. Once he dies and it gets out about her she won't be welcome there.'

'Oh, well, you'll only have to see her at the funeral, then.'

Raúl glanced up. He could never be sure if she was being flip or serious. 'When are you going to see your father?' she asked him.

She was being serious, Raúl quickly found out.

'He chose to live in the north—he chose to end his days with his other family. Why should I….?' He closed his tense lips. 'I do not want to discuss it.'

'Angela called again today.'

'I told you not answer to her.'

'I was waiting for my brother to ring,' Estelle said. 'It was Cecelia's cardiology appointment today. I didn't think to look when I picked up.' Estelle could not finish her dinner and pushed the plate away.

'You're not hungry?'

'Just full.'

'I was thinking...' Raúl said. 'There is a show premiering in Barcelona at the weekend. I think it might be something we would enjoy.'

'Raúl...' She just could not sit and say nothing—could not lie beside him at night and sleep with him without caring even a bit, without having an opinion. Surely he could understand that? 'I was riddled with guilt when my parents died.'

'Why?'

'For every row, for every argument—for all the things we beat ourselves up about when someone dies. Guilt happens whatever you do. Why not make it about something you couldn't have changed, instead of something you can?' On instinct she went to take his hand, but he pulled it back.

'You're starting to sound like a wife.'

She looked at him.

'Believe me, I don't feel like one.'

Estelle pounced on her phone when it rang.

'I need to take this.'

'Of course.'

It was Amanda, doing her best, as always, to sound upbeat. 'They're going to keep Cecelia in for a few nights. She's a bit dehydrated...'

'Any idea when she's going to have surgery?'

'She's too small,' Amanda said. 'They've put a tube in, and we're going to be feeding her through that. She might come home on oxygen...'

Raúl watched Estelle's eyes filling with tears but she turned her shoulders and hunched into the phone in an effort to hide them. He heard her attempt to be positive even while she was twisting her hair around and around her finger.

'She's a fighter,' Estelle said, but as she did so she closed her eyes.

'How is your niece?' Raúl asked as she rang off.

'Much the same.' She didn't want to discuss it for fear she might break down—Raúl would be horrified! Seeing that he'd finished eating, Estelle gave him a bright smile. 'Where do you want to go next?'

'Where do *you* want to go?' Raúl offered.

Home, her body begged as they walked along the crowded street. But that wasn't what she was here for. She'd been transferring money over to Andrew since he'd gone back to England. The first time she'd told Andrew it was money she'd been saving to get a car. The second time she'd said it was a loan. Now she'd just given him a decent sum that would see them through the next few months, telling Andrew that she and Raúl simply wanted to help.

It was time to earn her keep.

They passed a club that was incredibly loud and very difficult to get into. It was a particular favourite of Raúl's. 'How about here?'

Estelle woke to silence. It was ten past ten and Raúl would long since have gone to work.

She sat up in bed and then, feeling dizzy, lay back down.

How the hell he lived like this on a permanent basis, Estelle had no idea. All she knew was she was not going out tonight.

He could, she decided, dressing and heading out not for the trendy boutiques but for the markets. She just wanted a night at home—or rather a night in Raúl's home—and something simple for dinner. There must be some subclause in the contract that allowed for the occasional night off?

Marbella was rarely humid, the mountains usually shielded it, but it struggled today. The air was thick and oppressive and the markets were very busy. Estelle had bought the ripest, plumpest vine tomatoes, and was deciding between lamb and steak when she passed a fish stall and gave a small retch. She tried to carry on, to continue walking, tried to focus on a flower stall ahead instead of the appalling thought she had just had.

She couldn't be pregnant.

Estelle took her pill at the same time every day.

Or she had tried to.

All too often Raúl would come home at lunchtime, or they'd be in a helicopter flying anywhere rather than to his father's—the one place he needed to be.

She couldn't be pregnant.

'Watch where you're going!' someone scolded in Spanish as she bumped into them.

'Lo sierto,' Estelle said, changing direction and heading for the *Pfarmacia*, doing the maths in her head and praying she was wrong.

Less that half an hour later she found out she was right.

Raúl didn't get home from work till seven, and when he did it was to the scent of bread baking and the sight of Estelle in his underutilised kitchen, actually cooking.

'Are we taking the wife thing a bit far?' Raúl checked tentatively. 'You don't have to cook.'

'I want to,' Estelle said. She was chopping up a salad. 'I just want to have a night in, Raúl.'

'Why?'

'Because.' She frowned at him. 'Do you ever stop?'

'No,' he admitted, then came over and give her a kiss. 'Are you okay?'

'I'm fine. Why?'

'You didn't wake up when I left this morning. You seem tense.'

'I'm worried about my niece,' Estelle said, removing herself from him and adding two steaks to the grill.

She was curiously numb. Since she'd done the test Estelle had been operating on autopilot and baking bread, which she sometimes did when she didn't want to think.

She just couldn't play the part tonight.

They carried their food out to the balcony and ate steak and tomato salad, with the herb bread she had made, watching a dark storm rolling in.

Estelle wanted to go home, wanted this over. Though she knew there was no getting out of their deal. But she needed a timeframe more than ever now. She wanted to be far away from him before the pregnancy started showing.

She could never tell him.

Not face to face, anyway.

Estelle could not bear to watch his face twist, to hear the accusations he would hurl, for him to find another reason not to trust.

'I spoke with my father today.'

She tore her eyes from the storm to Raúl. 'How is he?'

'Not good,' Raúl said. 'He asks that I go and see him soon.'

'Surely you can manage to be civil for a couple of days?' She was through worrying about saying the wrong thing. 'Yes, your father had an affair, but clearly it meant something. They're together all this time later...'

'An affair that led to my mother's death.' He stabbed at his steak. 'Their lies left the guilt with *me*.' He pushed his plate away.

The eyes that lifted to hers swirled with grief and confusion and now, when all she wanted was to be away from him, when she must guard her heart properly, when she needed it least, Raúl confided in her.

'I had an argument with my mother the night she died. She had missed my performance at the Christmas play—as she missed many things. When I came home she was crying and she said sorry. My response? *Te odio.* I told her I hated her. That night she lifted me from my sleep and put me in a car. The mountains are a different place in a storm,' Raúl explained. 'I had no idea what was happening; I thought I had upset her by shouting. I told her I was sorry. I told her to slow down…'

Estelle could not imagine the terror.

'The car skidded and came off the mountain, went down the cliffside. My father returned from his so-called work trip to be told his wife was dead and his son was in hospital. He chose not to tell anyone the reason he'd been gone.'

'Did they never suspect he and Angela?'

'Not for a moment. He just seemed to be devoting more and more time to the hotel in San Sebastian. Angela was from the north and she resumed working for him again. Over the years, clearly when Luka was older, she started to come to Marbella more often with my father. We had a flat for her, which she stayed in during the working week.'

'He had two sons to support,' Estelle said. 'Maybe it was the only way he could see how.'

'Please!' Raúl scoffed. 'He was with Angela every chance he could get, leaving me with my aunt and uncle. Had he wanted one family he could have had it. Perhaps it would have been a struggle, but his family would have been together. He chose this life, and those choices caused my mother's death.'

'Instead of you?'

'I blamed myself for years for her death. I thought the terrible things I said...'

'You were a child.'

'Yes,' he said. 'I see that now. The night she died was two days after Luka's birth. I realise now that she was on her way to confront them.'

'In a storm, with a five-year-old in the back of her car,' Estelle pointed out.

'I thought she was trying to kill me.'

'She was ill, Raúl.'

He nodded. 'It would have been nice to know that she was,' Raúl said. 'It would have been nice to know that it was not my words that had her fleeing into the night.'

'It sounds as though she was sick for a long time, and I would imagine it was a very tough time for your father...' Estelle did not want involvement. She wanted to remove herself as much as she could before she told him. Yet she could not sit back and watch his pain. 'He just wants to know you're happy, that you're settled. He just wants peace.'

'We all want peace.' He was a moment away from telling her the rest, but instead he stood and headed through the balcony door. 'I'm going out.'

Estelle sat still.

'Don't wait up.'

'I won't.'

She didn't want him going out in this mood, and she followed him into the lounge while knowing he wouldn't welcome her advice. 'Raúl, I don't think—'

'I don't pay you to think.'

'You're upset.'

'Now she tells me what I'm *feeling*!'

'Now *she* reminds you that she read that contract before she signed it. If you think you're going to go out clubbing and carrying on in your usual way I'll be on the next plane home…' she watched his shoulders stiffen '…with every last cent you agreed to pay me.'

He headed for the door.

'Hope the music's loud enough for you, Raúl!' she called out to him.

'It could never be loud enough.'

There was a crack from the storm and the balcony doors flew wide open. He turned then, and she glimpsed hell in his eyes. There was more than he was telling her, she knew that, and yet she did not need to know at this moment.

He was striding towards her and she understood for a moment his need for constant distraction, for *she* was craving distraction now. She was pregnant by the man she loved, who was incapable of loving her. How badly she didn't want to think about it. How nice it would be for a moment to forget.

His mouth was, perhaps for the last time, welcome. The crush of his lips was so fierce he might have drawn blood. Yet it was still not enough. He wrestled her to the floor and it was still too slow.

Here beneath him there were no problems—just the weight of him on her.

He was pulling at his zipper and pressing up her skirt. She was kissing him as if his lips could save them both. The balcony doors were still wide open. It was raining on the inside, raining on them, yet it did not douse them.

He had taught her so much about her body, but she learned something new now—how fast her arousal could be.

He was coming even before he was inside her; she could feel the hot splash on her sex. Estelle was sobbing as he thrust inside her, holding onto him for dear life. Each thrust of his hips met with her own desperation. It was fast and it was brutal, and yet it was the closest they had ever been.

He was at her ear and breathing hard when he lifted his face. She opened her eyes to a different man.

'Come with me to see them?'

He was asking, not telling.

'Yes.'

'Tomorrow?'

'Yes.'

It felt terribly close to love.

CHAPTER FIFTEEN

THEY FLEW EARLY the next morning, over the lush hills of Spain to the north, and even as his jet made light work of the miles there was a mounting tension. Had they run out of time?

Far from anger from Raúl, there was relief when Angela came out of the door to greet them, a wary smile on her face.

'Come in,' she said. 'Welcome.'

She gave Estelle a kiss on the cheek, and gave one too to Raúl. 'We can do this,' she said to him, even as he pulled back. 'For your father. For one day…'

Raúl nodded and they headed through to the lounge.

If Estelle was shocked at the change in his father, it must be hell for Raúl.

'Hey,' he greeted his son. 'You took your time.'

'I'm here now,' Raúl said. 'Congratulations on your wedding.' He handed Antonio a bottle of champagne as he kissed him on the cheek. 'I thought we could have a toast to you both later.'

'I finally make an honest woman of her,' Antonio said.

Estelle watched as Raúl bit back a smart response. There really was no time for barbs.

'Your brother is flying in from Bilbao tonight. Will you stay for dinner?' Antonio's eyes held a challenge.

'I'm not sure that we can stay...'

'A meeting between the two of you is inevitable,' Antonio said. 'Unless you boycott my funeral. I am to be buried here,' he added.

She watched Raúl's jaw tighten as he told his son that this was the home he loved. Yet he had denied his first son the chance of having a real home.

'I will make a drink,' Angela said to Estelle. 'Perhaps you could help me?'

Estelle went into the kitchen with her. It was large and homely, and even though she was hoping to keep things calm for Raúl, Estelle was angry on his behalf.

'We will leave them to it,' Angela said as Estelle sat at the table. 'You look tired.'

'Raúl doesn't live a very quiet life.'

'I know.' Angela smiled and handed her a cup of hot chocolate and a plate of croissants.

Estelle took a sip of her chocolate, but it was far too sickly and she put the cup back down.

'I can make you honey tea,' Angela offered. 'That is what I had when...' Her voice trailed off as she saw the panic in Estelle's eyes and realised she must not want anyone to know yet. To Angela it was obvious—she hadn't seen Estelle since her wedding day, and despite the suntan her face was pale, and there were subtle changes that only a woman might notice. 'Perhaps your stomach is upset from flying.'

'I'm fine,' Estelle said, deliberately taking another sip.

'I am worried that when Antonio dies I will see no more of Raúl...'

Estelle bit her lip. Frankly she wouldn't blame him. Because being here, seeing first-hand evidence of years of lies and deceit, she understood a little better the darkness of his pain.

'He is like a son to me.'

Estelle simply couldn't stay quiet. 'From a distance?'
She repeated Angela's own words from the wedding day
and then looked around. There were pictures of Luka, who
looked like a younger Raúl.

'Raúl is here too.' Angela pointed to a photo.

'He wasn't, though.' Estelle could not stand the pretence. 'You had a home here—whereas Raúl was being
shuffled between his aunt and uncle, occasionally seeing
his dad.'

'It was more complicated than that.'

'Not really.' Estelle simply could not see it. 'You say
you think of him as a son, and yet…'

'We did everything the doctor said,' Angela wrung her
hands. 'I need to tell you this—because if Raúl refuses
to speak with me ever again, then this much I would like
you to know. The first two years of Luka's life Antonio
hardly saw him. He did everything to help Raúl get well,
and that included keeping Luka a secret. The doctor said
Raul needed his home, needed familiarity. How could we
rip him away from his family and his house? How could
we move him to a new town when the doctor insisted on
keeping things as close to normal as possible?'

Estelle gave a small shrug. 'It would have been hard
on him, but surely no harder than losing his mother. He
thought it was because of something he had said to her.'

'How could we have known that?'

'You could have spoken to him. You could have asked
him about what happened. Instead you were up here, with
his dad.'

There was a long stretch of silence, finally broken by
Angela. 'Raúl hasn't told you, has he?'

'He's told me everything.'

'Did Raúl tell you that he was silent for a year?' She

watched as Estelle's already pale face drained of colour. 'We did not know what happened that day, for Raúl could not tell us. The trauma of being trapped with his dead mother…'

'How long were they trapped for?'

'For the night,' Angela said. 'They went over a cliff. It would seem Gabriella died on impact. When the *médicos* got there he was still begging her to wake up. He kept telling her he was sorry. Once they released him he said nothing for more than a year. How could we take him from his home, from his bed? How could we tell him there was a brother?'

'Excuse me—'

Estelle retched and cried into the toilet, and then tried to hold it together. Raúl did not need her drama today. So she rinsed her mouth and combed her hair, then headed back just as Raúl was coming out from the lounge.

'Are you okay?'

'Of course.'

'My father is going to have a rest. As you heard, my brother is coming for dinner tonight. I have agreed that we will stay.'

Estelle nodded.

'Somehow we will get through dinner without killing each other, and then,' Raúl said, 'as my reward for behaving…' He smiled and pulled her in, whispered something crude in her ear.

Far from being offended, Estelle smiled and then whispered into *his* ear. 'I can do it now if you want.'

She felt him smile on her cheek, a little shocked by her response.

'It can wait.' He kissed her cheek. 'Thank you for today. Without you I would not be here.'

'How is he?'

'Frail...sick...'

'He loves you.'

'I know,' Raúl said. 'And because I love him also, we will get through tonight.'

She wasn't so sure they'd get through it when she met Luka. He was clearly going through the motions just for the sake of his parents. Angela was setting up dinner in the garden and Antonio was sitting in the lounge. It was Estelle who got there first, and opened the door as Raúl walked down the hall.

The camera did not lie: he was a younger version of Raúl—and an angrier one too.

Luka barely offered a greeting, just walked into his family home where it seemed there were now two bulls in the same paddock. He refused Raúl's hand when he held it out to him and cussed and then spoke in rapid Spanish.

'What did he say?' Estelle asked as Luka strode through.

'Something about the prodigal son's homecoming and to save the acting for in front of his father.'

'Come on,' Estelle said. There would be time for dwelling on it later.

He caught her wrist. 'You're earning your keep tonight.'

He saw the grit of her teeth and the flash of her eyes.

'Do you do it deliberately, Raúl?' she asked 'Does it help to remind me of my place on a night like tonight?'

'I am sorry. What I meant was that things are particularly strained. When I asked you I never anticipated bringing you here. Certainly I never thought I would set foot in this house.'

They could not discuss it properly here, so for now she gave him the benefit of the doubt. They went out to the garden, where Luka was talking with his father, and they all sat at the table for what should have been a most difficult dinner. Instead, for the most part, it was nice. It was little uncomfortable at first, but soon conversation was flowing as Estelle helped Angela to bring out the food.

'I never thought I would see this day,' Antonio said. 'My family all at the same table…'

Antonio would never see it again.

He was so frail and weak it was clear this would be the last time. It was for that reason, perhaps, that Luka and Raúl attempted to be amicable.

'You work in Bilbao?' Raúl asked.

'I do,' Luka said. 'Investment banking.'

'I had heard of you even before this,' Raúl said. 'You are making a name for yourself.'

'And you.' Luka smiled but it did not meet his eyes. 'I hear about your many acquisitions…'

Thank God for morphine, Estelle thought, because Antonio just smiled and did not pick up on the tension.

The food was amazing—a mixture of dishes from the north and south of Spain. There was *pringá*, an Andalusian dish that was a slow-cooked mixture of meats and had been Raúl's favourite as a child. And there was *marmitako* too, a dish from the Basque Country, which was full of potatoes and pimientos and, Antonio said, had kept him going for so long.

'So you study?' Antonio said to Estelle.

'Ancient architecture.' Estelle nodded. 'Although, I haven't been doing much lately.'

'Yes, what happened to your online studies?' Raúl teased.

'Sol's happened.' Estelle smiled.

Raúl laughed. 'Being married to me is a full-time job…'

Raúl used the words she had used about Gordon. It was a gentle tease, a joke that caused a ripple of laughter—

except their eyes met for a brief moment and it hurt her that he was speaking the truth.

It *was* a job, Estelle reminded herself. A job that would soon be over. But then she thought of the life that grew inside her, the baby that must have the two most mismatched parents in the world.

Not that Raúl knew it.

He thought she loved the clubs and the parties, whereas sitting and eating with his family, as difficult as it was, was where she would rather be. This night, for Estelle, was one of the best.

'You would love San Sebastian.' Antonio carried on speaking to her. 'The architecture is amazing. Raúl, you should take Estelle and explore with her. Take her to the Basilica of Santa Maria—there is so much she would love to see…'

'Estelle would prefer to go out dancing at night. Anyway,' Raúl quipped, 'I haven't been inside a church for years.'

'You will be inside one soon,' his father warned. 'And you should share in your wife's interests.'

Estelle watched thankfully as Raúl took a drink rather than delivering a smart response to his father's marital advice.

And, as much as she'd love to explore the amazing city, she and Raúl were simply too different. And the most bizarre thing was Raúl didn't even know that they were.

She tried to imagine a future: Raúl coming home from a night out to a crying baby, or to nannies, or having access weekends. And she tried to picture the life she would have to live in Spain if she wanted his support.

Estelle remembered the menace in his voice when he had warned that he didn't want children and decided then that she would never tell him while this contract was between them. When she was back home in England and there was distance, when she could tell him without breaking down, or hang up on him if she was about to, *then* she would confess.

And there would be no apology either. Estelle surged in sudden defensiveness for her child—she wasn't going to start its life by apologising for its existence. However Raúl dealt with the news was up to him.

'So…' Still Antonio was focused on Estelle. 'You met last year?'

'We did.' Estelle smiled.

'When he said he was seeing an ex, I thought it was that…' Antonio snapped his fingers. 'The one with the strange name. The one he really liked.'

'Antonio.' Angela chided, but he was too doped up on morphine for inhibition.

'Araminta!' Antonio said suddenly.

'Ah, yes, Araminta.' Estelle smiled sweetly to her husband. 'Was that the one making a play for you at Donald's wedding?'

'That's the one.' Raúl actually looked uncomfortable.

'You were serious for a long time,' Antonio commented.

Estelle glanced up, saw a black smile on Luka's face.

'Weren't you engaged to her?' he asked. 'I remember my mother saying that she thought there might soon be a wedding.'

'Luka,' Angela warned. 'Raúl's wife is here.'

'It's fine,' Estelle attempted—except her cheeks were on fire. She was as jealous as if she had just found out about a bit of her husband's past she'd neither known of nor particularly liked. 'If I'd needed to know about all of Raúl's past before I married him we'd barely have got to his twenties by now.'

She should have left it there, but there was a white-hot

feeling tearing up her throat when she thought of how he'd so cruelly dismissed Araminta—and that was someone he'd once cared about.

It was for that reason her words were tart when she shot Raúl a look. 'Though you failed to mention you'd ever been engaged.'

'We were never engaged.'

'Please!'

Antonio's crack of laughter caught them all by surprise and he raised a glass to Estelle. 'Finally you have met your match.'

It wasn't a long night. Antonio soon tired, and as they headed inside Luka farewelled his father fondly. But the look he gave to Estelle and Raúl told them both he didn't need them to see him to the door in *his* home.

They headed for bed. Estelle was a bit embarrassed by her earlier outburst, especially as everyone else seemed to have managed to behave well tonight.

'I'm sorry about earlier,' she said as she undressed and climbed into bed. 'I shouldn't have said anything about Araminta.'

'You did well,' Raúl said. 'My father actually believes us now.'

He thought she had been acting, Estelle realised. But she hadn't been.

It felt very different sleeping in his father's home from sleeping in Raúl's apartment or on his yacht. Even Raúl's ardour was tempered, and for the first time since she had married him Estelle put on her glasses and pulled out a book. It was the same book she had been reading the day she had met him, about the mausoleum of the First Qin Emperor.

She was still on the same page.

As soon as this was over she was going to focus on

her studies. It had been impossible even to attempt online learning with Raúl around.

'Read me the dirty bits,' Raúl said, and when she didn't comment he took the book from her and looked at the title. 'Well, that will keep it down.'

For his effort he got a half smile.

'You really like all that stuff?'

'I do.'

His hand was on her hip, stroking slowly down. 'They should hear us arguing now,' he teased lightly. 'You demanding details about my past.'

'I don't need to know.'

'My time in Scotland was amazing.' Raúl spoke on regardless. 'I shared a house with Donald and a couple of others. For the first time since my mother died I had one bedroom, one home, a group of friends. We had wild times but it was all good. Then I met Araminta, we started going out, and I guess it was as close to love as I have ever come. But, no, we were never engaged.'

'I really don't need to hear about it.' She turned to him angrily. 'Do you remember the way you spoke to her?' She struggled to keep her voice down. 'The way you treated her?' She looked at his black eyes, imagined running into him a few years from now and being flicked away like an annoying fly. She wasn't hurting for Araminta, Estelle realised. She was hurting for herself—for a time in her future without him.

'So, should I have slept with her as she requested?'

'No!'

'Should I have danced with her when she asked?'

Estelle hated that he was right.

'Anyway, we were never engaged. Her father looked down on me because I didn't come with some inherited title, so I ended things.'

'You dumped her for that?'

'She was lucky I gave a reason,' Raúl said.

Estelle let out a tense breath—he could be so arrogant and cold at times.

'Normally I don't.'

She returned to her book, tried to pick up where she had left off. Just as she would try to pick up her life in a few weeks' time. Except now everything had changed.

'Put down the book,' Raúl said.

'I'm reading.'

'You are the slowest reader I have ever met,' Raúl teased. 'If we ever watch a movie with subtitles we will have to pause every frame.'

She gave up pretending to read, and as she took off her glasses and put down the book he was suddenly serious.

'Not that we will be watching many more movies.'

She lay on her pillow and faced him.

'I could not have done this without you,' Raúl said. 'I nearly didn't come here in time.' He brushed her hair back from his face with her hand.

'You made it, though.'

'It will be over soon.' He looked into her eyes and didn't know if he was dreading his father dying or that soon she would be gone. 'You'll be back to your studies…'

'And you'll be back on your yacht, partying along the coastline.'

'We could maybe go out on the yacht this weekend?' Was he starting to think of her in ways that he had sworn not to? Or was he simply not thinking straight, given that he was here? 'We had a good time.'

'We did have a good time,' Estelle said, but then she shook her head, because she was tired of running away from the world with Raúl. 'But can we just leave it at that?'

She did not want to taint the memory—didn't want to

return to the yacht with hope, only to find out that what they had found there no longer existed.

But for one more night it did.

He held her face and kissed her—a very slow kiss that tasted tender. She felt as if they were back on the boat, could almost hear the lap of the water as he pulled her closer to him and wrapped her in his arms, urged her to join him in one final escape.

Estelle did.

She kissed him as though she were his wife in more than name. She kissed him as though they were really the family they were pretending to be, sharing and loving each other through difficult times.

He had never known a kiss like it; her hands were in his hair, her mouth was one with his, their bodies were meshing, so familiar with each other now. And he wanted her in his bed for ever.

'Estelle....' He was on the edge of saying something he must not, so he made love to her instead.

His hands roamed her body; he kissed her hard as he slid inside her. Side on, they faced each other as he moved and neither closed their eyes.

'Estelle?'

He said it again. It was a question now—a demand to know how she felt. She could feel him building inside her but she was holding back—not on her orgasm. She was holding back on telling him how she felt. They were making love and they both knew it, though neither dared to admit it.

She stared at this man who had her heart. She didn't even need to kiss him to feel his mouth, because deep inside he consumed her. She was pressing her hips into him, her orgasm so low and intense that he moaned as she gripped him. He closed his eyes as he joined her, then forced them open just to watch the blush on her cheeks, the grimace on her face, just to see the face he loved come to him.

She knew he would turn away from her afterwards. Knew they had taken things too far, that there had been true tenderness.

She looked at the scar on his back and waited till dawn for his breathing to quicken, for Raúl to awake abruptly and take her as he did most mornings.

It never happened.

CHAPTER SIXTEEN

HE WOKE AND he waited for reason.

For relief to flood in because he had held back his words last night.

It never came.

He turned and watched her awaken. He should be bored by now. She should annoy him by now.

'What am I thinking?' he asked when she opened her eyes and smiled at him.

'I wouldn't presume to know.'

'I *did* meet you that night,' he said. 'Despite the dress and the make-up, it *was* Estelle.'

He was getting too close for comfort. Raúl had never been anything other than himself. She, on the other hand, changed at every turn—he didn't actually know her at all. Sex was their only true form of communication.

Estelle could hear noises from the kitchen and was relieved to have a reason to leave. 'I'll go and give Angela a hand.' She went to climb out of bed, wondering if she should say anything about what Angela had told her last night. 'I spoke to her yesterday…'

'Later,' Raúl said, and she nodded.

Today was already going to be painful enough.

* * *

'Buenos días,' Raúl greeted Angela.

'Buenos días.' Angela smiled. 'I was just making your father his breakfast. What would you like?'

'Don't worry about us,' Raúl said. 'We'll have some coffee and then Estelle and I might go for a walk.'

'What time are you going back?'

'I'm not sure,' Raúl said. 'Maybe we might stay a bit longer?'

'That would be good,' Angela said. 'Why don't you take your father's tray in and tell him?'

He was in there for ages, and Angela and Estelle shared a look when at one point they heard laughter.

'I am so glad that they have had this time,' Angela said, and then Raúl came out, and he and Estelle headed off for a walk along the sweeping hillsides on his father's property.

'Have you been here before?' Estelle asked. 'To San Sebastian, I mean?'

'A couple of times,' Raúl said. 'Would you like to explore?'

'We're here to spend time with your father,' Estelle said, nervous about letting her façade down, admitting just how much she would like to.

'I guess,' Raúl said. 'But, depending on how long we stay, I am sure the newlyweds would like some private time too.'

'Wouldn't you be bored?'

'If I am I can wait in the gift shop.' Raúl smiled, and so did she, and then he told her some of what he had been talking about with his father. 'He has told my aunt and uncle about Angela and Luka.'

'When?'

'Yesterday. When he knew I was on my way,' Raúl said. 'He didn't want to leave it to me to tell them.'

'How did they take it?'

'He asked if we heard any shouting while we were flying up.' Raúl gave a small mirthless laugh. 'They want him dead, of course. He told them they wouldn't have long to wait.'

They walked for ages, hardly talking, and Raúl was comfortable with silence, because he was trying to think—trying to work out if she even wanted to hear what he was about to ask her.

'You miss England?'

'I do,' Estelle said. 'Well, I miss my family.'

'Will you miss me?' He stopped walking.

She turned to him and didn't know how to respond. 'I won't miss the clubs and the restaurants...'

'Will you miss *us*?'

'I can't give the right answer here.'

'You can.' He took her in his arms. 'You were right. I miss out on so much...'

It was a fragile admission, she could feel that, and she was scared to grasp it in case somehow it dispersed. But she could not deny her feelings any longer. 'You don't have to.'

His mouth was on hers and they were kissing as if for the first time—a teenage kiss as they paused in the hills, a kiss that had nothing to do with business; a kiss that had nothing to do with sex. His fingers were moving into her hair, touching her face as if he were blind, and she was a whisper away from telling him, from confessing the truth. Just so they could tell his father—just so there might be one less regret.

'Raúl...'

He looked into her eyes and she thought she could tell him anything when he looked at her like that. But for the moment she held back. Because a child was something far bigger than this relationship they were almost exploring. She remembered her vow to do this well away from their contract.

'Let's get back.'

They walked down the hill hand in hand, talking about nothing in particular—about France, so close, and the drive they could maybe take tomorrow, or the next day. They were just a couple walking, heading back home to their family—and then she felt his hand tighten on hers.

'It's the *médico*.'

They ran the remaining distance, though he paused for just a moment to collect himself before they pushed open the front door. Because even from there they could hear the sound of Angela sobbing.

'Your father...' Angela stumbled down the hall and Raúl held her as she wept into his arms. 'He has passed away.'

CHAPTER SEVENTEEN

ESTELLE COULDN'T BELIEVE how quickly things happened.

Luka arrived soon after, and spent time with his father. But it was clear he did not appreciate having Raúl and Estelle in his home.

'Stay,' Angela said.

'We'll go to a hotel.'

'Please, Raúl…'

Estelle's heart went out to her, but it was clear that Luka did not want them there and so they spent the night in a small hotel. Raúl was pensive and silent.

The next morning they stood in the small church to say farewell. The two brothers stood side by side, but they were not united in their grief.

'I used to think Luka was the chosen one,' Raúl said as they flew late that afternoon back to Marbella for the will to be read, as per his father's wishes. 'When I found out—when my father said he wanted to die there—I felt his other family were the real ones.' His eyes met hers. 'Luka sees things differently. He was a secret—his father's shame. I got to work alongside him. I was the reason he did not see much of his father when he was small. His hatred runs deep.'

'Does yours?'

'I don't know,' Raúl admitted. 'I don't know how I feel. I just want to get the reading of the will over with.'

It wasn't a pleasant gathering. Paola and Carlos were there, and the look they gave Angela as she walked in was pure filth.

'She doesn't need this—' Estelle started, but Raúl shot her a look.

'It was never going to be nice,' he said.

Estelle bit her lip, and tried to remember her opinion on his family was not what she was here for. But she kept remembering the night they had made love, their walk on the hill the next morning, and tried to hold on to a love that had almost been there—she was sure of it.

She sat silent beside him as the will was read, heard the low murmurs as the lawyer spoke with Angela. From her limited Spanish, Estelle could make out that she was keeping the home in San Sebastian and there were also some investments that had been made in her name.

And then he addressed Luka.

Estelle heard a shocked gasp from Paola and Carlos and then a furious protest started. But Raúl sat still and silent and said nothing.

'What's happening?'

He didn't answer her.

As the room finally settled the lawyer addressed Raúl. He gave a curt nod, then stood.

'Come on.'

He took her by the arm and they walked out.

Angela followed, calling to him. 'Raúl…'

'Don't.' He shrugged her off. 'You got what you wanted.'

Estelle had to run to keep up with his long strides, but finally he told her what was happening.

'His share of the business goes to Luka.' His face was grey when he turned and faced her. 'Even dying still he plays games, still he lies.' He shook his head. 'I get a vine-yard...'

'Raúl,' Angela had caught up with them. 'He saw how happy you two were the night before he died.'

'He did not change his will.'

'No, but it was his dream that his two sons would work side by side together.'

'He should have thought about that twenty-five years ago.'

'Raúl...'

But Raúl was having none of it. He strode away from Angela and all too soon they were back in his apartment and rapid decisions were being made.

'I'll sell my share,' he said. 'I will start again.' He would. Raúl had no qualms about starting again. 'And I will sell that vineyard too...'

'Why?'

'Because I don't want it,' he said. 'I don't want anything from *him*. I don't want to build bridges with my brother.' *His* mother's business was being handed over to her husband's illegitimate son—it would kill her if she wasn't dead already.

Raúl was back in the mountains—could hear her furious shouts and screams, the storm raging; he could hear the screech of tyres and the scrape of metal. He was over the cliff again. But that part he could manage—that part he could deal with. It was next part he dreaded.

It was the silence after that, and he would do anything never to hear it again.

'You don't have to make any decisions tonight. We can talk about it—'

'We?' His lips tore into a savage smile. '*We* will talk about *my* future? Estelle, I think *you* are forgetting your place.'

'No.' She refused to deny it any longer. 'The morning your father died, when were talking, we were *both* choosing to forget my place. If you want a relationship you can't pick and choose the times!'

'A relationship?' He stared at her for the longest time.

'Yes,' Estelle said, and she was the bravest she had ever been. 'A relationship. I think that's what you want.'

'Now she tells me what I want? You *love* me, do you? You *care* about me, do you? Have you any idea how boring that is to hear? I *bought* you so we could avoid this very conversation. You'd do well to remember that.'

Estelle just stood there as he stormed out of the apartment. She didn't waste her breath warning him this time. She refused to be his keeper.

CHAPTER EIGHTEEN

RAÚL SAT IN Sol's with the music pumping and stared at the heaving dance floor.

A vineyard.

A vineyard which, if he sold it, wouldn't even pay for his yacht for a year—would Estelle stick around then?

Yes.

He had never doubted his ability to start again, but he doubted it now—could not bear the thought of letting her down.

'Te odio.' He could hear his five-year-old voice hurling the words at his mother, telling her he hated her for missing his play.

He'd been a child, a five-year-old having a row, yet for most of his life he had thought those words had driven his mother to despair that day.

Could he do it?

Whisk Estelle away from a family that loved her to live in the hills with a man who surely wasn't capable of love?

Except he did love her.

And she loved him.

He had done everything he could think of to ensure it would not happen, had put so many rules in place, and yet here it was—staring at him, wrapping around him like a blanket on a stifling day.

He did not want her love, did not want the weight of it. Did not want to be responsible for another's heart.

She would stand by him, Raúl knew, but the fallout was going to be huge. The empire was divided. He could smell the slash and burn that would take place and he did not want her exposed to it.

His phone buzzed in his pocket but he refused to look at it, because if he saw her name he would weaken.

Raúl looked across the dance floor, saw an upper-class hooker, ordered her a drink and gestured her over.

He took out some money and as she opened her bag made his request.

'Lápiz de labios,' Raúl said, and pointed to his neck.

He did not have to explain himself to her. She delivered his request—put her mouth to his neck and did as he asked.

'Perfume,' he ordered next, and she took out her cheap scent and sprayed him.

'Gracias.'

It was done now.

Raúl stood and headed for home.

CHAPTER NINETEEN

'AMANDA.' ESTELLE ATTEMPTED to sound normal when she answered the landline. She was staring at the picture of them on Donald's wedding night, trying to fathom the man who simply refused to love.

'I tried your mobile.'

'Sorry…' Estelle had started to talk about the charger she'd left in San Sebastian, started to talk about little things that weren't important at all, when she realised that for once Amanda wasn't being upbeat. 'What's happened?'

'I tried to ring Raúl—I wanted him to break the news to you.'

Estelle felt her heart turn to ice.

'We're at the hospital and the doctors say that they're going to operate tomorrow.'

'Has she put on any weight?'

'She's lost some,' Amanda said. 'But if they don't operate we're going to lose her anyway.'

'I'm coming home.'

'Please…'

'How's Andrew?'

'He's with her now. He's actually been really good. He's sure she's going to make it through.'

'She will.'

'I don't think so,' Amanda admitted, and her sister-in-law who was always so strong, always so positive, finally broke down.

Estelle said everything she could to comfort her, but knew they were only words, that she needed to be there.

'I'm going to hang up now and book a flight,' Estelle told her. 'And I'll try and sort out my phone.'

'Don't worry about the phone,' Amanda said. 'Just get here.'

Estelle grabbed her case and started piling clothes in. Getting to the airport and onto a flight was her aim, but the thought of Cecelia, so small and so weak, undergoing something so major was just too overwhelming and it made Estelle suddenly fold over. She sobbed as she never had before—knew that she had to get the tears out now, so she could be strong for Amanda and Andrew.

Raúl heard her tears as he walked through the apartment and could not stand how much he had hurt her—could not bear that *he* had done this.

'Estelle…' He saw the case and knew that she was leaving.

'Don't worry.' She didn't even look at him. 'The tears aren't for you. Cecelia has been taken back into hospital. They can't wait for the surgery any longer…' She thought of her again, so tiny, and of what would happen to her parents if they lost her. The tears started again. 'I need to get back to them.'

'I'll fix it now.'

He couldn't *not* hold her.

Could not stand the thought of her facing this on her own, not being there beside her.

He held her in his arms and she wept.

And he could not fight it any more for he loved her.

'We'll go now.'

'No.' She was trying to remember that she was angry, but it felt so good to be held.

'Estelle, I've messed up, but I know what I want now. *I know…*'

She smelt it then—the cheap musky scent; she felt it creep into her nostrils. She moved out of his arms and looked at him properly, smelt the whisky on his breath and saw the lipstick on his neck.

'It's not what you think,' Raúl said.

'You're telling me what I think, are you?' Oh, she didn't need him to teach her to cuss in Spanish! 'You win, Raúl!' Her expression revealed her disgust. 'I'm out of here!'

The tears stopped. They weren't for him anyway. She just turned and went on filling her case.

'Estelle—'

'I don't want to hear it, Raúl.' She didn't even raise her voice.

'Okay, not now. We will speak about it on the plane.'

'You're not coming with me, Raúl.'

'Your brother will think it strange if I do not support you.'

'I'm sure my brother has other things on his mind.' She looked at him, dishevelled and unshaven, and scorned him with her eyes. 'Don't make this worse for me, Raúl.'

He went to grab her arm, to stop her.

'Don't touch me!'

He heard her shout, heard the pain—not just for what was going on with her niece, but for the agony of the betrayal she perceived.

'You can't leave like this. You're upset…'

'I'm upset about my niece!' She looked at him. 'I would *never* cry like this over a man who doesn't love me.' She didn't care how much she hurt him now. 'I'm not your mother, Raúl, I'm not going fall apart, or drive over a cliff-edge because the man I'm married to is a cheat. I'm far stronger than that.'

She was.

'All I want now is to get home to my niece.'

He'd lost her. Raúl knew that. Arguing would be worse than futile, for she needed to be with her family urgently.

'I will call my driver and organise a plane.'

'I can sort out transport myself.' Tears for him were starting now, and she didn't want Raúl to see—love was not quite so black and white.

'If you take my plane it will get you there sooner,' Raúl said.

And it would get her away from him before she broke down—before she told him about the baby...before she weakened.

It was the only reason she said yes.

CHAPTER TWENTY

RAÚL STOOD IN the silence.

It was the sound he hated most in the world.

It was his nightmare.

Only this was one *he* had created.

The scent that filled his nostrils was not leaking fuel and death but the scent of cheap perfume and the absence of *her*.

He wanted to chase Estelle—except he was not foolish enough to get in a car, and he could not follow her as his driver was taking her to the airport.

Raúl called a taxi, but even as he climbed in he knew she would not want him with her on the flight. Knew he would be simply delaying her in getting to where she needed to be. They passed De La Fuente Holdings and he looked up, trying to imagine it without his father and Angela, and with Luka working there. Trying to fathom a future that right now he could not see.

Noticing a light on, he asked the driver to stop...

'Raúl!'

Angela tried not to raise her eyes as a very dishevelled Raúl appeared from the elevator.

He was unshaven, his eyes bloodshot. His hair was a mess, and there was lipstick on his collar...

It was the Raúl she knew well.

'What are you doing here at this time, Raúl?'

'I saw the light on,' Raúl said. 'Estelle's niece is sick.'

'I am sorry to hear that. Where is Estelle?'

'Flying back to London.'

'You should be with her, then.' Angela refused to mince her words. He might not want to hear what she had to say to him—he could leave if that were the case.

'She didn't want me to go.'

'So you hit the clubs and picked up a *puta*?'

'No.'

'Don't lie to me, Raúl,' Angela said. 'Your wife would never wear cheap perfume like that.'

'I wouldn't cheat on her. I couldn't.'

Angela paused. Really, the evidence was clear—and yet she knew Raúl better than most and he did not lie. Raúl never attempted to defend the inexcusable.

'So what happened?' Angela asked.

He closed his eyes in shame.

'You know, when you live as a mistress apparently you lose the right to an opinion on others—but of course you have them.' Harsh was the look she gave Raúl. 'Over and over I question your morals.'

'Over and over I do too,' Raúl admitted. 'She got too close.'

'That's what couples do.'

'I did not cheat. I wanted her to think that I had.'

'So now she does.' Angela looked at him. 'So now she's on her own, dealing with her family.'

Angela watched his eyes fill with tears and she tried not to love him as a son, tried not to forgive when she should not. But when he told her what had happened, told her what he had done, the filthy place his head had been, she believed him.

'You push away everyone who loves you. What are you scared of, Raúl?'

'This,' Raúl admitted. 'Hurting another, being responsible for another…'

'We are responsible for ourselves,' Angela said. 'I have made mistakes. Now I pay for them. Now I have till the morning to clear out my office. Now your aunt and uncle turn their backs on me. I would do it all again, though, for the love I had with your father. Some things I would do differently, of course, but I would do it all again.'

'What would you do differently?'

'I would have insisted you were told far sooner about your father and I. I would have told you about your brother,' she said. 'We were going to before you went to university, but your father decided not to at the last moment. I regret that. I should have stood up to him. I should have told you myself. I did not. And I have to live with that. What would *you* have done differently, Raúl?'

'Not have gone to Sol's.' He gave a small smile. 'And many, many other things. But that is the main one now.'

'You need to go to her. You need to tell her what happened—why you did what you did.'

'She doesn't want to hear it,' Raúl said. 'There are more important things on her mind.'

He could not bring himself to tell Angela that their marriage was a fake. If this was fake, then it hurt too much.

And if it was not fake, then it was real.

'If you are not there for her now, with her niece so ill, then it might be too late.'

Raúl nodded. 'She has my plane.'

'I will book you on a commercial flight,' Angela said. 'You need to freshen up.'

He headed to his office, stared in the mirror and picked

up his razor. He called his thanks as she brought him in coffee and a fresh shirt.

'This is the last time I do this for you.'

'Maybe not,' Raúl said. 'Maybe your sons might have a say in that.'

Angela's eyes welled up for a moment as finally he acknowledged the place she had in his heart. But then she met his eyes and told him, 'I meant this is the last time I help you cover up a mistake. Estelle deserves more.'

'She will get it.'

'Your father was so pleased to see how you two were together,' Angela said. 'He was the most peaceful I have ever seen him. He knew he had not allowed time for you and Luka to sort things out, but you are brothers and he believes that will happen. The morning he passed away we were watching you and Estelle walking in the hills. We saw you stop and kiss.'

Raúl closed his eyes as he remembered that day, when for the first time in his life he had been on the edge of admitting love.

'He knew you were happy. I am so glad that I told him about the baby.'

Raúl froze.

'Baby?'

There was no mistaking his bewilderment.

'She has not told you?'

'No!' Raúl could not take it in. 'She told *you*?'

'No,' Angela said. 'I just knew. She did not have any wine; she was sick in the morning…'

Yes, Estelle was tough.

Yes, she could do this without him.

He did not want her to.

'Book the flight.'

CHAPTER TWENTY-ONE

'RAÚL!'

The only possible advantage to being in the midst of a family crisis was that no one noticed the snap to her voice or the tension on Estelle's features when a clean-shaven, lipstick-free Raúl walked in.

'I'm sorry I couldn't get here sooner.' He shook Andrew's hand.

'No, we're grateful to you for getting Estelle here,' Andrew said. 'We're very sorry about your father.'

It was strange, but in a crisis it was Andrew who was the strong one. Amanda barely looked up.

'Is she in surgery?' Raúl sat down next to Estelle and put his arm around her. He felt her shoulders stiffen.

'An hour ago.' Her words were stilted. 'It could be several hours yet.'

The clock ticked on.

Raúl read every poster on the wall and every pamphlet that was laid out. She could hear the turning of the pages and it only served to irritate her. Why on earth had he come? Why couldn't she attempt to get over him with him still far away?

'Why won't they give us an update?' asked Amanda's mother. 'It's ridiculous that they don't let us know what's going on.'

'They will soon,' Andrew said, and Raúl watched as Andrew put his arm around his wife and comforted her, saw how she leant on him, how much she needed him.

Despite everything.

Because of everything, Raúl realised.

'Why don't you wait in the hotel?' Estelle suggested when she could not stand him being in the room a moment longer. 'I've got a room there.'

'I want to wait with you.'

He headed out to the vending machine and she followed him. 'I need some change,' he said. 'I haven't got any pounds.'

'Why would you make this worse for me?'

'I'm not trying to make it worse for you,' Raúl said. 'I know this is neither the time nor the place, but you need to know that nothing happened except my asking a woman to kiss my neck and spray me with her perfume.' He looked her right in the eye. 'I wanted you gone.'

'Well, it worked.'

'I made a mistake,' Raúl said. 'The most foolish of mistakes. I did not want to put you through what was to come.'

'Shouldn't that be *my* choice?' She looked at him.

'Yes,' he said simply. 'As it should be mine.'

Estelle didn't understand his response, was in no mood for cryptic games, and she shook her head in frustration. She wanted him gone and yet she wanted him here— wanted to forgive, to believe.

'I can't do this now,' Estelle said. 'Right now I have to concentrate on my niece.'

As much as Raúl longed to be there for her, that much he understood. 'Do you want me to wait in the hotel or stay with you here?'

'The hotel,' Estelle said—because she could not think straight with him around, could not keep her thoughts where they needed to be with Raúl by her side. She wanted his arms around her, wanted the comfort only he could give, and yet she could not stand what he had done.

'Could I get a coffee as well?' Andrew wheeled himself over.

'Of course,' Raúl said as Estelle handed him some change.

'Estelle, could you take Amanda for a walk?' Andrew asked. 'Just get her away from the waiting room. Her parents are driving her crazy, asking how much longer it will be.'

'Sure.'

Estelle's eyes briefly met Raúl's, warning him to be gone by the time she returned, and Raúl knew the fight he had on his hands. He watched as Estelle suggested a walk to Amanda and he saw a family in motion, supporting each other, a family that was there for each other. A family who helped, who fixed—or tried to.

He looked to Andrew. 'You have the best sister in the world.'

'I know,' Andrew said. 'I'd do anything for her.'

As would Estelle for him, Raúl thought. She'd sold her soul to the devil for her family, but now he understood why.

'I am going to wait in the hotel,' Raúl said. 'I didn't sleep at all last night.'

'I know.' Andrew nodded. 'I'm sure Estelle will keep you up to date.'

'What hotel is she staying at?'

'Over the road,' Andrew told him. 'Good luck—I'm sure it's not at all what you're used to.'

'It will be fine.'

'You just wait.' Andrew gave a pale smile. 'I had to wait fifteen minutes just for them to find a ramp.'

They chatted on for a while—Andrew trying to keep

his mind out of the surgery, Raúl simply because Andrew wanted to talk.

'I had my reservations about the two of you at first,' Andrew admitted. 'You're so opposite.'

And then Raúl found out from his wife's brother just how much Estelle hated clubs and bars, found out exactly the lengths she had gone to for her family.

There was one length she would not go to, though. Raúl was certain of that now.

He walked alongside Andrew's chair, down long corridors, past the operating theatres and Intensive Care, and back again a few times over—until he saw Estelle returning and knew it was better for her that he leave.

He paced the small hotel room, waiting for news—because surely it was taking too long. It was now nine p.m., and he was sick to his stomach for a baby he had never met and a family he wanted to be a part of.

'She made it through surgery.'

Raúl could hear both the relief and the strain in Estelle's voice when the door opened.

'When did she get out of Theatre?'

'About six.' She glanced over to him. 'Was I supposed to ring and inform you?'

He could hear the sarcasm in her voice. 'I just thought it was taking too long. I thought…'

'I'm sorry.' Estelle regretted her sarcastic response—she could see the concern on his face was genuine. 'It was just a long wait till they let Andrew and Amanda in to see her. They've only just been allowed.'

'How is she?'

'Still here.' Estelle peeled off her clothes. 'I've lost my phone charger. I gave Andrew your number in case anything happens overnight.'

It was, though she would never admit it, a relief to have him here, to know that if the phone rang in the night he would be the one to answer it. It was a relief, too, to sink into bed and close her eyes, but there was something that needed to be dealt with before the bliss of sleep.

'I'm not going to tell them we're over yet,' Estelle said. 'It would be too much for them to deal with now. But after we visit in the morning can you make your excuses and leave.'

'I want to be here.'

'I don't want you here, though, and given what's happened you don't own me any more.' She stared into the dark. 'Exclusive, remember?'

'I've told you—nothing happened,' Raúl said. 'Which means I do still own you.'

'No,' Estelle said, 'you don't. Because whatever went on I've decided that I don't want your money. It costs too much.'

'Then pay me back.'

'I will…' she attempted, but of course a considerable amount had already been spent. 'I fully intend to pay you back. It just might take some time.'

'Whatever you choose. But it changes nothing now, Estelle…' He reached for her, wanted to speak with her, but she shrugged him off and turned to her side.

'I'd like the night off.'

'Granted.'

She woke in his arms and wriggled away from them, and then rang her brother. Raúl watched as she went to climb out of bed, saw the extra heaviness to her breasts and the darkening pink of her areolae, and he loved her all the more for not telling him, for guarding their child from the contract that had once bound them. It was the only leverage he had.

'You'll leave after visiting?' Estelle checked.

'Why would I leave my wife at a time like this?' Raúl asked. 'I'm not going anywhere, Estelle.'

'I don't want you here.'

'I don't believe you,' Raúl said. 'I believe you love me as much as I love you.'

'Love you!' Estelle said. 'I'd be mad to love you.' She shook her head. 'You might have almost sent me crazy once, Raúl, but if I possibly did love you then it's gone. My love has conditions too, and you didn't adhere to them. I don't care about technicalities, Raúl. Even if you didn't sleep with someone else, what you did was wrong.'

'Then we go back to the contract.' He caught her wrist. 'Which means I dictate the terms.'

'Your father's dead. Surely it's over?'

'We agreed on a suitable pause. You should read things more closely before you sign them, Estelle.' He watched her shoulders rise and fall. 'But I agree it has proved more complicated than either of us could have anticipated. For that reason, I will agree that the contract expires tomorrow.'

'Tomorrow?' Estelle asked. 'Why not now?'

'I just want one more night. And if I have to exercise the terms of the contract to speak with you—believe me, I shall.'

CHAPTER TWENTY-TWO

'SHE'S PINK!'

Estelle couldn't believe the little pink fingers that wrapped around hers. Even Cecelia's nails were pink—it was suddenly her favourite colour in the world.

'That's the first thing we said.' Andrew was holding Cecelia's other hand. 'She's been fighting so much since the day she was born.' Andrew smiled down at his daughter.

All were too entranced by the miracle that was Cecilia to notice how much Raúl was struggling.

Raúl looked down at the infant, who resembled Estelle, and could hardly believe what he had almost turned his back on.

'I have to go and do some work,' Raúl said. 'Do you want to get lunch later?'

Estelle looked up, about to say no, but he was talking to Andrew.

'Just at the canteen,' he added.

'That would be great.' Andrew smiled. 'Estelle, could you take Amanda for some breakfast? She wants one of us with Cecelia all the time but she needs to get out of the unit and get some fresh air.'

'Sure.' Estelle stood.

'I thought we could go for dinner tonight.'

This time Raúl *was* speaking to Estelle.

'I'm here to be with my niece.'

'Andrew and Amanda are with her. As long as she continues to improve I am sure they expect you to eat.'

'Of course we do,' Andrew said. 'Go out tonight, Estelle. You need a break from the hospital too!'

It was a long day. The doctors were in and out with Cecelia, and talked about taking her breathing tube out if she continued to hold her own. Amanda's parents went home, to return at the weekend, and after they had gone Estelle finally persuaded Amanda to have a sleep in one of the parents' rooms.

It was exhausting.

As she closed the door and went to head back to Cecelia she wondered if she had, after all, grown far too used to Raúl's lifestyle—she would have given anything to be back on his yacht, just drifting along, with nothing to think about other than what the next meal might be and how long it would be till they made love again.

Being Raúl's tart hadn't all been bad, Estelle thought with a wry smile as she returned to Cecelia.

It was being his wife that was hell.

'Amanda's asleep,' Estelle said. 'Well, for a little while.'

'Thanks for being here for us,' Andrew said. 'Both of you. Raúl's great. I admit I wasn't sure at first, but you can see how much he cares for you.'

She felt tears prick her eyes,

'Did you ask him to offer me a job?'

'A job?'

She couldn't lie easily to her brother, but instantly he knew that Estelle's surprised response was real, that she'd had no idea.

'Raúl said that when things are sorted with Cecelia there will be a job waiting for me. He wants me to check out his hotels, work on adjustments for the disabled. There will be a lot of travel, and it will be tough being away at first. But once Cecelia's better he says we can broaden things so it's not just about travelling with disabilities but with a young child as well.'

It was a dream job. She could see it in her brother's eyes. Soon he would be earning, travelling, and more than that his self-respect and confidence would start to return.

'It sounds wonderful.' Estelle gave him a hug, but though she smiled and said the right thing she was furious with Raúl—his company was about to implode, and she and Raúl were soon to divorce quietly.

How dared he enmesh himself further? How dared he involve Andrew in the chaos they had made?

She wanted it to be tomorrow, she wanted Raúl gone so she could sort out how she felt, sort out her life, sort out how to tell him that the temporary contract they had signed would, however tentatively, bind them for life.

There was a note from Raúl waiting for her when she reached the hotel, telling her that he was tied up in a meeting but would see her at the restaurant at eight.

'You signed up for this,' Estelle told herself aloud as she put on her eye make-up. She wondered if it would be just dinner, or perhaps a club after, or…

Estelle closed her eyes so sharply that she almost scratched her eyeball with her mascara wand. He surely wouldn't expect them to sleep together?

He surely wouldn't insist?

Then again, Estelle told herself as she took a taxi to the restaurant, this was Raúl.

Of course he would insist.

Worse, though, she knew she must comply—no matter the toll on heart.

* * *

He turned heads. He just did.

He was waiting for her at the bar, and when they walked into the smartest of restaurants he might as well have being stepping out of a helicopter in a kilt—because everybody was looking at him.

'You look beautiful,' Raúl told her as they sat down.

'Thank you,' she said.

He could feel the anger hissing and spitting inside her, guessed that she must have spoken to Andrew since lunchtime.

'It's a lovely dress,' he commented. 'New?'

'I chose it.'

'It suits you.'

'I know.'

He ordered wine. She declined.

He suggested seafood, which he knew she loved, but he had read in one of the many leaflets he perused in the hospital waiting room that pregnant woman were advised not to eat it.

'I thought you loved seafood?' Raúl commented when she refused it, wondering what her excuse would be.

'I've had enough of it.'

She ordered steak, and he watched her slice it angrily before she voiced one of the many things that were on her mind.

'Did you offer my brother a job?'

'I did.'

'Why would you do that? Why would you do that when you're about to walk away? When you know the company's heading for trouble?'

'We're not heading for trouble,' Raúl said. 'I have been speaking with Luka at length today, and Carlos and Paola too. There is to be a name-change. To Sanchez De La

Fuente... Anyway, if there is trouble ahead it will only be in the office. Your brother will not be dealing with it.'

'What about when we divorce? Will you use him as a pawn then?'

'Never. I tell you this: it is a proper offer, and as long as your brother does well he will have a job.'

'You say that now...'

'I always keep my word.' He looked at her. 'I don't lie,' Raúl said. 'From the start I have only been myself.' He watched the colour spread up her cheeks. 'You get the truth, whether you like or not. I think we both know that much about me.'

Reluctantly she nodded.

'It is only wives that I employ on a whim. I am successful because I choose my employees carefully and I don't give out sympathy jobs. Your brother pointed out a few things that could be changed at the hotel. He would like the menu outside the restaurant to be displayed lower too. He said he would not like to find out about the menu and the prices from a woman he was perhaps dating with.'

Estelle gave a reluctant smile. It was the sort of thing Andrew *would* say.

'He said that a lower table at Reception would be a nice touch, so that anyone in a wheelchair could check in there. That means I do not have to refurbish our reception areas. He has saved me more than his year's wage already.'

'Okay.'

'I don't want my hotels to be good, I want them to be the best—and by the best I mean the best for everyone: businessmen, people with families, the disabled. Your brother, as I told him, will soon be all three.' He looked at her for a long moment, wondering if now she might tell him. 'It is good to see Cecelia improving,' Raúl said. 'It must be a huge relief.'

'It is,' Estelle admitted. 'I think we're only now realising just how scary the last few months have been.'

'Does seeing your niece make you consider ever having a baby?'

She gave a cynical laugh.

'It's just about put me off for life, seeing all that they have had to go through.'

'But they've made it.'

She wasn't going to tell him about the baby, Raúl realised. But, far from angering him, it actually made him smile as he sat opposite the strongest woman he knew.

'Here…' At the end of the meal he smeared cream cheese on a cracker, added a dollop of quince paste and handed it to her.

'No, thanks. I'm full.'

'But remember the night we met…'

'I'd rather not.'

He saw tears prick her eyes and went to take her hand. He could not believe all that they had been through in recent weeks. As she pulled her hand away Raúl wasn't so sure they'd survived it.

'I'm sorry for hurting you. I overreacted—thought I was going to lose everything, thought I might not be able to give you the lifestyle—'

'Like I need your yacht,' Estelle spat. 'Like I need to eat out at posh restaurants seven nights a week, or wear the clothes you chose.'

'So if you don't want all that,' Raúl pointed out, 'what *do* you want?'

'Nothing,' Estelle said. 'I want nothing from you.'

He called for the bill and paid, and as they headed out of the restaurant he took her hand and held it tightly. He turned her to him and kissed her.

It tasted of nothing.

He kissed her harder.

She wanted to spit him out. Not because she loathed his mouth but because she wanted to sink into it for ever—wanted to believe his lies, wanted to think for a moment that she could hold him, that he'd want their baby as much as she did, that he'd want the real her if he knew who she was.

'Where now?' Raúl asked. 'I know...' He held her by the hips. 'You could show me Dario's...'

'I didn't meet Gordon at Dario's,' Estelle said. 'I told you that.'

'We could go anyway,' Raúl said. 'It's our last night together, and it sounds like fun.'

He saw the conflict in her eyes, saw her take a breath to force another lie. He would not put her through it, so he kissed her instead.

'Let's get back to the hotel.'

'Raúl...' She just couldn't go through with it—could not keep up the pretence a moment longer, could not bear to be made love to just to have her heart ripped apart again.

'What?' He took her by the hand again, led her to a taxi.

'Come on, Estelle...' He undressed speedily. 'It's been a hell of a day. I would like to come.'

'You can be *so* romantic.'

'But you keep insisting this is not about romance,' Raúl pointed out.

Her face burnt.

'I don't understand what has suddenly changed. We have been having sex for a couple of months now...' He was undoing her zipper, undressing her. He was down on one knee, removing her shoes. 'Tomorrow we are finished. Tonight we celebrate.'

'I don't want you.'

'So you did the other times?' he checked.

At every exit he blocked her. At every turn he made her see it had never been paid sex for her—not for one single second, not for one shared kiss. She had been lying from the very start. For she had loved him from the start.

'Estelle, after tonight you have the rest of the century off where we are concerned.'

He laid her on the bed and kissed her, felt her cold in his arms. His mouth was on her nipple and he swirled it with his tongue then blew on it, watching it stiffen and ripen. Then he took it deep in his mouth, his fingers intimately stroking her. He filled her mouth with his tongue and she just lay there.

This was what she had signed up for, Estelle reminded herself. She didn't have to enjoy it. Except she was.

It was like a guilty secret—a *filthy* guilty secret. Because she wanted him so—wanted him deep inside her. She turned her cheek away but he turned it back and kissed her. She did not respond—or her mouth did its best not to.

He felt the shift in her…kissed her back to him.

He felt the motion of her tongue on his, felt *her*.

'Tell me to stop and I will,' Raúl said.

She just stared at him.

'Tell me…'

She couldn't

'You can't stop this any more than I can…'

He moved up onto his elbows and she tried not to look at him, looked at his shoulder, which moved back and forth over her.

'Tell me…' he said.

She held on.

'Tell me how you feel…'

In a moment she would. In a moment she'd be sobbing

and begging in his arms. She lifted her hips, and then lifted them again, just so she could hurry him along.

'I'm going to come…' she moaned.

'Liar.'

He pushed deeper within her, hit that spot she would rather tonight he did not, for her face was burning, and her hands were roaming, and her hips were lifting with a life of their own as she let out a low, suppressed moan.

She felt a flood of warmth to her groin, felt the insistence of him inside her, the demand that she match his want.

'You couldn't pay for this…' He was stroking her deep inside and seducing her with his words. 'You could never fake this…'

He slipped into Spanish as she left the planet; he toppled onto her and bucked rapidly inside her as she sobbed out her orgasm. She didn't know where she started or ended, didn't know how to handle the love in her heart and the child in her belly. All belonged to the man holding her in his arms.

'You want me just as much as I want you.'

'So?' She stared back at him. 'What does that prove? That you're good in bed?' She turned away from him and curled up like a ball. 'I think you already knew that.'

'It proves that I am right to trust you. That it is nothing to do with contracts or money. That you *do* love me as much as I love you.'

'You don't know me, though.' She started to cry. 'I've been lying all along.'

'I know you far more than you think,' Raúl said.

'You don't. Your father was right. I like churches and reading…'

'I know that.'

'And I hate clubs.'

'I know that too.'

'I'm nothing like the woman you thought you met.'

'Do you not think I'd long ago worked that out?' Raúl kissed her cheek. 'My virgin hooker.'

He heard her gurgle of laughter, born from exhausted tears.

'I don't get how you're the one with no morals, yet I'm the one who's lied.'

'Because you're complicated,' Raúl said. 'Because you're female.' He kissed her mouth. 'Because you loved me from the start.'

She went to object, but he was telling the truth.

'Do you know when I fell in love with you?' Raúl said. 'When I saw you in those tatty pyjamas and I did not want you in Gordon's bed. It had nothing to do with me paying you. I deserved that slap, but you really did misinterpret my words.'

She was so scared to love him, so scared to tell him about the baby. But if they were to survive, if they were to start to trust, then she had to. It never entered her head that he already knew.

'When were you going to tell me you're pregnant, Estelle?'

She felt his hand move to her stomach, felt his kiss on the back of her neck. All she could be was honest now. 'When I was too pregnant to fly.'

'So the baby would be English?'

'Yes.'

'And you would support it how?'

'The same way that billions of non-billionaires do.'

'Would you have told me?'

'Yes.' She needed the truth from him now and she turned in his arms. 'Are you still here because of the baby?'

'No,' Raúl said. 'I am here because of you.'

She knew he was telling her the truth—not just because he always did, but because of what he said.

'I have had three hellish nights in my life. The first I struggle to speak about, but with you I am starting to. The second was the night after I'd found out about my brother and you were there. I went to bed not thinking about revenge or hate, but about a kiss that went too far and a slap to my cheek. I guess I loved you then, but it felt safer not to admit that.'

'And the third?'

'Finding myself in a nightmare—but not the one I am used to,' Raúl said. 'I was not in a car calling out to my mother. I was not begging her to slow down, and nor was I pleading with her to wake…'

Tears filled her eyes as she imagined it, but she held onto them, knew she would only ever get glimpses of that time and she must piece them together in the quiet of her mind.

'Instead I realised, again, that a woman I loved was gone because of my harsh actions and words. Worse, though. This time it *was* my fault.'

She heard him forgive what his five-year-old self had said as the past was looked at through more mature eyes.

'I went to Angela. She was always the one I went to when I messed up, and I had messed up again. I asked her what to do. I was already on my way to you. It was then that she told me that at least my father had known about the baby… It would seem I was the last to know.'

'I never told her.'

'I'm glad that she guessed. She told my father that morning. I'm glad that he knew, even if I did not.' He looked at her and smiled. 'Opposites attract, Estelle.' He kissed her nose. 'It's law. You can't argue with that.'

'I'm not arguing.'

'Did you hate every dance?' he asked.

She shook her head. 'Of course not.'

'We'll have to get babysitters when we want to go out soon.'

He blew out a breath at the thought of the changes that were to come and she saw that he was smiling.

'Who'd have thought?'

'Not me,' Estelle admitted.

'So, how do you tell your wife you want to marry her all over again?'

'We don't need to get married again,' Estelle said. 'Though a second honeymoon might be nice.'

'Where?'

He was going to make her say it.

'Where?'

'On the yacht.'

Yes, she could get used to that—especially when he made love to her all over again. Especially when he made her laugh about the maid's secret swapping of his DVDs.

No, he had never lied. But he'd never been more honest—and it felt so good.

'Do you think your family will notice a change in us?'

'No.' Estelle smiled. 'They think we met and fell head over heels in love.'

'They were right.' Raúl pulled her to him and then kissed her again. 'We were the only ones who couldn't quite believe it.'

EPILOGUE

IT WAS A beautiful wedding, held on the yacht, which had dropped anchor in Acantilados de Maro-Cerro.

It was Raúl's wedding gift to Gordon for bringing Estelle to him.

The grooms wore white and, contrary to Spanish tradition, there *were* speeches.

'I never thought I'd be standing declaring my love amongst my closest family and friends…' Gordon smiled, and then the dancing started.

Estelle leant against Raúl, feeling the kicks of their baby inside her.

'Is that Gordon's son Ginny is dancing with?' Estelle asked.

'They've been going out for a while.'

'Really?' Estelle smothered a smile. Raúl noticed everything. 'Gordon was once married before—ages ago, apparently.'

'How will they say they met? She can hardly admit she was his father's…' He stopped as Estelle dug him in the ribs. 'Sorry,' Raúl said. 'Sometimes I forget your other life.'

She didn't laugh this time, because the feeling was starting again—like a tight belt pulling around her stomach.

'Do you remember when we stopped here?' Raúl asked.

'When we took out a jet ski and you were scared and trying not to show it.'

'Of course I do.' Estelle attempted to answer normally. 'And I remember when we went snorkeling, and I—'

'Estelle?' He heard her voice break off mid-sentence.

Estelle had been trying to ignore the tightenings, but this one she could not ignore. Raúl's hand moved to her stomach, felt it taut and hard beneath his hands.

'I'll organise a speedboat to take us back to Marbella.'

'It might be ages yet. I don't want to make a fuss.'

'I think it would be a bit more awkward for Gordon if you have the baby here.' He glanced around at the guests and then went to have a word with Alberto, who soon organised transport.

'We are going to head off,' Raúl said when Gordon cornered them. 'Estelle is tired…' But then he couldn't lie— because Estelle was bent over.

'Oh, my!' Gordon was beaming.

'Please,' Estelle begged. 'I don't want everyone to know.'

There was no chance of keeping it quiet as she was helped down to the swimming platform, from where she was guided onto a speedboat. They sped off to the cheers and whistles of the wedding party.

'I wanted to have it in England…'

'I know.' They were supposed to have been flying there the next morning. 'But you wanted to be at the wedding too,' he reminded her.

'I know.'

'You can't have everything,' he teased. 'That's only me.'

She groaned with another pain and buried her face in his neck, wondering how much worse the pains would get, grateful that Raúl was so calm.

He *was* calm—he had everything he wanted right here on this small boat.

He looked up at the cliffs. He had long ago let go of that night, but there was a brief moment of memory just then. It didn't panic him. For a minute he thought of his mother and prayed for her peace.

It was the longest night, and her labour went on well into the next day.

Estelle pushed and dug her nails into his arms, and just when she was sure she could not go on any longer, finally the end was in sight.

'No empujen!'

'Don't push,' Raúl translated.

He had been incredibly composed throughout, but he was starting to worry now, watching the black hair of his infant and realising that soon he would be a father for real.

And then he saw her.

Red, angry, with black hair and fat cheeks.

And as he held her he was more than willing to be completely responsible for this little heart.

The midwife asked if they had a name as she went to write on the wristband and he looked at Estelle. They had chosen a few names, but had opted to wait till the baby was here before they decided. There was one name that had not been suggested till now.

'Gabriella?' Estelle said, and he nodded, unable to speak for a moment. The name that had once meant so much pain was wrapped now in love, and his mother's name would go on.

'Gabriella Sanchez Connolly,' Raúl said.

'She needs a middle name,' Estelle said.

'What about your mother's?' Raúl said, but Estelle already had her mother's name, and thanks to Spanish tradition Connolly was there, too.

Together they held and gazed at their very new daughter, quietly deciding what her full name would be.

'I want to ring Andrew and tell him he's an uncle,' Estelle said, her eyes filling with selfish tears—because though she could not be happier still she wanted to share the news. She wanted her brother to see Gabriella, as she had held Cecelia the day she was born.

'Why would you ring?' Raúl asked. 'They are waiting outside. I will go and bring them in now.'

Raúl stepped out into the waiting room.

His eyes were bloodshot, his hair unkempt, he was unshaven and there was lipstick on his collar—only this time Angela was smiling.

'It's a girl,' Raúl said. 'Both are doing really well,' he said.

Amanda burst into tears and Andrew shook his hand.

'Baby!' Cecelia said, pointing to her little cousin as Estelle showed off the newest arrival to the Connolly clan and thought that Raúl had somehow made an already perfect day even better.

'Come and see,' Raúl said to Angela, who was standing back at the door.

'She's beautiful.' Angela looked down and smiled at the chubby cheeks, seeing the eyes of Luka and Raúl. 'Just perfect—does she have a name?'

'Gabriella,' Raúl said, and looked at the woman who had been like a mother to him, even if it had been from a distance. 'Gabriella Angela Sanchez Connolly.'

Yes, Spanish names could be complicated at times, but they were very simple too.

It was a perfect day, and later came a blissful night, with

Estelle sharing a drink of champagne with her family till Cecelia was drooping in Andrew's arms.

'We're going to get back to the hotel,' Andrew said, looking down at Gabriella. He gave Estelle's hand a squeeze. 'Mum and Dad would have been really proud.'

'I know.'

And then it was just the two of them, lying in bed together, on their first night with Gabriella here.

'There is a text from Luka.' Raúl gave a brief eye-roll as he read the message. 'I have a feeling Angela may have hijacked his phone and typed it.' Raúl's voice was wry. Things were still terribly strained with Luka, but Raúl, very new to being a brother, was trying to work through it.

Not that Luka wanted to.

'You'll get there,' said Estelle.

'Perhaps,' Raúl said.

'Thank you for today.'

Gabriella, who was snuggled up in her cot beside them, made a small noise, and Raúl thought his heart might burst with pride and love as he gazed at his sleeping daughter.

'Thank *you*,' he said. 'I never thought I could feel so much happiness.'

'I meant for bringing my family over. It means so much to me to have them here.'

'I know it does.' He turned his gaze from his daughter to his wife. 'I know, thanks to you, the importance of family—even a difficult one.' He kissed her tired mouth. 'And no matter what happens I am never going to forget it.'

* * * * *

THE REAL ROMERO

CATHY WILLIAMS

To my fabulous and inspiring daughters.

CHAPTER ONE

'AMELIA? IS THAT Amelia Mayfield?'

Milly pressed the mobile phone against her ear, already regretting that she had been stupid enough to pick up the call. How many more instructions could Sandra King give about this job?

She was going to be a chalet girl! Two weeks of cooking and looking after a family of four! Anyone would think that she was being primed to run the country. It wasn't even as though she hadn't done this before. She had, two years ago, for three months before she'd started the hotel job in London.

'Yes.' She sighed, allowing her eyes to drift over the pure, dazzling canvas of white snow all around her. It had been a fantastic trip, just the thing to clear her head and get her mind off her miserable situation. She had travelled in style and she had enjoyed every second of it. It was almost a shame that she was now in the back seat of the chauffeur-driven SUV with her destination only half an hour away.

'You haven't been picking up your phone!' The voice down the other end was sharp and accusatory. Milly could picture the other woman clearly, sitting at her desk in Mayfair, her shiny blond hair scraped back with an

Alice band, her long perfectly manicured nails tapping impatiently on her desk.

Sandra King had interviewed her not once but three times for this job. It was almost as though she had resented having to give the job to someone small and round with red hair when there were so many other, more suitable candidates in the mix: girls with cut-glass accents, braying laughs and shiny blond hair scraped back with Alice bands.

But, as she had made clear with unnecessarily cruel satisfaction, this particular family wanted someone plain and down to earth, because the last thing the *señora* wanted was a floozy who might decide to start flirting with her rich husband.

Milly, who had looked up the family she would be working for on Google after her first interview, had only just managed not to snort with disbelief because the husband in question was definitely *not* the sort of man any girl in her right mind would choose to flirt with. He was portly, semi-balding and the wrong side of fifty, but he was filthy rich, and she supposed that that was as compelling an attraction as being a rock star. Not that she was in the market for flirting with anyone, anyway.

'Sorry, Sandra…' She grinned because she knew that Sandra didn't like being called by her first name. It was 'Ms King', or 'Skipper' to the chosen few. The other girls in the exclusive agency that dealt specifically with part-time positions to the rich and famous called her Skipper, one of those silly nicknames that Milly guessed had been concocted in whatever posh boarding school they had all attended.

'The service has been a bit iffy ever since I left London…and I can't talk for long because my phone's almost out of charge.' Not strictly true but she didn't need yet another check list of the various things the special family ate and didn't eat; or the favourite things the special little kids, aged four and six, insisted on doing before they went to bed. She didn't need to be reminded of what she could and couldn't wear, or say or couldn't say.

Milly had never known people to be as fussy with just about everything. The family for whom she had worked two years previously had been jolly, outdoorsy and amenable.

But she wasn't complaining. They might be fussy but the pay was fabulous and, more importantly, the job removed her from the vicinity of Robbie, Emily and heartbreak.

She had managed to push her ex-fiancé, her best friend and her broken engagement out of her head, but she could feel them staging another takeover, and she blinked rapidly, fighting back tears of self-pity. Time healed, she had been told repeatedly by her friends, who had never liked Robbie from the start and, now that she was no longer engaged, had felt free to let loose every single pejorative thing they had thought about him from day one.

On the one hand, their negative comments had been bolstering and supportive. On the other, they had shown up her utter lack of judgement.

'In that case,' the well-bred, disembodied voice informed her, 'I'm afraid I have to inform you that the job has been cancelled.'

It took a few seconds for that to sink in. Milly had been busy being distracted by the unfortunate turn of events that had catapulted her life from sorted and happy to humiliated and up in the air.

'Did you hear what I just said, Amelia?'

'You're kidding, aren't you? Please tell me that this is a joke.' But Sandra King was not the sort who had a sense of humour. Any joke, for her, would be foreign territory.

'I never joke,' the other woman said, on cue. 'The Ramos family has pulled out at the last minute. I only took their phone call a few hours ago and, if you had *picked up your phone* instead of *letting it ring,* you would not have wasted your time travelling.'

'Why? Why is it off?' Visions of slinking back into the flat she had shared with Emily, risking bumping into her one-time best friend clearing her stuff before she took off to America with Robbie, were so horrifying that she felt giddy.

'One of the kids has come down with chicken pox. Simple as that.'

'But I'm only half an hour away from the lodge!' Milly all but wailed.

They had left the exclusive village of Courchevel behind and the car was wending its way upwards, leaving the riff-raff of the lower slopes behind as it entered the rarefied air of the seriously rich. Hidden, private lodges with majestic views; helipads; heated indoor swimming pools; saunas and steam rooms by the bucket load...

There was an elaborate sigh from the end of the line. 'Well, you'll have to tell the driver to swing round and head back, I'm afraid. Naturally, you will be compensated for your time and trouble...'

'Surely I can spend *one night* there? It's getting dark and I'm exhausted. I have a key to the place. I can use it and make sure that I leave the lodge in pristine condition. I need to sleep, Sandra!'

She couldn't get her head round the fact that the one thing that seemed to be working in her favour, the *only*

thing that had worked in her favour for the past couple of horrific, nightmarish weeks, was now collapsing around her feet like a deck of cards, kicked down
by one of the odious rich kids from the family who had
bailed at the last minute. A wave of hopeless self-pity
threatened to engulf her.

'That would be highly irregular.'

'So is the fact that my job here has been cancelled at
the last minute, when I'm *fifteen minutes* away from the
lodge—having spent the past eight hours travelling!'

She could see the lodge rearing up ahead of them and
for a few seconds every depressing, negative thought
flew from her head in sheer, wondrous appreciation of
the magnificent structure ahead of her.

It dominated the skyscape, rising up against the
blindingly white snow, master of all it surveyed. It was
absolutely enormous, the largest and grandest ski lodge
Milly had ever seen in her life. In fact, it was almost an
understatement to classify it as a 'lodge'. It was more
like a mansion in the middle of its own private, snowy
playground.

'I suppose there's little choice!' Sandra snapped. 'But
for God's sake, Amelia, pick up when you hear your
phone! And make sure you don't touch anything. No
poking around. Just eat and sleep and make sure that
when you leave the lodge no one knows you've been
there.'

Milly grimaced as she was abruptly disconnected.
She leaned forward, craning to get glimpses of the mansion as it drew closer and closer to her, until the SUV
was turning left and climbing through private land to
where it nestled in all its splendour.

'Er…' She cleared her throat and hoped that the
driver, who had greeted her at Chambery airport in

extremely broken English and had not said a word since, would get the gist of what she was going to say.

'*Oui, mademoiselle?*'

Milly caught his eye in the rear-view mirror. 'Yes, well, there's been a slight change of plan...'

'What is that?'

She sighed with relief. At least she wouldn't have to try and explain an impossible situation using her limited French, resisting the temptation to fill in the gaps by speaking loudly. She told him as succinctly as possible. He would have to stay overnight somewhere and return her to the airport the following day... Sorry, so sorry for the inconvenience, but he could phone...

She scrambled into her capacious rucksack and extracted her wallet and from that the agency card that she had not envisaged having to use for the next couple of weeks.

She wondered whether he might stay at the lodge, it was big enough to fit a hundred drivers, but that was something he would have to work out for himself. She suspected that she had already stretched Sandra's limited supply of the milk of human kindness by asking if she could stay overnight in the place.

It was a dog-eat-dog world, she thought. As things stood, she was rock-bottom of the pack. She had been cheated on by her fiancé, a guy she had known since childhood and, as if that wasn't bad enough, she had been cheated on by her best friend and flatmate...

To top it off, she had been told that the reason he had become engaged to her in the first place was because his parents were fed up with his twenty-four-seven life-style of living it large and womanising. They had given him a deadline to find himself a decent girl and settle down or else he could forget about taking over the family business that had just opened a thriving branch in Philadelphia and was going places.

Banished from the family fortune and a ready-made job, he would have been faced, she assumed, with the terrifying prospect of actually buckling down and finding himself a job without Mummy and Daddy's helping hand. And so he had plumped for the slightly less terrifying prospect of charming her into thinking that they really had a relationship, proposing marriage whilst playing the field with her much taller, much skinnier and much prettier flatmate.

His parents had approved of her. She had passed the litmus test with them. She was his passport to his inheritance. She was small, round and homely; when she thought of Robbie and the angular Emily, every insecurity she nursed about her looks rose to the surface at the speed of light.

The only thing worse than catching them in bed together would have been actually marrying the creep, only to discover once the ring was on her finger that he had zero interest in her.

She gazed mournfully at her finger where a giant diamond rock had nestled only a few weeks ago.

Her friends had all told her that it was a monumental mistake to have chucked it back at him, that she should have kept it and flogged it at the first available opportunity. After all, she deserved it, after what he had put her through.

And the money would have stood her in good stead, considering she had jacked in her hotel job so that she could play happy families with him in Philadelphia. It was galling to think that he had had the nerve to tell her that he hoped she understood and that she could count on him if she ever needed anything!

As things currently stood, she was out of a job, banished from her flat until Emily cleared out and with a shockingly small amount of money saved.

And she had no one to turn to. Her only living relative, her grandmother who lived in Scotland, would have sold her cottage had she known about her granddaughter's state of near penury, but Milly had no intention of filling her in on that. It was bad enough that she had had to pick up the pieces when she had been told fifteen days ago that the fairy-tale wedding was off the cards.

As far as her grandmother was concerned, Milly was taking time off to work as a nanny for a family in Courchevel, where she would be able to do what she loved most, namely ski... She had glossed over the trauma of her breakup as just one of those things, nothing that a couple of weeks in the snow couldn't cure.

Milly had painted a glowing picture of a cosy family, practically friends, who would be there for her on her road to recovery. It had helped her grandmother to stop fretting. Furthermore, she had embroidered the recovery theme by announcing that she had another job lined up as soon as she was back in London, far better than the one she had jettisoned.

As far as her grandmother was concerned, she was as right as rain, because the last thing Milly wanted to do was worry her.

'Shall I call...er...the agency and see if you could stay overnight at the lodge...?' Her better instincts grudgingly cranked into gear and she resigned herself to another awkward conversation with Sandra, who would probably spend a ridiculously long time telling her that being let down was all her fault because she should have just *answered her phone,* having confirmed that the driver would not, definitely *not,* be allowed to sully the mansion, no way.

But, no; Pierre, the driver, was a regular at one of the hotels in Courchevel, where one of his relatives worked, and he would be fine there.

Milly was tempted to ask whether being let down by the special family came with the job. Maybe he had a permanent room there for when he got messed around.

She didn't. Instead, she allowed him to help her with her luggage, the luggage containing the clothes that would never be worn, and he only drove off when she had unlocked the imposing front door to let herself into the lodge.

It was blessedly warm and indescribably stunning, a testimony to the marvels of modern architecture and minimalism. The entire space was open-plan, with two sitting rooms cleverly split by a wall in which a high-tech, uber-modern fire caught the eye and held it. Beyond that, she could glimpse a vast kitchen, and beyond that yet more, although she was drawn to the floor-to-ceiling windows that captured the spectacular views of the valley.

She gazed out at the untouched, pristine snow, fast fading as night descended. It had been an excellent ski season so far—good accumulation of snow, which had collected on the roofs of the lodges lower down the mountain and lay there like banks and banks of smooth, marzipan icing.

Having no idea of the layout of the lodge, she decided to take her time exploring. She wasn't going to be there long, so why not enjoy the adventure of discovery? Her flat was small and poky. More than four people in the sitting area constituted a traffic jam. Why not pretend that this place belonged to her?

She explored each room exhaustively, one at a time. She admired the sparse, expensive furnishings. She had never seen so much chrome, glass and leather under one roof in her life before. Much of the furniture was white, and she marvelled at a couple confident enough to let loose two small children in a space where there was so much potential for destruction.

The kitchen was a wonder to behold: black granite counters, a table fashioned from beaten metal and an array of gadgets that made her culinary fingers itch.

She decided that she was glad she no longer worked at the Rainbow Hotel. It boasted three stars, but everyone there reckoned palms must have been greased to get that rating because the rooms were basic, bordering on the criminally dull, the restaurant should have been updated half a century ago and the two bars were straight out of the seventies but without a cool, retro feel.

Not to mention the fact that she had never been allowed, not once in a year and a half, to do anything on her own, Chef Julian, whilst only dabbling in the actual cooking, had specialised in peering over her shoulder and picking fault with her cooking whenever he got the chance.

Here, she could have let her imagination go wild—within the constraints of the various faddy food groups they did and didn't eat, of course. She trailed her hand over the gleaming, spotless counter and brushed a few of the marvellous gadgets, none of which bore the hallmarks of anyone ever having been near them. When she checked the fridge, it was to find that it was fully stocked, as were the cupboards. A horizontal metal wine rack groaned under the weight of bottles, all of which bore expensive, fancy labels.

Absorbed in her inspection of the kitchen, daydreaming about what it might feel like actually to have enough money to own a place like this as a second home, Milly was unaware of anyone approaching.

'And you are…?'

The deep, cold voice coming from behind crashed through her pleasant, escapist fantasy with the unwelcome force of a sledgehammer and she spun round, heart pounding.

Her brain, which had been lagging behind, caught up to point out mockingly that there was a stranger in the house and she should be looking for something handy with which she could defend herself.

Because the man could be….*dangerous*…

Her mind went blank. She forgot that she should be scared—terrified, even. She was in a bloody great rolling mansion packed full of valuables and the owners weren't there. The man standing in front of her, all six foot something of him, had probably broken in. She had probably disturbed him in the middle of ransacking the place, and everyone knew what happened to innocent people when they happened to interrupt a robbery.

But, God, had she ever seen someone so beautiful?

Raven-black hair, slightly longer than was conventionally permissible, framed a face that was, simply put, a thing of perfection: a wide, sensual mouth; chiselled features; eyes as dark and as fathomless as night. He was in jeans and a T-shirt and was barefoot.

It seemed unusual for a robber to take his shoes off to make off with the silver, but then it occurred to her that he had probably removed them so that he could sneak up on her unannounced.

'I could ask you the same thing!' She tried to keep the tenor of her voice calm and controlled—a woman in charge of the situation, someone who wasn't going to be intimidated. 'And don't even *think* of taking a single step closer to me!' Idiot that she was, she had left her mobile phone lying in her rucksack, which was currently reclining on the kitchen counter. It was infuriating, but how could she possibly have anticipated something like this?

In stark disobedience of her orders, the man took a couple of steps closer to her and she fell back, bumped into the counter and spun round to grab the nearest heavy thing to hand—which happened to be the kettle, a glass concoction that didn't look as though it could stun a flea, never mind the muscled man who was now only a metre away from her and had folded his arms, cool as a cucumber.

'Or else what? Don't tell me you have plans for using that thing on me…?'

'You'd better tell me what you're doing here or else I'm going to…call the police. And I'm not kidding…'

This had not been the way Lucas had anticipated his evening going. In fact, he hadn't actually banked on being here at all. He had lent the place to his mother's annoying friends, only for them to cancel at the last minute, which was when he had decided to head there himself for a few days.

He would get away from his mother, who was becoming more strident in her demands for him to settle down and get married. She had suffered a minor stroke three months previously, had been pronounced fit and able, yet had decided that she had stared death in the face, had become acquainted with her own mortality—and now all she wanted was to hold a grandchild in her arms before she died. Was that asking too much of her only beloved son?

Frankly, Lucas thought that it was, but he had not

been inclined to say so. Instead, he had wheeled out consultant after consultant, but no amount of reassurances from these top consultants could convince her that her fragile grasp on life wasn't about to be snipped.

Add to that an annoying ex-girlfriend who refused to believe that she had been dumped, and a few days' skiing had suddenly seemed like a brilliant idea.

Bracing conversations with his mother could be better faced after he had vented his frustrations in a few black runs.

Peace and quiet seemed to have nosedived, however, and he was not in the best of moods to be standing here, staring down a crazy woman brandishing his kettle and threatening to call the police.

A short, crazy woman, with red hair that was all over the place, and who thought he was looting the place. Hilarious.

'You don't really think you could take me on, do you?' With lightning reflexes, he reached out and relieved her of her dangerous weapon, which he proceeded to set back down on its base. 'Now, before *I* call the police and have you forcibly removed, you're going to tell me what the hell *you're* doing here.'

Deprived of the kettle, Milly stuck her chin out at a stubborn angle and stared at him defiantly. 'You're not scaring me, if that's your intention.'

'It's never been my intention to scare a woman.'

The man oozed sex appeal through every pore. It was off-putting. How could she get her thoughts in order when he stood there, looking at her with those darker-than-night eyes that were insolent and intransigent at the same time? How was she supposed to *think*?

'I'm actually *employed* here.' Milly broke the silence. A thin film of perspiration had broken out over her body and, try as she might, she couldn't seem to peel her eyes away from him.

He raised one enquiring eyebrow, and she glared at him, because she had every right to be here which he, almost certainly, did not.

What, she wondered, could possibly go wrong next? How could one person's life get derailed in such a short space of time? She should have been here recovering, looking forward to an essential break from normality while she mentally gathered her forces and rallied her troops in preparation for returning to London. She should have been using the splendid kitchen to whip something up that was gluten-free for Mrs Ramos, meat-based for her husband and healthily braised for their children! Instead, she was having a staring match with someone who looked like Adonis but behaved like a caveman.

'Oh, yes?'

'Yes,' she snapped. '*Not* that it's any of your business! I'm the chalet girl the Ramos employed to work for them for the next two weeks. And they'll be here *any minute now...*'

'Ah...chalet girl... Now, why am I finding that hard to believe when I know for a fact that Alberto and Julia won't be here because one of their children is ill?' He strolled over to the fridge and helped himself to a bottle of mineral water, which he proceeded to drink while keeping his eye on her.

'Oh.' The annoying, arrogant man wasn't a robber but, instead of rushing to reassure her, he had prolonged her discomfort by not deigning to tell her that he knew the family who owned the lodge. Were there *any* nice guys left in the world? 'Well, if you think that I'm going to apologise for...for...'

'Coming at me with the kettle?'

'Then you're mistaken. I don't know what you're doing here, but you shouldn't sneak around, and you should have told me that you knew the owners...' A thought occurred to her. 'I suppose they've let you down, as well?'

'Come again?'

'They let *me* down,' Milly expanded glumly. Now that she was no longer in danger of imminent attack, her breathing had more or less returned to normal, but she still found that she had to put a little distance between her and Adonis, who was still standing by the fridge and yet managing to have a very weird effect on her nervous system.

His legs, she noted absently as she sat down on one of the high-tech leather-and-chrome chairs by the table, were long and muscular and he had good ankles. Not many men had good ankles but he had excellent ones—brown like the rest of him...with a sprinkling of dark hair...

She surfaced to find that he had said something and she frowned.

'Not you, as well.' She groaned, because from the tail end of his sentence she gathered he had been pointing out the obvious—which was how it was that she had managed to make the trip without being notified that the job had been cancelled. 'I've had enough lecturing from Sandra about not picking up my phone; I don't think I have the energy to sit through you telling me the same thing. Anyway, why are *you* here? Didn't your agency let you know before you made a wasted trip here?'

Lucas had the dazed feeling of someone thrown into a washing machine and the spin cycle turned to full blast. She had raked her fingers through her wild red hair, which he now appreciated was thick and very long, practically down to her waist, a tumbling riot of curls and waves.

'Agency?' Never lost for words in any given situation, he now found himself speechless.

'Sandra's the girl at the agency that employed me. In London.' She permitted herself to look at him fully and could feel hot colour racing up to her face. He was obviously foreign, beautifully and exotically foreign, but his English was perfect, with just a trace of an accent.

'My job was to cook for the Ramos family and baby-sit their children.' It suddenly occurred to her that he had called them by their Christian names. She had been under strict instructions to use their full titles and to remember that they weren't her friends. It just went to show how different agencies operated; just her luck to have got stuck with snooty Sandra. 'What were *you* employed to do? No, you don't have to tell me.'

'I don't?' Fascinating. Like someone from another planet. Wherever Lucas went, he generated adulation and subservience from women. They tripped over themselves to please him. They said what they imagined he wanted to hear. Born into wealth, he had known from a tender age what the meaning of power was and now, at the ripe young age of thirty-four, and with several fortunes behind him—some inherited, the rest made himself. He was accustomed to being treated like a man at the top of his game. A billionaire who could have whatever he pleased at the snap of his imperious fingers.

What did this woman think he did? He was curious to hear.

'Ski instructor.' Milly discovered that this strange turn of events was having a very beneficial effect on her levels of depression. Robbie, Emily and the horror story that had suddenly become her life had barely crossed her mind ever since Adonis had appeared on the scene.

'Ski instructor.' He was parroting everything she said. He couldn't believe it.

'You have the *look* of a ski instructor,' Milly said thoughtfully.

'Am I to take that as a compliment?'

'You can if you want.' She backtracked hastily just in case he got it into his head that she was somehow trying it on with him, which she wasn't, because aside from anything else she was far too upset even to look at another man. 'Isn't it amazing how rich people live?' She swiftly changed the topic and watched, warily, as he dumped the bottled water on the counter, making no effort even to look for the bin, and sauntered towards the kitchen table so that he could sit on one of the chairs, idly pulling another towards him with his foot and using it as a foot rest.

'Amazing,' Lucas agreed.

'I mean, have you had a chance to look around this place? It's like something from one of those house magazines! It's hard to believe that anyone actually ever uses this lodge. Everything's just so…shiny and expensive!'

'Money impresses you, does it?' Lucas thought of all the other apartments and houses he owned, scattered in cities across the world from New York to Hong Kong. He even had a villa on an exclusive Caribbean island. He hadn't been there for at least a couple of years…

Milly leaned on the table, cupped her chin in the palm of her hand and gazed at him. Amazing eyes, she thought idly, with even more amazing lashes—long, dark and thick. And there was a certain arrogance about him. She should find it a complete turn-off, especially considering that Robbie had had his fair share of arrogance, and what a creep he had turned out to be. But Adonis's arrogance was somehow *different*... Just look at the way he had stuck his feet on that chair.

'No...' she admitted. 'I mean, don't get me wrong, money is great. I wish I had more of it.' *Especially considering I have no job to return to.* 'But I was brought up to believe that there were more important things in life. My parents died in a car accident when I was eight and my grandmother raised me. Well, there wasn't an awful lot of money to go round, but that never bothered me. I think people create the lives they want to live and they do that without the help of money...'

She sighed. 'Stop me if I'm talking too much. I do that. But, now that I know you're not a burglar, it's kind of nice having someone here. I mean, I'll be gone first thing in the morning, but... Okay, enough of me... Is this the first time you've worked for the Ramos family? I mean, I couldn't help noticing that you called them by their first names...'

Lucas thought of Alberto and Julia Ramos and choked back a snort of derisive laughter at the thought of working for them. In actual fact, Alberto had worked for his father. Lucas had inherited him when his father had died and, because of the personal connection, had resisted sacking the man, who was borderline incompetent. He found them intensely annoying but his mother was godmother to one of their children.

'We go back a way,' he said, skirting round the truth.

'Thought so.'

'Why is that?'

Milly laughed and it felt as though this was the first time she had laughed, really laughed, for a long time. Well, at least two weeks, although there had been a moment or two with her friends post-traumatic break-up. Manic, desperate laughter, probably…

'Because you've got your feet on the chair and you've just dumped that empty bottle on the kitchen counter! Sandra told me that under *no circumstances* was there to be any sign that I'd stepped foot in this lodge when I left. I might even have to wipe all the surfaces just in case they find my fingerprints somewhere.'

'You have a wonderful laugh,' Lucas heard himself say with some surprise. She did. A rich, full- bodied laugh that made him want to grin.

And looking at her…

That first impression of someone small and plump with crazy hair was being rapidly dispelled. She was small, yes, barely skimming five-four, but her skin was satiny smooth and her eyes were the clearest blue he had ever seen. And when she laughed she had dimples.

Milly went bright red. In the aftermath of her hor-rible, *horrible* broken engagement, her self-confidence had been severely battered, and his compliment filled her with a terrific sense of wellbeing. Even if he had only complimented her on the way she laughed, which, when you analysed it, was hardly a compliment at all. But, still, coming from Adonis…

'Must be great being a ski instructor,' she said, all hot and bothered now. 'Would you like to know some-thing? I mean, it's no big secret or anything…'

'I would love to know something…even if it's no big secret or anything…' Hell, this impromptu break was certainly proving to be a great distraction in ways he had never anticipated.

'I used to ski—I mean *really* ski. I went on a school trip when I was ten and somehow I took to it. When I was fifteen, I even thought I might try and go pro, but you know… We didn't have the money for that sort of thing. But it's why I was looking forward to this job…'

Her situation hit her like a blast of cold air: no fiancé, no job, no two weeks' chalet income with the bonus of skiing now and again. She shook away her sudden despondency, which wasn't going to get her anywhere. 'Frankly, it's why Sandra employed me in the first place when there were other better looking girls lining up for the job.' *That and my low levels of physical attractiveness.* 'I thought I might be able to sneak a little skiing in, but now… Oh, well, that's life, I guess. My luck's been crap recently so I don't know why I'm surprised this fell through.'

She smiled, digging deep to recover some of her sunny nature. 'Hey, I don't even know your name! I'm Amelia, but my friends call me Milly.' She held out her hand, and the feel of his cool fingers as he shook it sent a wave of dizzying electric charge straight through her body, from her toes to the top of her head.

'And I am…Lucas.' So she thought he was a ski instructor. How frankly refreshing to be in the company of a woman who didn't know his worth, who didn't simper, who wasn't out to try and trap him. 'And I think we might just be able to solve the matter of your lost job…'

CHAPTER TWO

IT WAS A SPUR-OF-THE-MOMENT decision for Lucas, but whoever said that he wasn't a man who could think creatively on his feet? How many times had he won deals because he had approached them from a different angle; played with a situation, found the loopholes, cracks and crevices and exploited them to his own benefit? It was the crucial difference between moderate success and soaring the heights. He had been bred with confidence and it had never once occurred to him that he might not be able to get exactly what he wanted.

Right now, he had made the snap decision that he might enjoy the woman's company on the slopes for a few days.

She obviously wasn't the type he normally went for. His diet was tall, thin, leggy brunettes from social backgrounds very similar to his own—because there was nothing worse than a tawdry gold-digger—but she had a certain something…

Just at this minute she was gaping at him as though he had taken leave of his senses.

'I beg your pardon?' Milly could scarcely believe her ears. In fact, she was on the way to convincing herself that she was trapped with a madman. He might be well in with the Ramos family if he happened to be their personal ski instructor, but how much influence did ski instructors have anyway? It wasn't as though they weren't disposable.

'But first, food.'

'Food?'

'I actually came to the kitchen to grab myself something to eat.' Originally he had toyed with the idea of just importing a chef from one of the hotels, the regular chef he was accustomed to using whenever he happened to be at the lodge, but in the end it had hardly seemed worth the effort when he hadn't planned to stay longer than a couple of nights. And when he knew for a fact that the fridge would be brimming over with food in preparation for the non-appearing Ramos family.

'You came here to grab something to eat? Are you completely *crazy?* You can't just go rummaging around in their fridge, eating their food and drinking their wine. Have you taken a look at the bottles in that wine rack? They look as though they cost the earth!'

Lucas was already heading for the fridge.

'Bread…' He opened the fridge door and turned to look at her. 'Cheese… Both in plentiful supply. And I'm pretty sure there'll be some salad stuff somewhere.'

Milly sprang to her feet. 'I can, er, cook you something if you like…if you're sure. After all, cooking *was* to be part of my duties.'

Lucas looked at her and smiled and that electric charge zipped through her again. It was like being struck by a bolt of lightning.

Had Robbie the creep ever had this effect on her? She didn't think so, but then again disillusionment might have put a different spin on her memories of their somewhat brief courtship.

She and Robbie had attended the same small school in remote Scotland until they were fourteen, at which point grander things had beckoned and he had moved with his family down to London. At fourteen, gauche and way too sporty to appeal to teenage boys whose testosterone levels were kicking in, she had had a secret crush on him.

They had kept in touch over the years, mostly via social network with the occasional visit thrown in whenever he'd happened to be in the city, but his sudden interest in her had only really kicked off six months ago and it had been whirlwind. Milly, still finding her feet in her job, had been first pleased to see a familiar face and then flattered when that familiar face had started take an interest in her. Ha! The reason for that had become patently clear after he had dumped her for leggy Emily.

Lucas had slammed shut the fridge in favour of opening a bottle of the expensive wine from the wine rack, much to Milly's consternation.

So, women cooking for him had never been part of the deal; tinkering in the kitchen smacked of just the sort of cosy domesticity he had never encouraged. On the other hand, this was a unique situation.

'I'm actually a chef by profession.' Milly grinned and joined him by the fridge, the contents of which she proceeded to inspect, although she made sure not to remove anything. She could practically feel Skipper Sandra peering down at her, about to ask her what the hell she thought she was doing.

'Would-be professional skier, chef... Is there no end to your talents?'

'You're teasing me.' Their eyes met and she blushed. 'I still don't feel entirely comfortable digging in their cupboards but I suppose we *do* have to eat. I mean, I'm sure Sandra wouldn't expect me to *starve...*'

'This Sandra character sounds like a despot.' Lucas removed himself from her way as she began extracting bits and pieces. He had no idea what she intended to do with the stuff. He himself had zero interest in cooking and had never really seen fit to do much more than toast a slice of bread or, in dire circumstances, open a can of something and put it in a saucepan.

'Like you wouldn't believe.' She began hunting down utensils whilst reminding him, just in case he reported back that she had made herself at home, that she still didn't feel 100 percent good about using stuff from their fridge. 'Want to help?' She glanced over her shoulder to where he was lounging indolently against the kitchen counter with a glass of red wine in his hand.

Talk about making himself at home!

'I'm more of a spectator when it comes to cooking,' Lucas told her. And from where he was standing, the view was second to none. She had removed her thick jumper and was down to a clingy long-sleeved T-shirt that outlined every inch of a body that had been woefully kept under wraps.

'We'll eat quicker if you help.'

'I'm in no hurry. You were about to tell me about Sandra the despot...'

'I had to have three interviews for this job. Can you believe it? Three! The Ramoses are just about the fussiest people on the planet. Oh, sorry; I forgot that you're their regular ski instructor. You probably see a different side to them.' She sighed, her throat suddenly thick as she thought of the neatly packaged life she had been looking forward to flying through the window.

And yet, in a strange way, she was sure that she should be feeling sadder than she actually was.

Mortified, yes. She was about eleven out of ten on the mortification scale, although less so here where her well-meaning friends weren't hovering around her, hankies at the ready, as though she was on the verge of a nervous breakdown.

But sad?

The presents had all been returned; the dress had been sold online because the shop had refused to have it back; the small church in Sunningdale where his parents had lived ever since they had moved from Scotland had been cancelled. But she didn't get a lump in her throat when she thought about the details.

The lump came when she thought about the fairy-tale future she had had planned, when she thought about being in love and then being let down...

'I doubt that.' Lucas recalled the last time he had seen the couple at his mother's house in Argentina, where Julia Ramos had spent most of the evening lording it over anyone she thought might be a lesser mortal.

Despite being wealthy beyond most people's wildest dreams, his mother had a very solid streak of normality in her and frequently hosted parties to which all and sundry were invited, regardless of their income or status. She had never forgotten that both she and his father had come from nothing and had made their fortune through hard graft.

'There aren't many complex sides to Alberto and Julia Ramos. They have money and they insist on showing the world, whether the world wants to know or not.'

'Poor you.' Milly looked at him sympathetically. 'I guess it must become a bit of a drag if you're having to deal with people you don't especially like...' She returned to her chopping and he dragged one of the bar stools over so that he could see her as she worked. By now, she had given up on being appalled at the liberties he took. Perhaps that was the relationship he had with his employers. Less of an employee and more of an equal.

'But,' she continued as she tried to focus on the onions in front of her and ignore the fact that his dark eyes roving over her were making her feel a bit dizzy, 'we all have to do stuff we don't particularly like for the sake of earning a living. What do you do when you're not instructing?'

'This and that.'

Milly didn't say anything. Maybe he was embarrassed because being a ski instructor might be glamorous but it was hardly a ladder-climbing job, and she wasn't sure why, but Lucas struck her as the kind of guy to have ambition.

'Why are you doing a two-week stint as a chalet girl when you're a professional chef? You're not drinking your wine. You should. It's an excellent vintage.'

'I hope you don't get into trouble opening that bottle…' But the cooking was now done so she wiped her hands on one of the towels by the range, took the proffered glass of wine and followed him out of the kitchen and into the sprawling sitting area, where, through the vast panes of glass, they could see the spectacular sight of night settling on the snowy mountain ranges.

'I never get into trouble,' Lucas assured her as he joined her on the sofa. The white sofa. The white sofa that she would probably have to pay for if she made the mistake of spilling her red wine on it.

She perched awkwardly on the edge and made very sure to keep a firm hand on the stem of her wine glass.

'You *never* get into trouble...ever? That's a very arrogant thing to say!' But strangely thrilling.

'I confess that I can be arrogant,' Lucas told her truthfully, eyes steady on her face as he sipped his wine.

'That's an awful trait.'

'Deplorable. Have you got any?'

'Any what?' Her glass appeared to be empty. How had that happened?

'Deplorable traits.' Not red, he decided; her hair was not red...more a deep, rich auburn with streaks of lighter auburn running through it.

'I tend to fall for creeps. In fact, you could say that I specialise in that. I went out with boyfriend number one three years ago for three months. Turned out he had a girlfriend, who happened to be doing a gap year leaving him free to play the field while she was away...'

'The world is full of creeps,' Lucas murmured. He himself always made it very clear to the women he dated that rocks on fingers were never going be part of the game. If, at any point, they got it into their heads that they could alter that situation, then they were very sharply brought up to date with his ground rules.

'You're not kidding.'

'And boyfriend number two?'

'Boyfriend number two was actually my fiancé.' She stared at her empty glass, wondering whether she dared risk another drink. She wouldn't want to face the trip back to London on a hangover. She sneaked a glance at Lucas, who was reclining on the leather sofa, utterly and completely comfortable in his surroundings.

'Fiancé?'

Milly stuck her hand out for inspection. 'What do you see?'

Lucas shifted position, leaned forward and looked.

'An extremely attractive hand.' He glanced up at her and was charmed by the dainty colour in her cheeks.

'It's a hand without an engagement ring,' she said mournfully. 'Right now, at this precise moment in time, I should actually be a married woman.'

'Ah...'

'Instead, here I am, drinking wine that doesn't belong to me—which the Ramos family will probably discover and report back to Sandra the despot—and pouring my heart out to a complete stranger.'

'Sometimes complete strangers make the best listeners.'

'You don't strike me as the sort of guy who pours his heart out to other people.'

'It's not a habit I've ever actively encouraged. Tell me about the ex-fiancé...'

Milly thought that she had spent the past two weeks offloading about the ex-fiancé. Her friends had been fertile ground for endless meandering conversations about Robert and *types* like Robert. Over boxes of wine and Chinese take-out, hours had been spent discussing every aspect of Robert and men in general. Anecdotes of various Mr Wrongs had been cited like a never-ending string of rabbits being pulled from a magician's hat.

'You're not really interested...' She couldn't see *him* ever going through the trauma of being dumped from a great height.

'You fascinate me,' Lucas murmured, reaching over to the bottle, which he had casually dumped on one of the spotless glass tables so that he could refill both their glasses. Milly noted that the bottle had left a circular stain on the table and she mentally made a note to make sure it was wiped clean before she went to bed.

'I do?' She decided that that rated slightly higher than the compliment he had paid her about her laugh.

'You do,' Lucas told her gravely. 'I have never known anyone as…open and forthcoming as you.'

'Oh.' Deflated, Milly looked at him. 'I suppose that's just a kind way of saying that I talk too much.'

'You also have amazing hair.'

Was he *flirting* with her? Milly made her mind up that there was no way that she would allow herself to be flattered, especially not by a ski instructor who probably slept with every woman he taught over the age of twenty. Weren't they notorious for that? The last time she had worked as a chalet girl, the other two girls who had also been working with her had both had flings with ski instructors. Ski instructors were usually young, cute, unnaturally tanned and extremely confident when it came to enticing women into bed.

She shot him a jaundiced look, which was not the reaction he expected on the back of a compliment. He wondered how she would react if he told her that what he would really like to do, right here, right now, was sift his fingers through that wonderful hair of hers and watch it as it rippled over them.

'So what was the ex called?'

'Robert,' Milly told him on a sigh. Determined to make this glass last as long as possible and thereby avoid any nasty early-morning consequences, she took a miniscule sip.

'And what did *Robert* do?'

'Fell into bed with my best friend. Apparently he took one look at her and realised that he couldn't resist her. It turned out that he had proposed to me because I fitted the bill. His parents wanted him to settle down and I was *settling down* material. But not in a good way.

More in an "if he could do as he pleased, he wouldn't settle down with me" sort of way. He thought his parents would approve, which they did.'

She sighed and swallowed a more robust mouthful of wine. 'He said he really *liked* me, which is the biggest insult a girl could have, because he obviously wasn't actually that attracted to me. At any rate, he must really have fallen for Emily because he braved his parents' wrath to tell them about her and now...what can I say? She'll be having the life I had planned on having.'

'Married to a bastard who will probably find another skirt to chase within two years of getting hitched? I wouldn't wallow in too much self-pity if I were you...'

Milly laughed. To the point. Where her friends would spend literally hours analysing, he had cut to the chase in a few sentences.

'And now shall we see how that food of yours is doing?' Lucas stood up and stretched and Milly tried not to let her mouth fall open at the ripple of muscle discernible under his clothes.

'Yes, the food; the stolen food.'

'And I shall make a few calls; do something about this job of yours that's disappeared under your feet.'

Milly hadn't forgotten about that but she had decided not to mention it again. People had a way of saying stuff they seriously meant at the time but five minutes later had completely forgotten. Sometimes she had been guilty of that particular crime. A wide, sweeping invitation to friends to come round for drinks only to realise afterwards that she would actually be at work on the evening in question.

'You're going to make a few calls?'

'Two, in actual fact.' He watched her cute rear as she preceded him into the kitchen. He knew more about her life after five seconds than he had about anyone he had dated in the past, but then he didn't naturally encourage outpourings, and the women he dated were all too conscious of the fact that they had to toe the line. No outpourings. No long life stories. No involved anecdotes.

Was it any wonder that he was frankly enjoying himself? He would never have imagined that being a ski instructor could be such a liberating experience. He wondered whether he shouldn't become a ski instructor for a week every year just so that he could refresh his palate with a taste of normality.

He disappeared, heading back to the sitting room so that he could make his calls as he stood absently looking down at the sprawling white vista outside his lodge.

One call to his mother, to tell her that he might be staying on slightly longer than originally thought. The other to Alberto, to tell him that his chalet girl had arrived to find herself jobless and that he would be digging into his pocket to pay her what she was due, because she would be staying on, and that he should contact whatever agency he got her from and relay the message. Lucas could easily have afforded to pay her himself but on principle he saw no reason why he should pick up the tab. The man was grossly over-paid by his company for what he did, and Lucas suspected that he had told the agency that the deal was off at the last possible minute because neither he nor his wife would really have given a damn if their chalet girl's nose was put out of joint.

He sauntered into the kitchen, snapping his phone shut just as she was dishing out two heaped bowls of pasta.

'Done.'

Alone and away from his overpowering personality, Milly had had a little while to consider the prospect of spending two weeks with a man she didn't know in a lodge that belonged to neither of them. The plan made no sense. Were they to deplete the contents of the fridge? Guzzle all the alcohol? Then leave with a cheery wave goodbye? Wouldn't a bill catch up with her sooner or later? There was no such thing as a free lunch, after all, not to mention two weeks' worth of free lunches.

And, also, what if the ski instructor with the drop-dead good looks turned out to be dodgy? He didn't seem the violent type but who was to say he was trustworthy? He could be a gentleman by day and a sex maniac by night.

Bracketing Lucas and sex in the same thought brought hectic colour to her cheeks. Even if he *was* a closet sex maniac, there was no chance he would look twice in her direction. Robert, who had been nice looking but definitely not in Adonis's league, hadn't found her attractive. That, in a nutshell, said it all as far as Milly was concerned.

But she still found herself hesitating, clearing her throat and sitting down at the sleek kitchen table with burning, self-conscious hesitation.

Would it be inappropriate to ask him for a CV? she wondered. Maybe a few references from women he had happened to be thrown together with inadvertently who had found him to be a decent, honourable man with upstanding moral values?

'The look of joy and satisfaction seems to be missing from your expression.' Lucas tucked into the pasta, which was as good as anything he had had in any restaurant. He had wondered about the 'professional chef' description of herself—had thought that maybe it was a bit of self-congratulation when, in fact, she worked behind the scenes at the local fast food joint—but she was a seriously good cook.

'Well....' Curiosity got the better of her. 'How did you manage to do that? I mean when you say *done*...'

'You'd be surprised at the things I can accomplish when I put my mind to it. Your job here is safe, and you'll be fully paid for the duration. Even if you decide to leave after two days.'

Milly's mouth dropped open and Lucas grinned wryly.

'Admit it. You're impressed.'

'Wow. You must have an awful lot of influence with the Ramos family.' A thought struck her and she went bright red and took refuge in her pasta.

'Why do I get the feeling that there's something on your mind?' Lucas drawled drily.

'What makes you think that?'

'Maybe it's because you've suddenly turned the colour of puce. Or maybe it's because you have a face that's as transparent as a pane of glass. Pick either option. The food's delicious, by the way. Were it not for the red hair, I would be tempted to think that you have a streak of Italian running through you.'

'Auburn, not red. I don't like the word "red",' Milly automatically asserted, still staring down at her plate.

'Spit it out, Milly of the "auburn not red" hair...'

'Well, you probably wouldn't like it.'

Lucas helped himself to more pasta, poured himself another glass of wine and allowed the silence to stretch between them. Eventually, he rescued her from her agonising indecision.

'Trust me, I'm built like a brick wall when it comes to being offended.' Not that he could think, offhand, of anyone who would dare say something offensive to him. The joys of wealth and power.

'You really *are* arrogant, aren't you?' Milly said distractedly and he delivered her a slashing smile that temporarily knocked her for six. 'Well, if you must know, I just wondered whether you managed to pull strings because you're sleeping with Mrs Ramos…' She said it in one rushed sentence and then held her breath and waited for a reply.

For a few seconds, Lucas didn't actually believe what he had just heard and then, when it *had* sunk in, he wasn't sure whether to be outraged, amused or incredulous.

'Well…' She dragged that one syllable out, licking her lips nervously. 'It makes a weird kind of sense.'

'In what world does it make a weird kind of sense?'

'How else would you be able to get me my job and ensure that I get paid for it?'

'Ski instructors can have a lot of influence, as it happens.' Lucas skirted over that sweeping and vague statement because it was one thing to delicately economise on the truth and another to lie outright, especially to someone who, he suspected, had probably never told so much as a white lie in her entire life. 'I've helped Alberto out on a number of occasions and, put it this way, he was more than happy to do as I asked. Furthermore, I would never go near a married woman.'

'You wouldn't?'

'Don't tell me—all the ski instructors you've met have been more than obliging with women whether they were wearing wedding rings on their fingers or not?'

'Their reputations *can* be a little racy.' But she breathed a sigh of relief. 'Just one other small thing…'

'You *do* take testing conversations to the outer limits, don't you?'

'I wouldn't normally…er…choose to be alone in a ski lodge with someone I actually don't know.'

This time Lucas *was* outraged. He flung his hands in the air in a gesture that was mesmerising and typically foreign and leaned back into his chair. 'So, not only do you clock me for a womaniser who doesn't bother to discriminate between single and married women, but now I'm a pervert!'

'No!' Milly squeaked, on the verge of telling him to keep his voice down because, with all the food and wine they had consumed, guilt was making its presence felt in a very intrusive way. It would be just her luck to find out that he hadn't made any phone calls at all, that he was in fact a burglar who had decided to make himself at home before getting down to the serious business of nicking the silver, and to top it off somewhere lurking behind a wall was Sandra and her band of blond-haired guard dogs.

'How do I know that you've actually spoken to Mr Ramos?'

'Because I just told you that I had.' Unaccustomed to having his word doubted, Lucas was finding the conversation more and more surreal. 'I can prove it.'

'You can? How?' She cast him a dubious look. What was it about the guy? Her instinct was just to believe everything he told her, zombie-style. She was pretty sure that if he pointed to the sky and told her that there were spaceships hovering she would be more than half-inclined to wonder if they contained little green men.

Lucas dialled a number on his cell phone and, when it connected, spoke rapidly in Spanish and then placed the mobile on the table and put it on speakerphone.

Then he sat back, a picture of relaxation, and spoke. Very slowly and very clearly. Without taking his eyes off her face. Which, when inspected in-depth, as he was now doing, was really an extraordinarily attractive face. Why was that? She didn't have the sharp, high cheekbones of a model, nor did she have the haughty, self-confident air of a trust-fund chick, but there was just something soft yet stubborn about her, sympathetic yet outspoken…

She was the sort of person who would never give in without a fight and for a few seconds he felt impossibly enraged at the unseen but much discussed ex-fiancé who had dumped her. He almost lost track of the conversation he was in the middle of having with Alberto, who, naturally, had adopted the usual tone of subservience the second he knew who was on the line.

Like someone pulling off a magic trick, Lucas waved to the phone and folded his hands behind his head as he listened to Alberto do exactly what he had been told to do, which, in actual fact, was simply to tell the truth.

Yes, of course she could stay on! On full pay. *No hay problema*. Furthermore, there was no need for her to replace any of the food eaten or wine drunk, nor was there any need to run herself ragged trying to keep the lodge clean. All that would be sorted at a later date. Meanwhile, he would be transferring her pay directly into her account, if she would just text him the details of her bank account, and furthermore there would be a bonus in view of the inconvenience she had suffered.

'I feel just terrible,' was the first thing Milly said as soon as Alberto had signed off, having wished her a very pleasant stay and apologised for any inconvenience caused.

'You feel terrible. You give new meaning to the word "unpredictable". What's that supposed to mean? Why do you feel terrible? I thought you would be leaping around this kitchen with joy! Face it, you don't have to return to London and risk bumping into your charming "best friend" and the loser ex…nor do you have to worry about money for the time being because you'll be paid for your stay here. You can take the time out you wanted and oh, what joy, you won't even have to slave over a hot stove catering to the Ramos family. In other words, you won't have to sing for your supper. From where I'm standing, you couldn't have wished for a better deal…yet you look as though someone's cancelled your birthday.'

'I haven't exactly been nice to poor Mr Ramos, have I?' She flung the rhetorical question at him in a voice laden with accusation.

'Have I encouraged that?'

'I made assumptions. I just thought that—because I had a list of a hundred different things I had to prepare for them individually to eat, and because I had so many strict instructions on what I could wear and what I couldn't wear, and what I could say and couldn't say—they were a pretty demanding, diva family. And yet…' She dug into her rucksack, grabbed her phone and texted the relevant information to Alberto.

'He couldn't have been more decent about the whole thing.' In record time she heard the ping of her phone as he confirmed that the money had been deposited into her account. 'After Robbie, it's nice to see that there are some decent people left in the world.'

Lucas was fighting down annoyance over Alberto and his ridiculous demands. He could kiss sweet goodbye to any further freebies at the lodge, whatever the family connection.

'So is the Dance of Joy and Happiness about to take place? Oh, no, I forgot, you still think that I'm a pervert you can't trust...'

'No.' Milly sighed. And anyway, had she really been conceited enough to imagine that he would make some kind of pass at her? Which was something she would obviously reject out of hand, because she was recovering from a broken heart! Not that he would anyway. Adonis types went for Aphrodite types—known fact.

'I'm weak with relief.'

'I guess we should clean here and then turn in for the night,' she said, standing up. The rollercoaster ride loosely called 'her life' was still looping her around in a million different directions. So now, unbelievably, she was staying on at the lodge for the full duration of her contract. From jobless and heading back on the first flight to still in work, earning her fabulous wage for two weeks of having fun and skiing...

'Clean?'

'Do the dishes.' She waved at the plates, the glasses, the saucepans. 'You might not be able to cook, but you can certainly help tidy this kitchen. I'm not doing it on my own. We both contributed to the mess.'

Lucas stood back, arms folded, and realised that 'do the dishes' had never been words applied to him, but he obligingly began clearing the table while she spent a little more time expressing completely unnecessary levels of remorse for having been uncharitable towards Alberto and his family.

As consciences went, hers appeared to be extremely overactive.

'Okay!' He held up one hand, cutting short yet another take on how kind the Ramos man had turned out to be. 'I get the general picture. Not,' he added darkly, 'that you actually know the first thing about Ramos… er…Alberto… But no point going down that road.' He leaned against the kitchen counter and folded his arms.

His contribution to tidying the kitchen had consisted of moving two plates and a glass from the table to the sink.

Good-looking men were always spoiled, first by their adoring mothers, who ran around doing everything for them, then by adoring girlfriends who did the same, and finally by their adoring wives, who picked up where the girlfriends had left off.

'Let's just cut short the Ramos eulogies. Now that you're here, I'm going to be here for a couple of days. We can talk about which runs we do.' She was someone capable, by all accounts, of skiing to a high standard, as opposed to dressing to a high standard with lamentably average skiing skills, which had always been the case with his girlfriends in the past. The actual process of skiing had always been an interruption to the more engaging business of looking good in skiing outfits.

A quirky, amusing companion who didn't know him from Adam. Who knew what the outcome of their brief, unexpected meeting of ways would be?

In his highly controlled and largely predictable life, the prospect of the unknown dangled in front of him like a tantalising carrot.

He smiled and closely watched the way she blushed and lowered her eyes.

Yes, coming here had definitely been the right decision…

CHAPTER THREE

'SOMETHING'S ONLY JUST occurred to me...'

The dishes had been done, mostly by Milly, while Lucas had relaxed and fiddled with the complicated coffee-making machine, eventually succeeding in producing two small cups of espresso that she was embarrassed to tell him would probably keep her up all night. It had taken him such a long time finally to get there that it would have seemed churlish to politely refuse. She had never met anyone more clueless when it came to knowing his way around a kitchen. Or less interested, for that matter.

Now they were back on the white sofa although, with permission granted to stay in the lodge, she felt a little less uncomfortable in her surroundings.

'And I take it that this sudden thought is one you want to share with me.' This was a brave, new world. She had already berated him for not helping enough in the kitchen and had then proceeded to give him a mini-lecture on the wonders of 'the modern man'. Apparently those were men who shared all the domestic chores, cooked and cleaned with the best of them and gave foot massages to their loved ones. He had told her that, quite frankly, he could think of nothing worse.

'I should have asked you this before but with everything going on my mind was all over the place…'

Lucas grunted. The emails that he had planned to spend the evening ploughing through had quickly taken a back seat to the girl now staring off into the distance with a thoughtful frown.

'I should have asked you whether you're…er…involved with someone or not.'

'Involved with someone…'

'Are you married?' she asked bluntly. 'Not that it makes any difference, because we're both just employees who happen to be stranded in the same lodge.' *The same empty lodge.* 'But I wouldn't want your wife to be worried. You know…'

'You mean you wouldn't want her to be jealous.'

'Well, *anxious*…' So he *was* married, despite the lack of a wedding ring. Lots of men didn't wear wedding rings. She felt a stab of disappointment. Why wouldn't he be married? she thought, restlessly pushing aside that awkward, uninvited emotion that had no place in her life. He was sinfully sexy and oozed just the sort of self-assurance and lazy arrogance that women went wild for.

'Interesting concept. A jealous and anxious wife worried about her beloved husband sharing a ski lodge with a total stranger…' He tried the thought on for size and tried not to burst out laughing.

When it came to women and commitment, he was the least likely candidate. Once bitten, twice shy and he had had his brush with his one and only near-escape. It had been a decade and a half ago but as learning curves went it had been a good one. He had been a nineteen-year-old kid, already with plenty of experience but still too green to recognise when he was being played. He'd been young, cocky and arrogant enough to think that gold-diggers all came wrapped up and packaged the same way: big hair, high heels, obvious charms.

But Betina Crew, at twenty-seven nearly eight years older than him, had been just the opposite. She had been a wild flower-child who went on protest marches and waxed lyrical about saving the world. He had fallen hook, line and sinker until she'd tried to reel him in with a phoney pregnancy scare, which he had so nearly bought, and had so nearly walked down the aisle. It was pure chance that he had discovered the packet of contraceptive pills tucked away at the back of one of her drawers and, when he'd confronted her, it had all ended up turning ugly.

Since then, he had never kidded himself that there was such a thing as disinterested true love. Not when the size of his bank balance was known. His parents might have had the perfect marriage, but they had both started off broke and had worked together to make their fortune. His mother still believed in all that clap trap about true love, and he hadn't the heart to disillusion her, but he knew that when and if he ever decided to tie the knot it would be less Cupid's bow and arrow than a decent arrangement overseen by a lawyer with a watertight pre-nup.

'No.' He shook his head. 'No anxious, jealous or whatever-you-want-to-call-it wife keeping the home fires warm.'

'Girlfriend?'

'Why the interest? Are you suggesting that there might be something for a woman to be jealous about?'

'No!' Milly nearly choked on her espresso. 'In case you'd forgotten,' she added, regaining her composure, 'I came over here to try and escape. The last thing on my mind would be involvement with anyone! I just don't want to think that there's anyone out there who cares about you and who might be alarmed that we happen to be stuck here together through no fault of our own.'

'In that case, I'll set your mind at rest, shall I? No girlfriend and, even if there was a girlfriend, I'm not a jealous guy and I don't encourage jealousy in women I date.'

'How can you discourage someone from being jealous?' She hadn't been at all jealous when it came to Robbie. Why was that? she wondered. Was it because she had known him off and on for a long time, and one was never that jealous when it came to people they were familiar with? She hadn't even thought twice about Robbie and Emily being alone together. And yet there was something deep inside telling her that surely jealousy was something that attacked at random and couldn't be debated or ordered out of existence?

'I've never found a problem with that. The women I date know my parameters and they tend to respect them.'

'You're the most arrogant guy I've ever met in my entire life,' Milly said with genuine wonderment.

'I think you've already told me that.' He drained his cup and dumped it on one of the coffee tables, then he stood up and flexed his muscles, watching as she uncurled herself from the sofa and automatically reached to gather his cup along with hers.

His automatic instinct was irritably to tell her to leave it, that someone would tidy it away in the morning, then he remembered that there would be no cleaner trooping along to make sure she tidied in his wake.

'I'll show you to your room.'

'Feels odd to be here without the owner in residence.'

Lucas had the grace to flush but he refrained from saying anything, instead scooping up her holdall, which had seen better days, and heading out towards a spiral staircase that led up to a huge galleried landing that overlooked the ground floor.

There, as on the ground floor, soaring windows gave out to the same spectacular views of the open, snow-covered mountains. It was dark outside and the snow was a peculiar dull-blue white against the velvety darkness.

For a few seconds, Milly paused to admire the vista, which was truly breathtakingly beautiful. When she looked away it was to find his dark eyes speculatively pinned to her face.

She was here with a guy she didn't know and yet, far from feeling threatened in any way, she felt *safe*. There was something silent and inherently strong about him that was deeply reassuring. She felt that if the place were to be invaded by a clutch of knife wielding bandits he would be able to dispatch them single-handedly.

'I have no idea where Ramos was going to put you,' Lucas told her truthfully. 'But I expect this room will do as good as any of the others.'

He flung wide the door and she gasped. It was, simply put, the most splendid bedroom she had ever seen. She almost didn't want to disturb its perfection by going inside. He breezed in and tossed her bag on the elegant *chaise longue* by the window, yet another of those massive windows designed to remind you of the still, white, glorious silence that lay outside.

'Well?' Lucas rarely noticed his surroundings but he did now because the expression on her face was so tellingly awestruck.

Playground for the seriously rich—this was what

the lodge was. He had had zero input into its decor. He had left that to a world famous interior designer. When the job had been done, he had dispatched three of his trusted employees to give it the once over and make sure that everything had been done to the highest possible standard, no corners cut. Thereafter he had used it a handful of times when the season was at its height and only if the skiing conditions were perfect.

It was a beautiful place. He looked at the cool, white furnishings, breathed in the air of calm, noted the quality of the wood and the subtlety of the faded Persian rug on the ground. Nothing jarred. In the bowels of the lodge, there was a comprehensive spa and sauna area. He'd used that once.

Now, he had an intense urge to take her down there and show it to her just so that he could see that expression of awe again, even though, regrettably, the lodge was not his as far as she was concerned. For the first time in living memory, he had an insane desire to *brag*. Hell, where had *that* come from?

'It's amazing.' Milly hovered by the door. 'Isn't it amazing? Well, I guess you're used to this, but I'm not. My entire flat could fit into this bedroom. Is that an *en suite* bathroom?'

Amused, Lucas pushed the adjoining door and, sure enough, it opened out to a bathroom that was almost as big as the bedroom and contained its own little sitting area. He wondered what the interior designer had had in mind when she'd decided on sticking furniture in the bathroom.

'Wow.' Milly tiptoed her way to the bathroom and peered in. It was absolutely enormous. 'You could have a party in here,' she breathed in a hushed voice.

'I doubt anyone would choose to do that.'

'How can you be so blasé about all of this?' She was too busy inspecting her glorious surroundings to look at him but she was acutely aware of his masculine presence next to her. 'I mean, do you teach lots of rich people? Is that it? You're accustomed to places like this because you're in them all the time?'

'I've been to a number of places along these lines...'

Milly laughed that infectious laugh that made him want to smile. 'Must be a terrific anti-climax when the season's over and you have to return to your digs.'

'I cope.'

Suddenly exhausted after a day of travelling and the stress of finding herself out of a job, then back in one, Milly yawned behind her hand and wandered over to her holdall, which was not the quality of bag that should have adorned the *chaise longue*.

'I've talked about myself all night,' she said sleepily. 'Tomorrow you can tell me all about yourself and your exciting life working for the rich and famous.'

A minute later she closed, and after a few seconds' thought locked, the bedroom door behind him and began running the bath. The ridiculously luxurious bath that was so big and so deep that it was almost the size of a plunge pool.

She wouldn't have believed it but she was having an impossible adventure and—okay, admit it—was so transfixed by Lucas that there had been no room in her head to feel sorry for herself.

She wondered what he did when he wasn't playing ski instructor to rich adults and their kids. Did he while away his summers in the company of wealthy social-ites? He was good-looking enough to be a gigolo but she dismissed that idea as fast as it entered her head be-cause she couldn't imagine that he could be that sleazy.

He'd said didn't sleep with married women and she believed him. There had been a shadow of repugnance when that suggestion had been mooted.

But he was a man of experience, from the way he had talked about the women he dated, in the casual voice of someone who was accustomed to getting a lot of attention and to dating a lot of women.

She thought about her own circumstances. When it came to experience with the opposite sex, she was wet behind the ears. She had never really been the kind of teenager who had become swept up in boys, in make-up, in short skirts and mini bottles of vodka at house parties. Maybe if she had had a mum; maybe if she hadn't been raised by her grandmother. She adored her grandmother, but she could reflect back and see that the generation gap had not been conducive to giggly conversations and experiments with make-up.

Nana Mayfield was a brisk, no-nonsense woman with a great love of the outdoors. Widowed at the age of forty-five, she had had to survive the harsh Scottish winters in unforgiving terrain and she had thrived. That love of the great outdoors was what she had brought to the relationship with her granddaughter and Milly had grown up loving all things to do with sport. She had followed sport on TV and had played as many sports as she could possibly fit into her school timetable.

Of course, she had been to parties, but hockey, tennis, rounders, even football, and later as much skiing as she could possibly do, had always come first.

And so the stages of infatuation, the teenage angst and disappointment, the adolescent broken hearts and the comparing of notes about boys with her friends, had largely passed her by.

Was that why she had fallen for Robbie in the first

place? Because her lack of experience had allowed flattery and compliments to blind her to the reality of a relationship that was built on sand? Had a crush at fourteen predisposed her to become the vulnerable idiot she had been when he had swanned back into her life ten years later? And then, had she held on to him because she had wanted someone to call her own?

He hadn't even shown much interest in getting physical with her. How did that fit into the equation of two love birds on the brink of a happy-ever-after life? And she hadn't pushed him. That should have sounded the alarm bells, but nope, she had merrily continued sleep walking her way to the inevitable.

She had made sure to keep that to herself. She knew, from listening to her friends, that they would all have read the writing on the wall and would have known that his only half-hearted attempts at touching her, and her cheerful acceptance of that situation, did not augur a healthy relationship. They had all been born and raised in London and they were streetwise in ways she couldn't hope to be.

She fell asleep to images of a dark, swarthy, sexy face. He wasn't replacement therapy, but he was a distraction, and maybe that was exactly what she needed right now: a harmless distraction.

The following morning it was snowing when she awoke. She hadn't drawn the curtains and from the bed she could look straight across to ceiling panes of glass to the winter wonderland outside. She itched to put on her skis and get out there.

Before she did anything, she telephoned her grandmother to tell her that she arrived safe and sound but that the family in question had had a slight change of plan, after which she managed to avoid directly lying about her new circumstances, about sharing the lodge with a stranger. Then she texted her friends, brief texts telling them that she'd arrived. No more.

Once changed, she went downstairs and after prowling through the lodge finally located Lucas in a big, airy room behind a desk. She came to a halt outside the door and looked at him. There were papers spread around him and he was peering at a thin laptop computer, frowning.

'You're going to express concern that I'm sitting here without due respect for the owner, aren't you?' he said, without looking away from the computer.

He had had time to question his motives in offering her the use of his ski lodge. She was a young girl recovering from a broken relationship. In short, she was vulnerable and vulnerable, along with married, was something he didn't do.

Was he so jaded that he was prepared to try and take something simply because it made a change? And was a change as good as a rest? Yes, she was refreshing, as was the fact that she had no idea who he was or what he was worth, but was that any reason for him to amuse himself with her?

In any equation where 'vulnerable' appeared, hurt was always its companion.

He was immune but she wouldn't be. He knew what it was like to have complete control over the outcome of his emotional life, whilst she clearly didn't.

And yet...he couldn't escape the tempting notion that it would be utterly relaxing to spend a couple of days in her company. He could look without touching. It was called restraint and, whilst it was something he had never had any need to practise, it should be something that he could manage.

He needed to take time out from the combined stresses of his mother, who would not let up on reminding him that he needed to settle down, and an ex-girlfriend who was still texting him in a way that was heading dangerously into stalker land. The fact that she knew his mother, albeit remotely, had foolishly led her to believe that their fling was more significant than what he'd had in mind.

He needed to take time out from being Lucas Romero. It was an elevated position he had occupied for his entire life. He had been born and bred to manage the family fortune and to add to it. He had never known what it felt like to be a normal person, with normal concerns. Wariness, suspicion, caution: those were the bywords in a life that was as wealthy and as powerful as his was.

'How did you know?' Overnight, Milly had wondered whether exhaustion and a build-up of stress were responsible for her exaggerating Lucas's overwhelming physical impact.

Not a bit of it. He was sprawled in front of his computer in all his devastatingly good-looking glory.

His near-black hair was swept back, accentuating the hard, chiselled lines of his face, and he was wearing a pale blue short-sleeved polo shirt that exposed the rippling, muscled strength of his arms and a glimpse of bronzed collarbone that made her mouth suddenly go dry.

'Because I'm getting the impression that you have a highly developed sense of guilt.' He stood up, dark eyes fixed on her face.

She was in a pair of jogging bottoms and a black base-layer long-sleeved T-shirt that clung to every curve of her small, sexy little body. It was just as well Ramos was not around. His wife would have spent the entire time trying to peel his eyes back into their sockets. The man was a notorious womaniser.

'What are you doing?'

Lucas logged off and leaned back, hands folded behind his head. 'Work.'

'Oh.' Milly looked at him, confused.

'A man has to get by.'

'What work?' Then her face cleared and she smiled. 'Oh, I remember. This and that. You didn't specify. How long have you been up?' It wasn't yet nine and he looked bright eyed and bushy tailed.

'I'm usually up by six.'

'Wow. Are you? Why?' Fascinated, she watched as he strolled towards her, pausing to stand directly in front of her so that she had to look up to him.

'What do you mean *why*?' Lucas asked, amused and puzzled.

'Why would you get up so early if you don't have to?' She felt breathless and exposed. 'I stay in bed as long as I can,' she confessed. 'Admittedly, my hours at the Rainbow Hotel are pretty long. *Were* pretty long. I'm out of a job now.'

She followed him towards the kitchen, chewing her lip, thinking about having to apply for more jobs as soon as she returned to London. How was she going to afford the rent on the flat? Emily would have disappeared off to her shiny new life that left her without a flatmate and with a disgruntled landlord. He might give her a little bit of leeway, if she explained the circumstances to him, but he wasn't a Good Samaritan and unless she found the rent money fast she would be out on her ear with nowhere to live.

'I like to be awake for as much of the day as possible,' Lucas murmured. Lie-ins were unheard of. Even if there was a woman in bed with him, he found it impossible to waste his time next to her, unless they were making love.

Sex got him into bed and kept him there. Sleep was something essential he had to grab. But, for him, those were the two main functions of a bed.

The kitchen was as they had left it. Milly stared around her, dismayed.

'You were up at six, made yourself a cup of coffee and yet you couldn't be bothered to tidy up?'

Lucas surveyed the kitchen as though seeing it for the first time. 'What's wrong with it?'

'Everything. The dishes need putting away...the counters need wiping...the milk's been left out...'

Lucas shrugged and looked at her with his head tilted to one side. 'I fail to see the point of tidying away anything that's going to make an appearance later on in the day. Same goes for the kitchen counters. Why wipe them? Unless you're planning on having a food-free day?'

'How can you be so blasé about someone else's property? You should respect the things that don't belong to you.'

'You're cute when you're being self-righteous,' he murmured and Milly stood stock still and folded her arms.

'You might think you're the hottest guy on the planet,' she said on an indrawn breath, 'and you might be bored because your job here with the Ramos family fell through, but that doesn't give you the right to flirt with me just because I happen to be around.'

'Who's flirting?' He surveyed her lazily. 'Simple statement of fact.'

'And I won't be running around cleaning up behind you like a maid either. I realise I'm being paid by Mr Ramos, who's been more than generous, all things considered—and I know that that's thanks to you—but I'm going to use my time here to really relax and try and forget about what I've been through. I don't want to feel as though I've got to be on full alert every time you're around.'

'I'm at a loss. What do you imagine I'm going to do?'

'Well, I just think we should lay down some boundary lines.'

'Agreed.' He held up both hands with a wicked grin that seem to utterly contradict what he had just said. 'Shall we have a spot of breakfast and then put our skiing skills to the test? The weather looks perfect. We could save the boundary line conversation for a little later.' He watched her hesitate, wondering whether to carry on the argument, maybe add to the 'boundary line' suggestion, but in the end the thought of taking to the slopes proved too much of a temptation and she smiled, her good humour restored.

Inexperienced.

Vulnerable.

He should be laying down more than just a few boundaries himself. He should be the one warning her off. He had the instincts of a born predator when it came to women and, however much she amused him, the last thing he wanted was for her somehow to get it into her head that he might be a worthwhile replacement for the vanishing ex-fiancé. The guy was obviously a complete loser, and she was well rid of him, but transference was a dangerous possibility and a complication he could do without.

As are women who have romantic notions of love and marriage, a little voice added. A complication he could do without...

Milly's face was flushed with happiness when, several hours later, they returned to the lodge.

The day's skiing had been exhausting, exhilarating, wonderful. It had been over a year since she had last taken to the slopes. The *real* slopes. She had managed to keep her hand in by going as often as she could to the nearest dry slopes, but nothing could come close to the feeling of euphoria when, poised at the very top of the mountain, you looked down to the naked, white beauty of snow-covered slopes. It was the closest you could get to your mind being empty, with just you and the infinite snowy space around you, your whole body yearning for the thrill of speed.

They had raced. She was good but he'd made her look like an amateur. He knew where to go to avoid all crowds. He would, she supposed. He would know these ranges like the back of his hand.

Dressed completely in black, including a black woolly hat and dark sunglasses, he was unbearably sexy, and she'd found her gaze drifting back to him repeatedly.

He moved as though he had been born to ski. He was skilled, fast, at times disappearing to reappear like a speeding bullet far ahead of her on the slopes.

They'd broken off for lunch at a tiny café nowhere near the hubbub of the town centre. This café was in the opposite direction, and there wasn't a single designer shop in sight—unlike the town centre, which heaved with rich and famous people spending money in the expensive shops that had sprung up to cater for their exclusive clientele.

Milly had loved it. She had never felt more relaxed as she'd sipped hot coffee and told him all about her childhood, her love of sports, the football team she supported. She'd told him about being brought up by her grandmother, the way it made you feel vulnerable to being left by the people you love.

It was weird but she knew that if she had met him under more normal circumstances there was no way she would ever have approached him. But here, things were different. She was recuperating from the humiliation of a broken heart, and he was the objective listening ear who didn't know her and so was not interested in tea and sympathy. In fact, he made no mention of Robbie except, when he could sense her drifting off, to tell her that the guy was a loser and she was better off without losers in her life.

'Tough times make you stronger,' had been his bracing observation when she had mentioned the uphill struggle of having to return to London to find work so that she could pay the rent on a house she couldn't really afford unless she found another lodger pronto.

Everything about him was as sexy as hell and by the end of the day she had stopped trying to pretend that she didn't want to just keep looking at him. She had stopped trying to figure out how it was that she could be broken-hearted and yet still open to his incredible, mind-blowing, raw animal magnetism...

Their joint love of skiing had banished her nerves. When she was moving on the snow, she was no longer the small, round red-haired girl who couldn't hold a candle to the tall glamorous models men found attractive. No, when she was skiing, she was at the top of her game and bursting with self-confidence.

* * *

Lucas had planned to stay no more than two nights at the ski lodge.

It was all the time he could spare. His high-octane life did not leave room for impromptu holidays. The impulse to go to the ski lodge where the isolation and privacy would recharge his batteries had been a good one.

The unexpected presence of Milly, her freshness and openness, had turned out to be even better for recharging his batteries.

By the second day, he had already made up his mind to take a couple more days off.

What was the point in having highly paid executives in place if you needed to hold their hand every time a decision had to be made? They could all do without him for a few days. Some of them could definitely do with an injection of backbone.

The truth was that he was enjoying himself. He was even enjoying his self-imposed rule of looking but not touching. He liked the way she coloured when he occasionally flirted with her. He liked the challenge of restraint when, the more he saw of her, the more he wanted to see. He liked her openness and he liked the way she confided, her pretty face pink and open and earnest.

The joy of restraint, however, was the certain knowledge that it could be broken at any given moment in time.

She fancied him. He had picked that up with finely tuned antennae: the way she sneaked sultry, stolen glances at him; the way she stilled whenever he got within a certain radius, as though ordering her body not to betray what she was feeling.

Her attempts to keep her distance were like constant

gauntlets being thrown down. His libido, jaded after a diet of the same type of woman, was being tested to its absolute limit.

It was invigorating.

It made him think that he had not faced up to any sort of challenge for a very long time. He had flat-lined. He made money, more than he could ever hope to spend in a lifetime. He owned things and occasionally even enjoyed some of his possessions. And he had women. However many he wanted and whatever variety he chose.

He was keeping his hands to himself but his determination to keep in mind that she didn't play by his rules, that she had been hurt once and he didn't want to be responsible for adding to the tally, was beginning to fray round the edges.

Right now, she was downstairs cooking something. It would be good. She would be moving around the kitchen in clothes that showed off a body she seemed to have downgraded to the lowest possible rating, despite the fact there wasn't a red-blooded man on this earth who wouldn't have appreciated those generous breasts, that tiny waist and those womanly hips.

Wouldn't it do her good to have a man—a *real man,* not a wimp like the vanishing ex—tell her how sexy she was?

Wouldn't it do her self-confidence a power of good for her to know what it felt like to be desired? From what he had read between the lines, the ex had been a waste of space from day one. They had met, gone to the movies, gone on walks, enjoyed meals out. From where he was standing, it had been a courtship that had shrieked 'boring'—and most women with a little more about them would have picked that up and moved on after deadly date number four.

But Milly hadn't and, now that fate had seen fit to bring them together for a few days, wouldn't he be doing her a *favour* if he showed her that she was a desirable woman? If he conclusively proved to her that she was well rid of the man, that she could have any guy she wanted…?

With the logical, clear-minded and concise brain any lawyer would kill for, Lucas made a mental list of all the many reasons why he could be justified in sleeping with her.

At the very end, he tacked on *no more restless nights for me wondering…*

He got downstairs to find the kitchen empty, with a note on the counter propped up against the salt shaker.

She had popped down to the town to get some stuff.

It had been snowing sporadically for the past twenty-four hours but the snow had gathered pace overnight. Optimum skiing conditions were bright-blue skies and good accumulation of snow. Too much falling snow could end up being inconvenient and, in some cases, downright dangerous to safe skiing.

He looked outside at what appeared to be a gathering snow storm. The lifts would be running at half-empty, if that. The line between safe and treacherous was slim. But she was a damned good skier. The best skiing companion he had ever had—courageous without taking unnecessary chances. He would wait for her to return and give himself a chance to catch up on work.

But there was no internet connection. Nor, when he tried his mobile phone, could he get a signal.

He waited a further twenty minutes and then realised that he had no choice but to hunt her down.

Chances were she was fine and on her way back but there was the very slender possibility that the sudden heavy snowfall had disorientated her, as it was wont to do with skiers unaccustomed to these slopes.

A disorientated skier very quickly became a skier at high risk. There had also been three avalanches in the past eighteen months. No casualties, but it only took one…

One disorientated skier, unfamiliar with the terrain, reacting without thinking, panicking…

When that happened, experience on a pair of sticks counted for nothing.

He dropped everything: the coffee he had just made; the historic files he had been about to review on his computer; the report waiting to be concluded.

He hit the slopes at a run, strapped himself into his skis and took off.

This was more than just a bit of fun for a couple of days. This was a serious case of *wanting* a woman and he was sick of playing mind games with himself. Hell, when he thought of her disappearing without him having bedded her…

He killed every single scruple that had been holding him back, because he was a man who was accustomed to taking what he wanted, and why bother trying to break the habits of a lifetime?

CHAPTER FOUR

THE GOING WAS slower than it would normally have been. Lucas was familiar with the slope down to the town centre but the thickly falling snow meant that he had to take it more carefully, which went against the grain when it came to skiing.

What the hell had she been thinking, venturing out when she must have known that there was the possibility of getting lost? She had never been here before and so far had only seen the slopes in his speeding wake.

He did his utmost to cover as much ground as possible, cross-skiing, eyes peeled for anything that might be a figure in distress. Or even a figure moving at a snail's pace, trying to get her bearings.

Nothing.

The slopes were virtually empty. The height of the tourist season was over and the falling snow would have kept most of the skiers indoors. Good food, good wine, expensive lodges—some, like his, with saunas and gyms. Being cooped up indoors would hardly be a hardship.

After twenty minutes, he saw the town approaching in the distance, a clutch of shops and restaurants, bars and cafés.

He hadn't planned to make this trip. He had planned

to stay put in the lodge, testing the less obvious ski slopes, maintaining his privacy. It was a small town and he was its wealthiest occasional visitor.

Cursing fluently under his breath, because he had no idea what 'stuff' she could possibly have needed to buy when the house was stocked with enough food for them to survive a sudden nuclear war, he resigned himself to a door-to-door search for her.

He hadn't signed up for this.

He was recognised within minutes of entering the first shop. He was stopped as he tried to progress through the town. His dark, striking looks halted people in their tracks, even those who didn't know who he was.

Somewhere, there would be someone with a camera. The place was a magnet for the paparazzi.

Hell! It made no difference to him whether some sleazeball with a camera snapped a photo of him but he would rather have avoided it. He valued his privacy, little of it as there was.

He found her in the very last café, huddled in front of a mug of hot chocolate, watching the snow storm. He had just spent the past hour trudging to find her and here she was, cool as a cucumber, sipping her drink without a care in the world!

He burst into the smart café and was, of course, immediately recognised by the owner. He might not have been a regular visitor but he was so extraordinarily high-profile that people went out of their way to garner his attention.

Even when, as now, he patently didn't want it. Especially not when she had spotted him and was frowning as she absorbed the café owner's deference.

The man was practically bowing as he retreated.

Lucas ignored him, choosing instead to hold her gaze as he strode towards her.

'What the hell do you think you're doing?'

'Enjoying a cup of hot chocolate.'

'Are you a complete idiot?' He remained standing, his face dark with anger. 'Have you noticed what's happening with the weather outside? Or are you in a world of your own? Come on. Let's go. Now!'

'Don't you dare order me around!'

Lucas leaned down, hands flat on the table, crowding her so that she automatically flinched back.

The café was half-empty but the few people there were whispering, looking covertly in their direction.

How dare he stride into this café and order her around like a schoolteacher telling a misbehaving kid what to do? *How dare he?* And where was the laid-guy who had listened to her rattle on about her life? The guy who had offered sparse but good advice, who had actually succeeded in helping her put her nightmare broken engagement into some kind of healthy perspective? Where had *he* gone? In his place, this was a dark, avenging stranger bossing her about, embarrassing her in front of other people.

Thanks to her lying, cheating ex-fiancé, she had spent the last two weeks smiling and putting on a brave face to mask her total humiliation. She wasn't about to let any stranger drag her back to that place!

'I am *not* ordering you around. I am very politely but very firmly telling you to drain the remnants of that hot chocolate and follow me out of here. Unless you want to find yourself spending the night in whatever hotel can fit you in!'

'I didn't ask you to come flying down here to rescue me!' Milly snapped, digging her heels in as a matter of principle, even though he was right. She had barely noticed the worsening weather. She should have. She knew all about worsening weather from growing up in Scotland—but she had been lost in her thoughts. 'And, for your information, it wasn't like this when I came out this morning.'

Lucas didn't answer. He pushed himself away from the table with the unswerving assumption that she would follow him, which she did.

'I haven't paid!' she gasped, catching up with his furious stride.

'There's no need to pay...' This from behind her.

Milly looked round, startled. 'Wh-what do you mean?' she stammered.

'Mr Romero is a very special visitor.' Like nearly every person working in the shops and cafés, the owner of this café was deferential to the wealthy and politely but condescendingly accommodating to everyone else. Money talked.

'A *very special visitor*...?' Milly's mouth wobbled on the brink of laughter because she wondered what a simple ski instructor could have done to have been awarded the title of 'very special visitor'. So he might have a handful of rich clients, but since when did their prestige rub off on him? Was he a *very special visitor* because of the way he looked?

'Enough, Jacques!' Lucas forced a smile but he could feel curiosity emanating from her in waves. 'Naturally your bill will be paid.' He turned to Milly. 'Did you have anything else? No? In that case, put it on my tab, Jacques.'

'Tab? What *tab*?'

She trailed out of the café behind him. The cable car was still in operation but for how long? Another hour and she might have been stranded downhill, unable to make her way back up to the lodge. 'I apologise if you felt you had to rush down to find me,' she offered grudgingly as they began the trip back up the hill. 'Like I said, conditions were a lot better when I started out.'

'And when they worsened, you intended to stay put, drinking hot chocolate and waiting for things to blow over?' Lucas turned to her, jaw clenched. 'I don't do rescue missions, so if you want to risk life and limb do me a favour and wait until I've vacated the lodge. Then you're more than welcome to take your life in your hands.' Not a very fair remark, but damn if he was going to retract it. When you went out to ski, you had to have your wits about you. One false move and you could end up endangering not just your own life but someone else's life, as well.

'I'm not responsible for you while you're out here,' he continued coldly.

'And I never asked you to be!' Her eyes flashed but he was right. She should have known better. That said, she had apologised, and he hadn't been big enough to accept it.

She turned away and stared off into the distance. What was it about her that was so poor when it came to reading men? Lucas had shown her a funny, charming side to him and she had been instantly captivated and disarmed. She'd have thought that experience, *very recent experience,* might have toughened her up a bit, made her just a little more jaundiced when it came to believing people and their motivations, but not so.

Apparently, he was fine when it came to her cooking for him and tidying up behind him like a skivvy. And if she wanted to chatter on inanely about herself, then he was happy enough to listen, because really, what choice did he have when he happened to be in the same room as her? But woe betide if she was stupid enough to think that any of those things amounted to him actually *liking* her.

She took people at face value. She always had. Growing up in a small town in remote Scotland where everyone knew everyone else had not prepared her for a world where it paid to be on guard. How many learning curves did one person need before they realised that having a trusting nature was a sure-fire guarantee of being let down? Especially when it came to the opposite sex?

Once back in the lodge, Milly stalked off to have a shower and get changed. The relaxed atmosphere between them had changed just like that after a silent trip back. She took her time having a very long bath and then changing into a pair of jeans and a comfortable cotton jumper. Her hair had gone wild in the snow and she did her best to tame it with the blow drier in the bathroom but in the end she resorted to tying it back in a loose braid down her back. Wisps and curly tendrils escaped around her face, but too bad.

For a few seconds, she looked at the reflection staring back at her in the mirror.

She couldn't remember ever having been envious of any of her friends when she had been growing up. They had been interested in cultivating their feminine wiles and getting with boys, and she hadn't. Not really. She hadn't been interested in make-up or skimpy clothes and she had been amused at how much time and effort some of her friends had devoted to their looks and to attracting boys. It had all seemed a bit of a waste of time, because they had all been in and out of relationships, spending half their time hanging around waiting for a text to come or else putting everything on hold because they were 'going steady' with a boy and somehow that left no time for anything else.

She was pretty sure that those girls would have matured into women who would be savvy enough to spot someone like Robbie for the fraud that he was—and would certainly have spotted Lucas for the arrogant kind of guy who thought he could say what he wanted and do as he pleased with the opposite sex.

He didn't *do* jealousy and he didn't *do* rescue missions and there were probably a million other things he *didn't do*. What it came down to was that he was someone who just did whatever he wanted to do and he didn't really care if he trampled on someone's feelings in the process.

It was not yet lunch time and the snow had already picked up a pace. Lucas was in the kitchen when she finally went downstairs, sitting at the table with a pot of coffee in front of him. Cut off from the outside world thanks to the snow storm, he had given up on trying to sift through paperwork he had brought with him.

She had sat in stony silence on their trip back, head averted, back rigid as a plank of wood as the cable car had carried them back up the slopes. There had been no pleading for him to listen to her and no trying to tempt him out of his foul mood. He had been spoiled by women who tiptoed around him. Despite her open, chatty nature, she was as stubborn as a mule.

'Perhaps I should have been a little less...insistent,' Lucas drawled, pushing aside the file he had given up on and watching the way she was deliberately avoiding eye contact with him. 'But you don't know this area and you don't know how fast and how severe these snow storms can be.' This was the closest he was going to get to an apology and it was a damn sight more than he would have offered anyone else.

'Is that your idea of an apology?' Milly asked, finally turning to look at him.

He must have showered during the time she had been upstairs, taking as long as she could in the bath without shrivelling to the size of a prune. His dark hair was slicked back and still damp, curling at the nape of his neck, and he was in loose grey jogging bottoms and a sweatshirt that managed to achieve the impossible—it was baggy and yet announced the hard muscularity of the body beneath it. He hadn't shaved and his jaw was shadowed with stubble.

He looked insanely gorgeous, which made her feel even more of a fool for having been sucked into thinking that he was Mr Nice. Since when were insanely gorgeous guys *ever* nice?

'Because if it is,' she continued, folding her arms, 'Then it's pretty pathetic. I told you that I was sorry for not having paid sufficient attention to the weather, but I left very early this morning so that I could do a little skiing before I went into town and, yes, it was snowing, but nothing like it's snowing now…'

Had she just told him that his apology was pathetic?

'I'm not going to waste time discussing whether you should or shouldn't have been on the slopes in bad weather.'

'*And…*' she carried on, because she wasn't ready to pack in the conversation just yet. They were going to be spending at least another night under the same roof and she might as well clear the air or else they would be circling one another like opponents in a boxing ring, waiting to see who landed the first blow.

'There's more?'

'You had no right to storm into that café and start laying down laws as though you're my lord and master. You're not.'

'I never said I was.'

'I've been taken for a mug by my ex and I haven't come over here for a complete stranger to pick up where he left off!' Okay, so some exaggeration here but, the more Milly thought about her idiocy in actually thinking that Lucas was a nice guy, the angrier she became. She thought of the high-handed, autocratic way he had delivered his command for her to follow him or else find herself stuck trying to get into a hotel—because she wouldn't be able to make it back to the lodge, presumably because *he* would have had no qualms about leaving her to her own devices, having made sure grudgingly that she hadn't died on the slopes…

Lucas was outraged at that suggestion. She had somehow managed to swat aside the small technicality of her rashly having ventured out without due care and attention because she had wanted to have a little 'early-morning ski' before 'dashing to the shops for something and nothing and a cup of hot chocolate'. While he had been worried, imagining her skiing round and round in ever decreasing circles in a wilderness of unfamiliar white, she had been gaily sightseeing! And, when he'd run her to ground, not only had she expected an apology but she had the barefaced nerve to compare him to an ex-fiancé who had made off with her best friend!

Was there a crazier way to join dots?

'So now I'm on a par with a guy who strung you along before he got caught in bed with your best friend?'

'I'm *drawing a comparison*.' Milly pushed herself away from the counter and turned her back on him so that she could make herself a cup of coffee. She could feel his eyes boring into her back. Typical! He was charm personified when she was obeying his rules but the second she so much as expressed an opinion that didn't happen to tally with his, the second she stood up to him and refused to let him treat her like a kid, he suddenly couldn't see her point of view!

'It's a ridiculous comparison and I'm not having this conversation. The phone lines are temporarily dead, and it looks as though I'm going to be staying on here a little longer than I originally anticipated, so you might want to rethink your sulkiness—because it's going to be a little charged if you're either jumping down my throat or stalking around in surly silence.'

Had he actually considered the challenge of bedding the woman? Was there a less appropriate candidate? He shot her a glance of pure exasperation. How much more illogical could one human being be? And how much more temperamental? One minute, she was as chirpy as a cricket, pouring out her life story with gay abandon. The next minute, she was a raging inferno, behaving as though his act of kindness in putting himself out to find her had been *offensive* somehow.

'I just bet you're like that with all those women who fling themselves at your feet,' Milly snapped, turning back to face him and plonking herself at the kitchen table with her mug of coffee in front of her.

'Are we still embroiled in this pointless argument?' Lucas flung his hands in the air and then raked his fingers through his dark hair and folded his arms. 'Like *what*?' He wondered why he was being drawn into this when there was nothing to stop him getting up and walking out of the kitchen, leaving her to stew. 'What am I like with all those women who fling themselves at my feet?'

Histrionic scenes annoyed him. In fact, he could think of nothing more unacceptable than a woman having a hissy fit. Women should be obliging, soothing, a source of undemanding pleasure to interrupt the ferocity and stress of his working life.

He assumed that the only reason he was putting up with the red-faced, throbbing little ruffled angel in front of him was because she wasn't *his* woman.

More to the point, he wasn't exactly awash with choices, considering she was in his lodge, sharing his space.

But you could always walk away, a little voice in his head pointed out, and Lucas brushed it aside. This was not an occasion for walking away.

'High-handed and annoying!'

'You're telling me that you find me *annoying*?'

'You think you can do whatever you like because of the way you look.'

Lucas smiled, a slow, devastating smile that made her pulses jump. 'Is there a backhanded compliment in there somewhere?'

'No. I bet you play the field and lead women on because you *can*...'

Lucas stifled a groan. 'You're like a dog with a bone.'

'I take it there's a backhanded compliment in there somewhere?' Milly parroted tartly and his smile broadened. How was she supposed to get on with the business of being angry with him when he smiled like that? How was she supposed to remember what an arrogant jerk he could be?

Lucas tilted his head to one side, as though seriously considering her rhetorical question.

'Possibly,' he said slowly, his dark eyes roving over

her flushed face. 'I'm surprised you stuck it out in a job where you were forced to take orders.'

Milly glared. It had taken a lot of tongue biting to work in a hot, understaffed kitchen where she had never been given the opportunity actually to produce anything of her own…but she still didn't care for him pointing that out to her.

'There are always up sides to any situation,' he told her, accurately reading the expression on her face and following her thoughts as seamlessly as if they were written in big, bold letters across her forehead. 'You can waste time feeling sorry about yourself and moaning about the job you've lost…'

'I wasn't moaning!'

'Of course you were. Or, you can see it as a good thing. So you no longer have to run around taking orders from someone you don't particularly like in a job that was going nowhere anyway. And, getting back to your sweeping generalisation that I lead women on because *I can,* I think it's wise for me to dispel that myth before it has time to blossom into another full-blown argument.'

His dark eyes were cool and Milly stiffened.

'I'm not interested in—'

'Well you'd better start working up an interest because, frankly, I wasn't interested in hearing you compare me to the bum who let you down.'

Milly reddened because she knew that she had been unfair.

'You were high-handed,' she began weakly in her defence and the temperature in his eyes dropped a few notches from cool to glacial.

'I've already told you that I would never sleep with any woman who was involved with someone else. Likewise, I would never sleep with any woman if *I* was involved with someone else. The thought of that disgusts me, so I couldn't be further from the unprincipled bastard you got yourself involved with.' He didn't take his eyes off her face. 'When I go out with a woman, she is safe in the knowledge that I'm not going anywhere else and I'm not looking anywhere else either.'

Milly shivered at the rampant possessiveness in his voice. She wondered what it would be like to have that possessiveness directed on *her,* to have this big, powerful man focus all his attention on *her,* to the exclusion of anybody else.

'And yet you're not a jealous guy.' She moved on the conversation to dispel the alluring thought of him wanting her so badly that he literally didn't have eyes for any other woman. Her skin tingled, as though he had brushed it with his fingers, and her whole body shrieked into heated response.

'I've never had cause to be.'

'Because all those women who come running when you snap your fingers wouldn't dream of ever giving you anything to be jealous about?' She thought of the way everyone had looked at him in that expensive café, on the street as they'd been leaving…

Something stirred at the back of her mind but she shoved it aside because she wanted to hear what he had to say.

'Because I have yet to meet anyone I'm interested enough in,' Lucas answered bluntly. He picked up his phone, searching for the signal that might or might not appear at any given moment. The lines were down but hopefully not for long. Like anywhere else where the weather could become suddenly and wildly unpredictable, there was no telling when normality would be restored.

The endless cry of the commitment-phobe, Milly thought. Men who could have whoever they wanted never had an interest in settling for one because why opt for one type of candy when there were so many jars and bottles to choose from? He could barely be bothered to have this conversation with her. He was searching his phone for a signal. She knew that. He was desperate for an outside line and connection with the real world. He'd already gone beyond the line of duty in putting himself out to stage a rescue mission for someone he happened to be stuck with.

'Am I boring you?' she asked and Lucas looked at her.

'You're the most demanding woman I have ever met in my entire life.'

'What's that supposed to mean?' Milly bristled.

'You're still annoyed because I rescued you?' Lucas had never done so much delving into any woman's psyche in his life before. Even in his wild and misspent youth, when he had been gunning for the wrong woman, he had let sex do the talking.

'Don't start thinking of yourself as a knight in shining armour,' Milly jumped in to correct him and he raised his eyebrows in an expression that was lazy and amused.

'Ah. Still annoyed. Where has Little Miss Sunshine gone?'

In a flash, Milly had insight into what he thought of her. While she had been shooting her mouth off, *confiding,* losing herself in the thrill of being in the company of a guy who was actually *listening* to her...not to mention thrilling her with those dark, saturnine good looks…he had not been similarly entranced. The opposite. She had been a spot of comic relief with her 'Little Miss Sunshine' personality.

She turned away, hurt.

'I apologise if you were embarrassed,' he said gruffly. 'I realise that, along with *arrogant,* I can be prone to occasionally lapsing into caveman tactics.' When she didn't say anything, he reached forward and, finger on her chin, turned her gently to face him.

Milly's eyes widened and her body was suddenly, horrifyingly, excitingly, in meltdown. She could barely breathe. Her mouth parted. Her nipples stiffened, poking against her bra, sensitive as they scraped against the cotton. Between her legs, she was dampening.

'Hell, you should be careful when you look at a man like that,' Lucas said roughly. But he didn't remove his finger. His libido had been in retreat for a while. Dealing with his ex had left a sour taste in his mouth and he had submerged himself in work because it was, frankly, blessed relief from the whining demands of a woman who didn't want to go away.

Milly, with her disingenuous ignorance of who he really was, with her open, confiding nature and her easy laughter—despite having come through circumstances that would have knocked back anyone else—had stirred his interest.

'Forget it. Not interested.' She pulled away and stood up. 'Just out of curiosity, when were you thinking of leaving?'

Lucas felt the reassuring buzz of his mobile as the outside world was once more connected. Normality could be restored within twenty-four hours. This unusual interlude could be left where it was and he could return to his formidably controlled and predictable life.

Since when had he ever been a fan of surprises anyway? Since when had he ever been interested in exploring anything that came in an unpredictable package? Hadn't he already been there? Done that? Got burned?

'I'm considering my options.'

'That being the case, I suggest we do our own thing. If I decide to go out skiing, then I don't expect you to instigate a search party if I happen to be a couple of hours late.'

Lucas shook his head and briefly closed his eyes. 'Demanding,' he drawled. 'And bloody stubborn.'

'Would that be because I disapproved of you making an idiot out of me in a public place?' She opened her mouth to fume a little bit more but his phone beeped with a series of incoming text messages, voicemails and emails.

Exasperated, she walked off towards the window where the furious snowfall was already showing signs of abating. Blue sky was doing its best to break through. By tomorrow, if not later in the day, the skiing would be good.

And who knew? Lucas might be gone.

She told herself that that would be the best possible outcome. She needed her time out, undiluted time to mourn the passing of a significant relationship. Under normal circumstances, if the Ramos family had showed up, she would have been busy but her busyness would not have distracted her from her thoughts. Lucas distracted her from her thoughts. Robbie had barely registered on her radar! In fact, when she tried to think of him, a darker, leaner image instantly superimposed itself.

Behind her, she was aware of Lucas talking rapidly on his phone. He seemed to be very well known in these parts. A man with connections. He was probably doing all sorts of networking right now, getting things lined up now that his stint here had fallen through.

'You were asking me,' a dark, sexy drawl said from behind her, 'how long I intended staying here and I told you that I was keeping my options open...'

Milly spun around, tensing up. 'I'm fine to stay here by myself,' she told him without hesitation.

'But would that require you to curb your keen sense of adventure?' Lucas couldn't help asking. He thought of her here, on her own, deciding to explore the slopes at midnight just for the fun of it. 'Tell me what your plans are when you leave this place. Do you intend to stay here for the full fortnight? Or will you return to London and start looking for another flatmate? What happens if you don't find one? '

Milly frowned, taken aback at his change of subject. 'I'm keeping my options open,' she mimicked, and Lucas smiled.

'Come and sit down. I want to have a talk with you.'

'What about?'

Lucas didn't answer. Instead, he strolled towards the sofa, his face revealing nothing of what was going through his head.

Was there anything more annoying than an actively functioning grapevine? He had been in the town no longer than an hour and the world at large seemed to know.

His window of freedom appeared to have shut and now he had a problem on his hands.

Of course, there was no problem that did not carry a solution, but he could definitely have done without this particular thorn in his side. His mouth tightened as he thought of the series of texts he had received, texts that had been in a toxic holding bay until service resumed and he could pick them up.

'What are the chances of you finding a job the second you return to London?' he asked, relaxing back on the sofa, his face revealing nothing of what was going through his head or of the vague plan slowly beginning to cohere into shape. 'In the catering arena? I'm guessing that there are a lot of jobs to work at burger joints but I'm also guessing that those jobs won't be top of your list.'

'I honestly don't see what my future job hunting has to do with you!'

'And then there's the little technicality of paying rent when you don't have a job. Difficult. Unless you have a stash of money saved...' He steamrollered over her interruption as though she hadn't spoken. 'Have you a stash of money saved?'

'That's none of your—'

'Business. Is that what you're about to say?'

'Where are you going with this, Lucas? Okay, so I may not have much money saved, but...I'll have what I've earned for this fortnight.' She frowned and wondered how long that would last. Why did he have to throw reality in her face? Had he no heart *at all*?

'"Water through fingers" is the thought that springs to mind,' Lucas said with what she thought was a callous lack of empathy. 'The cost of living is astronomical in London.'

'How would you know?' Milly muttered and again Lucas opted to ignore her interruption.

'I guess, in all events, you could always return to your grandmother's place in Scotland. Ah. I can see from the you way you blanched just then that that option lacks appeal.'

'Why are you doing this?'

'Doing what?' Lucas asked with a show of innocence that set her teeth on edge because it was so clearly false.

'Ramming all my problems down my throat. I wish I'd never confided in you.'

'I wasn't ramming your problems down your throat.'

'I didn't come here to…to…'

'Confront that awkward little thing known as *reality*?'

'You can be really horrible.' Okay, so obviously she would have to address the pressing issue of how she was going to survive without a job and, hard on the heels of that, probably nowhere to live either. But she had been quite happy to put that on hold, at least for a few days. Once she had sorted out the emotional mess she was in which, thinking about it, she realised she seemed to be sorting out rather nicely, all things taken into account.

'There's a point to my timely reminder of the problems you're facing,.' Lucas leaned forward, resting his forearms on his thighs. He wondered where he should start. Her mouth was pursed into a sulky downturn, her eternally upbeat personality dampened by the way he had forced unpleasant reality upon her.

'And that point being…?'

'Point being that I'm about to come to your rescue. In fact, I'm about to open up your world to tantalising new possibilities, and in return all you have to do for me is one small favour.'

CHAPTER FIVE

MILLY STARED AT Lucas in confusion. For a few seconds, she wondered whether he was joking, whether he was having a laugh at her expense, somehow getting his own back for the tantrum she had pulled earlier.

She dismissed that idea as fast as it had come. His face was impassive, deadly serious. And if her gut was telling her that he wasn't the sort of guy who liked tantrums, it was also telling her that he wasn't the sort of guy who would do anything to get his own back for something as silly as her snapping at him.

Whether he had deserved it or not. Which he had. More or less.

'Tantalising new possibilities?' she laughed a little weakly. 'Are you feeling okay, Lucas? How are you going to open up my world to *tantalising new possibilities*?' She wished he would stop looking at her like that, with such deadly calm.

'You might be a little…surprised by what I'm about to tell you.'

'Then don't tell me,' she said promptly. 'I hate surprises. They're never good.'

'Well, that's one thing we have in common,' Lucas murmured, momentarily distracted. He stood up and she followed the easy, fluid movement of his long body with something close to compulsion. He walked across to the window and stared out and, even with his back to her, she could tell that he wasn't really seeing what he appeared to be staring at. She could sense his distraction and that made her nervous because, and she could see this now, there was something so intensely *focused* about him. *Distracted* was not his normal frame of mind.

He spun round, caught her staring at him and allowed himself a small smile which immediately made her glower. And *that* was why he was just so damned arrogant, she thought. Because women followed him with their eyes, irresistibly drawn to mindless gazing.

'I'm not quite the person you think I am.'

For a few seconds, Milly thought that perhaps she had misheard him. Who on earth ever said stuff like that? Her mouth fell open and she stared at him in silence, waiting for him to enlarge on that enigmatic statement.

Lucas was taking his time. He walked slowly back towards her, maintaining eye contact.

'And, before your over-active imagination starts casting me in the starring role of homicidal maniac, you can rest assured that it's nothing like that.' He sat down and continued looking at her thoughtfully, trying on the various options at his disposal for telling her who he really was and what he wanted from her. And why. Much as he loathed justifying his decisions to anyone, he would have no choice in this circumstance.

'The Ramos family,' he began. 'This house…everything in it…doesn't belong to them.'

'Oh, please…' Milly raised her eyebrows in rampant disbelief. 'I don't know where you're going with this but I know for a fact that it does. You forget that snooty Sandra employed me to work for them. I was given all their details. Are you going to tell me that she made the whole thing up? That there are no such people? Plus, you're forgetting that Mr Ramos paid me for my time here!'

She shot him a look of triumph at winning this argument, mixed with pity that he had chosen to come out with such a glaring lie. The combination felt good, especially after the way he had hauled her out of the café in front of everyone. Triumph and pity…she savoured the feeling for a few seconds and threw in a kindly but condescending smile for good measure.

Lucas, she noted, didn't come close to looking sheepish.

'Of course he paid you,' he said, brushing aside that detail as casually as someone brushing aside a piffling point of view that carried no weight. 'He paid you because I told him to.'

'Because you told him to…' Milly burst out laughing and, when eventually her laughter had turned to broken giggles, she carried on, very gently, 'I think you might be delusional. I know you fancy yourself as some kind of hot shot just because you happen to work for loads of rich people and you probably have them eating out of your hand…' *Especially the women.* 'But the bottom line is that you're still just a ski instructor'

Lucas kissed sweet, rueful goodbye to his very brief window of normality.

'Not quite…'

'I mean,' Milly expanded, ignoring him, 'it's a bit like me saying that I own five Michelin-starred restaurants when in fact I just happen to work behind the scenes for an average hotel in West London.'

'Worked,' Lucas swiftly reminded her and she scowled at the reminder. 'You *worked* at an average

hotel in West London. Don't forget that you're now jobless.'

'I hadn't forgotten,' Milly said through gritted teeth. 'And I still don't know where you're going with this.'

Lucas sighed and raked his fingers through his hair, then he reached for his computer, which was on the glass table next to him.

With a start of surprise he realised that for the first time in a very long time indeed work had not been the overriding thought in his head. In fact, he had a back-log of emails to work his way through, emails to which he had given precious little thought. Dark eyes lazily took in the diminutive girl in front of him sitting in a lotus position, her long hair flowing in rivulets over her shoulders. Self-restraint with a sexy member of the opposite sex had clearly had an effect on his ability to concentrate to his usual formidably high levels.

He kick-started the computer and when he had found what he had been looking for he swivelled the com-puter towards her.

Milly looked at him sceptically. Did anything faze this guy? Whatever the situation, he was the very pic-ture of cool. Chewing her out in the middle of an ex-pensive café in one of the most expensive ski resorts on the planet: *cool.* Arranging for her to stay in the ski lodge: *cool.* Telling her a string of real whoppers about the extent of his influence: *cool.*

'You're not meant to carry on sitting there,' Lucas informed her gently. 'You're meant to get close enough to the computer so that you can actually read what I've flagged up.'

Accustomed to having the world jump to his com-mands without asking questions, Lucas had a brief mo-ment of wondering whether she intended stubbornly to stay put until he was forced to bring the computer to her. However, after a few seconds of jaundiced hesitation, Milly stood up and then sat on the sofa, back in her cross-legged position, so that she could read his extensive bio.

Lucas watched her. She didn't have to say anything; her face said it all: calm and superior, morphing into frowning puzzlement, then finally incredulity.

Then she did it all over again as she re-read the article, which, fawningly and in depth, traced his lineage and every single one of his achievements, from university degrees to acquisitions of companies. Much was made of his background and the limitless privileges into which he had been born.

He had been personally interviewed for this article. It had come hard on the heels of his unfortunate experience with his gold-digging almost-fiancée, and he had not been predisposed to be anything but brusque with the glamorous blonde whose job it had been to glean some scintillating 'heard it from the horse's mouth' titbits.

His coolness had not bothered her. She had practically salivated in his company and had crossed and re-crossed her long legs so many times that he had asked her at one point whether she needed to use the toilet.

At any rate, the finished article had been sent to him for proofreading before it had been put online, and he had been amused to note that he had somehow achieved a god-like status, even though he knew he had been borderline rude to the woman. Money: Was there anything in the world that talked louder and more persuasively?

'I don't understand.' Milly sat back, drawing her legs up and looping her arms around them.

'Of course you do.'

'Don't tell me what I do or don't understand,' she said automatically, because there was nothing worse than an arrogant know-it-all. But he was right. She understood. 'You're not a ski instructor at all, are you?'

'Correct.'

'In other words, you lied to me.'

'I wouldn't exactly call it a lie…' Naturally he had expected surprise, incredulity even, but at the end of the day the ski instructor had been swapped for a billionaire. He had taken it as a given that his new status would do its usual job and bring a smile of servile appreciation to her lips. None of it. She was scowling at him, eyes glinting with anger.

'Well, *I* would.' Milly was struggling to contain her anger. How dared he? How dared he play her for a complete fool? But then, she was just Little Miss Sunshine, wasn't she? Some comic relief for a man marooned in a ski lodge with her!

'You made false assumptions,' Lucas told her with barely concealed impatience. 'I chose not to set you straight.'

'In your world, that might be acceptable behaviour. In my world, that's called lying!' She sprang to her feet and stormed over to the window, stared out for a little while and then stormed back towards him, hands on her hips. 'I leave London to escape a creep who lied to me and what do I land up sharing space with? Another creep who lies to me!'

'That's the last time you're going to insult me by bracketing me with your loser ex!'

'Why? You seem to have a fair few things in common! Why didn't you just tell me who you were?'

Because I was enjoying the novelty of being with someone refreshingly honest… Because in a world where wariness and suspicion are bywords, it was a holiday not having to guard every syllable, watch every turn of phrase, accept instant adulation without being able really to distinguish what was genuine and what was promoted by a healthy knowledge of how much I was worth...

'When you're as rich as I am, it pays to be careful.'

'In other words, I could have been just another cheap, tacky gold-digger after your money!'

'If you want to put it like that...'

His dark eyes were cool, assessing, unflinching. She could have hit him. How could he just *sit there* and admit to lying to her without even batting an eyelid? As though it was just perfectly acceptable?

Although...

The man was a billionaire. He owned a million companies. He had a hand in pretty much every pie and he had come from money. There were no limits to his wealth, his power, his influence, it would seem. She could reluctantly understand that suspicion would be his constant companion.

That thought instantly deflated her and she had to summon up some of the old anger she had felt at the thought that he had cheerfully lied to her.

'I feel sorry for you,' she told him scornfully and he stiffened.

'Do I really want to hear you explain that remark?' No one, but no one, had ever felt sorry for him or, if anyone had, they had been at pains to conceal it. Money engendered quite the opposite response. Money combined with good looks—which was something about himself he accepted without any vanity whatsoever—was even more persuasive a tool in affording him the sort of slavish responses he got from other people. Particularly from women.

He looked at her carefully. She was as volatile and as unpredictable as a volcano on the point of eruption. It should have been a turn off and it was mildly surprising that it wasn't.

'How can you trust that anyone likes you for you?'

'My point exactly. But, before we deviate down some amateur psychobabble road, there's a reason I have brought this up.'

Milly stilled. There would be a reason, of course there would, or else he would have stayed a couple of nights and pushed on leaving her none the wiser. Certainly he would have spared himself the sort of awkward conversation he clearly wasn't relishing.

But before he got to that… She finally grasped the thought that had been niggling away at the back of her mind.

'At that café,' she said slowly, 'The owner… I wondered why he was so eager to please…why he said that I didn't have to pay the bill.'

'I'm known here.' He offered an elegant shrug. 'I don't come often but when I do I'm high-profile.'

High-profile and made of money. What had he thought of her? Babbling on and taking him for being a ski instructor? He must have thought that she was crazy. A crazy woman who chattered non-stop and had ruined his seclusion by landing on his doorstep.

'Why did you decide to come over?' she asked, feverishly pursuing her train of thought so that she could join the pieces of the puzzle together and get the complete picture.

Lucas hesitated. It was for the very reason that he had decided to descend on his ski lodge that he was now having this conversation. 'Everyone needs a break,' he informed her silkily. 'Alberto and his annoying family had pulled out and I decided that a bit of skiing would be just the thing. And, in case you're wondering, the Ramos family were over here as a favour to my mother. Alberto works for me.'

'Which was why you could engineer to have me paid for this this two-week holiday. You just had to pick the phone up and tell him and he had to obey. Is that what happens in your life, Lucas? You snap your fingers and people jump to attention and obey you?'

'In a nutshell.'

Milly wondered how she hadn't noticed before the way that he was sheathed in an invisible aura of power, the sort of power that only the super-rich had. Or maybe she *had* noticed but, in her usual trusting way, had shoved that to the back of her mind and chosen to take him at his word: Mr Ski Instructor who did a bit of *this and that* when he wasn't teaching people like the Ramos family to ski.

Maybe, just maybe, she would wake up one day and realise that people were rarely who they said they were.

'Sit down, Milly.' He waited until she was back on the sofa. Her eyes were guarded, the cheerful smile wiped off her face. He had done that. Whatever he told her, he would be just someone else who had lied to her. His mouth tightened; for once, he was finding it hard casually to dismiss someone else's emotions. Habits of lifetime, however, came to his rescue and he swept past his temporary discomfort. So he had punctured some of that bubbly sparkle. Cynicism was healthy. It prepared you for life's adversities. She would return to this very point in time and, in the years to come, she would thank him for bursting her bubble.

'I told you that I came here because I needed a break. Partially true. I'm responsible for the running of…countless companies that stretch across countless countries. I employ thousands…and I'm responsible for them, as well.'

So many revelations were piling up that she felt faint. He was a one-man employment agency. He was a guy who ruled the world, someone who dropped in now and again for a bit of skiing when he needed to unwind, someone who had the most amazing ski lodge on the planet, which he used for a few days in the year. She would stake her life on him having a house in every country, places like the ski lodge that he could use when and if it suited him.

'What do you mean when you say *partially*? You said that it was *partially true* that you came here to unwind. What other reason would you have for coming here?'

'I have been experiencing a few problems with an ex,' Lucas said heavily. Unaccustomed as he was to accounting for his actions, he was decidedly ill at ease with explaining himself to the woman sitting opposite him, but explain himself he had to.

'No, let me guess.' Milly's voice was a shade higher than normal. The whole situation felt surreal. In fact, the past few *weeks* had felt surreal. *You'd think I'd be used to dealing with surreal by now,* she thought with an edge of bitterness that was alien to her. 'The ex wasn't ready to be an ex. Did the poor woman start getting ideas about settling down with you?'

Lucas found it difficult to think of Isobel in terms of 'the poor woman'. She was anything *but* a helpless, deluded damsel with a broken heart. She was a sophisticated, hard-as-nails, six-foot model who had capitalised on the fact that, very slightly, she was acquainted with his mother. She had mistakenly figured that the connection carried weight. His parents had known her parents, both wealthy families living in Madrid, both mixing in the same social circles. The relationship had fizzled out when his father had died but she had done her utmost to resuscitate it during their six-month fling in the hope that familiarity would somehow guide him to a flashbulb moment of thinking that what they had was more than what it actually was. It hadn't but she still refused to let go.

'My relationship with Isobel was not of the enduring kind.'

'Don't you *ever* want to settle down? What was she like? Why wasn't it of the enduring kind?' Curiosity dug into her. 'Was she a gold-digger?' She pictured a kid who was too naive to comprehend all the things Lucas *did* and *didn't* do.

'I am a meal ticket for most women,' Lucas responded drily, not flinching from the absolute truth. 'Even for rich women who can manage quite happily on their trust funds. I have a lot of pull, a lot of connections. I offer a lifestyle that most women would find irresistible.'

'What sort of lifestyle is that?'

'What can I say, Milly? I have a passport to places only available to the rich and famous. It's not just about the limitless spending and the shopping sprees, it's also about the mixing and mingling with famous faces and people who appear in magazines.'

'It sounds hideous.'

'You don't mean that.'

'Being on show every minute of the day and living your life in a glass house with everybody looking in? Having to dress up for social affairs every night?

Wear war-paint and make sure you're shopping in all the right places and mixing with all the right people, even if they're dull and shallow and boring? I'd hate it.'

Which was why she had been such a breath of fresh air—enough of a breath of fresh air to make him alter his plans for leaving. Anonymity had brought him a glimpse of being the sort of man who could dump his cynicism for a minute...except cynicism was just much too ingrained in him for him ever really to do that. And besides, that glimpse of freedom was now gone.

Lucas gazed at her open, honest face and wondered whether she would be singing the same song if she were to be introduced to that life of glamour and wealth that she claimed she would hate. It was very easy to dismiss the things you've never personally experienced.

'All this is by the by,' he said with a shrug. 'The fact is that Isobel has been annoyingly persistent in thinking that we can salvage something and carry on. She's refused to fade away and, having finally reconciled herself to the end of our relationship, she's decided that a little healthy revenge might be called for. When I went looking for you in the town, I was snapped.'

'Snapped?'

'Surely you can't be *that* naive, Milly. The paparazzi are always on the lookout for candid shots of high-profile people. In fairness, I don't know whether I was snapped by the paparazzi or by some interested visitor who recognised me. Or maybe Alberto's wife just happened to let slip to someone who let slip to someone else that I was staying at the lodge with you... Whatever picture happened to be taken of us together consolidated the story. I would think that someone who knows Isobel posted it to her on a social network and it went from there...'

'Sorry, but you're losing me. What story? There *is* no story. Not unless it's the story of the ski instructor who wasn't a ski instructor.'

'Are we back to that?'

'Tell me what you're talking about,' Milly said because he was right. What was there to gain from going over trodden ground? So he had lied because he was suspicious of the human race and in particular of women. She could tell him a thousand times that she found it insulting and offensive but he would just look at her blandly, shrug and imply that her point of view was inferior to his.

'Isobel has somehow managed to get hold of the fact that I'm here with you.'

'You're not here *with me*.' She flushed hotly at the unspoken implication buzzing in the air between them like a live, dangerous electric current.

'And I'm perfectly sure,' Lucas intoned in a voice that was suddenly hard and devoid of emotion, 'that she is all too aware of that. But she's a woman scorned and she's decided that a little malicious mischief is just what I deserve. She can't have me so why not make life as hellish for me as she can, to teach me the valuable lesson that, when it comes to dumping, she's the one who decides to do it?'

Milly frowned in confusion. For someone who had an exceptional grasp of the English language and how to use it to maximum benefit, he seemed to be struggling with his words. 'Okay...' She dragged out that one word while trying to grapple with whatever he was attempting to say to her.

'There's something else I should mention,' Lucas

admitted. 'Another reason I came here was to have a break from my mother. She's been ill and, ever since her extremely successful operation, she's managed to convince herself that time is no longer on her side…'

'I'm sorry. Happens with older people sometimes,' Milly murmured. 'My granny had an operation on her hip two years ago and, even though she can run up a mountain faster than a goat, she still thinks that she'll wake up one morning and she won't be able to stand. Sorry. I interrupted you. What does your mother have to do with this? Lucas, I haven't got the foggiest what you're talking about.'

'Isobel,' he said heavily, striving to stem the anger in his voice when he thought of where his ex had landed him, 'has presented my mother with whatever picture was snapped of us in town and has intimated that…' he shook his head and cursed fluently under his breath '…we are somehow involved in some kind of romantic situation.'

He flushed darkly, remembering the way his libido had gone into orbit when he had looked at her. Yes, he had toyed with the tantalising thought of taking her to his bed. Had that thought somehow manifested itself in whatever expression he had been snapped wearing? Had he been looking at her with some kind of sexual intent? Had some idiot's camera caught him off-guard with a look in his eye that had lent itself to some kind of misinterpretation?

Milly's mouth fell open. She didn't know whether to be horrified, incredulous or just downright amused. No. Not amused. His expression was grim. If she laughed, then he wouldn't be laughing along with her.

'But that's ridiculous.' *Who in their right mind would link the two of us together romantically?* 'I've been here for a couple of days. How on earth would anyone suppose that we're somehow *romantically linked*?' She tried a laugh of sorts and, as expected, he saw nothing funny in the situation. 'Besides, I'm here recovering from a broken heart. Don't forget I was due to be married less than a month ago…'

'She's implied to my mother that we may have known one another longer than a mere couple of days. She knows how I feel about involvement and permanence because I told her, and she knows that the last thing I would want is to find myself trapped in a situation where my mother thinks that I may have ditched my bachelor ways…'

'How do you feel about involvement and permanence?'

'Another time, Milly. For now, you just need to know that they don't form part of my lifestyle choices.'

Milly burst out laughing. 'I just can't picture it!' She gasped. 'I just can't imagine you sneaking around my miniscule two-bed house, comforting me after my break-up. Somehow I don't think you're the kind of guy to go unnoticed! And then what? We planned a secret rendezvous here via snooty Sandra and her band of clones? It doesn't add up. Any fool would be able to see through that in seconds!' She sobered up. 'But that was a mean trick. I guess she fell in love with you. Poor woman.'

Lucas raised his eyebrows, momentarily disconcerted. If he hadn't had proof positive that Milly wasn't interested in what he brought to the table, he would have put her down as just another gold-digger with a slightly different approach. 'I'll cut to the chase,' he said tightly. 'She's told my mother that we're slightly more than an item. My mother is now under the impression that we're going to be married. Isobel showed her whatever candid snapshot got taken and presented her case as the utter truth because would I have gone for someone so…different from what I usually go for if it weren't for the fact that we were serious about one another?'

'What do you usually go for?' She mentally answered that question for herself before she had finished asking it. The guy was drop-dead gorgeous and rolling in money as an added bonus. Guys like that only went for a certain type and that type wasn't *her*. 'No, don't answer that,' she told him quietly. 'I'm thinking you like lots of supermodel types, stunning arm-candy. I'll bet your jilted Isobel was tall and skinny and looked like a model.'

'She *was* a model.'

'So she's pulled a pretty clever trick in showing your mum a picture of dumpy little me, because why else would you be in the same *room* as me unless it was serious. Am I right?'

'That's more or less the size of it. She must have glossed over the holes in the story and ran amok with the rest because my mother's fallen for whatever she's been told hook, line and unfortunate sinker.'

'Do you know what, Lucas?' She breathed in deeply and marvelled at how complicated her life had become ever since Robbie had entered it—lying, cheating Robbie who had come along and wreaked havoc with her perfectly enjoyable, uneventful, contented life. And, not satisfied with that, fate had decided to carry on where Robbie had left off and had thrown her a blinder in the form of the man now looking at her with dark, lazy intent.

'I think I need a break from the male species. In fact, I might take a permanent break from them. Anyway, I don't know why you've told me all this. I'm sorry your mother now thinks that you've found the love of your life but you'll just have to tell her the truth.'

'There is an alternative…' He stood and flexed his arms, stretching out from having sat in one spot for too long when he had wanted to move around, walk some of his restlessness away.

'Which is what, exactly…?' Milly looked at him cautiously as he prowled through the vast open space. *His* vast open space. She still found it hard to grapple with the reality that all of this belonged to *him.* That said, she had recognised a certain something the very first time she had met him: a certain air that spoke of power; a certain arrogant self-assurance that made a nonsense of him being someone as relatively unimportant as a ski instructor. Even a drop-dead, improbably gorgeous ski instructor.

Another telling example of her stupid ability to trust even when she was staring evidence to the contrary in the face.

'You're broke, you're out of work and you'll probably return to London to find all your possessions tossed onto the pavement, awaiting your urgent collection.'

'My landlord wouldn't do that,' Milly said coldly. 'Tenants *do* have rights, you know.'

'Not as many as a landlord whose primary right is the one to have his rent paid.' He paused to stare down at her and Milly grudgingly gazed back up at him. 'Here's the deal. I employ you for a couple of weeks—three, max—to play the role of loved-up wife-to-be. We will stay with my mother in her house in the outskirts of Madrid, a beautiful city by the way, and we can break up over there. My mother will be saddened but she will recover. Normally, I wouldn't go to this much trouble but, like I said, she's been ill and she's mentally not quite there yet. I don't want to present her with a litany of low tricks and lies. She will be upset and confused, especially coming hard on the heels of wanting me to settle down. I will give her what she wants and, when she sees how impossible I am, she will understand why marriage is off the cards for me for the foreseeable future.

'And here's what you get out of this: a fat pay cheque, a five-star, all expenses paid holiday in Spain and, afterwards, I will ensure that you're set up with a damn good job in one of the three restaurants I own in London, with full use of one of my company apartments for six months until you can find alternative accommodation to rent. Whatever you were earning in your last job... Put it this way, I'll quadruple the package.'

'And in return I lie to your mother.'

'That's not how I see it.'

'Plus I lie to my grandmother as well, I suppose? Because what am I supposed to tell her when I don't return to London? Plus I lie to my friends, as well? Thanks, Lucas, but no thanks...'

CHAPTER SIX

So why was she now, a mere day and a half later, sitting in splendid luxury on a private plane heading to Salamanca on the outskirts of Madrid?

Next to her, Lucas was absorbed in a bewildering array of figures on the computer screen blinking in front of him. The 'this and that' had kept billionaires busy and hard at it.

Milly sighed. She knew why she was here; she was just too soft-natured. It was an emotional hazard that was close cousin to the 'overly trusting' side of her that had propelled her into naively believing that the billionaire with the private jet had been a ski instructor—which in turn had been the same side of her that had encouraged her to think that Robbie the cheat had been in love with her rather than mildly fond and willing to exploit.

'You're sighing. Tell me that you haven't done a U-turn on your decision.' Lucas snapped shut his computer and sprawled back in the oversized seat, which was just one of the many perks of having his own plane— no unwelcome strangers crowding his personal space and as much leg room as he needed. He was a big man.

He looked at her, his dark eyes lazily drifting over the baby-smooth, soft curves of her open, expressive

face. She had tied her long hair back but, as usual, unruly curls were refusing to be flattened into obedience.

'What would you do if I told you that I had? We're
in mid-air. Would you chuck me out of your plane? I
still can't believe that you actually *own this,* Lucas.'

'I don't employ strong-arm tactics, Milly. So no, in
answer to your question, I wouldn't chuck you out of the
plane. And I'm getting a little tired of hearing you tell
me how incredulous you find it that I happen to be rich.'

'You can't blame me. I don't meet many people who
own ski lodges and private planes.' Her voice bore the
lingering remnants of accusation.

'I suppose I should be grateful that you're no longer
lecturing me for being a lying bastard like your long-
gone ex-fiancé. Why are you sighing? If we're going
to do a passable imitation of being a loved-up couple,
heavy, troubled sighs aren't going to sell it.'

In response, Milly released another sigh as she absently looked at the stunningly beautiful face gazing at
her with just the slightest hint of impatience.

'You never told me why you're so averse to settling
down.'

'You're right. I didn't.'

'Why not? I've told you loads of stuff. The least you
could do is fill me in, or am I supposed to be the clueless girlfriend?'

Lucas raked his fingers through his hair and stared
at her in silence for a few seconds. 'I don't confide.'

'And I don't pretend to be someone I'm not.'

'Bloody stubborn,' he muttered under his breath.
'Okay, if you really want to know, I had a poor experience when I was young. Take one pretty girl, making
me so out of my normal comfort zone that I didn't think
twice about believing the clap trap she concocted, add

a phoney pregnancy threat and I give you the sort of gold-digging experience that's made me realise that, when it comes to permanence, the only kind I will ever go for is of the business arrangement variety. I'm a fast learner when it comes to mistakes and never making them again.'

'That's awful,' Milly said, appalled. 'How old were you?'

'This isn't a continuing discussion, Milly.'

'But how old?'

Lucas shook his head, exasperated. 'Nineteen.'

'So you had a bad experience when you were a teenager and you've let it ruin your adult life and all the choices you make?'

'*Ruin?* Wrong word. I prefer *affect*. Like I said, I learn from my mistakes.'

And he wasn't about to budge. She could see that in his eyes and in the grim seriousness of his expression. It chilled her to the bone.

'But what if you one day fall in love?'

'Not on the cards. And, Milly, let's put this conversation to rest now.'

'I never thought that large scale lying was on the cards for *me,* yet here I am…' She rested back and stared off at nothing in particular.

Lying was just not part of her nature and ye here she was, immersed in the biggest lie of her life, and all because she had had a vivid image of his mother, frail, vulnerable, bitterly saddened and disappointed at having to be told that she was the victim of a lying ex-girlfriend. She knew first-hand how much lies could wound. She also knew that men could be utterly blind when it came to health issues. If someone had been recently mown down by a bus and, when asked how they were, replied, 'just fine,' the average man would be insouciantly inclined to accept the answer at face value.

The average man would also be highly likely to underestimate the impact of disappointment on a sick and elderly person. Who knew how Antonia, Lucas's mother, would react if she discovered the depth of the lies told to her? Stress killed. Everyone knew that. Whereas, if she were to see for herself just how unsuited Lucas was to her, Milly, then the termination of their so-called relationship would be no big deal. And unsuitable they most certainly were, especially after what he had just told her...

And, face it, there were all those other perks that would certainly make the horror story called her present situation so much easier to bear: job secured, accommodation secured, no nasty landlord banging on her door demanding to know when his rent would be paid.

She would be able to put her grandmother's mind at ease that her life was back to normal and *it would be.*

'I guess your mother was disappointed that you weren't prepared to tie the knot with your girlfriend. I guess she doesn't know about your hang-ups.' She turned to him, wanting to hear just a little more about her competition, because now that they were en route to unchartered territory she could feel butterflies beginning to take up residence in her tummy.

'My hang-ups. You really have a way with words. You conversationally go where no other woman has gone before. My mother may want me to settle down,' he said drily, 'But even she sussed that Isobel wasn't going to be the perfect candidate for the position of stay-at-home wife.'

'Because...?'

'Because Isobel was more jet-setter than home-maker. I think it goes with the territory of being a supermodel. Something about being treated like a goddess when, in fact, you're no more than a pretty face.'

'Jet-setter…'

'Glitz, glamour and an unnatural love of having cameras focused on her.'

'The sort of girl you tend to go out with.'

'Why the hundred and one questions, Milly?'

'Because I'm nervous,' she confessed. The way he described his ex was a fine example of a man who attached himself to just the sort of woman he was in no danger of wanting to commit to. Casual sex. She shouldn't even bother to speculate on his motivations or lack of motivations when it came to women.

'Think of the wonderful payback and your nerves will disappear. Trust me.'

Milly scowled because, however wonderful those paybacks were, they weren't the reason she had agreed to engage in this little game of fiction and, the closer the plane got to their destination, the more she wondered whether her impulse to do what had felt right at the time really was such a clever idea.

Her impulses *had* been known to let her down.

'I didn't agree because of the…paybacks.'

Lucas's eyebrows shot up and he gave her a slow, disbelieving smile.

'You're so suspicious,' Milly muttered.

'You're telling me that your sole reason for agreeing to pretend to be my soon-to-be-departed fiancée is because you felt sorry for my mother, a woman you've never met in your life?'

'Mostly. Yes.'

'Nice word, *mostly*. Open to all sorts of conflicting interpretations.'

'Sometimes you really annoy me, Lucas.' Right now he was doing rather more than annoying her. Right now she wished that he would return to his obsessive contemplation of whatever high-powered deal he was in the middle of making, because his attention on her was making her feel all hot and bothered.

Having travelled with nothing suitable to wear for warmer temperatures, she was in a thermal T-shirt, jeans, her thick socks and trainers and the whole ensemble made her skin itch.

'I'm just trying to... Wondering how...to pretend to be someone I'm not.'

'You mean how to pretend to be someone in a relationship with me?'

'I've never done anything like this before. I'm not the sort of girl who likes fooling people. It doesn't seem kind and, whether you want to believe me or not, yes, the paybacks will certainly make my life a whole lot easier when I get back to London but mostly I'm doing this because I hate thinking that your mother's had her hopes raised only to have them dashed, and cruelly dashed at that. I honestly can't believe that anyone could tell such a horrendous lie to someone who hasn't been well, just to get revenge because you let her down.

'Has your mother *ever* been keen on *any* of your girlfriends?'

'Not that I can recall offhand...' And that had never bothered him until she began making noises about wanting him to settle down because 'who knew what lay round the corner for her?'.

He knew what she thought of the Isobels of his life, the never-ending stream of decorative supermodels who enjoyed basking in his reflective glow; who simpered, acquiesced and tailored themselves to his needs. He, personally, had no problem with any of those traits; his work life was high-powered and stressed enough without adding more stress to the tally in the form of a demanding girlfriend. His mother, always grounded, was of a different opinion.

It occurred to him that this little game of make-believe might have an unexpected benefit.

Milly was as normal and as natural as the day was long. Were it not for his inherently suspicious nature, he would truly believe that, as she had stated, she had agreed to this well-intentioned charade from the goodness of her heart. She was just the sort of wholesome girl he would never seriously consider as a life partner in a million years. No; like it or not, if and when he decided to tie the knot, it would be with someone who saw marriage through the same eyes as his. It would be with someone who didn't need his money, someone who understood the frailty of the institution and recognised, as he did, that marriage stood a far better chance of success if it was approached as a business proposition.

If his mother saw for himself just how unsuited he was for a girl like Milly—and for Milly read all women like her—not only would she accept it when they 'broke up' but she would understand that her dreams of romance and falling in love were not his. She would get it that his plans for himself lay in a different direction. It would be a salutary learning curve that would succeed where explanations had in the past failed.

'My mother is a firm believer in true love and happy-ever-after endings,' Lucas intoned with a corrosive cynicism he made no attempt to disguise. 'She married the man she fell in love with as a teenager and they stayed married and in love until the day he died. She has high hopes that I might continue the tradition and she doesn't

see it happening in the arms of any of the supermodels
I've ever dated.'

'There's nothing wrong with true love and happy-
ever-after endings. You might have had *one* bad experience, but you can't knock the real thing because of that.'

'I'm surprised to hear you say that after what you've
been through.' But he wasn't. She struck him as just the
sort of hopeless romantic who nurtured secret dreams
of the walk down the aisle in a big wedding dress, with
a sprawling line of best-friend bridesmaids in her wake.
The sort of girl who eagerly looked forward to testing
her culinary skills in her very own kitchen while lots
of little Millies pitter-pattered at her feet. Just the sort
of girl his mother imagined for him and precisely the
sort of girl he would run a mile from, because he'd had
his learning curve when it came to all that nonsense
about love.

'Just because I was let down—'

'Dumped by a guy who absconded with your best
friend.'

Milly flushed hotly. 'There's no need to ram that
down my throat.'

'A little reality goes a long way, Milly.'

'If by that you mean that it goes a long way to turning me into someone who doesn't believe in love and
marriage, then I'd rather not face it.'

'Well, considering I have no time for any of that, it
should be a cinch demonstrating to my mother just how
incompatible we are.'

'If we're that incompatible, then I'm wondering how
we ever got involved with one another in the first place,'
Milly said tartly. 'I'm broken-hearted and vulnerable
after a broken engagement, and you swoop into my life
and decide that I'm the one for you even though I'm the

last person on the planet you would get involved with? How does that make sense, Lucas?'

'Like I said, my mother is a devotee of fairy stories like that.'

'Then she doesn't know you at all, does she?'

'Do you ever accept anything without questioning it out of existence?' He shook his head and sighed with a mixture of resignation and exasperation. 'People believe what they want to believe even if evidence to the contrary is staring them in the face. My mother believes in true love without any encouragement from me, I assure you. So she won't find it odd at all that you've swept me off my feet.'

Milly blushed and looked away. 'Does she know about your experience with that girl when you were still a kid? An excusable mistake when you were too young to know better.'

'Is that your way of introducing your analysis of the experience?' He shot her a glance of brooding impatience, which she returned with unblinking disingenuousness. 'Which I'm seriously regretting telling you abou. To answer your question, no, she doesn't.' His gaze became thoughtful. 'Which brings me to one or two ground rules that should be put in place.'

'Yes?' What would it take to sweep a man like Lucas off his feet? she wondered. Someone amazing. And that person existed, even if he didn't think so. His parents had been happily married, as had hers. Her grandmother had told her numerous tales of how much in love her parents had been. Inseparable, she had said. Growing up, Milly had never tired of looking at snapshots of them together; had never tired of hearing all the small details of the childhood sweethearts who had grown up together and had never wavered in their love for one another. Maybe those tales had formed the person she was now: idealistic and eternally hopeful that she would one day find the right guy for her.

If it was inconceivable that someone like Lucas, jaded and cynical, could ever be attracted to someone like her, then it was equally inconceivable that someone like her, optimistic and romantic, could ever be attracted to someone like him.

'Ground rules…' he repeated gently, snapping her out of her reverie.

'Oh, yes, you were about to tell me.'

'Ground rule number one,' he said, frowning, because never had he ever had to work so hard at getting a woman's attention, 'is the importance of remembering that this is just a temporary charade.'

Milly looked at him, eyes wide with puzzlement. 'I know *that*.'

'By which,' Lucas continued, taking advantage of her full, concentrated attention before she could drift off into one of those doubtless cotton-candy fantasies of hers, 'I mean that you don't get ideas.'

'What on earth are you talking about?' Enlightenment dawned as he stared at her with unflinching intent. 'Oh, I get it,' she said slowly, as colour crept into her face and her heart picked up angry speed. 'You don't want me to start thinking that the game is for real. You really are the limit! Do you honestly imagine for a second that I would be stupid enough to fall for a guy like you? Especially after everything you've told me?'

'Come again?'

'You think that because you happen to be okay looking, because you happen to have a lot of money, somehow you're an irresistible catch! And you may just be for all those supermodel women who like being draped over your arm, getting their pictures taken whenever they're with you, but I meant it when I told you that I can't think of anything worse! Least of all with a guy who's said that he sees marriage as a business transaction!'

'Sure about that?' Lucas's mouth thinned, a reaction to the unfamiliar sound of criticism.

'Quite sure,' Milly informed him scathingly. 'I could never be interested in a man like you. I'm sure you have wonderful qualities...' She paused for a heartbeat while she tried to imagine what those wonderful qualities might be. Certainly sensitivity and thoughtfulness didn't feature too high.

Although, a little voice pointed out, *isn't his attitude towards his mother an indication of just those qualities, lurking there somewhere underneath the cool, hard, jaded exterior?*

'But,' she continued hurriedly, 'I go for caring, sharing fun guys.'

'Caring? Sharing? Fun? This may come as a shock, but when it comes to fun I can't think of a single woman who's ever complained.'

'I'm not talking about *sex*,' Milly said derisively, scarlet-faced, because really what on earth did she know about sex? Her life had not exactly been littered with panting suitors desperate to strip her naked and climb into bed with her. Sure, there had been interest. She had even gone out with a couple of them. But none of those brief relationships had ever stayed the course. Either she was too fussy or she just wasn't clever enough to play the games that most women knew how to play, the games that trapped men. Not that she had ever had any inclination to trap any of the guys she had dated briefly.

She went a shade pinker as she wondered how Lucas

would react if he knew that she was a virgin. The virgin and the rake, poles apart, the most unlikely pretend couple in the world!

'I'm talking about the sort of caring, giving man who shares the same belief system as I do; the sort of man who wants the same things that I want—love, friendship, a soulmate for life...'

'Sounds thrilling,' Lucas said drily. 'You're omitting passion. Or is that sidelined by the friendship, soulmate angle?' He shot her a wolfish grin that made her skin prickle, made it difficult to keep her eyes focused on his lean, dark face. 'Never mind, I get the picture, and I'm glad that we're singing from the same song sheet. That being the case, you will have no need to pretend. I imagine our conflicting personalities will be enough to demonstrate to my mother that our relationship is not destined to last longer than it takes for you to rustle up a hot meal.' He shrugged elegantly and shot her a crooked smile. 'Feel free to share all your home truths about me!'

'I most certainly will! And...one other thing.' The plane began dipping, preparing to land. 'I'm afraid I didn't come prepared for warm weather.' She thought wistfully of the innocent little ski-resort job she had mapped out as part of her recovery programme. 'I hadn't expected to find myself on a plane to Madrid.'

'Believe it or not, there are shops there. A free wardrobe is part of the package.'

'I don't feel comfortable with that.'

'Then we can agree on a repayment schedule—although you might want to settle into your new job when you get back to London before you start working out how to transfer money into my account for a handful of clothes.'

'I wonder how it is that I never spotted just how *in-furiating* you could be.'

'That could certainly be one of the things you tell my mother that you dislike about me,' Lucas pointed out. 'Although who knows how she might react to the shock of hearing a woman speak her mind? You have to bear in mind that she's had a stroke.'

'You're telling me that no one ever speaks their mind when they're around you?'

'Frankly, no. Although you're more than making up for that.'

The small plane touched down smoothly, skimming over the landing strip like a little wasp before slowly grinding to a halt. Conversation was abandoned amidst the business of disembarking, after which a long, sleek car was waiting for them, complete with uniformed driver.

Cool, early spring temperatures greeted them. She was fine in what she was wearing but, stepping into the car, which was the height of luxury, she was suddenly and acutely aware of just not quite blending into her surroundings. What was appropriate gear for travelling in a luxury chauffeur-driven limo? She was sure that there would be some sort of dress code and, whatever it was, it certainly wasn't what she was wearing. His mother might disapprove of supermodel girlfriends, but supermodel girlfriends would match expensive limos; supermodel girlfriends would pull off luxury houses and private planes…

And suddenly she felt that tug of self-consciousness that had been her occasional companion growing up— the little pang of knowing that she really wasn't too sure when it came to the opposite sex, of knowing that she would never really make it into the inner sanctum of the cool set, even though she got along just fine with them. Lucas's mother might have whimsical dreams about her son finding a suitably wholesome, down-to-earth girl but she would discover fast enough that wholesome, down-to-earth girls were not fashioned for ridiculously wealthy lifestyles.

Her eyes slid across to where he was sitting, casually at ease in his expensive limo. His sense of style was so much a part of him that he could have been wearing a bin bag and he would still have looked stupendously sophisticated. Stupendously sophisticated and utterly, bone-meltingly, sinfully *sexy.*

He was right. There would be no need for her to pretend because there was no way his mother could fail to notice just how ill-suited they were as a couple. She wouldn't be deceiving anyone. She would just have to be herself. This was going to be a little adventure, nothing to get all worked up and anxious about. Life threw curve balls and she was catching one. When again would she find herself in this position—freed from all responsibility; no job, nothing waiting for her back in London, suddenly free to do exactly what she wanted to do?

She rested her head back and half-closed her eyes, and when she turned to look at him after a few seconds it was to find him staring right back at her. He had the darkest eyes imaginable and lashes most women would kill for. The perfect, beautiful symmetry of his lean face should have made him too…*pretty,* but there was a harsh, dangerous strength there that made him 100 percent alpha male.

Her heart skipped a beat. She was supposed to be romantically involved with the guy! What a joke. As though someone like him would ever look at someone like her! Even that gold-digger who hadn't been a supermodel had probably *looked* like one. But for a few heart-stopping seconds she imagined what it might feel like to be touched by him; to be seduced by that rich, dark, dangerous, velvety voice; to have him run his hands over her naked body.

She bit back a stifled gasp as moisture pooled between her legs and a heavy, tingling ache began in her breasts and coursed through her body until she felt hot and uncomfortable in her skin.

It was a physical reaction that was so unexpected and so blindingly powerful that she felt faint. Faint, giddy and slightly sick. She couldn't remember feeling anything like this when she had been with Robbie. In fact, she couldn't remember feeling anything like this *ever.* She was shockingly aware of her own body in a way she never had been before, aware that she wanted it to be *touched,* wanted the strange tickle between her legs to be alleviated.

She dragged her eyes away from his mesmerising face, mortified at the suspicion that he could see exactly what was going through her head, and even more mortified when she belatedly remembered what he had said about making sure she didn't start getting ideas.

'How long before we get, er, to your mother's house?' she asked because talking might distract her from what was going on with her body.

A little over an hour. An hour of sitting next to him in the limo, trying hard to rein in her wandering mind. An hour of pretending not to notice the muscled strength of his forearms; the taut pull of his trousers over his powerful thighs; the length of his fingers; the sexiness of his mouth; the way his voice curled around her, tantalising, tempting, as velvety smooth as the finest dark chocolate.

Every confusing sensation racing through her body

and running like quicksilver through her head crystallised to demonstrate, conclusively, just how inexperienced she was when it came to the opposite sex. And, as if that wasn't bad enough, she couldn't even rely on good old common sense to point her in the right direction or else she wouldn't be sitting here, pressed against the car door to create maximum space between them, babbling like the village idiot because it was better than letting any disturbing silences settle between them.

At the end of half an hour she knew more about Madrid than she did about her own village where she had grown up because she had plied him with questions. By the time they were drawing into Salamanca, she could have done a doctorate on the subject.

Not only did his mother have a house in Salamanca but she also had a house in Madrid for those times when she fancied an extended shopping trip to the city, or when she visited friends and wanted somewhere to stay over.

It hadn't been used in a while because ill health had interrupted her usual routine, she had been told.

'Relax,' Lucas told her wryly. She was staring at him, mouth parted on the brink of yet another question. There seemed to be no end to them. He politely refrained from telling her that he had never known any woman to talk as much as she did. 'You're not walking into a dragon's den.'

'I didn't think I was,' Milly lied.

'Oh, yes, you did. That's why you haven't drawn breath since you started asking me to give you a verbal guided tour of Madrid and its surroundings. If we'd been in the car for another hour, you would probably have extended your parameters to the rest of Spain, because you think that talking calms your nerves.'

'I'm not nervous. We've agreed that neither of us has to pretend to be anything other than what we are.'

'You're nervous. And you're the girl who wasn't nervous when she was plying me with questions about my past. Don't be.' He gently tilted her chin away from him, directing her to look through the front window, and her eyes widened at the mansion approaching them. She had barely noticed when the limo had pulled off the main road. 'We're here.'

Milly's mouth dropped open. The low white house with its red roof sprawled gloriously amidst a profusion of shrubs, flowers and trees. The intense blue of the sky picked up the even more intense, vibrant colours of the clambering flowers of every shape and variety, and everything melded harmoniously together into picture-postcard perfection.

Standing at the front door was a tall, striking woman leaning on a walking stick. Black hair was pulled back from an angular, handsome face.

'I have no idea why my mother can't let one of the maids get the door.' But there was affectionate indulgence in his voice and Milly had a vivid image of the boy beneath the man, the unguarded person beneath the cynical, hard-edged adult in control of an empire. He was a loving son and she had a moment of piercing happiness that she had agreed to this unexpected charade.

'She probably just can't wait to see you.'

'To see *us*...' The limo swerved smoothly to a halt and, as they emerged from the car, she felt the heavy weight of his arm sling over her shoulders. 'We are, after all, the loving couple,' he whispered into her ear and the warmth of his breath made her want to squirm. 'At least before the rot sets in...' And, to prove his point, he curved his hand under her hair to caress the nape of her neck.

And then, barely breaking stride, with such natural-ness that anyone would have been forgiven for thinking that what they had was real, he paused, dipped his head and covered her mouth lightly with his.

Just a brief meeting of tongues, enough to do dev-astating things to her body, then he was pulling away, hand still caressing her neck. The epitome of a man in love.

He couldn't have been more successful at killing her nerves because how could she be nervous about facing his mother when her thoughts were all over the place at that what that casual kiss had done to her body...?

CHAPTER SEVEN

ANTONIA ROMERO WAS an elegant, quietly spoken woman who immediately put Milly at ease. She ushered them in warmly, allowing Lucas to kiss her on the cheek and then fret at the fact that she had come to the door herself when she should be resting, when there was help in the house to do things like answer doors.

'I just couldn't wait to meet Milly...' she protested, drawing Milly into the living room, where tea and pastries were waiting for them on a low glass table while a pretty, smiling maid hovered in the background, ready to leap to service. 'And I know you must be tired after your trip but I'm dying to hear all about your romance. I knew it. I just knew that son of mine would end up finding true love with a real woman and not one of those plastic dolls he's spent his life fooling around with.'

Milly sneaked a surreptitious look at Lucas to see how he was handling his mother's criticism and he caught her eye and grinned, eyebrows raised.

'Didn't I tell you that my mother has no problem saying exactly what she thinks?' He shooed Antonia back to the sofa as she automatically rose to pour them tea and hand round the pastries. On cue, the maid leaped into action and refreshments were served before the maid vanished out of the room, shutting the door behind her.

With Antonia on the low, damask pink sofa facing her, Milly had a chance really to look at her hostess. There were fine lines of strain around her eyes and mouth and she was borderline too thin, barely filling the black, shapeless dress that hung down to her calves, yet it wasn't hard to see that she must have been a great beauty in her day. Not that she was exactly ancient now. At a guess, Milly would have put her in her mid to late sixties.

She tried to maintain the chirpy smile of a woman in love as Lucas helped himself to a few more pastries before subsiding right next to her on the sofa, a replica of the one on which Antonia was sitting, his thigh pressed against hers.

She had been leaning forward, perched on the edge of the sofa, her hand primly linked on her knees, and now he pulled her back so that she tumbled against him.

'What would you like to know?' Lucas's voice was teasing as he fondly addressed his mother. 'You have limited time for questions because you should be taking it easy.'

'I'm sitting,' Antonia retorted, smiling. 'How much easier can I take things? Please don't join the queue along with all my friends who have insisted on treating me with kid gloves ever since I got ill.'

'Why don't you explain…?' Lucas brushed aside Milly's hair and delivered a feathery kiss on the side of her cheek, just enough to send the heat spiralling through her.

Milly's eyes glazed over. If she wasn't under a microscope, she would have punched him, because he was the one who had propelled her into this awkward situation; how fair was it that she was now being dumped in the thick of it, having to concoct some vaguely realistic lie? Not very.

Antonia was watching her expectantly and Milly reluctantly stumbled into a suitable tale of sudden love and searing romance. She swept aside the minor detail of her broken engagement as just a bit of nonsense from which she had thankfully escaped because, had she not, how else would she have found herself with Lucas? Fate.

Good word. Antonia picked up the cue and reminisced over her own wonderful marriage. Fate had thrown her and her husband together from such a young age.

How could Milly resist confiding about her own parents, also childhood sweethearts? She couldn't. They had died too young but desperately in love; she felt scared at the thought of being deserted by those she loved, but she still believed in love with all her heart, whatever the risks it brought. She was thinking of Lucas and the mystery gold-digger when she said that. Belatedly, as Antonia nodded approvingly, Milly remembered that this was not supposed to be a bonding experience. She cleared her throat and wondered whether she should shove the man at her side into picking up the baton and continuing their fictional tale of love.

'Of course.' She decided against that course of action because who knew what he would say? He hadn't uttered a peep while she had been in confiding mode, although she had felt him edge a little closer to her, all the better to…*what*? Prolong his mother's incorrect assumptions? 'Wonderful though our sudden love is, I have to admit that your son can be a little…*forceful*.'

'Too forceful?' Antonia asked, and Milly ruefully inclined her head to one side, as though seriously giving the question house room, before erring on the side of tactful.

'Borderline arrogant,' she sighed, patting Lucas's thigh without looking at him. 'I guess it's something to do with having grown up in the lap of luxury. I'm afraid I grew up in the lap of, well, rubbing pennies together and trying to make ends meet...' She left Antonia to make the obvious deduction, which was that they were worlds apart and therefore incompatible in a fundamental area. The first of many, if only she knew.

Antonia seemed delighted with her admission. 'So good,' she murmured, tearing up, 'that you've finally come to your senses...' she smiled at her son and leaned forward '...and realised how much more fulfilling it is to have a real woman at your side. My dear, let me tell you about my dearest husband and myself. We rubbed many a penny together before Roberto's career began to take off! I could tell you a hundred tales of having to choose between paying the bills and buying food, especially in the beginning when we owed the bank so much money...'

'Thank you so much for helping me out there,' was the first thing Milly said when, an hour and three pastries later, they were being ushered up to their bedrooms. 'Why didn't you...why didn't you...?'

'Launch into a speech about why our fast and furious romance is destined to crash and burn within the next fortnight?'

He hadn't known about how she felt about her background. Orphaned as a kid and brought up by her grandmother, yet never looking back and blaming an unfortunate past. Still believing in the power of love even though abandonment issues should have made her wary and cynical, disinclined ever to trust anyone to get too close. Still ever-hopeful, the eternal optimist.

He had known women who had been blessed with the best life could offer and still managed to moan and complain about nothing in particular.

'Bit soon for the cracks to be showing, wouldn't you agree?'

At the top of the landing, the maid turned right and they both followed, Lucas breaking off to say something to the maid in rapid-fire Spanish that had her laughing. Their cases had been brought up whilst they had been in the sitting room.

'Your mother's really lovely,' Milly admitted. 'It's going to be a shame when she has to face up to the fact that you're so obnoxious that no one in their right mind would ever put up with you.'

Lucas looked down to see whether she was joking, but her expression was thoughtful and earnest.

'There are times when I can't actually believe that I'm hearing what you say correctly.'

Milly stopped and looked at him with a little frown. 'Do you have any idea how arrogant you were when you led me to believe that you were someone you weren't? I may only have been the chalet girl, but you just didn't see why you should be honest with me. For a start, you assumed that I was the sort of low life who would be out to see what I could get if I knew you were rich, and then you just didn't give a damn if you weren't honest. You didn't care about my feelings at all. I know you had one bad experience with a gold-digger but that's no excuse to just assume that everyone falls into the same category, guilty until proved innocent.'

'How did your feelings have anything to do with… anything at all?'

'You barely apologised for having duped me,' Milly told him flatly.

Where had that come from? Lucas, frustrated, raked his fingers through his hair and stared at her, lost for words.

'You just *assumed* that it was okay because you can do what you want to do without bothering to consider other people.'

'Is this conversation going anywhere?' he questioned in a driven voice. He glared at the maid, who seemed to be suppressing a smirk.

'I'm projecting…'

'You're *what*? I have no idea what you're talking about.'

'I'm projecting ahead to when you mother sadly discovers what a selfish, self-centred guy you've turned out to be.'

'I'm guessing she's probably wised up to those traits a while ago,' Lucas said drily, eyebrows raised. 'And, while we're on the subject of scrupulous honesty and caring about the feelings of others, have you mentioned to your grandmother what's going on in this part of the world?'

Milly flushed. 'I didn't see any point in worrying her by going into details.' It wasn't as though this was going to be a long-term situation. Two weeks—three, absolute max—he had told her when she had agreed to his plan. In those weeks, even if a dramatic break-up hadn't been staged, they should have covered the important phase of their fairy-tale romance revealing shaky foundations.

In those couple of weeks, he had privately thought, his mother would put to bed all ideas of trying to see him settled with the woman of her dreams. She would kill off notions of fairy-tale romances insofar as they pertained to him and she would resign herself to cheerful acceptance that what he wanted out of life, emotionally, was a far cry from what she thought would do him good.

She was his mother and he indulged her but, at the end of it, it was his life and he would choose its outcome whether or not it flew in the face of her ideals. This exercise in harmless fiction would be a gentle learning curve for her.

'I'm only going to be here for a short while and, when I return to London and my life's all sorted out, maybe then I'll let her in on some of the details.'

'You honestly think your life's going to be *all sorted out* when you return to London?'

'You said that...'

Lucas waved aside her predictable cry of protest. He had offered to have a formal agreement drawn up listing the conditions of this arrangement, what she would be given at the end of it, but she had airily told him that that wouldn't be necessary.

'I'm not talking about the job and the accommodation and the money, Milly. I'm talking about your blind faith in life always turning out for the best.'

'I don't have to listen to this.' She turned away and felt his hand gently stay her.

'If my mother's long overdue a little learning curve, then you should take this opportunity to put in place one of your own. Reality doesn't disappear because you decide that you'd quite like it to.' He nodded to the maid, who had tactfully moved to stare through one of the sprawling windows on the landing, ears blocked to any conversation—although Milly didn't think she spoke a word of English, so that probably was a step too far when it came to fulfilling her unspoken duties.

Milly watched, mouth open in anger, as he sauntered off, once again speaking Spanish, once again making the maid giggle. The maid might have been an old retainer well into her sixties, but it was obvious that he could still work the charm offensive on her.

Which was something he couldn't be bothered doing in *her* case.

How dared he think that he could bring his jaundiced views to bear on *her* life?

Placid by nature, she could scarcely credit the fury bubbling up inside her as her brain began functioning once again, and she tripped along behind him, barely paying attention to the magnificent surroundings.

The house was in the style of a rambling ranch. A short flight of stairs led up to the first floor, which, like the floor below, was wooden-floored, the wood gleaming from years of polish.

The corridor opened out in places into small sitting areas and curved round in other places, leading to nooks and crannies, various bedrooms and sitting rooms. It should have been disjointed and higgledy-piggledy but in fact there was an attractive coherence about the honeycomb nature of the layout, something whimsical and charming.

A lot of light poured in, thanks to large windows at regular intervals, a couple of which were fashioned of stained glass so that the bright sunlight was refracted into thousands of splintered shapes.

Through the windows, as she marched along in Lucas's wake, she could see extensive lawns and the bright turquoise of a swimming pool.

She stopped behind Lucas as the maid disappeared

into one of the bedrooms and she hovered, arms folded, still simmering.

'Good news and bad news.'

'Huh?' Snapping out of her reverie, Milly focused on his swarthy, handsome face. He leaned against the doorframe, the very picture of cool elegance.

'The good news is that it's a vast bedroom, complete with two sofas. There are even twin wardrobes. The bad news is that we're sharing it.'

The maid had vanished and Milly stared at Lucas, heat flooding her cheeks.

'You told me that there was no way your mother was going to...going to stick us in the room together! You told me that your mother was very old-fashioned, that she hadn't been brought up on a diet of sex before marriage. You *said* that she might know what you got up to but she'd always been adamant that you wouldn't get up to it under *her roof.*'

'I have a feeling that on those occasions when I showed up with a woman in tow she decided that the best way to avoid contributing to a loveless union was to locate us at opposite ends of the house.'

'Is that all you can say?' Milly hissed as her anger headed a little bit further north.

'At the moment, yes.' He pushed himself away from the doorframe and strolled into the guest suite.

Normally, he was given his usual room in the other wing of the house. He had barely noticed that they were being shown to a room in the opposite direction.

'How is this supposed to work?' Milly persisted, hands on hips as she followed him through.

'You should shut the door. The last thing we need is for wagging ears to hear us at each other's throats.'

'I thought that that was supposed to be the whole intention.'

'Not on day one. Now shut the door, Milly.'

'Bossy,' she muttered, stepping into the room with the unwillingness of someone entering a torture chamber.

How was she supposed to share a room with the man standing in front of her? How could he look so cool and collected when she was suddenly a bundle of nervous tension?

'You might want to freshen up,' Lucas said neutrally. He nodded in the direction of the *en suite* bathroom, which she saw was as big as the bedroom, which was huge.

'We can't share a room.'

'I won't be breaking that to my mother at this point in time, Milly, so you might as well settle into the idea. What's the problem anyway?'

'The problem is that I don't even *know* you...'

'It wasn't a problem when we were in Courchevel,' Lucas pointed out with infuriating logic. 'And frankly, thanks to your reckless habit of saying what you want and asking whatever questions you choose to ask, you probably know me a lot better than most.' And that was a shocking revelation. But true. A certain, intangible unease snaked through him.

'We weren't sharing a *bedroom* there. We were sharing a *mansion*.'

'But, on the upside, at least now you know that I'm not a homicidal maniac or a ski instructor on the lookout for a body to take to bed.'

'I didn't sign up for this.'

'For what, exactly?' His voice was silky smooth and those midnight-dark eyes watching her speculatively made her feel hot and tingly all over.

All those forbidden thoughts that had crowded into her head from the very first moment she had laid eyes on him surfaced with frightening ease.

Thoughts of him touching her, tasting her; crazy, stupid thoughts that were just the product of a fevered mind unbalanced by the trauma of a broken engagement.

Except, when was the last time she had thought about Robbie? How traumatised had she really been, exactly? If her heart had been broken, wouldn't she have still been cooped up somewhere, licking her wounds and thinking about a future that wasn't going to happen?

'Cling to the prospect of what you're getting out of this,' he advised her. 'And, if it puts your mind at ease, I'm happy to take the couch.' He'd contemplated the enticing prospect of taking her to bed—before she had discovered who he really was and all the advantages that came wrapped up with him. She might make a big deal of her maidenly virtue, but how long would it be before she began really looking round his mother's mansion; before she heard about all the other houses he owned, scattered across the globe like unused jewels waiting to be aired when the occasion arose?

Take one self-confessed romantic, tie it up with a broken heart and then into the mix throw one billionaire with a healthy libido and what did you come out with?

Complications. It didn't take a genius to figure that one out. And, when it came to complications of an emotional nature, well, that was something Lucas could do without.

So if that quirky *something* about her got to him…if there was something about her unruly hair and sexy little body that got his imagination firing on all cylinders…he would have to put it to rest. He was accustomed to getting exactly what he wanted with the opposite sex but, in this instance, his hands were tied and he wasn't about to untie them so that he could play with a bit of fire.

Milly eyed the couch with jaundiced eyes. Okay, so he wouldn't be sharing the bed with her—the gigantic king-size bed with its gauze canopy—but she would still be *aware* of him sleeping only a matter of metres away.

And that shouldn't be a problem. *He* certainly didn't see it as one. Maybe he had flirted slightly with her, in his few days as a ski instructor, but that was then.

'I'm not accustomed to sharing a bedroom,' she protested feebly and his face relaxed into a disbelieving, mocking half smile.

'You were engaged…' He drew that one sentence out as though it was explanation in itself that she wasn't quite telling the truth.

Milly reddened, mouth dry. 'You keep reminding me of that,' she said in a valiant attempt to change the course of the conversation because she didn't like where it was heading. 'I guess in a minute you'll start lecturing me about not facing reality and being a hopeless romantic and burying my head in the sand…'

Lucas narrowed his eyes on her. 'You didn't share a bedroom with the guy?' he asked, honing in on the truth with deadly accuracy. He watched the way she guiltily glazed over and licked her lips. He knew that he shouldn't pursue the topic because, frankly, there was no point. This wasn't a 'getting to know you' exercise, after all, although stable doors and horses sprang to mind, resuscitating that unease he had earlier felt. *They knew each other… Like it or not, weird though it seemed…*

'I don't think that's any of your business,' Milly said

haughtily. 'And I think I'll have that shower you mentioned...'

'Course it's my business,' he told her with just the sort of slow smile that implied that shrewd mind of his was leaping to all sorts of correct conclusions about her relationship with Robbie. 'We're in love. Isn't that what star-struck lovers do—share everything?'

'You...you're...' She spluttered furiously at him and he grinned.

'You're like a little spitting cat.'

'If your mother was a fly on the wall, she'd get a pretty good picture of how *not* star-struck lovers we are!' She could all but get the words out. The man was infuriating! There wasn't a human being on the planet who could work her up so fast and so effortlessly.

'Or...' Lucas held her gaze but he was still grinning '...she might decide that a little volatility is good when it comes to...being in love and star- struck...'

'Well, she'd be wrong,' Milly hissed, making a bee-line for her case and rummaging until she had located some clothes. 'And now, if you don't mind, I'm going to have a bath.'

Sure you don't want me to join you? The instinctive riposte was on the tip of his tongue but then the thought of actually doing that, of actually sliding into the warm water with her, soaping her, feeling her curves pressed against him, slammed into him with the force of a runaway train and his mouth tightened.

'I have work to do,' he said abruptly. 'Take your time. Dinner's usually served around seven-thirty. Early by Spanish standards but my mother's schedule is no longer what it was. I'll either come and get you, take you down to the dining room, or I'll dispatch one of the maids to show you the way.'

Running a bath, door firmly locked, Milly figured that this was how it must feel like to be a toy at the whim of an unpredictable owner. He had managed to rile her, provoke her and then, when it felt as though she actually *needed* to have some sort of full-blown argument with him, needed to wipe that annoying, laid-back grin from his face, he changed, just like that, for no particular reason.

Boredom.

She eased herself into the bath and closed her eyes. He had suddenly become bored. He enjoyed provoking her and he knew he could. It amused him. But, like a kid with the attention span of a flea, his amusement had a very short sell-by date because, however *different* he might find her, she just didn't have what it took to hold his attention for longer than five seconds. Thank goodness this was all just a fabrication! Because if it wasn't then she would never be good enough for him, would she? Being *different* didn't count. Being a *novelty* didn't count.

She mentioned that over dinner. A fabulous dinner served by a different maid. A typically Spanish meal of paella rich with seafood with lots of salad. Just a casual little remark when there was a lull in the conversation, a little throwaway observation about her *sheer amazement* that she and Lucas had become involved, because they were just so different, because she was just the sort of girl he would find boring…

Antonia had smiled and talked about opposites attracting and then, sensing something intense in Milly's expression, had kindly listed all the ways that relationships worked when two people complemented each other by bringing different personality traits to the union.

Lucas had failed to take the bait with the opening. Was he still of the opinion that his mother should have a honeymoon period before the cracks began showing?

When Milly thought of that bedroom, waiting for them to share it, she was of the opinion that the cracks should surface sooner rather than later.

She thought so even more when, over coffee in the sitting room, yet another room new to her, he draped his arm over her shoulders, sitting next to her with the indolent casualness of a man with his woman. His low, sexy voice was warm and teasing. He absently played with her hair. When she spoke, she could feel his breath warm on her cheek as he looked at her.

Antonia was taking in everything, eyes shrewd, and if *he* didn't see that then Milly certainly did and it was the very first thing she said to him when Antonia excused herself for the night, leaving the two of them alone in the sitting room.

'You *could* have helped me out when I began listing all the reasons why we didn't make sense as a couple.' She sprang to her feet and plonked herself down on a chair far away from him although, even though there was now distance between them, she could still feel the weight of his arm around her and the warmth of his thigh pressed against hers.

'Did you *see* your mother? She thought it was *cute* that I was pointing out all our differences!'

Lucas shrugged and Milly gritted her pearly-white teeth in pure frustration.

He hadn't seen his mother this happy in a while. How long had she been secretly harbouring hopes that he would meet the woman of his dreams and bring her home? She had dropped hints in the past but she had really only begun pressing him after her illness. But had she been fretting long before then?

'The time isn't right for a two-pronged attack.'

'There's no question of an *attack*.' Why did he have to be so dramatic? she wondered. Why did he have to make her out as the bad guy in this when she was only here because of him and only gently laying the foundations for their break-up because that was what she had been primed to do?

'And,' she continued, 'I'd rather you didn't sit so close to me...'

'Sit so *close* to you?'

'I just think that your mother might find such public displays of affection a little embarrassing, that's all.'

'We're sharing a bedroom. Somehow I don't think she's going to swoon because I stroke your thigh now and again. Did she look embarrassed?'

'That's not the point.'

'The point is, I have no idea what you're talking about. I'm not going to retreat to the furthest corner of the room. That would be unnatural. Furthermore, I don't see why it's such a big deal.'

'The big deal,' Milly said with a ferocious whisper, because how could he be so *cool* when she was all over the place? 'Is that I'm still in the process of getting over something pretty big and pretty horrible and maybe I need just a little more physical space than you're giving me. Lord knows what your mother must secretly think of me.' A sudden thought occurred to her. 'What if she thinks I'm a gold-digger? After all, one minute I'm engaged to one guy and the next minute I'm going out with a billionaire.' She wrung her hands in despair at the misconception.

'What if she thinks I *targeted* you...? It makes horrible sense in a way, doesn't it? What if she imagines that I'm just one of a long line of women who want you for what you can do for them...?'

Lucas raised his eyebrows and held up one imperious hand to stop her before she could begin exploring this new theme in exhaustive depth.

'She doesn't think that,' he told her flatly. 'Nor does she think that you're somehow emotionally unstable and fickle because you're going out with me hard on the heels of a broken engagement.'

'You can't say that.'

'Oh, but I can and I have.'

'What do you mean *you have*?'

'I told my mother that this was not a case of you jumping from one man to another without pausing for breath. I've explained that I'm not a rebound love affair—which, as you can imagine, would not have sat well with her.'

'When did all this explaining take place?' Milly asked in frank bemusement.

'When you were soaking in the bath for two hours,' Lucas said drily. *She thinks you're impossibly brave. As I do...*

'And she believed you?' Milly aimed for an incredulous laugh. 'I know you could sell ice to Eskimos, Lucas, but women are very intuitive when it comes to stuff like that; when it comes to matters of *the heart*...'

'Which is why she knows it's the truth,' Lucas told her with silky assurance. 'She's met you, talked to you and she knows—like we both do, Milly—that whatever you had with your ex-fiancé wasn't love. You may be the jilted girlfriend, and that's not a great place to be, but you're not the heartbroken jilted girlfriend. So your little speech about feeling uncomfortable sitting too close to me because you're nursing a broken heart is, frankly, a load of rubbish. Maybe you're scared of being too close to me because you think I'm going to make a move on you...'

And hadn't the thought crossed his head more than once? *Good job he had iron self-discipline and was smart enough to spot danger before it spotted him.*

'Not going to happen. Or maybe,' he mused thoughtfully, 'you're scared because you think *you* might make a move on *me*...'

Milly could feel herself burning up as he shoved his version of reality down her throat. There was nothing he said that had not occurred to her before, even if only in passing.

And that included the shameful fact that she found the man physically attractive, that she had flirted with silly fantasies...

'In your dreams,' she told him tartly. But she heard the faint wobble in her voice. She wasn't accustomed to playing these sorts of games. She was straightforward; she had never found herself in this kind of situation. She was walking in unchartered territory and it was only her survivor's instinct that told her that, whatever she did, she should not show him that he was right. That maybe, just maybe, that bed held unspoken terrors for her because she could picture, far too easily, what it might be like *to have him in it next to her...*

CHAPTER EIGHT

MILLY GAZED AT her reflection in the mirror but she
wasn't really focusing on the face staring back at her.
She was thinking of the past week and a half.

Behind her, the king-size bed that had filled her with
horror was just...a king-sized bed. Her fears had been
unjustified. At least, unjustified except in the deepest,
darkest corners of her mind where fantasies of Lucas
still swirled around with dangerous strength, powerful riptides lying in wait for the appropriate moment
to suck her under, or so it felt.

They barely shared this private space. Antonia always retired before ten, at which point Milly would head
upstairs, leaving Lucas downstairs, where he would
work until the early hours of the morning. She neither
heard nor saw him when he finally made it to the bedroom because she was always sound asleep. The only
evidence he left that he occupied the room at all was
the barely discernible imprint on the sofa where he had
slept, because he was always up and moving by eight
in the morning.

The man hardly needed any sleep at all. She, on the
other hand, had always been able to sleep for England.

The linen he used for the sofa was always shoved
neatly in the wardrobe.

Twice she had woken needing the bathroom and her heart had been pounding as she had tiptoed her way past where he had lain sprawled and asleep, half-naked, the thin duvet barely covering him.

That fleeting glimpse of him sadly had been yet more fodder for her very active imagination.

If only this stupid charade had done what it should have done and exposed his failings. At this point in time, shouldn't he have morphed into an arrogant bore with too much money for his own good? Shouldn't the impact of his good looks have done her a favour by diminishing?

She sighed and peered a little more closely at her reflection. The hair looked wilder than usual but she had given up trying to tame it. Was this the look she really wanted to go for? Wild hair and a strappy dress, and high-heeled sandals that were *so* not her thing?

She and Lucas, at his mother's urging, were going to have a supposedly romantic dinner out tonight. She had given Milly a stern talk on buying something pretty for the occasion, because she had not been shopping, and had managed to use what she had brought with her: jeans; T-shirts; more jeans; jogging bottoms.

So, despite lots of protests, she and Antonia had spent much of the day out. There had been no need to venture further afield into Madrid because Salamanca boasted designer shops for every taste. These were just the sort of things that were undermining the 'cracks in the relationship' that should have been happening by now.

Every crack Milly tried to break was papered over by Antonia, who seemed to think that her outspokenness was a charming and refreshing change from all the limpets who had cluttered her son's life before.

And in the meantime, while all this was going on, she was seeing sides to Lucas that chipped away at her defences.

He was ferociously intelligent and, whilst he was good at listening to other sides of an argument, he liked to win. Over dinner—which was usually when she saw most of him, because his days were spent working to make up for the fact that he wasn't actually in his office or on a plane going to meetings somewhere or other across the globe—they talked about everything under the sun. Antonia might generate the topic, but they would all contribute. And the topics flowed from one to another, from what was happening in the news to what had happened in the news, sometimes years previously.

He was a loving son without being patronising. He was very good at teasing his mother, and Milly's heart always constricted when she witnessed this interplay between them.

Of course, she and her grandmother were very close, as she had insisted on telling them a couple of nights ago, but it was still something to have grown up without a mother figure. Or a father figure, for that matter. She might have had a sip or two too many at this point, Milly recalled uncomfortably. She had held the floor for far too long and she might even have become a little tearful towards the end. She shuddered thinking about it.

He was also funny, witty and downright interesting. He had travelled the world. It helped when it came to recounting fascinating anecdotes about faraway places.

Her heart picked up speed as another treacherous thought crept into her head like a thief in the night: she looked forward to his company. She spent her days in

the grounds, sometimes by the swimming pool reading her book, often in the company of his mother. But,
when five o'clock came, she always felt a stirring in
her veins, as though her body was beginning to wake
up and come alive.

And that wasn't good.

In fact, it frightened her because, face it, Lucas was
as distant as he had promised. Yes, when they were in
each other's company he was warmth and charm itself but, the second his mother wasn't around, a shutter
dropped and he became someone else. Someone cool,
controlled and somehow absent.

Now, she noticed, he had stopped sitting quite so
close to her on the sofa and the physical shows of affection…the little touches on her shoulder, her cheek,
her arms…had dropped off.

She guessed that this was his subtle way of inform-
ing his mother that all was not quite right in the land
of wonderful love and happy-ever-afters.

Had Antonia noticed? Milly didn't know. She had
thought of trying to open a discussion on the subject,
maybe starting with a few vague generalities before
working her way up to her and Lucas and what they had,
and then ending by finding out what Antonia's thoughts
were. But she always chickened out because she wasn't
sure she would be able to hang on to her composure if
the questions became too targeted.

Right now Lucas was downstairs. He usually stopped
working around six so that he could spend some time
with Antonia while Milly was upstairs having a bath,
changing…analysing her thoughts and coming up
empty handed.

And, while Milly relaxed downstairs, usually with
a glass of freshly squeezed lemonade, he took the op-

portunity to get cleaned up. It was a clever game of avoidance that Antonia didn't seem to notice, but Milly noticed it more and more because she was noticing *everything* more and more.

Tonight, Milly entered the sitting room to find Antonia there sipping a glass of juice, her book resting on her lap.

Like all the other rooms in the splendid house, this one was airy and light with pale walls and furnishings and adjustable wooden shutters to guard against the blistering sun during the hot summer months. And, as with all the rooms, the air was fragrant with the smell of flowers, which were cut from the garden several times a week and arranged by Antonia herself in an assortment of brightly coloured vases to be dispersed throughout the house.

'I wanted to see how the dress looked.' She beamed and beckoned Milly across and then ordered her to do a couple of turns so that she could appreciate it from every angle. 'Beautiful.'

'I don't know about that,' Milly said awkwardly. 'I'm not accustomed to wearing dresses.'

'You should. You have the perfect figure to carry them off. Not like those scrawny women my son has dated in the past. Like boys! Simpering and preening themselves and looking in every mirror they pass! *Pah!* I tell him, "Lucas, those are not real women, they are plastic dolls and you can do better than that"...' She smiled smugly and waved Milly into a chair.

'We have our differences,' Milly said weakly, determined to head off an awkward situation at the pass. 'You might think that those model types are no good for Lucas but in fact...*in fact*...they suit him far more than you might imagine. I mean...' She leaned forward and stared earnestly at the handsome woman in front of her whose head was tilted to one side, all the better to grasp what was being said because, impeccable though her English was, she still became lost in certain expressions. 'It's okay to be outspoken but, in the end, it can get on a guy's nerves.'

'Is that what happened to your last boyfriend?' Antonia asked gently. 'Was that why it all fell apart, my dear?'

Milly blushed. She had breezily and vaguely skimmed over the details of the broken engagement that had supposedly encouraged her into the arms of her one true love, Lucas. Antonia had conveniently not dwelled on the subject. Now, she was waiting for some girlish confidence.

'It fell apart,' Milly said slowly, 'Because he didn't love me and, as it turns out, I didn't love him either.' This was the first time she was actually saying aloud what she had been privately thinking. 'I was just an idiot,' she confessed. 'I'd had a crush on Robbie when I was a teenager...' She smiled, remembering the gawky, sporty kid she had been, more at home with a hockey stick than a glass of vodka, which had been the in drink at the time with all the under-age drinkers: the alcohol could be camouflaged by whatever you happened to dilute it with and parents could never tell you were actually getting a little tipsy at parties.

'Robbie was the cutest boy in the class. Floppy blond hair, gift of the gab. Plus, he would actually take time out to chat to me. It felt like love, so when he showed up in London and asked to meet up I guess I remembered what I used to feel and somehow transported it to the present day and decided that those feelings were still there, intact. He was still cute, after all. He brought back memories.'

And he had known how to manipulate her weaknesses to his own benefit but, in the end, it took two to tango. He had made inroads into her common sense because she had allowed him to.

'But what was I saying...?' She gulped back the temptation to cry just a little.

'You were saying...' Lucas's voice from behind her made her temporarily freeze '...that you got suckered in to a dud relationship with some guy who was never suited to you in the first place.'

He had been standing by the door, unnoticed by both his mother and Milly, and he couldn't quite understand just why it gave him such a kick to hear her finally admit what he had suspected all along.

She had not been occupying Heartbreak Hotel, as she had fondly and misguidedly imagined. Of course she had known that, he had seen it on her face when he had chosen to point it out to her, but it was still gratifying to hear her admit it.

Not, he hurriedly told himself, that it mattered in any way that was significant. It didn't. She might be amusing, feisty, way too open for her own good...in short, all the things he never encountered in his relationships with women...but that didn't make her available. She had been available to a simple ski instructor but to the man he was? No.

But, hell, it was getting more and more difficult by the second. He always made sure that temptation was safely out of the way by burning the midnight oil in front of his computer, although he knew that his mind was only partly on work. Too much of it, as far as he was concerned, was preoccupied with visions of her in that bed—and those visions were all the more graphic because he knew how she slept, sprawled in sexy abandon with the duvet tangled about her body.

He'd bet all his worldly possessions that that was not the way she started out. No. He imagined that she tucked herself tightly underneath those covers, *swaddled* herself in them, but somewhere along the line, when she was happily gambolling about in deep REM, her body had other ideas on how it was most comfortable. And that was not wrapped up like an Egyptian mummy.

Twice she had gone to the bathroom in the early hours of the morning, tiptoeing past the sofa in such slow motion that it had taken all he had not to burst out laughing.

Her sleepwear would be a passion-killer for most men, but the baggy T-shirt with the faded logo, reaching mid-thigh, did crazy things to his system, sent it soaring into the stratosphere. She might wear the least flattering outfits known to womankind, but her body was luscious and sexy, the jut of her full breasts promising more than a handful, the shapeliness of her legs tempting him to find out what lay between them.

He flushed darkly now as he recalled the rigid erection those thoughts had induced as he had showered.

He wondered, with some irony, whether this was what happened when the guy who could have it all was denied the one thing he found he wanted.

The sooner this charade came to an end, the better. Not least because his mother appeared to have fallen in love with the woman and that had not been on the agenda. But they were going out tonight, just the two of them, and he wouldn't mince his words.

The time for pulling the plug had come.

He was sick of waging war with his libido. He had to return to the land of the living, his offices in London. His mother was getting far too involved in their pretend love affair for his liking. And, anyway, who knew whether Milly was getting a little too accustomed to the good life? That was a consideration that had to be taken into account. Surely. Wasn't it?

'How long have you been lurking by the door?' Milly said accusingly and Lucas strolled into the room to take up position by the window, perching against the broad window sill with his arms folded.

Here comes Adonis again, Milly thought absently, *and shouldn't I have become accustomed to this by now?* She could see him a million times and still be startled by his dark, stunning beauty.

'I don't *lurk*...' His features were perfectly controlled, as was the tenor of his voice, but he had to steer firmly away from the soft swell of her breasts jutting against the soft fabric of a flimsy, strappy dress. Hell, she wasn't even wearing a bra! It bordered on indecent, even though the style was modest enough.

There was something about the shimmering colours, though...blues and creams that made the fall of her curly red hair even more vibrant...and she was wearing make-up. Just a bit. Just sufficient gloss on her full lips to tease any red-blooded man to distraction.

He felt himself harden and he looked away from her momentarily, gathering himself, before indulging in his usual light-hearted banter with his mother. The fiercer his desire grew, the more distance he had to try and put between them. Those brief touches were like matches flung onto dry tinder.

'Now, make sure you use Carlos...' his mother was telling him as he walked towards Milly, who was rising to her feet, as graceful as a ballet dancer in some strappy little sandals that showed off newly painted toenails.

'Is this the drink-driving lecture?' Lucas slipped his arm around Milly's waist and felt her soft body against his, which was a predictable challenge to his self-control. 'Don't worry. I'll be using Carlos. If I remember correctly, he has a fondness for that little wine bar not a million miles away from the restaurant. He can enjoy himself with a plate of pasta and a big bottle of mineral water.' Her breasts were just above where his hand curved on her ribcage.

As soon as they were through the front door, he dropped his hand and moved away from her.

Talk about being obvious, Milly thought, stung because he was so clearly turned off by her. She slid into the back seat through the door that Carlos held open for her and didn't glance in Lucas's direction as he levered himself in and sat next to her.

He hadn't even commented on her dress. Her normally bubbly nature was flattened by that and she was cool as they drove towards the town, choosing to stare through the window at the scenery and replying to his attempts at conversation in stiff monosyllables.

'Are you going to tell me what's wrong?' Lucas drawled once they were out of the car and in the restaurant, which was a cosy Italian that obviously appealed to the beautiful and the wealthy.

'Nothing's wrong.' Milly reluctantly looked at him and her heart picked up pace. He was staring at her, his dark eyes lazy and unfathomable. Was he comparing her to the sort of women his mother disliked but he didn't?

'Spit it out.'

'Okay—what's wrong is that you're not making any

attempt to sort this business out. We've been here nearly two weeks.'

'I didn't think you were in any rush to get back,' Lucas said mildly.

'That's not the point. The point is that I don't like lying to your mother. I feel we're getting close to one another...'

'Then make sure you pull back, Milly. She's not a substitute mother because you lost yours.'

'That's a rotten thing to say!'

Lucas sighed and raked his fingers through his hair in frustration. 'It is and for that I apologise. In actual fact, I have been thinking the same as you. It's time to start letting my mother know that this situation between us isn't going to work. For one thing, I'm sick to death of sleeping on that sofa. I'm a big man. Far too big for a sofa. I never even did that in my teenage years.'

'You never slept rough?'

'Never. But we're getting off topic here. We will have to be a bit more proactive. I admit, I've been at fault here...' Yes, he had. He had preferred to enjoy the atmosphere in the house, his mother's delight with his latest conquest, so different from her reactions to the few women she had met over the years. Lazy. He had been lazy. 'Tomorrow, we stage an argument. It shouldn't be too difficult. We have precious little in common.' He shrugged with the usual graceful nonchalance that Milly found so seductive.

Milly drank some of the white wine that had found itself into the oversized glass in front of her. She had hardly been aware of a waiter pouring from a bottle.

'If we have so little in common,' she mocked, 'then how is it that we haven't been at each other's throats by now?'

Lucas flushed. It was a good question. 'It's called the route of least resistance. When my mother has been around, it has been all too easy to let her see what she has wanted to see, but I have a life to get on with. I can't afford to spend much more time here. Naturally, I will commute on weekends, but I need to be back in the saddle. I need to return to London. As do you. So that you can make good on the bargain you struck with me. Have you told your landlord that you will no longer be needing his flat? Or house? Or wherever it is you live?'

'House. I've already told you that.'

'My short-term memory can be occasionally short.' The house she had shared with her so-called good friend. Of course he remembered! He remembered everything, every little detail. Too much.

'And, no, I haven't told my landlord yet. I can email him in the morning but you have to give me your word that you won't renege on our agreement. I don't want to find myself without a roof over my head.'

'You did as you were asked. Naturally I will keep my end of the bargain.'

He was barely aware of ordering another bottle and, by the time they had finished eating, they were two bottles down and were making inroads into a third.

'And what do you think our staged argument should be about?' After a brief lull in hostilities, Milly picked up the thread of what they had been discussing earlier. The meal was finished, the bill paid; when she stood up, she had to focus, *really focus,* to stop herself from teetering on her unfamiliar heels.

He reached out to steady her and his hand remained there at her waist.

'You've had too much to drink,' Lucas murmured.

'Maybe we could weave *that* in. Maybe you could turn me into an alcoholic.'

'My mother would never buy it.'

'Because I'm such a *boring* girl-next-door type?'

'Where did *that* come from?' He stopped dead in his tracks and spun her to face him. Of their own volition, his fingers sifted through her hair and brushed her cheek.

Milly was transfixed by that gesture. He was staring down at her and she experienced a weird, drowning feeling. He was right. She'd drunk too much. She couldn't peel her eyes away from his handsome face.

'You should stop looking at me like that,' Lucas said huskily and Milly half-closed her eyes.

'Like what?' she breathed.

'Boring girl-next-door types don't look at men the way you're looking at me...'

Milly reached out and tentatively touched his cheek, and was blown away when she realised that that was what she had been longing to do since...*for ever.* She let her hand linger there, feeling the roughened stubble on his chin, while her heart carried on beating like a sledgehammer inside her.

'No,' Lucas said shakily. 'Come on. Carlos is waiting.'

And he meant it. However tempting she might be, he wasn't going to make love to her. No way. The prospect enticed and, yes, *frightened* him in equal measure. It was an unfamiliar feeling. It disturbed and unsteadied him. It smacked of a loss of control.

'I'm going to put you to bed as soon as we're back.' He was dismayed when she nodded and nestled against his arm. She smelled floral, clean, *young.*

'So, tell me what vices you're going to give me,' Milly encouraged, at once sleepy and yet never so wide awake. She felt alive to everything: to the scent of him; to the rough feel of the linen jacket he had flung on before leaving the house; to the way his chest rose and fell as he breathed. 'I've always thought it must be nice to have a few vices.'

Lucas wasn't doing much thinking at all. He cleared his throat, shifted, failed to budge her...knew that he didn't want to anyway, not really. The key thing was that he wasn't going to make a move on her.

'Not a cry I've often heard,' he remarked drily.

'I guess you heard what I was telling your mother about Robbie...having a crush on him. He was so cool when he was young.'

'And now less so,' Lucas reminded her shortly. 'A loser, in fact.'

'I bet you think that everyone's a loser compared to you,' Milly murmured, wriggling so that she could tilt her head and look him directly in the eye.

Her breath caught in her throat and her racing heart slowed, along with time, which seemed to stand still altogether.

Her kiss took him by surprise, reaching up on tiptoe as she did, and it was so sweetly, disarmingly innocent; the gentle, tentative probing of her cool tongue a breathless, feathery flutter against his lips..

He shuddered and stifled a groan. 'This isn't part of the deal,' he muttered unsteadily.

'I know. But remember those vices I wished I had? One of them was to just...*let go*, not take guys so *seriously*...' She traced the outline of his jaw, could sense him wanting more against his will and that filled her with a heady sense of power. When he pressed a button so that opaque glass separated them from Carlos, she smiled.

So the big break-up was going to start tomorrow. And then, in a heartbeat, she would be back in London, back to reality… But, right now, *this* was her reality and why shouldn't she grab it with both hands? If he pushed her away and stormed off in revulsion, then so be it, but deep inside she sensed that he wouldn't do that.

'You see them and you what…? Want to marry them?'

'I see them and I start wondering how they would fit in on a long-term basis.' Which was pretty badly in every case thus far, few though those cases had been. 'Sort of, "hi, how are you? What are your thoughts on big families…?"' She felt him shudder and laughed. 'I know. You're horrified. I bet you'd run a mile if a woman asked you a question like that. I mean, you gave your heart away and you got burned, right? So you're not up to giving it away again.'

'You got that right but, word to the wise, don't mention that particular bone of contention to my mother. She might not quite see my side of the story.'

'Oh, I won't mention anything that might give her the wrong idea about us,' Milly said with a hitch in her voice. She didn't want to think about going. Not right at this moment.

What she wanted…

She covered his big hand with her much smaller one and guided it to her breast, and she felt him slip a little lower in the seat.

'Hell, Milly! No. You…don't know what you're doing…' But he kept his hand there, felt the rounded fullness of her breast, and wanted to do so much more that it was a physical ache. His erection was so hard that he could barely move.

'I *do* know what I'm doing. For the first time in my

whole life, I know what I'm doing.' Her voice was insistent as she unbuttoned the top two pearl buttons of the dress, allowing him more access to her and loving, absolutely *loving,* the way he was making her feel. 'I'll be gone in a few days and I won't be seeing you again… And…you make me feel…'

'How do I make you feel, Milly?' *More than a handful.* She was well endowed; if Carlos hadn't been in the front seat, driving them slowly with an impeccable lack of interest in the goings on behind him, he would have taken her right here in the car.

'Curious,' she confessed with the honesty that was so much a part and parcel of her personality. 'You make me feel curious.'

CHAPTER NINE

THE KING-SIZE BED that had been her hiding place for nearly two weeks seemed suddenly to have expanded until now she felt as though it was consuming all the space in the room. It was the only thing she could see.

Milly's body was on fire. 'Sexually daring and adventurous' were not descriptions that could ever have been applied to her. The truth was that she had never felt particularly bothered by her lack of experience in this field. She had kissed a few guys and had been content enough to leave it right there. Now, though, her head was filled with possibilities.

'This…isn't a good idea.' Common sense half-heartedly tried to prevail but Lucas recognised it for what it was: a flimsy attempt to hold off something that felt inevitable. He had already dumped his jacket downstairs and his fingers were hooked under the polo shirt, ready to yank it over his head. He was breathing fast as he stared at her, not trusting himself to get any closer, because that flimsy attempt at common sense wouldn't stand a chance.

'Why not?' Milly asked with reckless abandon. She took a couple of steps towards him.

They hadn't switched on the light, and the bedroom was bathed in pale moonlit rays sifting through the big windows. His beautiful face was a mix of shadows and angles, his eyes glittering as he watched her nervous progress.

He felt nervous, as well. Unbelievable.

'Don't you fancy me at all?' she asked, placing the palm of her hand on his chest and feeling the steady beating of his heart underneath it.

'What sort of stupid question is that?' Lucas returned roughly. He covered her hand with his and guided it to the bulging hardness of his erection pushing against the zip of his jeans.

Milly shivered, unbelievably turned on. So turned on that she forgot to be scared that this was going to be her *first time*. With trembling fingers, she hitched down the zip and heard his sharp, indrawn breath with a jab of pure satisfaction.

She had taken a chance, had been prepared to stomach his rejection because her own shameless craving felt like something requiring satisfaction before she packed her bags and walked away. The feel of his arousal was proof that he wanted her, too, even if he didn't think it was a good idea.

With a growl of impatience, Lucas pulled off the polo shirt, revealing a bronzed, muscular body that was as exquisite and as perfect as the rest of him. Any wonder she had dumped all her reservations? Breathing shallow, she ran her fingers lightly over his torso, pausing to circle the tight, brown nipples.

'We're supposed to be lovers...' She looked up at him with a wry smile. 'Aren't we?'

'How is it that you haven't felt this pressing need to touch me before?'

'Who says I haven't?'

Lucas's smile was triumphant. Common sense flew

through the window. He began unbuttoning the tiny pearl buttons, taking his time, until the top half of the dress was gaping, allowing him to see tantalising glimpses of her soft breasts.

'You weren't wearing a bra,' he murmured huskily. 'That was the first thing I noticed when I saw you this evening.'

'I had no idea you even noticed what I was wearing, considering you didn't say anything.'

'The sight left me speechless.'

Milly smiled. 'Speechless in a good way?'

'Speechless in a way that made me want to do what I'm about to do now.' He hooked his fingers under the spaghetti straps of the dress and slowly pulled himself down until he was feasting his eyes on the proud jut of her breasts.

Milly stood absolutely still, which was the only way she could think of to restrain herself from pulling the dress back into position. She didn't want to think of all the lovely bodies he had looked at before because she was not built like one of them.

'Don't say anything.'

'Not hard. I find...' He circled one rosy nipple with his finger and felt her shudder. 'I find myself without words...'

'I'm not tall and skinny. I'm short and well-endowed... Sorry.'

Lucas looked at her in genuine amazement at her self-denigration. 'I've never heard anything so ridiculous in all my life.'

'Thank you for that.' Romantic fool she might be but she could also be as realistic as he assumed she was not, and she was realistic enough to know that what he saw was the novelty of a differently shaped body and a differently fashioned personality from those to which he was accustomed. But the moment would be lost if she embarked on that sort of conversation. It was a topic best left alone.

She walked shakily towards the bed and seconds later he joined her, tossing the condom he had sourced onto the small bedside table.

'Take off the dress,' he commanded. 'No, just let it fall open… Yes, like that. I want to see you…' He straddled her prone body and just watched, savouring the tight buds of her nipples. He removed his jeans and enjoyed the way her eyes skittered away from his pulsing erection before looking once again. 'Feel free to touch.' He barely recognised his voice.

Milly gulped and tentatively tugged down the boxers. He was impressive in his girth, his erection as big, as powerful and as striking as he was. She took it in her hand and instinct took over. At first, she kept her eyes half-closed, but then opened them and looked at the shiny head in her hand then, growing braver, she sat up and took him into her mouth.

She tasted him and felt him shudder, move and arch back. His fingers had coiled in her long hair. The salty taste of him was an aphrodisiac, sending waves of pleasure and yearning through her in equal measure.

She moaned when he pushed her back. Her underwear was wet, her own arousal soaking through the cotton, and she wriggled and kicked herself free of it, parting her legs in an attempt to cool between them.

'You're burning up for me.' Lucas slipped exploring fingers into her and her breath caught in her throat as he found her clitoris and began rubbing it, gentle, persistent strokes that made her arch her body up, transported like she had never been before in her life.

She didn't want to come. Not like this. She pulled him to her and kissed him and Lord…it was beautiful. It was a kiss meant to be lost in. His tongue against hers was gentle and demanding at the same time. She could taste the essence of the guy who wanted to move slowly and yet was desperate to sate his hunger. His steel shaft brushed against her and she opened her legs a little wider so that she could feel its hardness against the parted, delicate folds. She moaned softly into his mouth, quivering when his erection pressed against her clitoris, threatening to push her over the edge.

She broke apart and captured his face between her hands. 'There's something I should tell you.'

'Now isn't the time for sharing confidences,' Lucas breathed shakily. He pinned her arms above her head and ordered her to keep them there.

Then he lowered his head to taste her succulent nipples, circling first one then the other with his mouth, drawing them deeply in then teasing the stiffened bud with his tongue.

Milly couldn't bear it. It was beyond pleasurable. It was also a completely new experience. She wanted to tell him that she was a virgin. He deserved to know, didn't he? Or else he might expect her to…be like all his other women. She wasn't sure what that meant, exactly, but she thought that creative gymnastics might be involved.

She half-opened her mouth and a gasp of pure pleasure came out instead of the haltering admission she had been formulating.

He was licking her nipple, watching her, enjoying the hectic colour in her cheeks, enjoying the way she couldn't keep still, all her little soft moans and whimpers.

Her full breasts jiggled as she writhed under him and he was driven to capture her other nipple, suckling on it until the moans became husky and uncontrolled.

He'd never felt the need to rush his love-making. Sex was an art form and pleasure had to be given and taken in equal measure. He was a master of taking things slowly, of the languorous intimate exploration, but right now it required a great deal of self-control not to grab the condom on the bedside table, stick it on and just...*take her*. Where his skinny supermodels were all sharp angles and jutting hip bones, Milly was soft, silky smooth and sensually rounded.

He curved his hand along her side, mouth still firmly clamped on her breast, then over the gentle swell of her stomach to slip between her legs, although once there he simply smoothed her inner thigh. His knuckles brushed the soft down of her pubic hair, and he itched to delve deeper, but all in good time.

Very slowly...and trying hard to douse his raging libido by concentrating on something, anything, other than the sex bomb squirming under him...he licked a trail along her stomach, starting from underneath her heavy breasts and working all the way down to her belly button.

He tipped his tongue into the sensitive indentation and felt the whoosh of her breath as she inhaled sharply. She had pressed her legs together and he gently but firmly eased them apart in preparation of tasting her but she tugged him by his hair and he glanced up to meet her feverish eyes.

'What are you doing?' Milly whispered, yearning for his mouth to touch her in her most private part, yet horrified at this outrageous show of intimacy.

'Nothing while you're pulling my hair out.'

'It's just that…'

'Don't tell me that no one has ever tasted you… there…' Could his libido get any more out of control? he wondered.

'I…' Confession time—but her vocal cords protested at ruining the moment and what difference would it make anyway? She still wanted him, wanted *this*.

Lucas slanted a bone-melting smile at her and her fingers slackened their grip. She fell back, eyes closed, cautiously opened her legs then sucked in deeply and held her breath as his tongue began to tease her open, flicking over the stiffened nub of her clitoris. She exhaled but had to breath in quickly again because sensations were running rampant through her.

She was burning up all over and panting. No part of her could keep still under the force of the fire spreading through her body, wafting through her in waves, making her arch up against his mouth, and there he kept her by placing his hands firmly under her butt.

He brought her close, so close that she wanted to cry out, then pulled back, teasing her body in a way that had her breathless and shamefully pleading for him to enter her.

She felt rather than saw him fumble for the condom he had earlier fished out. She watched, cheeks hot, as he expertly slipped it on, never taking his eyes off her face. She felt that she should have done more—clambered over him, perhaps, enticed him with the promise of new, acrobatic positions—but she dismissed that jag of insecurity. The hunger blazing in his dark eyes left no room for her to doubt that he was as turned on as she was.

He nudged the thick head of his arousal into her, and she tensed and stifled a little yelp as he inserted more of his tremendous girth into her, plunging deep and hard. She stiffened, eyes wide and panicked, and he stopped as realisation dawned.

'Tell me you're not a virgin,' he gasped, his whole body so still that it sent a ripple of alarm racing through her.

'You said that this was no time for confiding.' Milly pulled him down to her, raising herself slightly so that she could kiss him.

'Oh, Milly of the not-red hair, I'll take my time... I'll be gentle...'

He did, teasing her with his arousal, nudging it slowly in, withdrawing it, enticing her until her little whimpers became pleading moans. It was agony. But there was no way that he was going to hurt her, no way that she would ever think back to this night as anything but utterly memorable. Why that meant so much to him was something he shoved away.

She was wet and slippery as he eased himself deeper, taking his time as he had promised, until she was crying out for him to take her and take her *now*.

With a groan, Lucas thrust deep into her, and after the first sharp shock of his entry her body settled around him, responding to his deep, fierce thrusts, and the orgasm she had come so close to having when his mouth had been exploring her built into something wild and unstoppable.

She cried out and he placed a hand gently over her mouth, lifting his hand and grinning, then kissing her and coming as his mouth was still on hers, tasting her as his big body shuddered.

Spent, he backtracked and registered what she had confessed earlier.

'You're a virgin.' He eased himself off her and

flopped onto his side then immediately propped himself on one elbow to stare at her.

And this was why he had stayed away. Not that he'd known that, but still, he'd known enough: had known that she wasn't tough like the women he dated; had known that she was one of life's romantics; had known that she was still in a vulnerable place. That she was a virgin took a stupid situation and threatened to turn it into a very messy one.

But, hell, the sex had been good.

A virgin. He'd never placed any value on that particular virtue at all but now he wanted to take her all over again, show her things she had never experienced before, teach her, make love to her with all the gentle command at his disposal.

None of it made sense but he couldn't fight the realisation. Since when had he become a he-man bore who got a chauvinistic kick out of bedding virgins? What next? Belting out a Tarzan yell and looking for a vine to swing on?

But he couldn't contain a deep sense of mystifying satisfaction.

'You should have told me.'

'I was going to. Does it matter?'

'What I don't understand is *why*?'

'I don't want to talk about this.' Milly rolled onto her back and stared up at the ceiling. This had been the most wonderful experience in her entire life. Nothing had prepared her for all the amazing sensations that had bombarded her entire body; nothing. And yet all he could take away from it was the fact that she hadn't told him that he was her first.

Lucas propped himself up, invading her space so that she was forced to look at him. 'I apologise if I wasn't up to your high standards,' she managed to choke out and his eyebrows shot up.

'What the heck's going through your head, Milly?'

'What do you think?' She drew in a deep breath and said what was on her mind. 'We've just made love, and I know that it's probably not a big deal for you, but the only thing you seem to care about is the fact that I've never done this before. Is it because you're... I know those women you dated...supermodels...'

'Don't *ever* run yourself down to me, Milly. Ever. That has nothing to do with...anything.' He sighed his frustration. Even the way she *looked* at things was different. Why the instant rush to denigrate herself? In so many areas she was the most outspoken, cheerful and upbeat woman he had ever met...and yet there was an insecurity there that was reflected in the wounded, accusing eyes looking at him.

He had a moment of disturbing tenderness that threw him for a few seconds and then he rationalised that it was because he didn't usually do this, didn't usually have cosy conversations with women after sex. But naturally Milly would want to have that conversation because this had been her first time and by nature she was confiding and talkative. Of course she wasn't going to keep quiet and uncomplaining when he rose from the bed to have a shower and check his emails.

'I expressed puzzlement that you were still a virgin because you're so damned hot, Milly.'

She allowed her hurt to dissipate a little. 'I'm not.'

'Are we going to waste time playing the "no, I'm not—oh yes, you are" game?' He brushed a lock of hair from her cheek and hardened at the thought of taking her again.

Milly was tempted to tell him that she quite liked the

idea of that game. 'I practically threw myself at you. Most men would take what was on offer even if they didn't fancy it.'

'I'm not most men and we seem to be coming back to the fishing for compliments game. I fancied you the minute I laid eyes on you at my ski lodge.'

'You did?' Now she *definitely* wanted to hear more.

'And now here we are, in bed together, and trust me—I enjoyed every second of the experience. In fact, if I didn't think you were sore, I would repeat it right now all over again...' He cupped her with his hand and her eyelids fluttered. 'Why me?'

'Sorry?' Milly dragged her addled brain into some sort of functioning order and frowned.

'You're hopelessly romantic...'

'Not *hopelessly*.'

'Romantic enough for me to wonder why you would choose your first experience to be with me, under these circumstances. I'm curious as to why you didn't sleep with the man you presumed you were going to marry but you were happy to hop in the sack with a guy you definitely won't be ending up with.'

'I haven't sat down and analysed it but...I guess, maybe, I just needed...'

'A tonic? A pick-me-up? And I happened to be the nearest suitable medication to hand? Wasn't the ex man enough to entice you into bed?'

'The ex didn't fancy me,' Milly said bluntly. 'So he didn't put much effort into trying.'

'And you didn't bother to try either.'

'I...' *I was never the sort of girl to make the first move.* Yet she had made the first move with Lucas, hadn't she? Was it because she'd had nothing to lose?

Or was it because she had never grasped the full meaning of lust until she'd met him?

'I suppose I was waiting for the big night.' In love with the thought of being in love, but she'd never fancied Robbie. Lucas had shown her that; lust and love were two separate things, miles apart. She stared at his lean, dark face for a few disorientated seconds. 'You're right. Stupidly romantic. This is real life. Maybe subconsciously that's what I wanted, to connect with real life…'

'A man could be hurt.'

'I can't picture you ever being hurt. I mean, so hurt that you wanted to cry.'

'Oh, Milly. The things you come out with. So, ironically, we're lovers for real but still on course for self-destruction…' He brushed his fingers over her nipple, which hardened in fast response. 'Shall we think about how we do that while we rediscover each other again…? Or maybe we'll have to do the thinking *after* the rediscovery has finished…because I guarantee you won't be thinking when we're making love…'

Lucas pushed himself away from his desk and restively strolled towards the bank of windows that overlooked the city. He was back in London, back in his towering office, back in the thick of it. This was his reality. The two-and-a-half weeks spent with his mother playing Romeo to Milly's Juliet had been a mirage, flimsy and insubstantial, easily blown away after a fortnight. Then, business as usual.

So what the heck had happened?

He raked fingers through his hair frustratedly and silently cursed himself for letting things get out of hand. It was a mess. They had returned to London, his mother none the wiser that their relationship, whilst it had become physical, was just a sham. Marriage was not on the cards. *Longevity* was not on the cards.

But that was nearly two months ago and now...

Entrenched. And in a place from which an exit had to be made. Accustomed as he was to making the most of a bad situation, Lucas decided that this was something from which a positive could be drawn. Perhaps it had been foolish to imagine that he could take Milly to Spain and, in the space of a mere week or two, manage to convince his very astute mother that their brief romance was drawing to its sad but inevitable close.

Wasn't it better this way? The relationship had lasted long enough for its demise to be more credible. They had got to know one another and unfortunately familiarity had bred contempt. His mother would not have witnessed the decline in their relations. It would be easy to report back that they were no longer an item. Disappointment all round, but that was life.

He prowled restlessly through his vast office. It was late. He was probably the last man standing in the office. Milly, now settled into her new apartment and her new job, was having an evening out with her new colleagues. A drink at some pub somewhere with a meal to follow.

What colleagues?

Lucas impatiently pushed away any line of pointless speculation. It was good that she was making lots of friends. So what if some of them were men? It was to be expected. She had smartened up her act when it came to her dress code. He had, she had told him more than once, given her confidence in the way she looked, in her body. She had had a ritual getting rid of most of her old clothes, which, much to his amusement, she had insisted in showing him piece by deplorable piece. He had never seen such a vast collection of shapeless items of clothing in one place in his life before. Then she had dragged him out shopping.

He gritted his teeth at the thought of some guy seeing her in some of the stuff they had bought together. The red dress with the plunging back; the tight black jeans; hell, some of the sexy underwear...

He only had himself to blame for the situation he now found himself in. He had known from the very beginning that she was vulnerable. He had known that she was the sort of romantic who got lost in house and garden magazines and gazed longingly into the windows of bridal shops. She had a strong nesting instinct and was a home-maker by nature. She had loved cooking for him and he, who had never allowed any woman the privilege of cosy home-cooked meals in his kitchens, had found himself trying out new recipes and working while she sat cross-legged next to him, watching rubbish on television.

Was it any wonder that she had fallen in love with him? Was it any wonder that she had risen to the futile challenge of trying to make him see that his teenage error of judgement was just a little something that 'true love' could overcome?

Before she had even told him, he had *known*. She wasn't good when it came to hiding things. She wore her heart on her sleeve, and he had seen it in her eyes but had chosen to ignore it because he enjoyed her company and the sex was better than brilliant.

But he wasn't going to marry her and just the thought of being the object of her love, just the memory of those hopeful, trusting, *adoring* eyes on him, filled him with a sense of claustrophobia.

Love was for fools. He had learnt that the tough way. She knew that and if she had chosen to ignore it, then, *hell*!

The long and short of it was that he had taken his eye off the ball...and now...

He made his mind up, grabbed his jacket and left the office before he had time for any weakness to seep in.

He, of course, had a key to the apartment. It *was* his, after all; why wouldn't he? On a couple of occasions, he had left work early and headed straight there, letting himself in and working until she returned.

In a short space of time, she had made inroads into the decor. The perfectly cool, bland apartment now bore just the sort of homey touches that should have warned him that she was settling into it, just as she was settling into him.

Pictures on the mantelpiece. Scraps of paper with handy recipe titbits pinned to the stainless steel American-style fridge-freezer with jokey magnets. Lots of flowers because, she told him, it had always been her grandmother's habit to fill the rooms with things from outside. Good Feng Shui, apparently. He had laughed and drily told her that he had lived quite happily without such touches in his own place. She had suggested some kind of water feature; he had firmly squashed that idea, but he suspected that its absence was only short lived.

He had to wait for over an hour and a half before he heard the turn of the key in the door and, in that hour and a half, his mind had been everywhere but on work. For once, the joys of deal making had failed in its duty to distract him.

'Where've you been?' was his opening question as

she entered the sitting room and Milly started, then smiled as her breathing returned to normal.

He had been on her mind all evening. So she had told him, just blurted it out; she hadn't been able to help herself. She had fallen in love with him and it had been just too big a deal for her to keep inside. She didn't even know when the process had begun. Maybe the seeds had been sown in Spain, when she had glimpsed sides of him that were so curiously appealing. Certainly, she now knew that her fate had been sealed by the time they had fallen into bed together that first time and she had sunk deeper and deeper the longer she had spent with him.

It was crazy, she had known that, but love was crazy, wasn't it? It wasn't something you could explain on a sheet of A4 paper, like a maths problem with a solution. If love made sense, she would never have fallen in love with Lucas. But she had. And, the minute she had told him, she had wished that she could yank the words back into her mouth and swallow them down. He had gone perfectly still, hadn't replied, and when he *had* spoken it was as though he had chosen to ignore what she had said.

And his eyes were grave now as she tentatively walked towards him.

'We need to talk.'

'Why?' Milly smiled quickly. 'You always tell me that there are far better things to do than talk.'

'But, first, where have you been?' That question hadn't been on the agenda.

'I told you, Lucas, that I was going out with some people from work.'

Lucas scowled and tried not to let his imagination run away with thoughts of who those people were. She looked bloody amazing. Just the right side of tousled, her red hair trailing down her back, her tight jeans showing off every succulent inch of her body, as did the clingy long-sleeved top. The fact that she was wearing a pair of flat sneakers did nothing to detract from the look and he angrily felt himself harden in automatic response.

He dismissively waved aside her explanation just in case she thought that a detour down that road was going to happen.

'What's going on, Lucas?' As if she didn't know. One sign of love and he was getting ready to bolt. Things were just fine as long as they were having sex. The charade was well in place then! But she had crossed a line; she had forgotten what he had told her about not getting involved and had committed the mortal sin of not only disobeying the edict, but of telling him that she had.

'I think you know. And sit down; stop hovering.'

'I'm not sorry I said what I said,' Milly imparted with just the sort of driven honesty that he felt had landed them in this mess. 'And I never said that I was asking you to love me back.' *But she was.*

'This is no longer a working proposition.' He was somehow angry and bewildered as to how it was that these seemed to be the hardest words ever to have left his mouth. He had known that it was going to end sooner or later. So why did each syllable feel like broken glass? Maybe it was because he hadn't been the one to determine the timing of the end. He had been pushed into it because unforeseen circumstances had forced his hand. That made sense. He, of all men, did not like having his hand forced.

Milly opened her mouth but nothing emerged. She stared at him, wide-eyed, not daring to speak in case she started doing something really humiliating…like pleading and begging. Because, for the life of her, she couldn't envisage life without him.

Stupid Robbie and her broken engagement had been a walk in the park in comparison. This was the real thing. This was love, and hearing him tell her that their relationship was over was like staring down the barrel of a gun and waiting for the trigger to be pulled.

Did she regret her honesty? No. Was she going to compound her horror and dismay by really pushing the boat out and bursting into tears? Absolutely not!

'I get it,' she told him quietly. 'And I agree.'

CHAPTER TEN

A WEEK AND a half later, Milly could still scarcely believe that she had shown such fortitude in the face of the groundswell of misery that had been gathering at her feet.

So she had hung on to her pride, but at what cost? He was on her mind twenty-four-seven. She thought of him when she was working, when she was relaxing, and she dreamed of him when she was asleep.

He hadn't argued with her when she had conceded defeat. He had wanted out and she hadn't fought to bar him from the exit he was desperate to take. But he had been as quick to rush through the open door as she might have expected. He had continued the conversation: had told her in a cool, detached voice that he had never been in it for the long term; that he had warned her that commitment was off limits for him; that she should have known that after everything he had told her. His voice had been thick with accusation.

She had agreed with him.

'Off the cards and especially with someone like me,' she had obliged him by pointing out. All the time, her heart had been beating so hard and so fast that her breathing was short and raspy.

'With anyone. I'm not interested in a long-term relationship and I should never have allowed myself to be swept into something with a woman who was vulnerable and in search of a life partner.'

'I may have been vulnerable but I was *not* in search of a life partner! And I may have fallen in love with you, but has it occurred to you that I'm not as ditzy as you think I am? Has it occurred to you that I *know* we're not suited?'

Of course it hadn't occurred to him.

'We're different people from different backgrounds,' she had persisted. 'And that might not make a difference, but we're also like oil and water. You're darkness to my light. I'm not suspicious and distrusting of everyone; I like giving people chances. And I know you think I'm naive and stupid because I should have learned from Robbie and what happened but maybe, just maybe, that makes me a happier person than you, Lucas! You had one crappy experience and you've let it dictate the rest of your life! How does that make sense?'

'So you're prepared to carry on as we are with no expectations?' he had mocked. 'You're fine if I tell you that I'm more than happy to take you to my bed but that's all there is to it?'

Naturally she wouldn't have been fine with that and her brief hesitation had given him all the answer he had needed.

But what if she *had* agreed? What if she had buried her feelings under the sort of hard veneer that he would have been able to deal with? What if she had taken up his proposition and shut away the side of her that had wanted more, that would always want more? Would that have been a better decision than the one she had made? She wouldn't have spent the past week and a half thinking about him whilst staring at the walls of his apartment and thinking that she would have to move out sooner rather than later.

She almost, but didn't quite, regretted that she hadn't thrown his stupid job and his stupid free apartment right back in his face but common sense had thankfully kicked in because she would have been in an even worse position than she was now. She would have been hurting emotionally, and positively haemorrhaging financially, because a cursory glimpse at the ads for jobs in the catering industry had told her that there were no jobs to speak of. She would have been on the first train back to her grandmother, and there would have been no jobs there either, so she would have ended up doing something and nothing just to make ends meet.

It had left a sour taste in her mouth because the last thing she had wanted to do was to accept the terms and conditions of the proposal that had so roundly backfired in her face. But sometimes pride just had to take a back seat, and she was very glad that it had, because she loved her job and loved living in the heart of London, such a far cry from her former digs.

Her friends had all been mightily impressed as well, although she had omitted to tell them the details of how she had landed up where she had.

She had simply said that she had been lucky enough to have found herself in the company of a guy who had felt sorry enough for her to have lent her a helping hand. It was bad luck to have found herself at the ski chalet without the job she had anticipated, but it had been extremely good luck to have found herself there in the company of the guy who actually owned the ski chalet, along with a whole load of other stuff; a guy who had heard her unfortunate story and had been kind enough to lend a helping hand.

Ha. She had nearly choked when she had expanded on his *kindness*. She had turned him into a benevolent, avuncular, father-figure type, which couldn't have been further from the truth!

If they had been a little curious as to why she had suddenly decided to become the stay-at-home type who no longer needed to talk incessantly about her misfortunes, they had not said anything, and she knew they figured that she was just experiencing the aftershocks of what had happened with Robbie.

In time, she would confess all, but right now she needed time out from...*everyone.*

She had just showered and climbed into a pair of baggy joggers and an even baggier T-shirt—because she had lost the desire to wear tight and sexy clothes now that she was back to being on her own—when she heard the ring of the doorbell, and she froze, because there could be only one person who would ring that doorbell, having got past Eddy, the porter who manned the desk downstairs.

Lucas.

He had a key to the apartment, which made sense bearing in mind it belonged to him, but he always used the doorbell, only letting himself in if he knew that she wasn't going to be in.

Her mouth went dry and she gulped in deep breaths because the thought of seeing him again filled her with pleasure and trepidation at the same time.

In the length of time it took her to traverse the wooden floor from sitting room to door, she had dissected, dismissed and re-dissected a hundred possible reasons for this unexpected visit.

In the starring role on her wish list was the tiny ray of hope that he had miraculously decided that they were suited after all, that he had made a terrible mistake. Or even, she was ashamed to concede, that he had missed her and would she climb back into bed with him? She would say no, she was pretty sure of that, but it would do her a power of good just to think that he, in some small way, missed her as much as she was desperately missing him.

Her heart was preparing to soar and she had to school her features into just the right level of indifference as she pulled open the door.

'My dear!'

'Antonia…' Milly forced a smile but she was taken aback to find his mother on the doorstep. She hadn't spoken to Antonia since the split, and she felt guilty now about that, because they had developed a strong bond in the short time they had been in each other's company. 'I…eh…have been meaning to get in touch with you…'

'You look a little peaky, my dear.'

'Please, come inside. I… What brings you to London? I didn't think that you would be okay to travel overseas…just yet. Can I offer you something? Tea or coffee?'

'I thought I might surprise my son with a visit,' Antonia confided. 'And a cup of coffee would be lovely, my dear. Decaf, if you have it. Caffeine any time after six in the evening ruins my sleeping patterns.'

'That reminds me: well, I guess you've come… I would have called…' *To further compound your disappointment by filling in all the gaps Lucas might have left in the saga of why we had broken up? Added to the story of personality clashes, simmering rows and different hopes and dreams?*

'It's even nicer seeing you face to face, Milly, my

dear. I've missed having you there at the house. It felt rather empty and quiet after you and Lucas left. Of course, I was in tremendous spirits, but nevertheless... How quickly we become accustomed to having pleasant company around us.'

Milly could feel her face getting redder and redder and her body hotter and hotter.

'Well, you look amazing,' she said truthfully, *even though the tremendous spirits may have taken a recent battering.*

'I feel it. I guess I'm just buoyed up by Lucas's turnaround.'

'His turnaround...?'

'Finally coming to his senses and seeing the value of settling down.'

For a confusing few seconds, Milly was appalled at the question that had instantly sprung into her head: *Who* was he planning to settle down with? How fast could one man move when it came to women?

'So—and I know I'm being an interfering old witch here—but I came over so that I could sit you both down together and find out when I can start looking forward to the big day...'

'*The big day,* Lucas...and I'm quoting here. So *what* in heck's name is going on?'

Milly had finally managed to get hold of Lucas, who was personally protected from hassle with anyone he might not wish to talk to by an army of people in charge of security checks. She actually had his direct line but, the second she had been redirected, she had had to engage in the usual barrage of questions from his guard dogs.

She was in a filthy temper by the time she actually

heard his dark drawl at the other end of the line, which was possibly why her stomach didn't instantly go into nervous knots.

For the first time since he had walked out, Lucas felt alive at the sound of her voice and that, in itself, was bloody infuriating.

'I have no idea what you're going on about, Milly. You can't commence a conversation in mid-sentence and expect me to instantly be clued up.'

'You *know* what I'm talking about! Guess who I just had a visit from?'

'Can't think. No time for guessing games.'

'Your *mother*!'

Lucas sat up and digested this piece of information. 'My mother...' he said slowly.

'Strangely,' Milly all but shrieked down the end of the line, 'she seems to be under the impression that we're still an item!'

'Where are you?'

'Where do you think I am, Lucas?'

'How would I know?' he answered with silky smoothness. 'It's after seven on a Friday evening and you're a single woman...'

'I'm at home.' How could he think that she would physically be able to go clubbing when she was in love with him? Or was he just judging her the way he judged himself? He would have no problem doing that. If he possessed a heart instead of a lump of cold where a heart should be...

'I'm on my way.'

Milly fought the temptation to get a little more dolled up than she was. Maybe swop the baggy jogging bottoms, which she knew he loathed, for something a little more attractive. He could take her as he found her, she decided. He could explain why his mother was still in the dark and then he could be on his way.

She was as cool as a cucumber until the doorbell went half an hour later and there he was. All dark, tall and broodingly, sinfully gorgeous. Just the right side of dishevelled with the sleeves of his white shirt rolled to the elbows and his jacket slung over one shoulder. A sight for sore eyes and she just wanted to stand there and stare.

'So...' She pulled open the door and stepped away from him, not trusting herself. 'Mind explaining...?'

Lucas couldn't peel his eyes away from her. She was wearing just the sort of outfit he had always teased that she needed to wean herself away from. It hid every delectable curve, and yet she was still so enticing, still so damned *sexy*.

He'd missed her. It was as simple as that. He hadn't been able to focus, had lost interest in deals that should have netted all of his undivided attention, could not even be bothered to rifle through his little black book for other women. And he had told his mother nothing because...

'I need a drink. Something stronger than a cup of tea.'

'You *need a drink*? This isn't a social call, Lucas.' Milly finally looked at him and her treacherous eyes skittered away. She clasped her arms around her body, hugging herself.

'No. It's not.' He headed straight for the kitchen, directly to the cupboard where he knew she kept a practically full bottle of whisky, and he poured himself a hefty glass, keenly aware that she had padded in behind him. He imagined her arms were still folded and her full mouth would be pursed in a moue of frustration.

She loved him. She *had* loved him. Did she still?

'I intended to tell her...'

'But somehow you didn't manage to get round to it? Even though you speak to her every other day? That titbit just managed to *get lost* amidst the chit chat?'

'No.'

'Okay...' She looked at him hesitantly, picking up vibes which, for once, he wasn't bothering to hide. He had sat down at the kitchen table and was nursing his drink, not looking at her—again, a little weird, because it smacked of the sort of indecision not associated with him. She felt in need of a stiff drink as well but instead made do with a glass of juice from the fridge before sitting opposite him at the chrome-and-glass table.

'I could have told her but...I needed time.'

'Time for what?'

'Time to come to terms with the fact that we were really no longer an item.' He looked at her with serious intent and swallowed a mouthful of the whisky, not taking his eyes from her flushed face. 'I thought...when you told me that you loved me...'

'I don't want to go there.'

'We don't have a choice.'

'We do!' she cried. 'I said what I said and there's no point going over it!'

'I've never believed in love.'

'I told you—I get that.'

'You don't. You don't because, as you said, I let one crappy experience dictate my future where you, my optimistic Milly, would never have allowed that to happen. So, no, you didn't understand. Not really.'

He shot her a crooked, hesitant smile.

'Do you know that you were the first person I ever told about Betina and my youthful error of judgement?

And I knew that every time you raised the subject, which was often, you were trying to come to terms with the way I thought, because it was so unlike the way *you* would think. I should have been enraged at having that one confidence thrown back in my face time and again. I wasn't.'

He looked at his glass, circled the rim with his finger.

'We're all creatures of habit to some extent. My habit lay in the way I thought, the way I conditioned myself to think. For me, marriage would be about something that made sense because love made no sense. My head told me that you made no sense. You were just so damned young, you wore your heart on your sleeve, you were looking for the same happy-ever-after ending my mother believed in—the same happy ever ending I had no time for. I had built my box and I had no intention of stepping out of it, even though I knew you wanted me to. Am I losing you?'

He shot her the ghost of a fleeting smile that made her world tilt on its axis.

'I'm following you and you're right—I didn't understand, not really. Plus I was, well, I've never been that secure about my looks and I was…'

'Jealous?'

'No. Yes. Maybe.'

'Just maybe? Because I've been eaten up with jealousy thinking about all those men you might have been seeing behind my back in the last week or two.'

Milly's heart soared. She wondered whether she was hearing correctly. She half-leaned forward just in case she missed something and that devastating smile broadened as he read her mind.

'You can't let go, and I'm sorry about that, but…but you don't have to explain.'

'I do, my Milly, because I find that I let go a long time ago. I never realised it because I was just waiting in a holding bay for the right woman to come along and mess with my heart.'

The silence stretched between them. When she finally extended her hand along the table and he linked his fingers through hers, she experienced a rush of so many emotions, all vying for prominence, that she felt faint.

'I ran scared when you told me how you felt. I didn't know how to deal with it, Milly. And yet, I couldn't bring myself to tell my mother that it was over between us. I had the strangest feeling that if I said it out loud, if I vocalised it, then I would find myself in a place of no return. I couldn't face the thought of losing you but I didn't know how to make it right between us. My head was still waging war with my heart. The fact is, I love you. I was falling in love and I didn't even recognise the symptoms because I was so stubbornly and arrogantly convinced that I was immune.'

He absently played with her fingers in a way that was thrillingly intimate. 'You came into my life and you woke me up, Milly of the not-red hair, and my life is nothing without you in it.'

'And I love you,' Milly said with wrenching earnestness. 'I never loved Robbie, but you knew that, didn't you? When I think of what my life could have been if I hadn't found out the truth…' She shivered. 'I didn't want to fall in love with you either,' she admitted. 'I know you think I'm a hopeless romantic…'

'You are and I thank God for that.'

'But I still knew that you weren't a good bet and I was still fighting my own silly demons; still thought that you were just, well, that you'd never look at someone like me. Even though…' she dimpled at him '…you cured me of that.'

'Would you have felt that if I had continued being a harmless ski instructor?'

'You're never harmless and why, out of interest, didn't you tell me your true identity from the start?'

'It was liberating. You had landed there, like someone from a different planet, no airs, no graces and no knowledge of just how wealthy I was. You fascinated me from the very first moment I met you. And now, here we are. You are the love of my life, Milly, and I can't imagine life without you in it.'

'Okay.'

Lucas laughed. 'Is that all you have to say? When you're usually a woman of so many words?'

Milly grinned. 'I'm full of surprises.'

'And I want to be the one to find them all out, every day, for the rest of my life. Will you marry me? I'm asking that on behalf of both me and my mother…'

Milly laughed and rose, moving to sit on his lap so that she could feel his arms around her, holding her close, never letting her go.

'In that case, since you've brought your mother into the equation, what can a girl do but accept?'

* * * * *

A PRICE WORTH PAYING?

TRISH MOREY

CHAPTER ONE

FELIPE WAS DYING. Six months to live. Maybe twelve at a stretch.

Dying!

Simone swiped away a tear from her cheek, stumbling a little as she ran between the rows of vines clinging to the mountainside. Her grandfather would hate it if he knew she was crying over him. 'I am old,' he'd said, when finally he'd let her learn the truth, 'I've had my time. I have few regrets…' But then his eyes had misted over and she'd seen the enormity of those 'few' regrets swirling in their watery depths.

The sorrow at losing his wife of fifty years to her battle with cancer.

The despair when his recently reconciled daughter and her husband—*Simone's parents*—were lost in a joy flight crash whilst holidaying not three months later.

And the shame of succumbing to drink and then to the cards in the depths of his resultant depression, gambling away three-quarters of the estate before he was discovered and dragged bodily from the table by a friend before he could lose his own home.

It was the regret that was killing him. Oh yes, there was cancer too—that was doing its worst to eat away at his bones and shorten his life—but it was the regret that was sucking away his will to fight his disease and give in to it instead; regret that was telling him that there was no point because he had nothing left to live for.

And nothing anybody could say or do seemed to make a difference. Not when every time he looked out of his window he saw the vines that were no longer his, and he was reminded all over again of all that he had lost.

She stopped at the edge of the estate, where the recently erected fence marked the new border between her grandfather's remaining property and the neighbouring Esquivel estate. Here, where there was a break between the rows of vines staked and trellised high above her head, she could look down over the spectacular coastline of northern Spain. Below her the town of Getaria nestled behind a rocky headland that jutted out into the Bay of Biscay. Beyond that the sea swelled in brilliant shades of blue that changed with the wind and with the sun, a view so unlike what she had at home in Australia that it took her breath away every time she looked at it.

She inhaled deeply of the salt-tinged air, the scene of terraced hills, the tiered vines, the ancient town below all too picture perfect to be real. It wouldn't seem real when she was back home in Melbourne and living again in one of the cheap, outer-city student flats she was used to. But Melbourne and her deferred university studies would have to wait a bit longer. She'd come expecting to stay just a few weeks between semesters. Then Felipe had fallen ill and she'd promised to stay until he was back on his feet. But after this latest news, it was clear she wasn't returning home any time soon. Because there was no way she could leave him now.

Dying.

Hadn't there been enough death lately without losing Felipe too? She was only just getting to know him properly—the long-term rift between him and his daughter keeping the families apart ever since she was a child, Felipe and his wife here in Spain, their wayward daughter, her forbidden lover and their granddaughter living in self-imposed exile in Australia.

All those wasted years, only to be reunited now, when mere months remained.

How could she make those last few months better for Felipe? How to ease the pain of all he had lost? She shook her head, searching for answers as she gazed across the fence at the acres of vines that were once his and that now belonged to others, sensing the enormity of his loss, his guilt, his shame, and wishing there was some way she could make things better.

For there was no way to bring back his wife or his daughter and son-in-law.

There was no money to buy back the acreage he had lost.

And given the long-running rivalry between the two neighbouring families, there was no way the Esquivels were going to hand it back when they had seized such a powerful advantage.

Which left her with only one crazy option.

So crazy there was no way it could ever work.

But was she crazy enough to try?

'You sacked her!' Alesander Manuel Esquivel forgot all about the coffee he was about to pour and glared incredulously at his mother, who stood there with her

hands folded meekly in front of her looking as cool
and unflurried in the face of his outburst as a quintes-
sential Mother Superior. Her composure only served
to feed his outrage. 'What the hell gave you the right
to sack Bianca?'

'You were gone the entire month,' Isobel Esquivel
countered coolly, 'and you knew what a dreadful
housekeeper she was before you left. This apartment
was a pigsty. Of course I took the opportunity to sack
her and engage a professional cleaner while you were
gone. And just look around you,' she said with a flourish of her diamond-encrusted fingers around the now
spotless room. 'I don't know how you can possibly be
so irritated.'

His mother thought him irritated? Now there was
an understatement. After a fifteen-hour flight from
California, he'd been looking forward to the simple
pleasure of a hot shower before tumbling into bed and
tumbling a willing woman beneath him in the process.
He suppressed a growl. During her brief tenure, Bianca had proven to be particularly willing.

Finding his mother waiting for him in Bianca's
place had not been part of his plans. And so he dredged
up a smile to go with the words he knew would irritate his mother right back. 'You know as well as I do,
Madre *querida*, that I didn't employ Bianca for her
cleaning skills.'

His mother sighed distastefully, turning her face
towards the view afforded by the large glass windows
that overlooked the Bahia de la Concha, the stunning
bay that made San Sebastian famous. 'You don't have
to be crude, Alesander,' she said wearily, her back to
her son. 'I understand very well why you "*employed*"

her. The point is, the longer she was here, the less interested you were in finding a wife.'

'Oh, I assumed finding me a wife was your job.'

Her head snapped back around as the seemingly cool façade cracked. 'This is not a joke, Alesander! You need to face up to your responsibilities. The Esquivel name goes back centuries. Do you intend to let it die out because you are too busy entertaining yourself with the latest *puta-del-dia*?'

'I'm thirty-two years old, Madre. I think my breeding potential might be good for another few years yet.'

'Perhaps, but don't expect Ezmerelda de la Silva to wait for ever.'

'Of course I would expect no such thing. That would be completely unreasonable.'

'It would,' his mother said speculatively, her eyes narrowing, but nowhere near enough to hide the hopeful sheen that glazed their surface. She took a tentative step closer to her son. 'Do you mean to say you've come to your senses while you've been away and decided to settle down at last?' She gave a tinkling little laugh, the sound so false it all but rattled against the windows. 'Oh, Alesander, you might have said.'

'I mean,' he said, his lips curling at his mother's pointless hopes, 'there is no *point* in Ezmerelda waiting a moment longer when there is no way on this earth that I'm marrying her.'

His mother's expression grew tight and hard as she crossed her arms and turned pointedly back towards the window. 'You know our families have had an understanding ever since you were both children. Ezmerelda is the obvious choice for you.'

'Your choice, not mine!' He would sooner choose a shark for a wife than the likes of Ezmerelda de la Silva.

She was a beauty, it was true, and once in his distant past he had been tempted, but he had soon learned there was no warmth to her, no fire, indeed nothing behind the polished façade, nothing but a cold fish who had been raised with the sole imperative to marry well.

Whether married or not, he would settle for nothing less than a hot-blooded woman to share his bed. Was it any wonder he had populated his bed with nothing less?

'So what about grandchildren then?' Isobel pleaded, changing tack, her hand flat over her heart. 'If you won't consider marrying for the sake of the family name, what about for my sake? When will you give me grandchildren of my own?'

It was Alesander's turn to laugh. 'You overplay your hand, Madre. I seem to recall you don't like children all that much. At least, that's how I remember it.'

The older woman sniffed. 'You were raised to be the best,' she said without a hint of remorse. 'You were raised to be strong.'

'Then is it any wonder I wish to make my own decisions?'

His mother suddenly looked so tightly wound he thought she might snap. 'You cannot play this game forever, Alesander, no matter how much you seem to enjoy it. Next week it is Markel de la Silva's sixtieth birthday celebration. Ezmerelda's mother and I were hoping that you might accompany Ezmerelda to the party. Couldn't you at least honour the friendship between our families by doing that much?'

To what end? To have the news of their 'surprise' betrothal announced the same night as some bizarre kind of birthday treat? He wouldn't be surprised. His mother was particularly fond of concocting such treats.

She would love to put him on the spot and force the issue.

'How unfortunate. I do believe I'm busy that night.'

'You have to be there! It would be a deliberate snub to the family not to appear.'

He sighed, suddenly tired of the sport of baiting his mother. Because of course he would be there. Markel de la Silva was a good man; a man he respected greatly. It wasn't his fault his daughter took after her grasping mother.

'Of course I will be there. But what part of "there is no way I'm marrying Ezmerelda", did you not understand?'

'Yes, you say that now, but you know there is no one else suitable and sooner or later you will have to fulfil your destiny as sole heir to the Esquivel estate,' his mother said, giving up any pretence that securing a marriage between their two families wasn't her ultimate goal. 'When are you going to realise that?'

'I can't give you the answer you want but, rest assured, Madre, when I do decide to marry, you'll be the first to know.'

His mother left then, all bristling indignation and pursed lips in a perfumed, perfectly coiffed package, her perfume lingering on the air along with his irritation long after she'd gone. He stared out of the same window Isobel had blindly stared out of a short time ago, but the view didn't escape him. Between the mountains Igueldo and Urgull, with its huge statue of Christ looking down and blessing the city, sprouted the wooded Isla de Santa Clara, forming a magnificent backdrop to the finest city beach in Europe.

He'd bought this apartment some years ago sight unseen after yet another argument with his mother. At the time he'd simply wanted a bolt-hole away from the family estate in Getaria, a twenty-minute drive away.

He'd got more than a bolt-hole as it turned out. He'd got the best view in the city. Today the white sandy curve of the bay was less crowded than it had been when he had left a month ago at the height of summer, most tourists content in September's milder weather to promenade around the Concha rather than swim in its protected waters.

His gaze focused in on the beach, the insistent ache in his groin returning. Bianca used to spend her days on the sand, working on her tan. To good effect, if he remembered correctly, even if his mother couldn't see the advantages of long tanned limbs over a spotless floor.

He scanned the beach. Maybe Bianca was down there right now. He pulled his phone from his pocket and searched for her number. Isobel must have paid her extremely well for her to keep the news of her sudden eviction from him. But if she was still in the area…

Halfway to calling he paused, before repocketing the phone. What was he doing? It was one thing to have her waiting here for him. It was another entirely to go searching for her. Did he really want to give her the wrong idea? After all, she'd been almost at her use-by date as it was.

Bianca had known that. He'd made it plain when she'd started that she'd be looking for another position inside three months. Which probably explained why she'd gone so quietly. Because she'd always known the position was temporary.

Still he growled his displeasure as he tugged at his tie and pushed himself away from the windows. Because on top of having to find himself a new live-in cleaner, it meant that tonight he'd just have to settle for a cold shower.

CHAPTER TWO

It wasn't just crazy. It was insane.

Simone stood with her back to the bay and looked up at the building where Alesander Esquivel lived and felt cold chills up her spine despite the warm autumn sun. His apartment would have to be on the top floor, of course, and so far above her she wondered that she dared to think he would lower himself long enough to even let her in, let alone seriously consider her proposal.

And why should he, when it was the maddest idea she'd ever had? She'd get laughed out of San Sebastian, probably laughed out of Spain.

She almost turned and fled back along the Playa de la Concha to the bus station and her grandfather's house in Getaria and certain refuge.

Almost.

Except what other choice did she have? Getting laughed out of the city, the country, was better than doing nothing. Doing nothing would mean sitting back and watching her grandfather's life slide inexorably towards death, day by day.

Doing nothing was no choice at all. Not any longer.

How could she not even try?

She swallowed down air, the sea breeze that toyed

with the layers of her favourite skirt flavoured with garlic and tomatoes and frying fish from a bayside restaurant. Her stomach rumbled a protest. She could not stand here simply waiting to cross this busy road for ever. Soon she must return to her grandfather's simple house and prepare their evening meal. She had told him she needed to shop for the paella she had planned. He would be wondering why she was taking so long.

And suddenly the busy traffic parted and her legs were carrying her across the road, and the closer she got to the building, the larger and more imposing it looked, and the more fanciful her plan along with it.

She must be crazy.

It would never work.

He'd just stepped out of the shower when the buzzer to his apartment sounded. He growled as he lashed a towel around his hips, wondering what his mother had forgotten, but no, Isobel was not the sort to give advance warning, not since he'd once lent her the key she'd made a habit of forgetting to return.

So he chose to ignore it as he swiped up another towel to rub his hair. He did all his work at his city office or out at the Esquivel estate in Getaria. Nobody called on him here unless they were invited. And then the buzzer sounded again, longer this time, more insistent, clearly designed to get his attention.

And he stopped rubbing his hair and wondered. Had Bianca been waiting for his return, keeping a safe distance from his mother? She had known his travel plans. She'd known he was due back today.

Serendipity, he thought, because she could hardly read anything into one last night if she'd invited herself back. Why not enjoy one last night together for old time's sake? And tomorrow or the next day, for that matter, he could tell her that her services were no longer required.

'Bianca, *hola*,' he said into the intercom, feeling a kick of interest from beneath his towel and thinking it fortuitous he wouldn't have to waste any time getting undressed.

His greeting met with silence until, 'It's not Bianca,' someone said in faltering Spanish, her husky voice tripping over her words and making a mess of what she was trying to say. 'It's Simone Hamilton, Felipe Otxoa's granddaughter.'

He didn't respond for a moment, his mind trying to join the dots. Did he even know Felipe had a granddaughter? They might be neighbours but it wasn't as if they were friends. But no—he rubbed his brow— there was something he remembered—a daughter who had married an Australian—the one who had been killed in some kind of accident some months back. Was this their daughter, then? It could explain why she was murdering his language. 'What do you want?' he asked in English.

'Please, Señor Esquivel,' she said, and he could almost hear her sigh of relief as the words poured out, 'I need to speak to you. It's about Felipe.'

'What about Felipe?'

'Can I come up?'

'Not until you tell me what this is about. What's so important that you have to come to my apartment?'

'Felipe, he's… Well, he's dying.'

He blinked. He'd heard talk at the estate that the old man wasn't well. He wasn't unmoved but Felipe was old and he hadn't exactly been surprised at the news. He still didn't see what it had to do with him.

'I'm sorry to hear that, but what do you expect me to do about it?'

He heard noises around her, of a family back fresh from the beach, the children being scolded by their mother for tracking sand back to one of the lower apartments, a father, grunting and grumpy and wearying of his so-called holiday and probably already dreaming about a return to the office. She tried to say something then, her words drowned out by the racket before she sighed and spoke louder. 'Can I please come up and explain? It's a bit awkward trying to discuss it like this.'

'I'm still not sure what I can do for you.'

'Please. I won't stay long. But it's important.'

Maybe to her. As far as he was concerned, Felipe had been a cantankerous old man for as long as he could remember and, whatever the distant reason for the feud between their two families, Felipe had done nothing to build any bridges over the intervening decades. But then, neither had his father during his lifetime. In a way it was a shame he hadn't been alive the day some lucky gambler had knocked on Alesander's door and offered him the acres of vines he'd won from Felipe in a game of cards. His father had been trying to buy the old man out for years.

He raked his fingers through his hair. The vines. That must be why the granddaughter was here. Had Felipe sent this hesitant little mouse with some sob story to plead for their return? He would have known he'd get short shrift if he tried such a tactic himself.

Maybe he should let her in long enough to tell her exactly that. He glanced down at his towel. Although now was hardly the time. 'I'm not actually dressed for visitors. Call me at my office.'

'My grandfather is dying, Señor Esquivel,' she said before he cut the connection. 'Do you really think I care what you are wearing?' And the hesitant mouse with the husky drawl sounded as if she'd found a backbone, and suddenly his interest was piqued. Why not humour his neighbour's granddaughter with five minutes of his time? It wasn't as if it was going to cost him anything and it would give him a chance to see if the rest of her lived up to that husky voice.

'In that case,' he said, smiling to himself as he pressed the lift release, 'you'd better come right up.'

Simone's heart lurched as the lift door opened to the small lobby that marked the entrance to the top floor apartment, her mind still reeling with the unexpected success of making it this far, her senses still reeling from the sound of Alesander's voice. Her research might have turned up his address and told her that Alesander Esquivel was San Sebastian's most eligible bachelor, but it hadn't warned her about his richly accented voice, or the way it could curl down the phone line and bury itself deep into her senses.

Yet even with that potent distraction, she'd somehow managed to keep her nerve and win an audience with the only man who could help her right now.

Alesander Esquivel, good-looking heir to the Esquivel fortune, according to her research, but then how he looked or how big his fortune was irrelevant. She was far more interested in the fact he was unmarried.

Thirty-two years old, with no wife and no fiancée, and he'd agreed to see her.

She dragged in air. It was a good start. Now all she had to do was get him to listen long enough to consider her plan.

'Piece of cake,' she whispered to herself, in blatant

denial of the dampness of her palms as she swiped them on her skirt. And then there was nothing else for it but to press on the apartment's buzzer and try to smile.

A smile that was whisked away, along with the door, somewhere between two snowy towels, one hooked around his neck, stark white against his black hair and golden skin, the other one lashed low over his hips.

Dangerously low.

She swallowed.

Thought about leaving.

Thought about staying.

Thought about that towel and whether he was wearing anything underneath it and immediately wished she hadn't.

'Simone Hamilton, I presume,' he said, and his delicious Spanish accent turned her name into a caress. She blinked and forced her eyes higher, up past that tightly ridged belly and sculpted chest, forcing them not to linger when it was all they craved to do. 'It is a pleasure to meet you.'

His dark eyes were smiling down at her, the lips on his wide mouth turned up at the corners, while the full force of the accent that had curled so evocatively down the telephone line to her now seemed to stroke the very skin under her clothes. She shivered a little as her breasts firmed, her nipples peaking inside her thin bra and, for the first time in a long time, her thoughts turned full-frontal to sex, her mind suddenly filled with images of tangled limbs and a pillow-strewn bed and this man somewhere in the midst of it all—minus the towels…

And the pictures were so vivid and powerful that she forgot all about congratulating herself for making it this far. 'I'm disturbing you,' she managed to whisper. *I'm disturbed.* 'I should come back.'

'I warned you I wasn't dressed for visitors.' He let that sink in for just a moment. 'You said you didn't care what I was wearing.'

She nodded weakly. She did recall saying something like that. But never for one moment had she imagined he'd be wearing nothing more than a towel. She swallowed. 'But you're not... I mean... Maybe another time.'

His smile widened and her discomfort level ratcheted up with every tweak of his lips. He was enjoying himself. At her expense. 'You said it was important. Something about Felipe?'

She blinked up at him and remembered why she was here. Remembered what she was about to propose and all the reasons it would never work. Added new reasons to the list—because the pictures she'd found hadn't done him justice—he wasn't just another good—looking man with a nice body, he was a veritable god-and because men who looked like gods married super-models and heiresses and princesses and not women who rocked up on their doorstep asking for favours.

And because nobody in their right mind would ever believe a man like him would hook up with a woman like her.

Oh God, what was she even doing here?

'I'm sorry,' she said, shaking her head. 'Coming here was a mistake.' She was halfway to turning but he had hold of her forearm and, before she knew it, she was propelled inside his apartment with the promise of fresh coffee on his lips and the door closed firmly behind her.

'Sit down,' he ordered, gesturing towards a leather sofa twice the length of her flat at home and yet dwarfed here by the sheer dimensions of the long, high-ceilinged room that seemed to let the whole of the bay in through one expansive wall of glass. 'Maybe now you could tell me what this is all about.'

She sat obediently, absently rubbing her arm where he'd touched her, the skin still tingling as if his touch had set nerve endings dancing under her skin. But then, why wouldn't she be nervy when she didn't know which way to look to avoid staring at his masculine perfection; when every time her eyes did stray too close to his toned, bronzed body, they wanted to lock and hold and drink him in?

How could she even start to explain when she didn't know where to look and when her tongue seemed suddenly twice its size?

'All right,' she said, 'if you insist. But I'll give you a minute to get dressed first.'

'No rush,' he said, dashing her hopes of any relief while he poured coffee from a freshly brewed jug. He didn't ask her how she wanted it or even if she wanted it, simply stirred in sugar and milk and handed it to her. She took it, careful to fix her gaze on the cup, equally careful to avoid brushing her fingers with his and all the while wondering why she'd ever been crazy enough to think this might work. 'So tell me, what's wrong with Felipe?' he asked, reminding her again of the reason why she was here, and she wondered at his ability to make her forget what should be foremost in her mind.

Giving Felipe a reason to smile.

She'd made it this far. She owed it to Felipe to follow through. She'd return to Melbourne one day after all. The humiliation wouldn't last for ever...

So much for wondering if she matched her husky voice. Instead she looked like a waif, he thought, lost and lonely, her grey-blue eyes too big and her mouth almost too wide for her thin heart-shaped face, while her cotton shirt bagged around her lean frame. She stared blankly at the cup in her hands, whatever fight she'd called upon to secure this interview seemingly gone. She looked tiny against the sofa. Exactly like that mouse he'd imagined her to be when she'd first spoken so hesitantly on the phone.

'You said he was dying,' he prompted. And suddenly her chin kicked up and she found that husky note that had captured his interest earlier.

'The doctor said he has six months to live. Maybe twelve.' Her voice cracked a little on the twelve and she put the cup in her hands down before she recovered enough to continue, 'I don't think he'll last that long.'

She pushed honey-blonde hair that had fallen free from her ponytail behind her ears before she looked up at him, her eyes glassy and hollow. 'I'm sorry,' she said, swiping a rogue tear from her cheek. 'I've made a complete mess of this. You didn't need this.'

He didn't, but that didn't mean he wasn't a little bit curious about why she thought it so necessary to knock on his door to ask for his help. He had his suspicions, of course—but he had to admit that the whole granddaughter turning up on his doorstep to plead her case was unexpected. 'Why do you think Felipe won't last that long?'

She shrugged almost impatiently, as if the reason was blindingly obvious and there was nothing else it could be. 'Because he's given up. He thinks he de-serves to die.'

'Because of the land?'

'Of course, because of the land! It's about losing his wife and daughter too, but don't you see, losing the land on top of everything else is killing him faster than any disease.'

'I knew it.' He padded barefoot to the window, strangely disappointed, regretting the impulse to let her in, and not only because his curiosity about Feli-pe's long lost granddaughter with the husky drawl had been satisfied with one look at this skinny, big-eyed waif. But because he'd been right. Of course it had to be about the land. And yet for some reason being right gave him no pleasure.

Maybe because he knew what would come next, and that any moment now she'd be asking for the favour she'd obviously come here to ask—for him to either return the land out of the goodness of his heart, or to lend her the money to buy it back.

He should never have let her in. Felipe should never have sent her. What had the old man been thinking, to send her to plead his case? Had he been hoping he'd feel sorry for her and agree to whatever she asked? A coiling anger unfurled inside him that anyone, let alone his father's old nemesis, would think him so easily manipulated.

'So that's why he sent you, then? To ask for it back?'

Maybe his words sounded more like accusations than questions, maybe he sounded more combative than inquisitive, because she flinched, her face tight, her eyes clearly on the defensive. 'Felipe didn't send me. He doesn't even know I'm here.' She hesitated be-fore saying anything more, before she glanced at the watch on her slim wrist and looked up again, already gathering herself, her face suddenly resolute, as if she'd decided something. 'Look, maybe I should go—'

He stalled her preparations to leave with a shrivelling glare. 'You do realise it wasn't me who gambled the property out from underneath him, don't you? I bought it fair and square. And I paid a hefty premium for the privilege.'

'I know that.'

'Then surely you don't expect me to hand it calmly back, no matter how ill you say your grandfather is.'

Her blue eyes flashed icicles, her manner changing as swiftly as if someone had flicked a switch. 'Do you think I'm that stupid? I may be a stranger here, but Felipe has told me enough about the Esquivels to know that would never happen.'

He bristled at her emphasis on the word 'never'. It was true, Felipe and his father had had their differences in the past, and yes, the Esquivels took their business seriously, but that did not mean they did not act without honour. They were Basques after all. 'Then why did you come? Is it money you want?'

She gave a toss of her head, setting her ponytail lurching from side to side, the ends she'd poked behind her ears swinging free once more. 'I don't want your money. I don't care about your money.'

'So why are you here? What other reason could you possibly have for turning up on my doorstep demanding a private hearing?'

She stood up then, all five feet nothing of her, but with her dark eyes flashing, her jaw set in a flushed face and an attitude that spoke more of bottled rage than the meek little mouse who had turned up on his doorstep.

'All right. Since you really want to know, I came here to ask if you would marry me.'

CHAPTER THREE

'MARRY YOU?' HE didn't wait for her to say any more. He'd heard enough. He laughed out loud, the sound reverberating around the room. He'd known she'd wanted something—land or money—and she had wanted something, but a proposal of marriage had never been on his radar. 'You're seriously proposing marriage?'

'I know.' His visitor clenched and unclenched her hands by her sides, her eyes frosty and hard with anger, her features set as if she didn't hold it all together, she would explode. 'Crazy idea. Forget I said anything. Clearly I was wrong to think you might lift so much as a finger to help my grandfather. Sorry to bother you. I'll see myself out.'

She wheeled around, her skirt flaring high as she spun to reveal legs more shapely than he would have imagined she possessed before they marched her purposefully towards the door, her words rankling more with each stride. How dare she come out with a crazy proposal like that and then make out that he'd let her down?

He caught up with her as she pulled the door open, slamming it shut the next second with the flat of his hand over her shoulder. 'I don't remember you asking me to lift a finger.' She wasn't listening. Either that or she simply took no notice. She worked the handle frantically with both hands, her slim body straining as she pulled with all her might, while the door refused to budge so much as an inch with his weight to keep it closed.

'Let me out!'

He stayed right where he was, with the tiny fury beneath him working away on the door, bracing herself against the wall for leverage. 'On the other hand, I do recall you asking me to marry you.'

'It was a mistake,' she said, frantic and half breathless from her efforts.

'What, you mean you meant to ask someone else?'

She gave up on the handle, staring at the door as if willing it to disappear with the sheer force of her will. 'I thought you might help. Turns out I was wrong.'

'And so now you make out that I've somehow let you down? Because I'm honest and laugh when you suggest something as ridiculous as marrying you?'

'Ridiculous because you're such a catch, you mean? God, you're unbelievable! Do you actually believe I *want* to marry you?'

She gave the door a final kick and spun around and almost immediately wished she hadn't, suddenly confronted by the naked wall of his chest just inches from her face. Bronzed olive skin roughened with dark hair and two hard nipples jutting out at her. God, why the hell couldn't the man just put on some clothes? Because this close she could see his chest hair sway in the breeze from her breath. This close she could smell the lemon soap he'd used while bathing; could smell the clean scent of masculine skin.

And she really didn't need to know that she liked the combination.

'You tell me,' he answered roughly. 'You're the one doing the asking.'

He had her boxed in on two sides, one arm planted beside her head, the door at her back, with only one avenue of escape left to her. Tempting as it was, she got the distinct impression this man would love it if she tried to flee again. He would no doubt feed off the thrill. So she stayed exactly where she was and forced her eyes higher to meet his.

'A few months,' she said. 'I wasn't asking for forever. I'm not that much of a masochist.'

Something flickered in his eyes as he leaned dangerously down over her, and she wondered at the logic of throwing insults at the only man who could help her. Though that had been before he'd laughed her proposal down without even bothering to listen to her. Now there was obviously nothing to gain by being polite—and nothing to lose by telling him exactly how little she wanted this for herself. 'If there was any other way, believe me, I'd grab it with both hands.'

His dark eyes searched hers, his chin set, the tendons on his neck standing out in thick cords. 'What kind of game are you playing? Why are you really here?'

She might have told him if she thought he might actually listen. 'Look, there's no point going on with this. Let me go now and I promise never to darken your door again. Maybe there's even a slight chance we might forget this unfortunate event ever took place.'

'Forget a scrawny slip of a girl I've never met asking me to marry her? Forget a proposal of marriage that comes dressed in barbs and insults from a woman who, by her own admission, wishes there was some other way? I don't think I'm going to forget that in a hurry. Not when she hasn't even explained why.'

'Is there any point? I'd say you made your position crystal clear. Obviously there's no way you'd lower yourself to marry "a scrawny slip of a girl".'

Her eyes flashed cold fire as she spat his words back at him, anger mixed with hurt. She was smarting at his insult, he could tell, and maybe she had a point. Maybe she was more petite than scrawny, though it was hard to tell, her body buried under a chain-store cotton skirt and top that left everything to the imagination. But she was no mere girl. Because, from his vantage point above her he could see the slight swell of her breasts as her chest rose and fell. This close he could see her eyes were more blue than grey, the colour of early morning sky before the sun burned away the mist from the hillsides. And this close he could smell her scent, a mix of honey and sunshine and feminine awareness, the unmistakable scent of a woman who was turned on.

His body responded the only way it knew how, surprising him, because she was nothing like his usual type of woman and he wasn't interested. If he had been interested he would have known it the moment he'd opened the door and laid eyes on her, the way it usually worked.

And once again he regretted the sudden absence of Bianca. Clearly it had been too long if he was getting horny over any random big-eyed waif who turned up on his doorstep. He willed the growing stiffness away, his decision not to put any clothes on intended more to amuse himself rather than any attempt at seduction. And then his eyes drifted down again, lingering over the spot where the neckline gaped, exposing skin that looked like satin.

Admittedly a big-eyed waif with unexpected curves...

'Then again, maybe not so scrawny,' he said, unable to resist putting a hand to her shoulder in spite of the fact he wasn't really interested, his thumb testing the texture of her skin, finding it as smooth as his vision had promised.

She shivered under his touch, her blue eyes wide, her bottom lip trembling, right before she shot away sideways. 'Don't touch me!'

He turned, amused by his unexpected visitor and her propensity to move from flight to fight and back again in a heartbeat. 'What is this? You ask me to marry you and then say I can't touch? Surely you must have come prepared for an audition.'

She wrapped her arms tightly around her waist. 'No! There will be no audition! The marriage is for Felipe. Only for Felipe.' Outside the windows the light was starting to fade, the afternoon sun slipping away, while inside her cheeks were lit up, her eyes flashed cold blue flame and her hands were balled in fists so tight that, unlike the rest of her, her knuckles showed white. 'Haven't you got a robe or something?'

He smiled at the sudden change in topic, holding his arms out by his sides innocently. 'Do you have a problem with what I'm wearing?'

'That's just it. You're not really wearing anything.' She paused suddenly, biting her lip, almost as if she'd said too much and revealed too much of herself in the process. Then she hastily added, 'I'd hate for you to catch cold or something.'

As if that was her reason. His amusement was

growing by the minute, his visitor unexpectedly entertaining. It wasn't just because the idea was so crazy he wondered how this woman, who seemed more timid than tigress despite her attempts, had found the courage to carry it off, but maybe because his mother had been here not an hour ago berating him on his reluctance to find a wife. He half wished she'd been here to witness this. Though no doubt she would be more appalled than amused, but then, that thought only amused him even more.

'Then you will be relieved to know I have a very healthy constitution,' he said, 'but the last thing I wish is for you to feel uncomfortable.' He excused himself for a moment to pull on fresh clothes, though not so much for her comfort level but because it suited him to do so. He'd had his sport and the last thing he wanted was for her to think he was interested in her sexually. He was intrigued, it was true, and now that the shock of her surprise proposal was over, he was curious to hear more, but there was no point encouraging her.

She was still here. Simone let out a breath she hadn't realised she'd been holding and turned to gaze out of the windows over the million euro view. He hadn't thrown her out and neither had he let her flee. She was still here and he was going to cover himself up.

Surely that counted as success on two counts?

And now, for whatever reason, he actually seemed willing to listen to her.

Even better, maybe once he had covered up that chest and all that toned olive-gold skin, she might even be able to think straight. She could only hope. Being forced to look at all that masculine perfection without actually looking like she was looking at it was one hell of a distraction otherwise. When he'd had her backed against the door and touched his fingers to her shoulder, she'd felt the sizzle shoot straight to her core. Although maybe it was the hungry look in his eyes that had turned his touch electric…

God, what must it be like to be a woman who actually wanted him to touch her? She shivered, her body remembering the electric thrill. Dangerous, she thought, definitely dangerous. Thank God she wasn't going there.

'I apologise for keeping you waiting.'

His richly accented voice stroked its way down her spine, almost convincing her that he meant every word he said. She turned to find him dressed not in a robe, as she'd been half-expecting, but in light-coloured trousers and a fine knitted top that skimmed over the wall of his chest in a way she really didn't want to think too much about. So she pushed her wayward hair behind her ears and looked elsewhere and found his feet instead. 'Nice shoes,' she said lamely, for want of anything better to say.

He glanced down at his leather loafers. 'I have a man who makes them for me. He is very good.'

Handmade shoes, she pondered, really studying them this time, wishing she could hide away her own scuffed ballet flats. She'd known he had money, sure, but what was this world she'd dared enter, a world where he probably spent more on a pair of shoes than she had on her entire wardrobe? And it wasn't as if he wouldn't know that. It was a wonder he hadn't let her flee while he'd had the chance. It was a wonder he hadn't slammed the door in her face.

'But you didn't come here to compliment me on my footwear,' he prompted, gesturing towards a sofa as he sprawled himself into a wide armchair, 'I am curious to hear more—a marriage between you and me, but for Felipe? How does that work, exactly?'

She lowered herself down tentatively on the edge of the sofa, her heart racing with the possibilities. He wanted to hear more. Was he was simply curious, as he claimed, or was he actually entertaining her proposal? 'You really want to know? You won't laugh this time?'

'You took me by surprise,' he admitted with a shrug. 'It is not everyday a woman asks me to marry her while at the same time claiming she would rather be torn apart by wild horses or eaten by sharks.'

She pressed her lips together, not bothering to deny she'd used those words, knowing he was poking fun at her and yet thoroughly disconcerted by his smile. He was good-looking even when he was angry, the strong lines of his face too well put together to be distorted by rage, but when he smiled he was absolutely devastating. 'I'm sorry. It's not every day that I ask a man to marry me.'

He nodded. 'I'm flattered,' he said, sounding anything but. 'So tell me, what is this marriage all about? Why is it so necessary, you believe, to marry me? What are you trying to achieve?'

'I want to make Felipe's last days happy.'

'You think you will make him happy by marrying the son of a man he was in dispute with almost his entire life?'

'I believe it will make him happy to believe his vineyard is reunited.' And when she saw her words made no impact on him, she continued, more passionately, this time. 'Don't you see, those vines you bought were Felipe's life. And right now every time he looks out of his window he's reminded of his mistake.

Every time he looks out of his window, he's reminded of all that he lost.' She shook her head. 'And right now he doesn't care about the remaining vines. He doesn't care about anything.' She gazed up at him, wanting to make him understand. Desperate to make him understand. 'I know it sounds mad, but if he could see a marriage between our families, he would also see the vineyard reunited, and whatever mistakes he made— well, they wouldn't matter any more. He might smile again, if he realised that all was not lost.'

'And so Felipe dies happy.'

She winced at his words and he found himself wondering if she was acting. How could she care so much about a man who must be almost a stranger to her? 'It would only be for a few months. The doctors said—'

'You told me.' He stood suddenly and wandered to the windows, his back to her. 'Six to twelve months. But why should I believe what you say? It seems to me that you have the most to gain out of this arrangement. How do I know you won't try to get pregnant and find yet another reason to "reunite" our families, this time on a more permanent basis?'

He thought her capable of doing that? God, what kind of people was he used to dealing with? She gave a tight shake of her head, feeling sick at the thought of there being any chance a pregnancy would result from this union. 'There is no chance of that. This would be purely a business arrangement. Nothing more.'

'So you say, but how can I believe you?'

'Quite easily.' She looked at him levelly, her blue-grey eyes as cold as the deepest sea. 'There will be no pregnancy because there will be no sex.'

He looked back at her over his shoulder in surprise,

one eyebrow arched. 'No sex? You really think a marriage can work without sex?'

'Why not? It's not a real marriage so there's no need for sex. What I'm proposing is a marriage in name only. Besides, it's not as if we even like each other. We barely even know each other, for that matter. Why would we need or even want to have sex?'

He shrugged aside every one of her objections as irrelevant. He'd never actually considered whether he actually liked someone as a barrier to having sex with them. Then again, from what he could ascertain, his father hadn't slept with his mother for the last thirty years of their marriage, which proved marriage without sex between husband and wife was possible, even if his father hadn't gone without, by all accounts.

Which was probably a point worth making…

'If I agreed to this marriage,' he said, pausing when he noticed the sudden flare in her eyes and wanting to damp it down before she got too excited, 'that's *if* I agree, and I agreed to your condition of a marriage in name only, you do understand that there will be other women? That I would need to have sex with someone.'

Her lips tightened. Her entire posture tightened. 'I'm sure you have no shortage of friends and acquaintances who would be only too happy to accommodate your needs. I wouldn't stand in your way, so long as you were discreet, of course.'

He stroked his chin thoughtfully and her eyes were drawn again to the strong lines of his face, the dramatic planes and dark-as-night eyes and wished his features weren't anywhere near as well put together. 'Then possibly it might work,' he said, 'And possibly you are also right about not having sex. It's not as if you're my type, after all.'

'Fine!' she snapped, her eyes wide, her cheeks flaring with colour. 'So much the better!'

'*Bueno,*' he said, smiling at her snippy response because, for her all her eagerness to announce that she had no interest in having sex with him, it was clear she didn't want to hear the reasons why he might not be interested in having sex with her. 'So long as we understand each other. As you've mentioned, we don't know how long such a marriage might last. Several months. A year. You couldn't expect me to remain celibate for the duration.'

'I would hate you to have to suppress your natural desires, although perhaps you might try exercising just a little more control.'

'Why should I? I like sex.'

'I don't want to hear it! All I know is that if you agree to this, there will be no sex between us. So there will be no chance of a child. So there can be no "complications".'

He sighed as he turned back towards the window, the light fading from the sky, the lighting around the Bay coming on, turning the shoreline to gold. Perhaps she was right. Without sex there could be no unwanted pregnancy. No complications, just as she said. Which meant no chance for her to claim against the Esquivel estate.

And meanwhile this marriage would get his mother off his back into the deal.

He almost laughed. There would be no point in Ezmerelda continuing to wait for him to propose because he'd already be married. It was utterly delicious. He couldn't remember when he'd ever been tempted by such a crazy deal. But would anyone believe it? Would anyone actually believe that, of all the women in the world, he had chosen this particular one to marry? Because he hadn't been joking. She was nothing like his usual kind of woman. He preferred his woman more overtly sexual, whereas this woman looked like a waif in her baggy clothes.

And even though there was something about her cool blue eyes and her husky voice, and there was something of feminine shape hidden away that he'd caught a glimpse of, if he was to agree to anything, the terms would definitely need some work. He would need a bit more of an incentive if he was going to bother to make their arrangement look convincing.

'It's very noble of you, sacrificing yourself on the altar of marriage for your grandfather's benefit. But why should I go along with it? What would be in it for me, given you've ruled out sex?'

She blinked up at him and he could tell she was completely unprepared for the question. He wondered at her naivety. Did she imagine he would go along with this out of the goodness of his heart? 'Well,' she began, 'you do now have most of Felipe's vineyard.'

'I told you, I bought that land, fair and square. That land is mine already.'

'But you knew how he'd lost it. You took advantage of an old man's misfortune because it suited you.'

'If I hadn't bought it, someone else would have.'

'But *you're* the one who bought it and don't tell me you didn't jump at the chance. Felipe told me your father had been trying to get him off his land for decades.'

'And you think that my agreeing to this will ease my conscience over the fact a large chunk of his estate is now mine?' He shook his head. 'No, my conscience is clear. I don't have any trouble sleeping at night. In which case, you're offering me nothing. And if I'm going to agree to this, I need a real incentive.'

Her heart jumped in her chest. *'If I'm going to agree to this'?* Was he serious? Was she that close to getting him to agree to her crazy plan? She licked her lips. 'So what would it take to secure your agreement?' she asked tentatively, almost afraid to breathe as she waited for his response.

'Am I right in thinking Felipe will leave the balance of the estate to you, as his sole beneficiary?'

She blinked. 'Um, yes, he still has to see a lawyer to change his will, but he's mentioned that's what he wants to do.'

'Then that's my price. When Felipe dies and you inherit, I want you to agree that you'll sign over the rest of the estate to me.'

'All of it?'

'There's not a whole lot left—and you do want me to marry you, don't you, so Felipe believes his precious vines are reunited once more?'

'Of course I do.'

'Then, subject to your final agreement of my terms, I'd say that makes us officially engaged.'

CHAPTER FOUR

'WHAT'S IT TO BE, my prospective wife? You decide. Do we have a deal?'

Did they? Her heart was hammering so loud she could scarcely hear herself think. Half of her was already celebrating. She'd done the unthinkable and secured Alesander's agreement. Soon Felipe would see his precious vines reunited under the mantle of their marriage.

But after he was gone—after their marriage was dissolved—they would stay reunited. Alesander would own the entire estate.

He was waiting for her answer, his half-smile telling her that he was already anticipating her agreement.

Should she accept his terms?

Felipe had promised her what was left of the estate when he died, wanting the vines to stay in the family, wanting to ensure that she would be taken care of financially. After her spendthrift parents had left her with nothing but a few trinkets, it would have been all that she owned. And now, if she agreed to Alesander's terms, she'd be left with nothing again.

But what good were the vines to her anyway when her plan had always been to return to her studies in Melbourne? What point was there in her keeping them, other than as a link to a past and a life she'd been denied most of her life? She didn't belong here. Not really. She was no vigneron, whatever her heritage. She couldn't even speak the language. Not properly. 'All right,' she said, her voice little more than a whisper, knowing that ultimately she had no choice. 'You have a deal.'

'Good, I'll get my lawyers to draft up the agreement.'

'This can't get out! Felipe must not suspect.'

'You think I want it to become public knowledge? No, my legal people will not breathe a word of this. Nobody will know our marriage is not real.'

She nodded, feeling her shoulders sag and her very bones droop, suddenly bone-weary. She'd come here and achieved what she'd never thought she'd achieve— the impossible had happened and Alesander Esquivel had agreed to her crazy plan. Soon the vineyard would be reunited and Felipe would have a reason to smile again. She should be over the moon ecstatic right now. And yet instead she felt wrung out, both emotionally and physically. 'I must go,' she said, shocked when she glanced out of the window and realised how the light was fading from the day. 'Felipe will be wondering where I am.' She looked back at him. 'I imagine you'll be in touch when the papers are ready to sign.'

'I'll get my jacket. I'll drive you home.'

'There's no need,' she said, even as he was disappearing into his room. She would be fine on the local bus. She would be even later home but she could do with the time to think. And right now she could do with the space to breathe air not spiced with this man's scent, a blend of citrus, musk and one hundred per cent testosterone.

'There's every need,' he said, returning with a jacket he shrugged over his shoulders, a set of keys in his hand. 'There are things we need to discuss.'

'Like what?'

'Like how we met, for a start. We need to get our stories straight and I'm assuming you'd prefer I didn't go around telling people you knocked on my door and asked me to marry you. Plus we need to work out how quickly to progress this arrangement. Given the state of Felipe's health, I'm guessing you're not after a long engagement?'

'Well, no…' She hadn't really thought about it. He was right, of course, it was just that she hadn't given herself the luxury of thinking that far ahead. Not when she'd never actually been confident of pulling this plan off and securing his agreement.

'Then let's make it next month—it'll take that long for the legalities, and meanwhile we need to be seen together and in the right places. We can work that out on the way.' He snatched up car keys from a drawer. 'Besides, I think it's about time I reacquainted myself with my prospective grandfather-in-law.'

His car was low and lean and looked more as if it belonged on a racetrack than on any road. It didn't help that it was black. She regarded it suspiciously. 'Are you sure this is street legal?'

He laughed, a low rumbling laugh that she felt uncomfortably low in her belly, as he ushered her into the low-slung GTA Spano that seemed filled with leather and aluminium and cool LCD lighting.

Safe in her leather seat, the car wrapped around her like an embrace, the panoramic glass roof bringing the outside inside.

He didn't so much drive through the busy streets of San Sebastian as prowled, driver and machine like a predator, waiting for just the right moment to switch lanes or to overtake, using the vehicle's cat-like manoeuvrability and power to masterfully take control of the streets, until they hit the highway and the car changed gears and ate up the few miles before the turn-off to the coast and small fishing village of Getaria.

Along the way they sorted the story of how they'd met by chance in San Sebastian when she'd stopped him on the street to ask directions. Or rather, Alesander sorted their story, while she tried hard to ignore the blood-dizzying effect of sharing the same confined space with him. She didn't have to turn her head and see him to know he was right there beside her, she could taste him in the very air she breathed, and somehow the scent of leather only added to the heady mix. She didn't have to watch his long-fingered hands to know when they were on the steering wheel or when he changed gears because she could feel the whisper of air that stirred against her leg.

It was disconcerting. She couldn't remember when she'd ever been so aware of anyone in her entire life.

Or especially any man.

But then she'd never asked anyone else to marry her before either, much less have them agree. This was brand new territory for her. Little wonder she was so on edge.

The closer they got to Getaria, the more anxious she grew and she found herself wishing she'd caught the bus after all. Now she'd have no chance to warn Felipe that she'd bumped into Alesander, no chance to let him get used to the idea before having him turn up on the doorstep. He would come around, she was sure, but he was bound to be a little unreceptive at first.

'Don't be surprised if Felipe is a little gruff towards you,' she warned. 'Given what's happened, I mean.'

'Given the fact I own three-quarters of his estate now, you mean?' He shrugged. 'As long as I have been alive and, indeed, for a long time before, things have never been easy between our two families.'

'Why is that? What happened?'

'What is the reason behind any family rivalry? A cross word. A dark look. And, in this case, a bride stolen out from under my great-great-grandfather's nose and married to another before he could stop her.'

'Who did she marry?'

'Felipe's grandfather.'

'Oh, I see. Wow.' She shook her head. 'But still, that must have happened years ago. Surely something that happened a century ago isn't still a sore point. The families are neighbours after all.'

'Honour is very important to the Basque people and memories are long. One does not forget when one's pride has been trampled upon.'

'I guess not.' And she wondered how she would be remembered when she was gone, after probably the shortest marriage in Esquivel history. It would, no doubt, add cause to keep resentment towards the Otxoa name simmering for the next century or more. Just as well she could disappear home to Australia when the marriage was dissolved. 'What about your family? How will they take the news of you marrying an Otxoa?'

He smiled. 'Not well. At least not initially. But I will tell them it is time to move on. I will make them come around and see that we cannot hold a grudge between

our families for ever. And then, when it is over, they
will delight in telling me that they told me so and that
they were right all along.'

'Will you mind that?'

'I don't care what anyone says, not when I'm going
to end up with the land.'

'Oh, of course,' she said. The land that made it
all worthwhile. *The land she'd bargained away.* His
family would probably forgive him anything for that.

'Tell me,' he said, changing the topic, 'is there a
boyfriend at home in Australia waiting for you to return home? Who might be upset about your getting
married and turn up suddenly to stop the wedding?'

She laughed. She couldn't help it, the thought of
Damon turning up to claim her from the clutches of
marriage to another man too funny not to laugh out
loud. But Damon wouldn't have the guts to show his
face, even if he had decided he wanted to get back with
her. 'No. No boyfriend.'

He looked across at her. 'You make it sound like
there was one.'

'There was, for a while. But he's history and he's
staying there. Believe me, he won't be turning up to
stop the wedding.'

'What about other friends or family? Won't they be
concerned for you?'

'There's no family to speak of. Not now.'

'But your father's family?'

She shook her head. 'I know it sounds odd, but I
never met them. Dad discovered he was adopted when
he was thirteen and he never forgave his adoptive family for keeping the secret from him for so long. And
he never met his birth parents but he hated them for
abandoning him in the first place. I think that's why

he and Mum got on so well together. They understood each other. They were alone in the world and they were all each other had.'

'Surely they had you?'

'They did but…' She raised her head, searching the night sky through the clear glass roof for the words. How did one go about explaining such personal things to someone who was a virtual stranger, and yet who should not be such a stranger, given they were now engaged to be married? How much did he need to know? How much did she need to tell him?

And yet there was something liberating, too, about sharing something about your family with a total stranger, knowing that it would never matter. After all, it wasn't as if he'd ever have to meet her parents. Not now.

'I always thought Mum was all Dad ever wanted or needed.'

He looked her way and she caught his frown.

'Don't get me wrong, he was a good dad, sometimes great,' she said wistfully, remembering a particular father and daughter three-legged race on the one primary school sports day. They'd come last but it didn't matter, because at least that year he'd actually bothered to turn up, despite the fact he'd never had a job to go to like the other dads and had always made excuses and she'd spent every year watching her friends run with their fathers. But he'd turned up that year and she'd been beside herself, bursting with pride.

He'd done it for her, she'd realised years later, because she'd pleaded for the weeks and days before with him to go, and finally she'd worn him down, but at the time it had felt like Christmas.

'Really, it was okay. I just got the impression he

would have been perfectly happy never having kids. I
guess I always just felt a little surplus to requirements.'

'You have no other family? No brothers or sisters?'

'No.'

He didn't reply and she didn't mind because she was
more than content to look out of the window, looking
at the rows of vines trellised so high above the hillside
that you could walk beneath them, so different to the
style of vineyard she was used to seeing at home. And
it was easier for a moment to think about the tangle of
vines than the tangle of families.

For a moment. Until she remembered another tangling thread.

'Dad didn't want Mum to come back to Spain, you
know, when she heard that her mother was dying. He
didn't want her to rebuild any bridges and reconnect
with a father he said had abandoned her. In all honesty, I think he only let her come in the end because
he figured Felipe was old and it might result in an inheritance that might pay off their debts.

'What he didn't figure on was Mum and Felipe
actually getting on okay. He expected they'd pick up
where they'd left off last time and they'd shout the
house down, but this time was different, I think because her mother had died. And Mum had grown up
a bit and Felipe had mellowed and both she and Felipe
were starting to realise all the things they'd missed.'

'He must have been happy to have you around, after
losing Maria.'

He shouldn't have had to wait that long. She
clamped down on a boulder of guilt she'd felt, heavy
and weighted inside her from the day she'd heard
Maria had died. Sometimes she could lock it away
and almost forget it was there, and other times it would

escape and roll awkwardly through her gut, crushing her spirit and making her remember a promise that she'd made to herself so many years ago.

A promise she'd broken.

She dragged in air. But she was here now. It wasn't too late to make things better; to make up just a little bit for all that had gone before.

'He was. We all were, all apart from Dad. He resented Mum talking in a language and laughing at jokes he couldn't understand.' Tears once again stung her eyes and she clamped down on the urge to cry. He was her father and she'd loved him but there were times she'd wanted to shake him too, and make him see that he didn't have to take on the whole world to enjoy it. 'And now they've both gone and Felipe is dying too.' She turned her head away as two fat tears squeezed their way from the corners of her eyes, swiping the wetness from her cheeks.

'The last few months have been rough on you.'

She squeezed damp eyes shut, wishing away the sting, trying to block out his rich, low voice from worming its way into anywhere it could do some damage. She wished to hell he didn't sound so...*understanding*. She wasn't looking for sympathy. She was looking for a solution. 'Anyway,' she said, huffing out air, shaking off her gloom, 'I'm not planning on telling anyone at home about this—about our arrangement. Nobody need know. Because then I don't have to go home and explain what went wrong with my quickie marriage. It might not bother you, but there's no way I want to listen to everyone telling me, "I told you so".'

'You'll have nobody? Don't you think it will look strange if you have no one in attendance? Isn't there a friend you can confide in and trust?'

That earned him a snort. She'd had a best friend she'd trusted. Ever since primary school, she and Carla had day-dreamed about the day they'd each get married and had sworn to be each other's chief bridesmaids. They'd shared everything in life—the good times and the bad—and the job had always been Carla's—right up until the day Simone had found her sharing her cheating boyfriend.

And not only sharing her boyfriend but sharing him in her bed, which, to her way of thinking, made the betrayal even more damning.

As for asking any of her other friends—there was no way she could expect photos or news of the wedding not to leak out onto social media, no matter how much she wanted to keep it quiet. And it would be unfair and unreasonable to ask her friends to keep it a secret, simply to protect her own need for privacy. They'd want to know why and they'd deserve to be told.

And that wouldn't work when she didn't want anyone to know. This marriage was hardly going to be one of her finest moments. She wasn't sure she wanted witnesses to the event. 'I don't know,' she said, thinking it was all getting too difficult. 'Maybe we should just fly off to Las Vegas and not bother with a wedding here at all. Just come back and say it's a done deal.'

'And cheat Felipe out of the pleasure of walking his granddaughter down the aisle? How would it brighten his days to know you had been whisked away to marry a man whose family he has been in dispute with his entire life?' He hesitated a moment to let that sink in, and sink in it did. As much as the idea appealed, how could she do that when this was all about convincing him this was real and making him happy?

'Besides,' Alesander continued, 'why should anyone believe it? Whereas if they see us married before their eyes, surely that will be more convincing.'

Convincing. What did that mean in Spanish terms? She looked out of the window, biting her lip as the car wended its way along the narrow road up the hill towards Felipe's shrunken estate. Her plan had seemed so easy when she'd come up with it. Marry Alesander and let Felipe end his days thinking his precious vines were reunited. What could be more simple?

But there was so much she hadn't considered; so many details where her plans could come unstuck.

Convincing.

But she didn't want a big church wedding with all the trimmings. Somehow a small civil affair seemed easier to undo. Less false, if there even was a scale of falseness.

Right now she wanted to believe it.

But maybe she'd been kidding herself all along. Maybe her idea had been doomed from the start and she was finally starting to realise it.

Except he must believe it was possible or why would he have gone along with it?

She turned to him, needing to hear what he thought. 'Do you really think we can make this work?'

He looked over at her. 'Having second thoughts?'

'No, not really. It's just that…it seemed like such a simple idea but there's just so much to consider. So many tiny details to sort out.'

'Ideas are the easy part. It's making them happen that takes work.'

Wasn't that the truth? 'So you think we can do it?'

'I'm banking on it.'

The land, she thought, sitting back in her seat. He

will make it happen because he's banking on the land. And she couldn't resent the price he'd demanded or the deal she'd made, because right now having Alesander Esquivel on her team was her plan's biggest asset.

If she had nothing else going for her, he would make it happen.

Oh yes, Alesander thought, he was banking on it. The way he figured it, he had nothing to lose and everything to gain.

He turned the car into the driveway leading to the small estate and immediately knew that something was wrong. Very wrong. In September one expected the vines to be dense, the foliage protecting the fruit hanging in clusters beneath, but the vines either side of the driveway were overgrown and tangled, the supporting trellises broken in places so that the vines had collapsed onto the ground.

The small house at the end of the driveway had the same air of neglect.

'What is Felipe doing about the harvest? The grapes will be ready in a month or so.'

'Not a lot. Even if he cared, I don't think he'd have the strength to do much.'

'But he has people working for him, surely?'

She gave him a pointed look as she undid her seat belt and pushed open her door. 'Seriously? Does it look like he has an army of people working for him?' He wasted the time it took to curse and she was almost out of the car before he stopped her with a hand to her arm.

'Hey!'

She swung around, cold flame erupting from her blue eyes.

'I'll get those trellises fixed.'

'Whatever.' She tugged on her arm and he tightened his grip and pulled her closer.

'We're supposed to be friends, right—friends who might be a little keen on each other. So get angry with me, sure, but do it on your own time. Right now we've got a job to do.'

'A snow job, you mean.'

'Do you want this? I can leave right now if you don't. Because I can wait a few months for this place to completely fall apart and then buy you out for a rock-bottom price if you'd prefer. Or we can do it your way. It's up to you.'

She blinked and looked up at the house, where a grizzled face craned his neck to make sense of what was going on in the driveway outside. She smiled at him and waved from inside the car before turning back to Alesander. 'Of course I do.'

'Okay, so share that smile with me, and look friendly.'

She turned on a smile so sickly-sweet she must have added a cup of saccharin to the mix. 'Thank you so much for the lift, Señor Esquivel,' she said in a voice designed not to carry, merely to convey an impression to the man sitting at the window. 'I'd like to say it's been a pleasure meeting you but that would be an out-and-out lie.'

He took her hand before she could get out and pressed the back of her hand to his mouth, loving the way her eyes threw heated sparks at the graze of his lips on her skin. 'I'm beginning to think this marriage might be more entertaining than I first thought.'

Her smile widened. She even managed a little laugh. 'Lucky you. I'm beginning to think it's going to be a real pain in the backside. Or maybe that's just you.'

'I aim to please.'

She pulled her hand free as she stepped from the car.

'Don't forget to smile,' he said behind her.

'Zer egiten ari da hemen zuen?' Felipe said from his chair near the window as she entered.

'What did you say, Abuelo?' Simone said, leaning over to give him a kiss first to one and then the other of his hollowed white-whiskered cheeks.

'He wants to know what I'm doing here.'

She nodded her thanks to Alesander behind her, and turned to invite him in. She was still angry that he could be so entirely oblivious to the contribution he'd made to Felipe's decline, but she was grateful for the translation. When her grandfather spoke in Spanish it was hard enough to keep up, but when he reverted to the regional Basque language she had no hope of understanding.

But when she looked around she had to do a double take. The room seemed to have shrunk and the modest cottage that was perfectly adequate for the two of them now seemed tiny, the roof hovering low over their visitor's head. She blinked and turned back to her grandfather. 'I ran into Alesander in San Sebastian,' she said, reeling out the story they'd concocted in the car. Not too many untruths to trip over. 'We got to talking and found out we were neighbours and he offered me a lift home so I didn't have to catch the bus.'

Her grandfather grunted and turned back to look pointedly out of the window towards the land and the vines he'd lost, his message clear, but before he'd turned away she'd seen there was more than resentment in his eyes. There was sadness too, and hurt.

Simone turned to their guest and shook her head. He shrugged, as if he'd been expecting such a lack of welcome all along.

'How go the grapes, Felipe?' he asked. 'People are saying it will be the best harvest for years.'

Another grunt from the window.

Alesander gave up. 'I should be going.'

'You won't stay for dinner?' She wasn't sure she wanted him to—the little exchange in the car had left her feeling unsettled—but maybe he'd been expecting to be asked after driving her home. And it would make a change to have younger company for a little while.

He shook his head. 'I won't impose on any more of your time. Felipe, it was good to see you again. It's been too long.'

The old man gave a flick of his gnarled hand without bothering to look around.

'But if there is one favour I might ask you before I go?'

The old man's head turned by only the barest of fractions towards their guest. 'It is Markel de la Silva's sixtieth birthday party on Saturday evening. I was wondering if you might let your granddaughter accompany me.'

The neck that seemed comprised entirely of cords twisted around until his flat glassy eyes met hers. 'Is that what you want?' he asked her pointedly.

'I would love to go,' she said, liking the fact Alesander had asked Felipe for his permission. Their families might have been rivals for years but there was a note of respect in his request that had sounded sincere. Although she wondered what he would do if Felipe said no. 'If it's all right with you, of course.'

Felipe merely grunted. 'You can do what you like, while you are here.'

'In that case, yes,' she said, already panicking about what she would wear. Party dresses hadn't been a high priority on her packing list when she'd come, expecting to stay just a couple of weeks, not that she'd had many to choose from anyway. She'd just have to head into San Sebastian again and find something that would fit into her limited student budget.

Alesander must have been wondering the same thing, a telltale frown bringing his two dark brows closer together as if he could tell from what she was wearing that she would own nothing suitable for a posh Spanish party. 'Did you bring a gown with you?'

A gown? 'No,' she confessed. Although he might just as well have asked if she even possessed a gown. 'But I'm sure I'll find something.'

'I'll take you shopping,' he said. 'Tomorrow. There is work I have to do in the morning first, but shall we say three o'clock?'

'Watch that one,' Felipe said between spooning up his paella. His appetite had been waning lately, and it was the one dish she could guarantee he would do more than pick at. 'Be careful with him.'

'You mean Alesander? I thought he seemed—' she searched for words that didn't include arrogant and bastard '—very pleasant.'

'You think he is interested in you? Bah! He only came to see how close to death I am.'

'No, Abuelo, why would you say such a thing? Why would he do that?'

'Why else? He is after the vines. He already has

three-quarters of them and now he wants the rest, you mark my words.'

She put her fork down, unable to swallow another mouthful, the ball in her stomach like lead and not only weighted with guilt. For, after the agreement she had made with him, Alesander as good as owned the vines. What would her grandfather say if he knew what she had done?

What she had done with good reason, she reminded herself, certain that once the marriage was announced, Felipe would be celebrating to know his precious vines were once again reunited, the fortunes of the Otxoa family restored.

Besides which, did it really matter who owned the vines after Felipe died? It might as well be someone who knew what to do with them.

'I'm sure you're wrong. I know you have had your differences with his father in the past, but I am sure Alesander is not as ruthless as you make out.'

'He is an Esquivel. Of course he is ruthless!'

'I could have met you in San Sebastian,' she said when Alesander opened the car door for her the next afternoon. 'You didn't have to come all this way.'

'I didn't come for your benefit.' He looked up at the window, where he caught the old man scowling at him before turning his head away. He waved, letting him know he'd seen. 'Felipe needs to get used to seeing us together.'

'Oh,' she said, looking suddenly contrite, 'of course,' before falling quiet as she got into the car, and warning bells went off in his brain. If she was going to start thinking he was being considerate towards her because he was interested in her...

There was no way he wanted her thinking that. He waited until the car was at the end of the driveway so they were well away from the house and Felipe's inquisitive gaze.

'Perhaps I should remind you that we are actors in this masquerade. We are expected to convey an image—first that we are a couple—and second that we are in love.

'But this is a marriage of convenience and it remains a marriage of convenience. A marriage in name only. That's what you wanted and that's what you will get. And if I show you any courtesy, and of course I will because it is all part of the act, it is not because I have suddenly fallen in love with you. It is merely to convince everybody else that I have.'

He looked across at her. 'Do you understand?'

'Yes. Of course I do. My mistake. I'm sorry for ever imagining you were simply being nice.'

He managed a brief smile at her response. On the one hand he found her Australian openness appealing, but at the same time he was concerned at her willingness to embrace something as simple as picking her up from her home as being a sign he cared, and he wondered anew about her long-term plans. She'd said she was doing this all for Felipe, but why should she give up her inheritance for a grumpy old man she barely knew and who he'd never seen happy and would probably never would?

Unless she'd had other plans from the start—other plans that involved making a fake marriage real and trading a modest inheritance for a luxury lifestyle. Was her demand that there be no sex just a way to lull him into a false sense of security?

It had better not be.

'I warn you now, it would be a mistake to ever go thinking I was nice.'

'Don't worry,' she said snippily. 'I won't make the same mistake again.'

CHAPTER FIVE

THE BOUTIQUE WAS just off La Avenida, the main street of San Sebastian, tucked away in a small *calle* closed to motor vehicles, and filled with planter boxes dotted down the *calle* spilling with bushes and greenery while the attractive three- and four-storey buildings that lined the street were home to exclusive boutiques and Michelin-starred restaurants topped by private hotels. The place screamed of money.

Alesander led her towards one of the boutiques now, and she hesitated, thinking of her limited budget. When he'd said he'd take her shopping, she'd imagined he would take her somewhere a little more generic. 'It looks expensive.'

'It is. Only the filthy rich can shop here.'

She stopped completely. There was no way she was setting foot in the place, let alone thinking about buying anything. 'That's not my kind of store.'

'Which is why I brought you. Because I know you could not be trusted to buy the kind of gown you will need to pull this off.'

'But I don't have to step inside to know I can't afford anything in that shop!'

He pulled her aside, leaning down close to her face to keep his words and, no doubt, hopefully hers out of the public realm. 'And we can't afford to get this wrong. If we're going to convince people that you are worthy of being an Esquivel bride, we cannot have you looking like you dressed yourself in some discount department store rags. People would not believe it.' She opened her mouth to protest and he held up one hand, silencing her. '*Especially* not for something as important as Markel's birthday party. Now, we are wasting time.'

'You can't make me go in there—'

'I do not expect you to pay. Of course I will pay. And it will be worth every euro. And, just for the record,' he added for good measure, 'I am not being nice.'

She found the nerve to smile up at him. 'Now that was the one thing I wasn't about to accuse you of.'

She had no time to celebrate her oral victory, for instead she found herself herded, rather than led, into the hushed boutique, where garments hung in spartan clusters around the otherwise minimalist walls. Even so, what was on display was enough that she immediately felt underdressed, the cut-off capri pants and soft lemon cardigan she'd thought suitable for this shopping expedition now feeling decidedly underdone in this world of hand-printed silks and designer denim.

Not that the two sleek shop attendants seemed to notice or care. They were too busy welcoming Alesander to their store with their wide smiles and gleaming eyes. If he wasn't as good-looking as he was, she'd think they could almost smell his money.

He rattled off something in Spanish too fast for her to understand and the two women threw a glance her way, sizing her up, chatting excitedly between themselves before one breezed past a rack of gowns and disappeared into a back room while the other introduced them both. Alondra and Evita promised to be of every assistance, she said, nothing would be too much trouble. 'And you are in luck, *señorita*,' the woman called Alondra said excitedly, 'we have some very special gowns delivered just today. They are exclusives. You will not find them anywhere else in all of Spain.'

Her colleague returned a few moments later, her arms laden with four exquisite gowns in rich colours that she hung side by side on a rail to compare. 'What do you think of these?'

They were all different in style, cut and colour, from strapless to asymmetrical to one-shouldered; from lilac to silver to fiery red, but with one thing in common— they were all exquisite.

'Stunning,' she said, overwhelmed by the detail of each of the gowns, whether in the beading or skilful pleating or the soft feminine drape of the skirt, finding it hard to believe that she might soon actually possess anything so beautiful—but, more than that, have an occasion to wear it.

'What about that one?' Alesander said behind her, but when she turned to see which one he meant, he was looking elsewhere, towards an aqua-coloured gown hanging by itself to one side. It was strapless with a pleated bodice, fitted through the body to the hip, where it finished emphatically in a ruffled skirt split high up one thigh. It was dramatic and sexy and seemed to convey the very essence of Spain, understated and yet over the top at the same time. And undeniably the most beautiful dress she'd ever seen.

Ordinarily her eyes would have already bypassed it, knowing there was no point giving it a second glance, knowing there was no way she could afford to even look at it, but these were no ordinary times and besides, she heard him say, 'It would go with your eyes.'

And she shivered and looked back at him uncertainly. When had he noticed the colour of her eyes?

The women descended again into rapid Spanish, to which Alesander simply responded, 'Who?' And when they answered, he smiled and issued a series of instructions to the women and finished with one to her. 'Try it on,' he said.

Heels were produced, and accessories and one woman zipped her into the dress while the other turned her ponytail into a messy knot that looked halfway to evening glam and when she was finally dressed she stared at the result in the mirror. My God, was that really her? Apart from being a little long, the gown fitted her as if it had been made for her, but instead of it emphasising how much weight she had lost in the last few months, like her other clothes did now they were too big, the fact this gown hugged her curves seemed to make the most of them.

'I love it,' she said, wondering at a dress that had the power to transform her from discount department store cheap to designer chic.

'The hem can be altered,' Alondra said. 'That is no problem.'

'And this before make-up and jewellery,' the other clucked, beaming her delight. 'You must show your boyfriend.'

She almost denied it. Almost said that Alesander wasn't her boyfriend, but stopped herself short. Because he kind of was now, even if it was only make-believe.

He was on the phone when she stepped from the dressing room, his back to her and she said nothing, not wanting to disturb him, but he must have heard something because after a few seconds he stilled and, still talking into his phone, he turned, only for the torrent of words to stop as his dark eyes drank her in. And then he said something short, punched a button to punctuate the call and pocketed the phone.

She smiled nervously, wanting him to like what he saw, if only to show him that she could pull this off. She didn't care what he thought about her, but she did want him to be confident that she could carry off her side of the bargain before they signed the paperwork linking them together. 'What do you think? Will it do for the party?'

It seemed to take an eternity for him to answer, an eternity that had her wondering if he was regretting this deal because she would never be up to the task. '*Sí,*' he said dispassionately at last, 'it will do. And now you will have to excuse me for an hour or so. I have a meeting that will not wait. The *señoritas* have instructions to find you a range of outfits for day and evening and I will leave you in their clearly capable hands.' And with that he was gone.

She clamped down on a bubble of disappointment as she returned to the changing room, the women eagerly rushing around to gather up more garments for her to try on. Alesander approved of the dress. That should be enough. That *was* enough. There was no reason to be disappointed with his reaction.

On the other hand, there was plenty of justification for the resentment that simmered and bubbled away inside her.

Because she'd come here looking for a dress and she'd found one and now he calmly instructed her to find a 'range of outfits'. Clearly he didn't think her existing wardrobe lived up to the necessary Esquivel standards in order to convince the world they were an item. And yes, she understood that the world he inhabited was located somewhere high in the dizzy stratosphere compared to her own, but it still rankled to be so constantly reminded of that fact. It rankled even more to be given instructions without discussion, as if her opinion was not worth either hearing or seeking. After all, they were supposed to be in this together.

'You will be very happy with that gown,' Alondra said.

'Your boyfriend thinks you look very sexy,' said the other.

He still wasn't her boyfriend and she very much doubted he thought about how she looked other than to gauge whether she would pass muster and be accepted in his company. 'Well, he sure didn't say much.'

'Didn't you see his eyes?' The women looked at each other with a smile. 'His eyes, they said plenty. He thought you were hot.'

Shop girl talk, she figured as she slipped out of the dress, the same the world over and designed to make you feel good about whatever you were trying on. If they saw anything in his eyes, it was most likely the greedy prospect of getting his hands on the rest of Felipe's vines.

Besides, he didn't think her hot. She wasn't his type and that was fine. That was good. It made it so much easier to deal with him, knowing he wasn't in the least bit interested in her.

She only wished she could be as impartial to him. Maybe then she wouldn't spend so much time thinking how good he'd looked dressed only in a towel. And God, how he had. And then there was his evocative scent and the curl of his long tapered fingers around the steering wheel and the way her skin had sizzled when they touched...

No, thank God he wasn't interested in her because it made the whole no-sex deal workable. Knowing the terms of their contract would stipulate that condition was comforting. But knowing she could rely on him not to try anything was the clincher.

At least one of them would be thinking straight.

His meeting had been interminable as plans were made for the upcoming harvest, and he wondered at the sense of leaving her for so long with a blank credit card. But she wasn't still shopping. Instead, he found the three women sitting at a table outside the nearby restaurant, eating pintxos and sipping on Mojitos. 'I do hope,' he said, joining them and only half joking, 'this doesn't mean Simone has bought everything in the shop.'

She coloured and gave a guilty smile, as if she'd been caught in the act, and he smiled too, not just because he couldn't remember the last time he'd seen a woman blush, but because somehow she looked different. She'd changed her top—out of whatever nondescript rag she'd been wearing before, for a flirty silk blouse patterned in orange and teal that he liked—but he was sure there was something else.

'It's our fault,' one of the shop assistants said. 'We have kept Simone so busy, we felt she deserved a treat.'

'So busy,' the other said, 'but so efficient that we even managed to get her into the salon across the street. Do you like Simone's new look?'

So that was what was different about her? Now he could see not only that her hair had been professionally styled, but that highlights had been added, whis-per-thin streaks of chilli and cinnamon that gleamed in the light and blended in with the natural honey-gold of her hair. Somehow it seemed to give her hair depth. He nodded. 'I approve.'

'I won't hold you up,' she said, her cheeks flaring now under his scrutiny as she awkwardly stood, reach-ing for her shopping.

'Is that all there is?' he asked, surveying the small collection of carrier bags nearby.

'The gown needs to be taken up,' said one of the women, 'It will be delivered tomorrow.'

'But that's the rest of it?'

One of the women laughed. 'Your girlfriend is a very reluctant shopper, *señor*. We tried to convince her but she would not buy a fraction of what we picked out for her.' She nodded. 'You are a very lucky man.'

The women excused themselves to return to their shop while she gathered up her bags.

He leaned past her to collect up the last of them and he breathed in her scent, like warm peaches on a sunny day. Liking her perfume, even though it was probably just the shampoo the salon had used. Still, he liked the changes he was noticing about her. She was still not his type, but it would make it so much easier to pretend. 'They think we are a couple.'

'I know. I couldn't see the point of correcting them.'

'No, it is good,' he said, leading her back to where he'd parked the car. 'That is what everyone is meant to think. If they assume simply because we are seen shopping together that we are a couple, imagine what people will believe when they see us kiss.'

See us kiss? 'You *were* actually fitting me out with a wardrobe,' she said, trying to find a shred of logic in a mind that wanted to hone in and focus on the prospect of him kissing her instead. When? How? *How soon?* 'We weren't "simply shopping" at all.'

He shrugged. 'Still, I think we will have no trouble convincing people.'

They were almost at Getaria when she remembered to ask, 'What was that about in the shop before, when you first asked about the dress?'

He looked across at her. 'When?'

'You said something like "What about that one?" after they brought the first batch of gowns over and that one was set apart. But you were all speaking so fast, I couldn't understand.'

He shook his head. 'I don't understand what you're asking. We have the dress, don't we?'

'I mean, was there a reason they didn't include it in the first place? Did they think it wouldn't suit me?'

'Ah,' he said. 'Apparently another of their clients had expressed interest in seeing it, that was all.'

'Oh, you mean they had it reserved for someone?'

He shrugged. 'It makes no difference now.'

'But won't that person be disappointed that it's sold?'

He smiled. 'Probably.'

She settled back into her seat, tangling fingers in her lap, newly manicured fingernails painted bright red if he wasn't mistaken. He had to hand it to her, she had been busy this afternoon.

'I should thank you, of course,' she said, 'for the clothes and everything.'

'I'm not sure you got anywhere near enough.'

'You must be kidding,' she said with a shake of her head, 'there's heaps, really there is. I just hate to think how much it cost. But in case you're wondering, I paid for the salon. I don't want you thinking I'd take advantage…'

Was she serious? Or was this just another tactic to lull him into taking her and her story at face value and believing she wanted nothing more than to make an old man die happy? Because none of the women he knew were anywhere near as naive or horrified at the prospect of spending someone else's money on themselves.

But then none of the women he knew would go to such extraordinary lengths that she was going either. Why was she going to such trouble for her grandfather? He didn't like that he didn't know, but if he ended up with the vines and she ended up not pregnant and with no claim on the estate, he didn't really care.

What he did like was the way she blushed. Whether it was because of her fair colouring, or because she was harbouring some guilty secret, that was one thing he wasn't used to. He glanced sideways at her. And he liked whatever the salon had done to her hair and how the sunlight through his roof turned her highlights to glistening threads of copper and gold. Not that he was about to admit that to her.

In fact, given his misgivings about her motives, he was better off not giving her too much encouragement at all.

He changed down gears as he headed into a tight bend, changing down gears on his thoughts at the same time.

'You might want to save your money,' he said, probably sounding more gruff than he intended, 'for when you get home. You might need it.'

Cold.

He might just as well have tossed a bucket of icy water over her. And why?

Moreover, why did she even care?

Alesander was nothing to her but a solution to a problem.

She was nothing to him but a means to an end.

It was a mutual arrangement.

So why did he feel it so important to remind her that this arrangement was not permanent?

Didn't he think that was how she wanted it?

She turned to him, or rather to his profile, strong and noble and too utterly perfect to be real, as he negotiated the winding track up the hill towards her grandfather's vineyard. 'What are you so afraid of?'

'What do you mean?'

'Only that every chance you get, you feel the need to remind me that this arrangement is temporary. "You might want to save your money for when you get home," you said. Well, I do know this is temporary because I was the one who insisted it would be from the start.'

'I don't know what you're talking about.'

'Just that you seem to be operating under the misapprehension that I either want or expect this arrangement to become permanent.'

He scoffed her protests away. 'I have only your word that you don't want it to be.'

'I am expecting to sign a contract saying exactly that! A contract which includes the condition *I* specifically demanded when I brokered this agreement— a condition that precludes sex between us. So when will you believe me? Because as clearly wonderful a catch as you so evidently are, I would rather not have to marry you. I don't want to be your wife, other than to convince Felipe that his vines are as good as re-united. And when Felipe is no longer with us, I expect the quickest divorce from marriage with you that it is possible to get. I expect the contract terms to reflect that fact.'

He changed down gears as he rounded the bend before climbing the hill up towards Felipe's estate. 'I will ensure it will be provided as quick as is humanly or inhumanly possible. I will not make you wait to be free.'

'Excellent. So we understand each other then.'

'Oh yes,' he said through gritted teeth, 'we understand each other perfectly.'

The banging started the next morning while she was cooking breakfast. 'What is that?' a grumpy Felipe demanded, peering out of the window, searching for the cause.

'I don't know,' she answered as she put a plate of eggs on the table for him. 'I'll go and find out.'

The morning air was crisp and clean. It would be warm later, but for now the cool air prickled the skin of her bare arms and her nipples turned to tight buds. She should have grabbed her jacket before she'd set off, she thought, hugging her arms over her chest as she followed the sound down the driveway.

Around a bend she found a four-wheel drive parked and someone working under the vines where part of the trellis had collapsed under the weight of the vines. And she remembered that Alesander had said something about getting that fixed. She hadn't paid any heed to his words at the time but he must have meant it and sent someone after all, no doubt to ensure there was no more damage done before he took over the vineyard completely.

But even if he was doing it for his own reasons, she could still be hospitable.

'*Buenos dias,*' she called out over the hammering. 'Is there anything you need that I can get you?'

'Coffee would be good,' a familiar deep voice said, as Alesander pushed aside the tangle of vines with one arm to peer out at her.

'You? What are you doing here?'

'I told you I'd get this fixed.'

'But I thought you'd send someone. I didn't expect you.'

'Well, you got me.'

His eyes raked over her and her bullet-hard nipples suddenly had nothing to do with the cold because she was suddenly feeling hot.

'I'll get you that coffee,' she said, discomfited, her cheeks flaring with heat.

He smiled as she turned away. 'You do that.'

'Who is it?' asked Felipe as she returned to the cottage. 'Who's making all that noise?'

She poured coffee into a mug. 'It's Alesander. He's fixing some of the broken trellising.'

'Why? What is he doing meddling with my vines?' He swayed backwards and forwards in his chair, gaining momentum and looking as if he was intending to get up and go and take issue with him. 'They're not his to meddle with!'

'Abuelo,' she said with her hands to his shoulders, squeezing gently, feeling a pang of guilt in her chest, knowing that soon they would be his to do anything he liked with them, 'he's being neighbourly, that's all.'

'Neighbourly? Pah!' But he settled back in his chair, already wheezing under the strain of his efforts.

'Yes, neighbourly. It's about time this feud between the Esquivels and the Oxtoas was put to bed once and for all, don't you think?'

He muttered something in Basque under his breath. Normally she'd ask him what he meant, but not this time. This time she had a fairly good idea what he meant without the translation. 'I'm taking Alesander some coffee. I'll be back soon.'

'It's the vines,' he called out in his thin voice as she left. 'He doesn't want you.'

She didn't answer. Felipe might be right, but she didn't have to tell him that. Not when she needed him soon to believe the exact opposite.

Alesander was busy under the vines when she returned, intent on the task of replacing a broken upright, and she leant against his car and watched him work. She hadn't pegged him as someone good at manual work, but he seemed to know what he was doing, every action purposeful and certain.

She watched him manhandle the new post into position, liking the way his body worked and the muscles bunched in his arms.

She watched him twisting broken wire together, increasing the tension on the wire supporting the heavy vines.

He was good with his hands.

And then she deliberately looked away while he finished the job, turning her gaze towards the view out to sea because she didn't want to think of the man having clever hands, not when that was something she didn't need to know.

It was better not to know.

It would be better if she didn't think about it.

What was it about this man who turned her thoughts carnal when her intentions were anything but? Thank God he'd agreed that there would be no sex between them. Never again would she have sex with a man who didn't love her one hundred per cent. Never again would she experience that sickening fear that she might be carrying the child of a man she didn't love with all her heart.

She wouldn't let it happen.

'Is that for me?' he asked, startling her, so lost in her thoughts she hadn't heard him approach. She turned to see the job done, the once fallen vines now lifted high off the ground again.

'Oh, yes,' she said, handing him the mug, pulling her hand away quickly when their fingers brushed. He sipped the coffee, thoughtfully watching her, and nodded.

'*Bueno*. How's Felipe this morning?'

'Mistrustful. He wonders what you're about.'

Alesander smiled. 'He'll come around,' and put the coffee to his lips again—good lips, wide and not at all thin—and she suddenly felt awkward, standing here, watching a man drink a cup of coffee. She wondered if she should go. She'd delivered the promised coffee after all. Then again, she'd only have to come back for the cup…

'Why are the vines grown so high?' she asked, finally falling on something to say. 'It must make looking after them more difficult.'

He shrugged. 'It's the way here. The weather from the sea can be harsh. This way the vines form a canopy that protects the fruit beneath, making it more suitable for the grapes to flourish. And of course—' he smiled '—up high they get a much better view of the sea.'

And she blinked as she remembered a phrase from her childhood, a sliver of a memory she'd forgotten until now, some words an old man had told her as she'd trailed behind him around the vineyard asking endless questions while he'd snipped and trimmed the vines, answering her in faltering Spanglish. He'd told her his grapes were magic grapes and she'd asked him what made them magic and he'd told her what made them magic.

'The sparkle of the sea.'

His eyes narrowed as he regarded her. '*Sí*. The grapes with the view make the best wine. They say that is why our *txakoli* wine sparkles when it is poured.'

'Is it true?'

'Of course it is true. And also it is to do with the fermentation process as well. But why wouldn't grapes be happy with a view such as this?'

They stood together for a moment, looking out over the vista, as the vine-covered hillside fell away to the low rolling countryside to the coast. And the sea did indeed sparkle under the morning sun, just as her skin tingled where it was touched by the heat of him.

'But I am boring you,' he said. 'When you care nothing for the vines. Thank you for the coffee. I should get back to work here.'

She took the cup, still warm, cradling it in her hands. She didn't care for the vines. And yet there was something about them that tugged at her. Maybe it was just the remnants of a short time in her childhood when the vineyard had been her playground. 'Surely you have more important things to do? I thought you had a business to run.'

'I grew up doing this work. I like it and these days I so rarely get a chance to do it. But it is good to be closer to the grapes.'

'How are they—can you tell?' And she surprised herself by caring to know the answer, even as she knew she was putting off returning to the house. 'Do you think there will be any point harvesting them?'

He nodded and looked back at the vines above his shoulder, where bunches of small grapes hung down from the vines. She tried to look at the grapes and not the Vee of skin at his neck where his white shirt lay open. She couldn't help but notice the man made an innocent white shirt look positively sinful, the way it pulled over his shoulders and turned olive skin darker. 'It would be a crime not to pick them. The vines should have been pruned in the winter, of course, which is why they are such a mess now, but they are good vines—old but strong—they have still produced good fruit. Has Felipe had the grapes tested at all?'

She looked blankly back at him.

'No,' he said, 'I assumed not. But soon they should be tested for their sugar and acidity levels. That will tell when they are right for harvest. But it is only a matter of weeks. Two, maybe three at the most.'

Her teeth found her lip. She shook her head. 'Could I manage it, do you think? I've never done anything like this before.'

'You can help, but the job will be bigger than just you.'

She smiled stiffly. 'Will you talk to Felipe about it, then? You know so much more than me about what is needed to be done.'

'You think he will listen to me?'

'At least you speak the same language. With me, our conversations are limited to the basics. I want him to see that all is not lost, that life goes on, that the vines go on.'

'Then I will talk with him. I will come up to the house before I go.'

'Thank you.'

She turned to leave but he caught her hand. 'I could ask you the same question.' And when he caught her frown, 'Why are you doing this?'

'You know already. So he has a chance to smile before he dies.'

'*Sí*.' He nodded. 'But why? Why do you care so about a grumpy old man who lives halfway around the world and who you barely know? Why have you given up an inheritance for him?'

She smiled at the 'grumpy old man' reference. There was no point in objecting to that. 'He's all I have left in the world.'

'Is that enough to do what you are doing? I ask myself if it is enough and still it makes no sense. Why do you care so much?'

Why did she care? She turned her face up to the wide blue sky. And suddenly she was back, that seven-year-old child with long tangled hair and an even more tangled family and a promise she'd made when her screaming mother had wrenched her in tears from her grandmother's arms, their one brief attempt at bridge-building over, with a vow never to see them again.

Simone had witnessed the pain in her grandmother's eyes, had witnessed the anguish in her grandfather's and understood nothing of what was going on, except the raw agony that these new people in her life—people that she had grown to love and know that they were important to her—were feeling.

Anguish that had transferred to her.

'My parents brought me to Spain when I was seven,' she said. 'Felipe paid the fares. He was trying to reach out to my mother but, of course, I know he wanted to meet me too, as his only grandchild. The visit started well. I remember a week or two of relative peace—or maybe they were just trying to hide the worst from me as a child—but then it ended badly. It was always bound to end badly.'

Horribly.

She could still hear her father's shouting and accusations. She could still hear her mother's shrill cries that she had never been welcome in her own home.

And most of all she could remember the look of desolation on Felipe's and Maria's faces as she'd been ripped from their arms, as if they knew this was the last time they would ever lay eyes on any of them ever again.

She hadn't understood what was going on, but she'd been torn. She'd loved them all and she couldn't understand why they couldn't love each other. And she couldn't understand the hurt. She would make up for it one day, she'd promised then and there. She would come back and make up for their pain.

'I said I'd come back,' she said. 'In the midst of all the shrieking, I promised them I'd return.'

'You did,' Alesander said. 'You're here now.'

She dipped her shaking head. No. She'd meant to come back years before now. She'd meant to return when she was old enough to make the travel plans herself. But life and university and lack of funds had meant that promises of years gone by were overtaken by the needs of the present. She would still go back to Getaria, she'd repeatedly told herself—one day.

Except that she hadn't. She'd let life get in the way of good intentions. And now Maria had died without ever seeing her again, and Felipe was dying too.

And good intentions, she realised, were not enough.

Not when guilt that she had done nothing weighed so heavily upon her.

'I'll see you back at the house,' she said.

He watched her go, lonely and sad, and just for a moment he was almost tempted to go to her. But why? What would he say? They were nothing to each other, even if he understood why she was doing what she was doing a little more.

But her demons were her own.

It was not his job to fix them.

CHAPTER SIX

'HE'S HERE AGAIN,' Felipe growled as Alesander arrived for the sixth time in as many days, but this time his voice contained less censure, more tolerance. Alesander had called by the vineyard every day. On one day he'd brought the contracts for her to sign and she'd read them in the privacy of his car parked out of sight, carefully checking to ensure the agreement included all the terms she'd asked for—the no sex clause, the termination, the consideration. Then, and only then, she'd put her signature to the contract.

But every day he'd stopped by the house to talk to Felipe and always finding something to repair while he was there, and for all his gruffness, the old man was enjoying talking to another man, she could tell.

'Of course, he's here, Abuelo,' she said, emerging from her room. 'He's come to take me to the party. How do I look?'

Felipe craned his head around and blinked, his jaw sagging open. 'What have you done with Simone?'

'It is me,' she protested before she caught the glint in her grandfather's eyes and realised he was joking, the first time she'd heard him joke since she'd arrived. 'Oh, Abuelo,' she said, laughing, giving his shoulders a squeeze, trying to stop a tear squeezing from her eyes and ruin her eye make-up, 'stop teasing.'

'Who's teasing?' Alesander said from the open front door.

'Felipe, the old rogue,' she said without looking up. 'He's wondering what I've done with Simone.' And then she lifted her head and saw him, in a dark-as-night evening suit and snow-white shirt, his dark hair rippling back from his sculpted face. Her mouth went dry. He looked—*amazing*.

'You'd better go tell her to hurry up,' Alesander said, 'I don't want to be late for Markel's party.'

Felipe snorted beside her while Alesander's mouth turned upwards into a smile.

She smiled back, a smile of thanks. 'I'll just go and get her in that case,' and went to fetch her wrap.

'Don't keep her out too late,' she heard Felipe tell him. 'She's a good girl.'

'Don't give away all my secrets, Abuelo,' she gently chided, dipping her head to kiss his grizzled cheeks. 'And you behave yourself while I'm out.'

Markel's home looked more like a palace than any house she had ever had reason to visit, complete with porticoes and balconies and tall arched windows and doors, and all lit up so the pale walls turned to gold against the evening sky, every open window glowing a warm welcome. Strategically placed palm trees softened the bold lines of the exterior while a fountain tinkled musically in the centre of the driveway turnaround.

'Help,' she said softly to herself as he pulled the car up next to waiting doormen who smoothly pulled open their doors. She'd known she was out of her depth from the first time she'd looked up at Alesander's apartment, but once again she was reminded just how far. This was a world where houses were palatial and came complete with tinkling fountains and where uniformed men waited on you hand and foot. This was so not her world.

She took a deep breath, careful not to trip on her gown, as she stepped from the car. There was music coming from inside, and the hum of conversation punctuated with the occasional peal of laughter, the note of which seemed to match the tinkling fountain. 'Nervous?' he said as he joined her, while his car was whisked away behind them for parking by the valet.

She nodded and smiled tightly, her fingers biting down on her evening purse. This was it. The night she not only met his family and friends, but paved the way for him presenting her soon as his fiancée.

Of course she was nervous.

'Relax,' he told her, his eyes massaging her fears away. 'Tonight you look like you were born to this. You look every inch an Esquivel bride. You look beautiful.'

She blinked up at him. Did he really mean it or was it just one more of his build-her-up pep talks to make her believe they could do this—before he pulled the rug out from under her feet again, just in case she actually got to thinking this could become permanent?

He'd barely spoken in the car after she'd thanked him for playing along with Felipe's joke and she'd guessed it was because he didn't have an audience he needed to impress any more.

'It's true,' he said, as if he was attuned to her unsaid thoughts and fears, his face perilously close to hers as he squeezed her hand so hard that she almost felt as if she wanted to believe him. But this was Alesander, she reminded herself. Alesander wasn't in the business of being nice. He bestowed upon her courtesies to convince everyone else that they were a couple, and he needed her to believe enough to carry it off.

Nothing more.

And that was *exactly* the way she wanted it. Business, she reminded herself, taking a deep breath. This is business. She could do this if she remembered it was business. 'Okay,' she said with a determination she wished would stop wavering, 'I'm ready. Let's get this show on the road.'

But if arriving at Markel's home had been daunting, inside was terrifying. So many people, so many women, all of whom seemed to know Alesander. All of whom were apparently keen to discover who she was.

Right now she might just as well have been a butterfly stuck with a pin inside a display case.

'Alesander, you came.' A woman's voice broke through the laughter. 'I knew you would.'

He leaned down and they kissed, cheek to cheek. 'Of course, Madre, I wouldn't have missed it for the world.'

The woman's gaze didn't linger on her son, moving at laser speed over his guest, appraisal, judgement and summary execution in one rapier-sharp movement. 'Oh, I see you found another cleaner.'

Cleaner? She looked up at him, waiting for an explanation, but Alesander only laughed.

'Allow me to introduce you to Simone Hamilton, granddaughter of Felipe. Simone, my mother, Isobel Esquivel.'

Simone's greeting was cut off, her proffered hand left hanging.

'Felipe?'

'Felipe Otxoa—our neighbour in Getaria. Remember?'

'Oh, *that* Felipe. I didn't realise he had a grand-daughter.'

'I'm from Australia,' Simone offered in her rusty Spanish. 'I haven't been here long.'

The older woman smiled for the first time. 'Oh,' she said, giving Simone's hand the briefest of acknowledgements with hers, 'I hope you enjoy your holiday,' and took Alesander's arm, effectively excluding her from the conversation as she turned away to look for someone in the crowd. 'By the way, darling, have you seen Ezmerelda yet? She looks fabulous tonight.'

Simone hooked a glass of champagne from a passing tray and almost had it to her mouth before Alesander claimed her arm and drew her back into the group. Wine sloshed over the rim of her glass at the sudden change of direction. His mother noticed, sending her a look of *oh-you-so-don't-belong-here*, and she thought how terrified she'd be if Isobel was to be her real mother-in-law. Fortunately she didn't have to be terrified.

'Alesander's always grabbing me at inopportune times,' she shared with a conspiratorial smile. 'It's quite embarrassing.'

As if to agree, he smiled and pulled her in close to his body. She didn't mind the display of affection. Not really. Other than what it did to her internal thermostat. But she could imagine worse places to be than against the hard wall of his body. And it was for a good cause. 'Simone is actually staying a while,' he said. 'As long as Felipe needs help.'

His mother looked anywhere but at the places they made contact. 'What's wrong with Felipe?'

'He's ill, I'm afraid. He's not doing so well lately.'

For a moment she almost thought she saw something like sympathy reflected in the older woman's eyes but just as swiftly it was gone as she caught sight of someone in the crowd. 'Oh, there she is. Alesander, I'll be right back.'

'So who's Ezmerelda?' she asked, easing herself away from the disturbing proximity of his body heat when his mother was out of earshot. 'Should I be afraid?'

'Markel's daughter, to answer your first question, and probably a resounding yes to the second.'

'And why, exactly, should I be afraid of her?'

He leaned close to her ear and whispered, 'Because you're wearing her dress.'

Shock forced her jaw to fall open. She stared at him, disbelieving. 'What? So you knew all the time who wanted this dress? What kind of person would do that?'

'A person who thought the dress would be wasted on her and look better on you. And it would have been and it does. Much better.'

She barely had time to digest that justification—for she could hardly call it a compliment, surely—when his mother was back with two people in tow. 'Here they are,' she said. 'I told you Ezmerelda looked fabulous.'

Simone caught her breath. Not just fabulous, but stunning as she smiled a greeting to another couple as she passed, her bearing regal if not haughty, looking every inch a Spanish society princess with her black hair pulled back and woven into an intricate up-do, and wide dark eyes and flawless skin. Simone felt pale and uninteresting in comparison.

Markel reached them first, bowing a ruddy-cheeked

face lower to catch her name, his smile wide as she wished him a happy birthday before he drifted off into the crowd for more congratulations. She liked the man on sight.

And then Ezmerelda turned her head and her smile widened as her gaze fell on Alesander, a smile that slid away when her eyes found her standing alongside, especially when she saw what she was wearing. Simone saw confusion in her beautiful eyes, and anger and something else that looked like hurt, and she wished the floor would open up and swallow her whole.

'Alesander,' she said, turning away once she'd recovered, 'how lovely of you to come.'

They kissed cheeks. 'You're looking beautiful, as usual, Ezmerelda. I'd like you to meet Simone Hamilton.'

'How lovely you brought a friend,' she said with barely a glance in her direction, 'but then when do you not have a friend? You're simply too popular, Alesander.'

She wanted to run. It was like being in a lion's den with a lioness whose cub she was trying to steal. A hungry lioness. But Alesander wouldn't let her run. He had her pinned in tight next to his body and he wasn't letting her go.

It was a relief when a band started playing. 'Ah,' Ezmerelda said, 'the tango display is about to begin, a special treat for my father. I must find him.'

Simone almost sagged with relief, thankful now that he had such a tight hold on her.

'Come,' he said, ushering her to a balcony overlooking the floor below, where two dancers posed dramatically, metres apart, on the marble floor. The woman was stunning, her gown like a sheath that flared into a sequin-studded skirt slit to the hip. The man looked equally potent.

And they watched as the music became more dramatic and the dancers circled each other almost warily before starting their attack. And it almost seemed like an attack to Simone—a chase, a seduction, rejection and sex. The dance was unmistakably about sex.

She felt it through each dramatic gesture, each silken caress, all of them purposeful and part of the game. They were exhilarating. But the last was the best, the music evocative and sexy and the dancers, now gleaming in the light with sweat, turned the music physical with their bodies. 'What is this music?' she whispered, moved by its powerful emotion.

'It's called *Sentimientos*,' he whispered back, close to her ear, his warm breath fanning her ear and throat while his thumb traced lazy circles on the back of her hand. 'It means feelings.'

It didn't surprise her. It was the most beautiful music she had ever heard.

Just as the dancers' physical expression of the music was the sexiest thing she had ever seen. She felt breathless with the spectacle, and never before had she been so acutely aware of the man standing beside her, of his steady breathing, of all the places where their bodies touched.

She liked how it felt.

She hated that she liked it.

And when the dancing was over and Alesander released her to applaud, she took the opportunity to flee to the powder room, closing the door behind her and hushing out the sounds of the party. She leaned both hands on the counter and breathed deep. She would have to go back out soon and smile and try to look relaxed, as if she was enjoying herself, but for now, for just a few short moments, she didn't have to pretend.

She heard the door open and close behind her but didn't bother looking up. It wasn't as if she knew anyone. 'I like your gown.'

Except maybe her.

She opened her eyes. Ezmerelda was standing by the door, watching her. Would it be paranoid of her to think the woman had followed her in here? She tossed up whether or not to apologise, to say she hadn't known it was her dress when they'd bought it, but that would mean she knew and maybe it was more politic to pretend to know nothing. 'Thank you. As it happens, I like yours.'

She shrugged the compliment aside. 'In fact I almost bought one similar to yours recently. Remarkably similar, in fact. Until I decided it was too trashy for such a significant event such as this. It suits you, though.'

Ouch. Mind you, she could hardly blame Ezmerelda being irate after the stunt Alesander had pulled. Not that it meant she'd take this woman's ire lying down.

'What a coincidence,' she replied evenly. 'I do believe I saw one like yours too. But I decided this one was so much sexier.'

Ezmerelda's eyes glittered as she swept a path to the counter, digging a lipstick from her purse, touching it to her blood-red lips. 'I expect Alesander bought it for you?'

Simone smiled at the other woman. Did anyone here not believe it? She shrugged. 'So what if he did?'

'You're sleeping with him then.' She nodded. 'I thought as much.'

Simone didn't bother denying it as Ezmerelda

calmly went back to checking her make-up. She'd clearly made up her mind and, besides, wasn't that what they wanted people to think? And then, just as abruptly, the woman stopped preening and stared at her in the mirror.

'I like you, Simone. You don't pretend to be anything that you're not and I really do understand. You sleep with him—he buys you a dress and takes you to a big party. It's a simple arrangement. I can see the appeal.' She shrugged. 'And because you have been honest with me, I, in turn, will be honest with you.'

'I appreciate it.' Simone waited as the other woman reshaped two perfectly arched eyebrows with her finger.

'Alesander likes his women. Everybody knows that. But everybody here also knows that family comes first, whatever distractions he finds along the way.' She tilted her head and smiled sympathetically. 'And believe me, there have been plenty of distractions along the way. But our two families have always had an understanding and perhaps you should also understand. Alesander and I are to be married.'

Really? Funny how Alesander hadn't mentioned that little fact along the way. 'Do you love him?' she ventured uneasily. She suspected not— Ezmerelda didn't look as if she was pining for a man who didn't seem to know she was alive, but she'd already inadvertently stolen a gown out from under her. She didn't want someone's broken heart on her conscience as well. That hadn't been part of her plans.

For a moment the other woman looked perplexed. 'I like him, yes, and it is a good match,' she said before nodding, as if agreeing with her own words. 'Together our families will create a new dynasty. He will love me, of course.'

Simone found a smile for Ezmerelda and this time it was genuine. What kind of life must she have, waiting for a man who showed no inclination to marry her—indeed, who flaunted his women in front of her? 'Then I do understand. Thank you so much for taking the time to share that with me.'

The Spanish woman sighed and swivelled in front of the mirror, checking the view from every angle, before snapping her purse closed, her smile back on and in full force. 'I'm so pleased we had this little chat. I should get back to the party now.'

'You should,' Simone agreed as the other woman headed for the door. 'Oh, and Ezmerelda?'

'*Sí?*'

'You look stunning in that gown. You are far and away the most beautiful woman here tonight.'

And the other woman smiled. '*Sí*,' she said, and slipped out of the room, leaving Simone staring blankly at the door, trying to get her head together. Alesander had asked if she had a boyfriend, but she hadn't thought to ask him if there was someone in his life who would be upset by his marriage. She'd assumed he would never have said yes if there was.

But now there was Ezmerelda, who clearly thought she was first in line to marry him. And she might not love him, she might be all kinds of crazy to wait for a man who clearly had no intention of marrying her, but when their engagement was announced, she was going to be devastated.

How could she do this?

'I thought I'd lost you,' Alesander said when finally she emerged from the powder room, handing her a fresh glass of wine before walking her slowly towards French windows that led to a terrace overlooking the garden.

'I would have been back much sooner, but your girlfriend and apparently my new best friend wanted to have a little heart-to-heart with me.'

'My girlfriend?'

She rolled her eyes. Were there so many of them that he lost track? 'Ezmerelda, of course.'

'About the dress?'

She sipped her wine as she stepped out into the balmy night air and a courtyard strung with fairy lights. 'Words were spoken about the dress, it's true, although strangely enough the main topic of the conversation was you.'

'Should I be worried?'

The lights reflected in his eyes, turning them playful. She wanted to smack him.

'I was warned off you because apparently your families have an "understanding" and you're practically betrothed. Imagine my surprise.'

He took her hand in his and lifted it to his mouth, his hot lips like a brand upon her skin. 'Imagine Ezmerelda's surprise when she learns that we are to be married.'

She pulled her hand away, wishing he wouldn't do that thing with her hand and his mouth. Wishing even more that she didn't shiver every time he did.

'You're not planning on telling her our arrangement is only temporary, then?'

'Why would I do that?'

'Why wouldn't you, if you cared anything for this woman who claims to be the next best thing to your fiancèe? Unless, of course, you don't care anything for her. Then again, given you're the man who bought the dress she had reserved for another woman to wear to the same party and then stood back to watch the fireworks, I'd conclude you don't care much for her at all. I'd even be willing to conclude you don't even like her.'

He looked around, checking to make sure they were not overheard, before dipping his head and continuing in a low voice that rumbled over her skin. 'Let's just say Ezmerelda is not my idea of a happily ever after, whatever our respective mothers may have concocted during their regular coffee mornings.'

She shrugged the stroke of voice on skin away. 'So you really played me for a fool. You didn't really need the vines to seal this deal at all, did you?'

'Excuse me?'

'That whole "What's in it for me?" argument of yours was a crock all along. My proposal was just what you needed to get Ezmerelda off your back.'

'I am quite capable of dealing with Ezmerelda with or without your intervention.'

'But marrying me does provide you with a handy out. She can't marry you if you've already got a wife. I bet you're hoping she's got her talons in someone else before our marriage is over.'

'I admit there may have been an element of that in my deliberations.'

'So I didn't have to sign over the vines at all. There was already plenty in it for you.'

'But you did sign them over.'

'But if I'd known about Ezmerelda—'

'That's just it,' he said, downing the rest of his glass and placing it on the tray of a passing waiter. 'You didn't.'

She turned away, feeling as if she'd been duped.

Worse, she felt used. She'd thought they'd negotiated a deal when he'd held all the cards to begin with. Felipe had told her to watch him and he was right. Alesander was as ruthless as they came.

And it didn't matter to know that her future waited for her half a world away. A vineyard halfway up a mountain in northern Spain was no good to her as it was, but she could have sold it. Alesander would have bought it, even if it was overgrown and neglected. She could have got something for it. Instead she'd practically given it to him and now she'd be going home as penniless as when she'd arrived.

'Cheer up,' he said. 'You don't look like you're having fun.'

'Oh, I am,' she lied. 'I'm having immense fun debating when to confide to my new best friend that all is not lost, that maybe things aren't as dire as they seem and that she may well still get her man, slightly used but none the worse for wear. But do I tell her before the wedding, or after?'

He bristled. She saw it in the flex of his shoulders and the set of a jaw that had gone from smug to stiff in a heartbeat. 'You wouldn't dare risk the news getting out and getting back to Felipe.'

'You're right, I wouldn't. But it was so worth the look on your face to say it.'

'You have a strange sense of humour, Miss Hamilton.'

'Miss Hamilton? We are formal, aren't we? I suspect I must have made you angry for some reason.'

'On the contrary, but you do have a habit of taking me by surprise at times.'

'Do I? That's actually a good thing, isn't it? It would

be awful being stuck together for even ten minutes if we bored each other senseless.'

Oh, there was no chance of that, he thought.

'Anyway,' she continued, 'I won't have to tell Ezmerelda anything, because you're going to tell her that you're getting married and to someone else first.'

'What?'

'Before you make any public announcement of our impending marriage, you will take Ezmerelda aside and let her know that we are getting married. And I don't care what you think of her or what kind of person she might be, she deserves to hear it from you first. She deserves that much consideration at least.'

Now he was angry. He looked down at her coldly. He wasn't used to being told what to do, let alone by a pint-sized woman who without her spiky heels barely came up to his shoulder. But, worst of all, he supposed she might actually be right. The last thing they needed when he made the announcement was a scene.

Though he'd wager that wasn't what was motivating Simone. If he didn't know better, he'd actually think she felt sorry for Ezmerelda, which made no sense at all, given the way she hadn't hesitated to warn her off.

And that was something new. As far as he knew, she'd never done that before. Or maybe nobody else had ever been game enough to tell him. This woman was, not to mention game enough to tell him to put her out of her misery as part of the deal. His doorstep bride really was turning out to be a surprise package indeed.

He looked around at the thinning crowd. He'd thought about making the announcement tonight when there were still enough people to witness the news to guarantee its rapid spread, but Simone did have a point. He didn't want to ruin Markel's party by creating a scene.

'Will you be all right if I leave you for a few minutes?'

She raised one eyebrow in question—a question he chose to ignore. 'I'll be fine. And look, here comes Markel.' The older man joined them, his ruddy cheeks even redder, his greying hair spiking up above one ear. 'Markel,' she said, 'I don't suppose you could look after me while Alesander runs off to take care of some business?'

'Gladly,' he said, looping her arm through his. 'Nothing would give me greater pleasure. You can tell me all about Australia. Tell me, is it true they sell wine in cardboard boxes there?'

'It is true, though it created all sorts of problems in the industry.'

'Oh,' he said, all ears. 'Why is that?'

'Nobody could work out how to make square grapes.'

It was the lamest attempt at a joke she'd ever made, but Markel roared with laughter, his good birthday humour clearly alcohol assisted.

Remarkable, Alesander thought as he drifted out of earshot, searching the crowd for a familiar face— now she told jokes? What other hidden talents did the woman possess?

There were some that weren't so much hidden as suggested. Just thinking of her in that dress, there were some he wouldn't mind having revealed. From the moment he'd arrived to pick her up and seen her wearing it again, the split from toe to thigh over one leg and the bodice wrapped low over her breasts, he'd wanted to do nothing more than to peel it off. He'd stewed the whole way here, wondering how he was going to do just that and still comply with the terms of the agreement. He'd held her close during the tango display, wishing it would go on for ever so he could feel her close to him.

He knew he wasn't the only man who'd lusted after her tonight. He knew the look and he'd recognised it in other men's eyes. And just the thought of others thinking the same made his breath growl in his throat. He needed them to know she was his—truly his.

His eyes scanned the ballroom.

So why had he agreed to this no-sex rule? What was the point of it? Forced contraception? They could easily prevent an unwanted pregnancy—people did it all the time.

No, she'd turned up on his doorstep looking like a stray—no wonder he'd agreed to her no sex condition. But that was then.

Now he could see what she'd been hiding under her too big clothes. Now he wanted to see more.

And it wasn't enough to marry her. He needed to stamp her with his ownership so that everyone would know, without a shadow of a doubt, that she was his in every sense of the word.

She would agree.

There was no question she would agree.

Because he'd make sure she had no choice.

He caught sight of a familiar flash of colour across the room, heard a familiar laugh and saw greedy eyes turn his way, lighting up when they saw he was alone.

Yes, he looked forward to the coming contract re-negotiations with another woman, but first he had a job to do.

CHAPTER SEVEN

THE DRESS WAS definitely the problem. Alesander watched her entertaining her circle of admirers and thought he should have let her choose one of the other gowns, as spectacular as they had been. But they had been nothing in comparison with this one, that turned woman into siren, hinting at what lay beneath if one was only reckless enough to try.

He was reckless enough to try.

Maybe if Ezmerelda had worn this dress tonight, nobody would have noticed Simone.

Then she laughed at something Markel had said and he saw the sparkle in her eyes and the warmth in her smile and he knew the dress would have made no difference. It was Simone who made the difference. Maybe the dress caught people's eye, but it was Simone herself who held their attention. The trouble was, there were too many people taking notice.

Correction—there were too many men.

He'd left her for what? All of fifteen minutes and yet now she was surrounded by them, Markel still there in the midst of them, no doubt wishing he was thirty years younger.

And he knew why they were there.

Because she was beautiful and desirable and they

all thought she was his latest plaything and they were lining up for a piece of her when he was done.

And it was his fault. Because he'd never before been seen with a woman on his arm who he wasn't sleeping with and meaning to dispose of. He'd never before been seen with a woman who wasn't temporary.

He swallowed back on the bitter taste of bile at the back of his throat. Well, this woman might be temporary but he wasn't sleeping with her.

Not yet.

But he'd soon fix that.

He made his way across the room towards them, knowing it was right to have decided what he had, already anticipating the pleasures that were to come. Finding a smile came easily, so easily in fact that she looked up at him and frowned and he realised he'd already forgotten about his little chat with Ezmerelda.

That made his smile widen even further.

Anticipation was a fine thing.

There must have been something in his eyes, for the other men drifted away, back to their own women, leaving only Markel, who snagged his arm as soon as he came close. 'You are a lucky man, Alesander. Simone is not only a beautiful woman, but she is clever and entertaining. Promise me you will not deprive us of her company in the future.'

'You're in luck, Markel, as it happens,' he said, sliding a proprietorial arm around Simone, who looked more confused than ever. 'I wasn't going to say anything—it is your birthday celebration after all, but there will be another party very soon and one to which you're invited, because a little earlier tonight Simone agreed to become my wife.'

'Your wife?' Markel blinked his surprise. 'But this is wonderful news!'

'I hoped you'd think so. I know Isobel and your wife had other plans.'

Markel waved the younger man's concerns away before laying his hand on Alesander's shoulder. 'As much as I would love to have you as my son-in-law, it was clear to me it was never going to happen. There was never any spark between you two. I tried to tell Ezmerelda that.' He shrugged. 'She chose not to listen. Her mother had put all kinds of fanciful notions into her head and she preferred to believe those.'

'I've already spoken to her tonight to let her know before she heard via other means.'

'*Bueno.* That was thoughtful of you.' Markel sighed wistfully. 'And perhaps it is good you are getting married because now she will forget her foolish dreams and finally see that there are other men in the world. I can only hope.

'As for you two,' he said, taking both their hands in his meaty hand, 'I wish you every success and many, many fine sons.'

'How did Ezmerelda take it?' she asked when they were in the car and heading towards Getaria. 'Was it rough?'

He changed gears to take a bend, the car sticking to the road like glue. 'She cried.'

'Oh.'

'And then she pleaded.'

'Ah.'

'And then she wished us all the best in our married life.' He didn't tell her the rest, that she'd said she'd noticed they had a connection from the moment she'd

seen them together and that was why she'd followed
Simone to warn her off, because she'd never before
felt so threatened. There were some things that sat uncomfortably with him. There were some things that
Simone didn't need to know.

'That was nice of her, in the circumstances.'

'*Sí*, but it was good of you to think of telling her.
That would not have occurred to me. It shows a generous spirit.'

She laughed at that. 'I don't know about that. I just
wish we didn't have to deceive everyone this way. I
never thought it would be so complicated. I was thinking only of Felipe when I came up with this plan and I
never realised other people might get hurt by it. Like
Markel. He's a nice man. I like him.'

'Markel is a good man.'

'I'm truly sorry he's going to be disappointed.'

'You mean because of the marriage ending?'

'Yes.' She sighed. 'But also because of all those fine
sons you're not going to have.'

He smiled. He was in too good a mood not to. Tomorrow he would ask Felipe for Simone's hand in marriage. He didn't expect the old man to be happy about
it, but he'd come around, just as soon as he realised it
would mean the Otxoa family fortunes finally shifting in the right direction.

And then, as soon as he'd secured his agreement,
he'd tell Simone he was changing the terms. She might
not like it—no, more like it, she would hate it—but by
then it would be too late.

And she would be his, in every sense of the word.

'What's the rush?' demanded Felipe at lunch the next
day. 'You barely know each other.'

The three of them were sitting outside, the table set under an ancient pergola creaking under the weight of overgrown vines, sunlight filtering through the dense forest of leaves while far below them the sunlight turned the sea sparkling. Alesander had come over ostensibly to do some more work on the vines when she'd lured Felipe outside to enjoy the mild weather while it lasted. Over lunch, after they'd shared a bottle of last season's Txakolina wine that she was beginning to acquire a taste for, Felipe pouring it from a great height into tumblers to give life to the bubbles and clearly enjoying himself. And after lunch Alesander had asked Felipe for permission to marry her.

'Sometimes you just know, Abuelo.' Simone had expected the request to come as a shock and it had. Felipe's initial prejudices towards Alesander were softening each and every time he visited, she could tell, but there were still too many decades of rivalry between the neighbouring families to be calmly put aside.

'But marriage? Already?'

'It's not so soon. It will still take a month for the paperwork to be processed. The wedding won't take place until after harvest.'

He frowned. 'Do you love her?' he asked Alesander pointedly.

Simone winced. More lies, she thought, hating it. How many lies would they have to tell before this was over?

Except Alesander seemed unfazed. He took her hand in his, covering it with his other, while his eyes held hers, dark and rich and so deep a person could drown in their depths. 'I admit, I did not expect this to happen. But Simone blew into my life and how could

I not love her, Felipe? She is very special. One of a kind. How could I let her slip through my fingers?'

There was no stopping the bloom of heat in her cheeks. She smiled, deeply touched that he would take the trouble to find the words to put Felipe at his ease.

'I thought you wanted the vines,' he said, and there was a tear in his eye. 'I thought you were looking to take the rest of them away from me. But it is my granddaughter who brings you here day after day.'

Alesander looked at his feet and Simone knew she had to fill the silence. 'We want you to be there at our wedding, Abuelo. I was hoping you would agree to give me away.'

Her grandfather puffed up before her eyes, blinking away the moisture. 'And you think I won't be there to walk my only granddaughter down the aisle on her wedding day? Of course I will be there.'

He lifted his empty tumbler in his bony claw-like hand. 'More wine,' he demanded. 'This calls for a toast!'

'Thank you for that.'

She'd walked Alesander to his car, their lunch over, Felipe snoozing under the vine covered canopy.

'For what?'

'For putting Felipe's mind at ease about us getting married. When he asked you if you loved me, I thought the game was up.'

He cocked one eyebrow, one side of his mouth turned up. 'You imagined I would simply say no?'

'I didn't know what you would say.'

He took her hands in his and she thought nothing of it, given they were still in sight of the house if Felipe happened to wake up and see them. Besides, she was getting to like the feeling of him touching her. If only because that meant she was getting used to it and that made the pretence easier to pull off. 'It was not hard to think of words I could say about you. It is true you are one of a kind, and you definitely blew into my life by turning up on my doorstep with your crazy proposal. And how could I let you slip through my fingers when you had such a juicy incentive?' He paused and looked out over the sparkling sea. 'Felipe was right all along about that.'

'He doesn't think so now.'

'No. And hopefully he will never find out.'

'I know. I feel bad about the lies. But it's worth it. You can see how happy this has made him. For the first time he has something to look forward to. He's smiling again. Thank you so much for not only agreeing to this, but for actually going to the trouble of making him believe it.'

He looked back at her and smiled, squeezing her hands to tug her a little closer as he dipped his head towards hers. She held her breath as his mouth came closer; held her breath as she wondered whether he would kiss her—and whether she should let him—it wouldn't mean anything after all, just a token gesture and probably meant for Felipe's benefit in case he was watching and so why should she stop him?

And then he kissed her forehead and breath rushed out of her on a whoosh.

From relief, she told herself. Not disappointment, despite that sudden inexplicable pang in her chest.

Except he didn't let her go. His lips lingered on her forehead, she felt his breath fan against her skin and he let one hand go, only to take her chin in his fingers as slowly he pulled away, tilting up her head at the same time.

Her eyes met his and held. 'I have to kiss you,' he said, 'but properly this time and, I warn you, it may take some time.'

'For Felipe's benefit?' she managed to say. 'In case he is watching.'

He growled, the corners of his mouth turning up the tiniest fraction. 'For my benefit.'

If such a confession wasn't enough to make her senses sing, the sensation of his lips meshing with hers was. Her breath hitched again at their impact, before she was assailed by the feel of his mouth against hers and the sheer complexity of it all—the unexpected contrast of lips that felt so warm and yielding and yet came from a face that could have been sculpted from stone. And the way he tasted…a heated blend of the wine they'd shared at lunch with coffee and all overlaid on the flavour of his own hot mouth.

He was addictive.

He was incendiary.

Her heart rate kicked up as she felt his hand draw her closer and she let herself be drawn as his tongue searched out hers and invited it into a dance—a dance that soon turned into a heated frenzy that had her temperature soaring and her heart beating even faster and her flesh throbbing in secret places situated a long way geographically from her mouth.

If the man knew nothing else, he sure knew how to kiss. Every place they touched seemed hyper-aware— her breasts jammed close to his chest, her hips hard against his thighs, her legs interwoven with his.

It was far more than any kiss she'd ever experienced.

And it was the last thing she'd wanted, but right now it made it too damned good to leave.

Instead it was Alesander who pulled away suddenly, putting her at arm's length, leaving her mouth hungry and desperately seeking his. Desperately seeking more. He was breathing hard, but she was breathing harder, and struggling hard to show she was not as affected as she was.

Failing miserably.

'We need to plan,' he said, his breathing choppy and desperate against her face. 'Are you taking precautions?'

For a kiss? Now she had to struggle with the meaning behind his words. She wasn't sure she'd heard right. 'Excuse me?'

'Are you on the Pill? Do you call it that where you come from—the contraceptive pill?'

She eased away. Even managed to laugh a little, while she put distance between them, though nowhere near enough to let him go completely. She wasn't ready for that yet and, besides, he was showing no intention of letting her go any time soon. 'What business is that of yours?'

'Because we will need precautions.'

'Against—what exactly? We've agreed we're not having sex. Why would we need precautions?'

'Because I've changed my mind. I'm not marrying you and not having sex with you.'

This time she found the strength to shove him away. 'No! You signed a contract! We both signed a contract. We agreed there would be no sex.'

'And I'm renegotiating the terms.'

'You can't do that. It's too late.'

'Of course I can. I don't like the terms and I'm changing them.'

'And I refuse to agree to your changed terms. There will be no sex in our marriage.'

'And I say there will.'

'What? And you think you can make me? I don't think so. I'm not changing anything. I don't want it.'

'Are you sure of that? I just got the impression you would quite happily have had me, right here, right up against the car next to the vines if I hadn't stopped, and you would have let me.'

Shock forced her jaw wide open. 'You imagine this because I let you kiss me just now?'

'You did more than let me kiss you. Your body told me it wanted me.'

'You flatter yourself,' she said, shaking her head, in denial because she had to be. He had felt good, it was true. Maybe very good. But he could not know what she had been thinking. 'You're wrong. I don't want you. Sure, we shared a kiss, and maybe it was okay, but it was only for Felipe's benefit.'

'Now who's kidding themselves? You weren't thinking about Felipe when I kissed you.'

'That doesn't mean we're having sex. There's no way I want sex with you. No way at all.'

'Fine.' He took a step back from her. 'I must have been mistaken. If that's the way you want it, I will go back up there and tell Felipe this marriage is off.'

'What? Why? I don't understand. You make one arrangement and then you insist on another? You can't do that to him! How could you do that after everything we've done? Felipe believes it now. He believes we're getting married. He thinks he's walking me down the aisle. How could you do this to him?'

'How could I do that to him?' he said. 'No. You should be asking how *you* could do this to him. You're the one suddenly wanting to deny him his happy ending.'

He was shifting the blame onto her? 'I can't believe you're doing this. Though maybe I should, because Felipe warned me from the very start that I should be careful. He said you were an Esquivel and that I shouldn't trust you, that you would be ruthless. I should have listened to him all along.'

'Maybe you should have.'

His cold, hard words floored her. Where was the man who had sucked her into his kiss, and whose heat had damned near melted her flesh? Where was that man? Had he been an entire fiction? She felt sick just thinking about how much she'd wanted him. 'I hate you. I don't think I've ever hated you more than in this moment.'

'That's fine. I told you I wasn't nice. Hating me will make it so much easier when you leave.'

CHAPTER EIGHT

SHE WANTED TO hate him after that. She did her best to. Late at night atop her single bed she did all she could to hate him. But hate disappeared in the overwhelming truth.

She should never have let him kiss her.

Now her body ached to make love to him and yet she didn't want to make love to him. She couldn't make love to him. Making love made a person vulnerable. She'd learned that with Damon, their relationship going from boyfriend and girlfriend, moving with their lovemaking to a higher level. To love. Or so she'd thought.

Damon's betrayal had ripped all sense of wanting intimacy out of her. Keep it platonic, she'd learned. Keep it simple, and you couldn't be hurt.

Keep it platonic—businesslike—and there could be no complications.

She knew this to be true. She knew she'd been right to insist on a sex-free marriage. She didn't want to go through what she had with Damon again. She couldn't live with the fear and the gut-sickening uncertainty.

And yet still the thought of Alesander's threatened lovemaking left her breathless and hungry. She tossed and turned in the small bed, tangling in the sheets, thinking about sheets tangled for other, more carnal, reasons.

Wishing that she didn't look forward to it as much as she dreaded it.

Wishing she could simply hate him and be done with it.

She tossed again. Oh God, why the hell couldn't she sleep?

The season shifted inexorably towards the harvest, and Alesander was busier, managing both his own business and yet still finding time to spend in Felipe's vineyard, repairing trellises and filling in pot-holes in the driveway and, even though she knew he was doing it because the land would soon be his, she could not hate him for it when she saw how it made Felipe happier, to see his vines and the vineyard looking cared for again.

She tried to keep her distance as much as she could but somehow he was always there, shrinking the tiny cottage with his presence, talking to Felipe about the grapes, or comparing techniques to manage the vines.

And there could be no avoiding him because, as the harvest drew closer, so too did their wedding. Alesander appointed a wedding planner charged with the task of organising a wedding extravaganza in less than a month. Simone was happy to leave her to it, but there was no escaping the endless questions. There were meetings to be had, decisions to be made, plans to be drawn up.

And nothing could wait. Every little thing was urgent.

'I can't get a church,' the wedding planner admitted at one of their first meetings, looking harried and stressed. 'You've waited too long. San Sebastian's churches are booked up months in advance and the village churches are full.'

Alesander brushed the problem aside. 'Then we'll get married in the Esquivel vineyard. It's unconventional, but everyone will understand.'

The wedding planner looked noticeably relieved and turned to Simone. 'Have you decided on who will be your attendant?'

Simone blinked. 'Do I really need one?'

The planner looked askance at Alesander. 'Who have you chosen as your best man?'

'A friend from Madrid. Matteo Cachon.'

Simone's ears pricked up. The name sounded vaguely familiar.

'Not the football player?' asked the woman, and Simone realised where she'd heard it. On the evening news. Matteo Cachon had just been signed in a massive deal that made him Spain's most valuable football player. In the same report came the news he'd just dumped his long-term girlfriend, so he was also Spain's most eligible bachelor.

He nodded. '*Sí*. He's an old friend from university. We don't see each other much these days but it fits in his schedule and he's agreed.'

'I have an idea about an attendant,' Simone said, and when the wedding planner looked expectantly back at her, pen poised, added, 'I'll ask her and get back to you.'

Meanwhile Felipe was the happiest she'd ever seen him. He seemed to have dropped twenty years overnight. He even seemed to have more energy, demanding to be taken into town to be fitted out with a brand new suit, his first new suit since his marriage to Maria more than fifty years before.

It made it all worthwhile, even after the visit to his doctor, who'd taken her aside while Felipe was getting dressed to warn that while Felipe was feeling happier, she shouldn't make the mistake of thinking he was getting better. There would be no getting better.

She'd thanked the doctor and swallowed back on a bubble of disappointment. Deep down inside she'd known that to be true, that there would be no sudden miracle or remission. She just hadn't wanted to give that knowledge oxygen.

But the doctor's warning made up her mind. She would stop this Cold War approach to Alesander. She would stop trying to make herself hate him and instead try to make this marriage look as happy for Felipe as she possibly could, although she hated the changed terms.

Because she would not let Felipe down.

The grapes tested perfectly one crisp day early in October and from then on it was madness. Swarms of workers filled the Esquivel vineyards, filling boxes with bunches of grapes, boxes emptied into a tractor drawn behind a trailer to be taken straight to the press.

Simone worked in Felipe's vineyard as part of a team sent by Alesander, wearing oversized gloves and with a pair of thin-bladed snippers, perfectly designed for separating the bunches from the vines. If you knew what you were doing. In no time she knew she was the slowest person on the team. But she was determined to catch on, filling box after box with bunches of grapes.

Felipe sat on the vine-covered terrace and kept an eye on the progress, muttering to himself.

They took a break halfway through the morning, sitting amidst the vines, talking and laughing amongst

themselves while they shared the most magnificent
view on earth, and Simone felt privileged to experience this; to be part of something so utterly unique
that she would never share in again. It made her sorry
that she would ever have to leave.

And then they were back at work and there was no
time for regret, only time for the grapes.

Alesander turned up at lunch time, with platters of
food from a local restaurant, which the pickers shared
around a big trestle table set up for the job.

'Thank you for this,' she told him near the car when
he was leaving, and it didn't matter this time whether
she thought he was being nice or not, or whether she
thought he was only doing it because he would soon
own these vines, because she appreciated the gesture
just the same. 'Thank you for so much.'

He scooped her into his arms and dipped his head
down and kissed her lightly on the lips, to the delight of
everyone at the table nearby. 'I've missed you,' he said,
and she knew he meant how she'd held herself separate from him while she'd told herself she hated him.

Because, in spite of all her reservations, she'd
missed him too.

'We get married in three days,' he said.

'Do you think the harvest will be finished?'

He growled and she felt it reverberate through her
bones while his eyes held her hostage. 'I don't care.
I'm marrying you anyway.' And then he kissed her
again.

It was because they were all watching, she told herself, as she snipped grapes for the next day and a half.
He'd only said it because people were watching.

But still, regardless of what he'd meant, or whatever his motivation, she'd cherish forever the look in his eyes when he'd uttered those words.

Three mornings later, the harvest completed, she donned the dress that would make her the Esquivel bride. Her gown was by the same designer as the one she'd worn to Markel's birthday party. Alesander had insisted on it and she'd argued that it wasn't necessary, right up until she'd seen the gown paraded before them and wished it could be hers and before she'd had a chance to say she loved it, he'd said, 'That one,' and she'd known they were both right even before she'd tried it on.

And it was perfect. With its fitted bodice and tight waist and pleating across her hips, it echoed in so many ways the gown she'd worn to Markel's party, but then this gown was so much more, the layers filmy and soft and the perfect foil to the fitted bodice.

Simone didn't have to ask how she looked. Today there was no joking. Tears sprang from her grandfather's eyes as she emerged from her room—tears that said it all. Tears that made all the lies she'd told suddenly worthwhile. It was worth it, she told herself, to see how happy Felipe looked today.

It was all worth it.

'You look beautiful,' he said in his thready voice. 'You have made me the proudest man in the world.'

'And you look wonderful, too.' And he did, freshly shaved and in his new suit. She worried about his role, walking her down the aisle, and wondered if he was up to it, but today he looked ready for anything.

'Come on,' he said, offering her his arm, 'the car is waiting for us.'

* * *

They arrived at the Esquivel vineyard to find most of the village waiting expectantly for her outside the vaulted cellars where the wedding was to take place.

'Don't be worried,' her attendant said from the front seat. 'Celebrations always follow the harvest. This is just one more cause for celebration.'

It was, apparently, as cameras clicked and buzzed around her as the bridal party made it from the car. Felipe took the longest time, untangling his legs but still smiling as he took his granddaughter's arm for the walk down the short aisle.

Ezmerelda set off first, serene and magnificent and so calm it lent Simone strength. She followed on Felipe's arm, his steps faltering and slow, but he beamed proudly to everyone along the way.

This is his moment, she thought, much more than mine, and she slowed her steps to match his, and let him have his moment. He was back, celebrating with the people he'd lived with all his life, the people he'd been cut off from, first with his wife's illness and then with his own disease.

He was in his element and he was lapping it up.

And then she saw Alesander waiting for her.

So tall and broad, and so breathtakingly handsome beyond belief, and smiling indulgently, as if he knew what she was doing taking so long making her way down the aisle.

His smile worked its way into her bones. No wonder it was so hard to tell herself she should hate him.

Finally they were there and she kissed Felipe on the cheeks as he left her with her husband-to-be. She'd done it, she thought as she listened to her vows. Her crazy plan had worked out.

Or almost worked out.

And minutes later, as they were declared man and wife and they kissed, now it was almost done. Now there was just the reception and Alesander's contract amendments to work through…

The reception was the easy bit. Ezmerelda was right, the village was in the mood to celebrate, and Felipe was not missing out on anything. She saw him stagger his way onto the dance floor as Alesander whirled her around the floor, and she wondered how long his strength would last, but how could she stop him when he was having so much fun?

Alesander whisked her past. 'However did you do it?' he asked. 'However did you get Ezmerelda on side to be your attendant?'

She smiled and looked across to the couple who had danced non-stop since the music had started, the couple the photographers were almost one hundred per cent focused upon. 'All I had to do was tell her I knew nothing about weddings and I needed her help.'

'That's all?'

'Okay, it did help when I mentioned who your best man was.'

He laughed. 'You are an amazing woman, Señora Esquivel.'

She blinked up at him and wished things could be different. 'And you are an amazing man.'

He pulled her to him and they shared that moment as he spun her around the dance floor, and this time she let herself relax and be held because it felt so good when this man held her and she knew it wouldn't last.

It didn't last. Barely a minute into the dance they heard the cries of panic.

It only took a second to work out why the music and dancing had stopped.

Felipe had collapsed on the dance floor.

CHAPTER NINE

'YOU SEEM tense,' Alesander said, as the car cruised through the quiet streets, his arm wound around her shoulders, his warm fingers tracing patterns on her skin.

'Do I?' She wasn't really surprised. She'd thought she was relaxed when they'd left the hospital. She'd accepted his arm around her shoulders and let herself tap into his strength, but on reflection she hadn't been relaxed at all. She'd just been relieved—that Felipe, in his weakened state, had simply overdone things and would be released after a night's observation. But the relief hadn't lasted long. Because almost as soon as the car had left the hospital she'd realised where they were headed.

To Alesander's apartment.

To Alesander's bed.

And the relief at knowing Felipe was in good hands for the night was no match for the apprehension that had followed. The pressure of his arm around her shoulders—the stroke of his fingers across her skin— the press of his strong thigh against hers—all of these sensations only served to ratchet up her tension and heighten her anxiety.

Because he had decreed that in spite of the agreement they'd both signed—the agreement that stipulated that this was a marriage in name only—that he intended to exercise all of his marital rights and bed her.

No, she thought on reflection, not decreed. Because this man had blackmailed her to make it so.

The fact he'd waited until their wedding night for it to happen didn't help at all.

Not now that night was here.

'The doctors say Felipe will be all right,' he said beside her, squeezing her shoulder, trying to reassure her, misinterpreting her nervousness. And that only made her angrier. Because this marriage was a device—a convenience—nothing more. Alesander didn't know the first thing about her. He didn't know what made her tick. He had no concept of what was troubling her like a man who loved her—like a real husband—would.

And yet he was expecting to take her to his bed and share the ultimate intimacy, as if he were that real husband—as if he actually cared about her.

Damn him! They'd made an agreement. They'd both signed it, only for him to go and change the rules midplay, and all because he couldn't handle the thought of a woman who wasn't interested in him, who didn't throw herself at his feet as he was used to.

'That must be a disappointment for you,' she countered, shifting herself as far as she could along the seat, wanting to put distance between them, or at least distance between their warm thighs, 'or it might have been the shortest wedding in history. You could already have been halfway to owning the entire vineyard.'

Something hard and sharp glinted in his eyes as

they met hers. 'I guess we are stuck together a little longer, in that case. And as much as that might bother you and inconvenience us both, luckily there is a silver lining attached to every dark cloud.'

She gave an unladylike snort. 'Really? So name it.'

'That's easy,' he said as he smiled and touched his hand to her forehead, where the ends of a stray curl had tangled in her lashes. With an all too gentle swipe of his fingers against her brow, he pulled the offending curl free. She shivered under the touch of his fingertip on her skin, and at the tug of hair against lash. She shivered again when she realised how much his touch affected her and how very much she didn't want it to. 'Because I get to make love to you, of course. What else could it be?'

And if she didn't already harbour enough resentment towards this man, she could hate him for the smug certainty that tonight it would happen. That tonight they would make love.

And even as he sought to relax her with the touch of his hand and the stroke of his fingers across her skin, instead his hand felt like the weight of obligation on her shoulders, his fingers heavy at the expectation of what this wedding night should bring.

A wedding night that should never be.

It was all so wrong.

It was all so false.

She looked out of the window, silently fuming, breathing deep, pretending interest in the buildings of the Platje de la Concha rather than look anywhere near him—at this man who was now her husband in name and who very shortly intended to make himself her husband in every intimate sense of the word.

And yet still not a husband at all. A real husband

would marry you because he loved you. Because he wanted to be with you and wanted to spend the rest of his life with you.

Not just because he thought he could get the vines you would inherit and get into your pants in the same deal.

'Stop the car,' she vaguely registered hearing, confused when they were still blocks away from his apartment.

The driver pulled in along the kerb. 'What are you doing?' she asked as he stepped from the car and held out his hand to her.

'Making an executive decision,' he said, his smile at odds with his tight features. 'It's such a beautiful night I thought we might both benefit from a walk along the beach.'

She looked up at him, searching his eyes in the night light, searching for meaning or another, darker, motive, but she could find none. And while it was a relief to know he wasn't so desperate to get her on her back that he would head straight to his apartment, it was disturbing too, that perhaps he wasn't as oblivious of her feelings as she had assumed. 'Thank you,' she simply said, because a walk along the beach suited her too, if only because it gave her much needed breathing space. She slid across the seat and took his hand to join him in the dark night air. 'I would appreciate that.'

The car pulled away, the driver dismissed, as Alesander tucked her arm into his and led her along the wide lamplit walkway. The mild night air kissed her skin, whispering in its salty tongue, while a fat moon hung low, sending a ribbon of silver across the water. From somewhere came the sounds of music, the strains of a violin to which the low waves whooshed in and out along the shore. Beside her Alesander said little, seemingly content also to absorb the evening, their war of words and wills temporarily suspended.

He was right, she thought, as they strolled their slow way around the bay. It was a beautiful night, a night made for lovers, a night where the air held a note of expectation, almost as if it was holding its breath waiting for something. And that thought left her sad, that this night and all its romance was wasted on them. Because she had no expectations. Hers was an obligation. Hers was nothing to look forward to.

Although…

She stole a look at his strong profile. His was not a face you would be disappointed waking up to after the night before. His body was not one you would regret reaching out for. And then she shivered a little, turning her eyes back to the path and trying not to think too much about that night before.

The night to come.

Was she pathetic to feel so nervous? She'd got naked with a man. She'd had sex. She knew how it worked and where the various bits went. Sometimes she'd even enjoyed it. But that had been with Damon, and they'd been a couple for almost a year. She'd even imagined she loved him at one stage—before she'd found out he was happily having sex with her best friend behind her back. But they'd been friends before they'd become lovers. Of course there had been times it had been good with him.

But sex with a virtual stranger?

Sex with a man who had blackmailed her into his bed?

There was no way she could enjoy that.

And there was no way she could trust her feelings

when she did. Intimacy came with a price, one she wasn't sure she wanted to pay again.

'Are you cold?' he asked, as if he'd sensed her tremor.

'I'm fine,' she replied, wishing he hadn't noticed, not wanting him to know anything about her, uncomfortable with the thought he was reading her body.

'Then why don't we walk on the beach?'

'Take our shoes off, you mean?'

'Unless you can walk in high heels on the sand.' And his smile caught the moonlight and his teeth glinted white to match the spark in his eyes and the idea was so unexpected that she laughed.

'Why not?'

She slipped off her silver sandals and unhooked the stockings from her suspenders, slipping them down her legs while he shrugged off his shoes before taking her hand. The sand was cool under her feet and tickled the sensitive skin between her toes. His hand was warm, his long fingers curled around hers, his thumb drawing lazy circles on her wrist.

She tried to concentrate on the sand and the squeak of their steps on the sand, on the lights of the buildings reflected into the bay, on the stars and moon above, but his touch wasn't easy to ignore. Damon hadn't liked holding hands. He'd said it signalled possessiveness and argued that people weren't possessions.

Was Alesander being possessive or just...neighbourly? Whatever, he had nice hands and a nice touch. She didn't mind the feel of her hand wrapped in his as they walked along the sand. And meanwhile the silver ribbon on the water shimmied, the shoreline spun with gold of the reflected city and the night air was fresh and clean.

She sighed wistfully. 'It's so beautiful here. You're lucky to live so close to the bay.'

'Do you live near the sea?'

'No, not really. I live in a shoe box of a flat near the university where I'm studying. It's about an hour to the coast, probably two to get to a decent beach.' She sighed again. 'The beach there is nice enough but it's nothing like this.'

They walked a few more steps, the strains of the violin haunting in the night air.

'What are you studying?'

And the question took her so unawares that she laughed.

'What's so funny?'

She shook her head. 'I don't know. It just seemed odd—we just got married and here you are, asking me what I do. Normally you'd ask that before you got married.'

'Normally a woman wouldn't turn up on your door-step and propose.'

'Yeah,' she said, looking at her feet. 'I take your point. I'm studying psychology. I'm in my final year.'

They neared a building that jutted out onto the beach—the same restaurant near where she'd crossed the road that first day—which meant his apartment must be just across the road. Here the music was louder, and she could see a small band of musicians playing on a balcony overlooking the sea, scattered patrons lapping up the last of the evening's musical fare. The music tugged at her as they passed by, the violin so sweet over the piano and drums, so richly emotional that she stopped to listen. 'What is that tune?'

'That one?' He smiled. 'It's an old folk song. The lyrics tell of the mountains and the sea and the people who settled here originally and made it home. But most times they don't bother with the lyrics. They let the violin sing the words.'

'It's so beautiful,' she said as she watched the violinist coax his instrument to even sweeter heights.

For a moment it was just the music and the tide that filled the space between and all around them, until he uttered the words, 'You are,' and she felt the night air shift sensually around her. 'Very beautiful.'

She looked back up at him, startled, to see him smiling down at her, and maybe it was the music that she could hear, the music that sounded so poignant and bewitching against the rhythmic shush of the tide, or maybe it was the velvet sky and the silver ribbon of moonlight on the water, but she caught the spine-tingling impact of his smile full on and then immediately wished she hadn't. Because she didn't want him to smile at her like that. She didn't want him to smile at her at all. She didn't want him to tell her she was beautiful and make out this marriage was something more than it was.

And suddenly she regretted letting him take her hand and walk her along the sand as if they were friends or even lovers. They were neither. They had a business arrangement, that was all it was, the terms of which he'd changed to suit himself, and only after it was too late for her to get out of it, once she was already committed. And now this whole 'walk on the sands holding hands' episode spoke of nothing more than lulling her into some false sense of security—to make her think he actually cared—when his apartment was right across the street and it was clear that was where they were headed next—so he could finish this thing he'd started.

She wasn't having it. She shook her head, saying no to whatever it was he was offering, vaguely aware of another tune, violin over drumbeat, half familiar.

Momentarily it threw her. Until she realised it was the music that had played at Markel's birthday party, the tango to which the dancers had danced so seductively. So passionately.

The music he'd told her was called *Feelings*.

And the music told her what a marriage should be. The music told her what was missing from this marriage and could never be a part of it.

Emotion.

Powerful, strong emotion.

It was the final straw.

'I'm sorry. I can't do this any more.'

'You cannot walk along the beach?'

She wanted to lash out at him. Did he deliberately go out of his way to misunderstand her? Surely it was obvious? 'The moon. The beach. Holding hands. All of it. I don't want it. I cannot pretend to be some blushing bride. I cannot look forward to a wedding night that I wanted no part of, that you have blackmailed me into.'

'Is it such a dire prospect that you face, making love with me?'

'When it was unwanted all along? When it remains so? Of course it is!'

'Unwanted?'

'Haven't I made that clear from the start?'

He paused a moment, looking into space, almost as if listening to the building music, the evocative violin, before he looked back at her. 'You're the one who agreed to change the terms.'

'Only because you threatened to tell Felipe our marriage was a sham! Do you know how much I hate you for that? You left me with no choice and then you have the gall to think I will happily fall into bed with you! I cannot believe how arrogant you are. You are everything I hate in a man and nothing I want in a husband!'

She finished her tirade breathless and panting and mentally preparing herself for his next shot, expecting to receive the full force of his fury.

'Dance with me,' he said instead.

'What?'

His flashing eyes sent out a challenge as the instruments merged, their sound weaving together on the night air. He took a purposeful step. Or more a glide across the sand. And then another, his body straight, his head held high. 'Dance with me.'

'No. It's too crazy. I don't know how.'

'You do,' he told her, changing direction. 'You are doing it now, with your tongue. With your words. Do it instead with your body. Show me how angry you are.'

'No!' she insisted, turning away, the idea of dancing with this man on the beach too ridiculous to consider. 'There is no point.'

But she'd barely taken a step before he'd grabbed her wrist and spun her bodily back into him, her shoes and stockings flung far from her grip. She collided bodily against his chest, her hands between them, the air knocked from her lungs and angry as hell at being plastered full length against him.

'I said no!' She shoved hard against his chest and wheeled away but he had hold of her hand and she was at arm's length again before he snapped her breathlessly back into his embrace.

'You bastard!' With her hands at his shoulders, she pushed herself away as far as she could, but his arms were wound around her waist, his eyes intent on hers, and she could do nothing as he moved in a circle around her, his body as tight, his movements as purposeful as the dancer they'd seen. 'What the hell do you think you're doing?'

'I am dancing. With my wife. Do you have a problem with that?'

'Yes!' When it meant his hands were like steel bands around her and his muscled chest like a wall under her hands. She'd seen that chest naked and in all its glory and now her fingers drank in every detail of the feel of him. He was so hard and lean and magnificent and she wanted to be nowhere near him because she didn't want her hands to tell her these things.

'I can't dance. Not this.'

'You will find it easier if you put your arms around my neck.'

Easier? Perhaps, but at least her hands wouldn't be subjected to the play of muscle under skin. Her grip relaxed, her hands sliding their way around his neck. He growled, a low sound of appreciation that rumbled its way into her bones as he spun her in a circle around him.

And then he slid one hand up behind his neck and took one of her hands in his own, drawing it down to his mouth to kiss the palm of her hand. She gasped, the sensation of his tongue flicking across the sensitive skin, the look of his eyes so darkly intent on hers, the music made for couples, the feel of his arm wrapped tightly around her waist—it was too much.

He took one slow step, and then another, drawing her across the sand. Long purposeful steps. Powerful. Dramatic. He guided her back, leading her with his touch and his body before he spun her around and dropped her low over his arm, holding her so securely that even for one so inexperienced she was never in any danger of falling. 'You see,' he said, drawing her slowly up again, held tight against his body, setting up a delicious friction in her breasts and her belly and the aching place between her thighs, 'you can do this.'

'I hate you,' she said, because she was enjoying it too much, this feel of him hard against her as they moved across the sand.

'That's what makes it so good,' he told her, turning her slowly in his embrace. 'Conflict and desire in one explosive package.'

'Who said anything about desire?'

He spun her then, her wedding gown spinning out in layers with her, and pulled her back first against his chest, his arms locking her so close she gasped when she felt the hard ridge of his arousal against her behind. Blatant. Shameless.

Arousing.

And every muscle inside her contracted in response.

She should be outraged. She should demand to be let go. But instead heat pooled between her aching thighs, her breasts felt heavy and hard and it was all she could do not to squirm her bottom harder against him.

'Your body does, every time we touch.'

She shuddered, knowing there was no denying it but not wanting him to take any satisfaction from it. 'It doesn't mean anything. It doesn't mean I like you. It's purely a physical reaction.'

Behind her he laughed, the sound rippling through her flesh, his warm breath fanning her ear. 'Oh, I'm good with old-fashioned lust.'

And she realised the enormity of what she'd just admitted to, the admission she'd made. 'No!' she cried, fighting her way out of the prison of his arms, desperate to flee. He was too confident, too damned smug, too damned right. 'It doesn't mean—'

But once again she was no match for his speed and strength, no match for his determination. He caught both her wrists as she fled, snaring her back, plastering her against him, hip to hip, chest to chest, his face just inches from her own as his fingers curled through her hair.

'It means you want me.'

'No.'

'And I want you.'

'No.' But this time her voice was more a plea than a protest.

He smiled then, his eyes locked with hers, his thumb stroking her parted lips. 'What does it take, I wonder, to make you say yes?'

'Never,' she breathed, knowing it would do no good, her eyes already locked on the mouth hovering over hers, already contemplating his coming kiss, anticipating it, already tasting him.

Even so, when his kiss came, when his fingers tangled in her hair and his mouth meshed with hers, still she was unprepared for the maelstrom that followed, the storm that was unleashed inside her. Like a flooded river bursting its banks, her need spilled over, threatening to swamp her under the deluge.

She clung to him like a drowning person clung to a rock, as sensation ruled her world and threatened to sweep her away on the sensual tide of his taste and hot mouth and how he made her feel.

Desirable.

Desired.

Delicious.

He feasted on her and she let him, because that gave her licence to feast upon him, to taste his mouth and his salty skin, to relish the texture of his whiskered jaw as it rubbed against her cheek.

She clung to him because she did not want to let him go, now she had finally unleashed her hands on him and could drink in his perfect body through thirsting, seeking fingers.

She clung to him because she could not let him go and stop this thing now that it had started, this thing she had denied herself for so achingly, pointlessly long.

Her lips parted easily under the assault of his feasting mouth and tongue, her hands clinging to him as she opened to his kisses and passion became her master.

Passion, and the music she could still hear, the drumbeat that called to her on some primitive level and that guaranteed this moment was all important; that promised that this moment was pivotal to her entire existence.

She believed it as he swept her into his kiss, and swept any remaining logic away in the process. His breath was hot as his mouth slipped from her mouth to her throat and she gasped in the night air. His hands left hot trails on her back and she arched against him, no longer bothering to pretend it wasn't exactly where she wanted to be.

He was hot. So hot. And her need turned suddenly combustible, from flood into flame, threatening to consume her with its heated promise.

And pressed against him, her thigh between his, her belly against his hip, the rigid column of his erection promised more heat. Promised all she needed and more.

Much more.

She wanted it. She wanted him to fill her and to feel him deep inside her and that need was premier.

Despite his blackmail. Despite his smug certainty that it would happen.

And she learned something about herself then, in the scorching heat of his hot mouth and stroking tongue and seeking, inquisitive hands. She learned that she could tolerate blackmail, forgive arrogance and sweep aside the worst character faults, if this was to be her reward.

'I want you,' he said, wrenching himself breathlessly from his kiss, one hand curled around her breast, his fingers stroking over her nipple until it was achingly hard, his other hand sliding down to tantalisingly cup the curve of her behind. And his declaration was so raw and honest that even if his touch hadn't already been electric and set her senses on fire she could not deny it.

'I know,' she gasped.

'You want me,' he said, a statement rather than a question, and there was a challenge in his eyes, a challenge for her to give in and admit it and utter the word she could not say.

She did, but still she shook her head, if you could call the half-hearted movement a shake. 'It doesn't mean anything.'

'That's just the point,' he growled, low in his throat, hesitating just a moment before sucking her into the whirlpool of his kiss. 'It doesn't have to.'

CHAPTER TEN

IT SHOULD MEAN something. She wanted so much to disagree with him, she wanted to argue the case for the affirmative. Except with her body jammed tight up against his and his mouth locked on hers, his seeking tongue like an inferno to her senses, it was hard to think straight. It was hard to remember why it was so important.

And in the end logic got swept away by the tide of need. Making love with this man wasn't just a contract condition—an obligation. Making love with Alesander was as inevitable as the constant whoosh of the tide or the falling of the night or the rising of the moon. There was no stopping it. It was always going to happen.

She was in the lift before she realised they'd somehow crossed the road, barefoot and locked in each other's arms, lost in sensation. She was consumed with heat and him and a need that threatened to engulf her.

The lift was slow.

Alesander was faster.

He had her backed against the wall, one hand tangled in her hair, the other sweeping aside the layers of her skirt in a bid to reach her heated flesh. She gasped, the touch of his hand on her thigh searing, electric, and her body pulsed and ached and vaguely she thought that if the lift didn't hurry up he might just take her here and now.

His hand glided higher, his thumb skimmed her mound and a million nerve endings screamed inside her and she wished he damned well would.

But before he could the lift doors opened and they tumbled out together across the private lobby. He pulled off his jacket while he fumbled for the key, still locked in their kiss. His tie followed as the door opened and he put his hands to her shoulders and put her away from him, his dark eyes almost black with need, his breathing choppy. 'I was going to do this slowly,' he said, 'but I don't think I can wait that long.'

Her simmering blood rejoiced. She didn't want to wait. She couldn't. Now that she was on this course, now she had made her choice, she didn't want time to reflect or analyse or allow logic to intervene. There would be time for reflection later. Maybe even time for regret.

But that was later.

Right now she had other priorities.

'I don't want to wait either.'

And he growled as he swept her up into his arms and kicked the door closed behind them on his way to his bed.

If he noticed her weight in his arms, he didn't show it; he was so strong and powerful as he strode purposefully through the apartment, and she was nervous, her heart pounding, knowing and yet not knowing what was to come. She was no innocent. She'd had sex before and there had been times it had been good. Essentially it was the same act of intimacy. There was nothing new.

And yet something told her that this time was different.

Maybe because this time she was with a man, who made Damon seem like a boy in comparison.

Was it wrong of her to imagine just for a moment that this was real? Would it hurt to pretend, just for a little while, that she was a real bride and that this was a real wedding night?

His room shared the same magnificent view as the living room, the waters of the bay dark with a foaming white edge, framed by the lights of the city and the mountains that stood guard, and all frosted in silver from a lovers' moon.

Her view was better.

Dark-featured and olive-skinned, he was beautiful, this arrogant Spaniard, his hot mouth ripe for pleasure, his body built for sin.

He let her down slowly and set her on her bare feet without letting her go. Almost—she wanted to believe—almost, as if he couldn't bear to. His eyes locked with hers, dark eyes storm-tossed and brimming with need—*need for her*—and the knowledge was as precious as it was empowering.

When she was back home in her tiny flat in Melbourne, where San Sebastian and arrogant Spaniards and endless sunshine would be nothing but a distant memory, just knowing she'd had a man like Alesander wanting her would be something to pull out on a cold wintry night to warm her frigid bones.

His dark eyes burned for her. And she might be nothing to him, she knew, but she was the one with him here now. She was the one he wanted now.

His hands slipped over her shoulders and down the bare skin of her back. Hot. Seeking. She felt the slide of the zip and her strapless gown loosened around her. It was all she could do not to reach for it as it fell away from her breasts. It was all she could do to let the weight of her skirt drag the gown to the floor without trying to cover herself. Until it was too late to do anything and she stood nervously before him, naked but for a lace garter meant for stockings abandoned somewhere with her shoes upon the sand, and the tiny scrap of silk that was her underwear.

Breath hissed through his teeth as his eyes raked over her, her nipples hardening at the cool caress of air after being constrained by her tight bodice. Her breasts firming, her nipples peaking more with his heated gaze. 'Beautiful,' he murmured and she let the word sink in and float down like a leaf to some special place deep inside. He touched the pads of his fingers to her throat and like an echo she could feel her heartbeat in his touch. Their gazes locked as he followed the line of her collarbone to her shoulder. His touch was electric, torturous and yet simultaneously exquisite, too damned good to bear, too damned good to stop.

And when his knuckles drifted lower, her world waited, breathing hitched, her nipples aching to be touched, as his fingers skimmed the curve of her breast.

It was ecstasy.

It was agony.

'I thought you were in a hurry.' Her protesting voice sounded thin and desperate and trembled like her knees.

'Forgive me,' he said. 'Do you know how perfect you are? I am in awe.'

She closed her eyes to stop the words getting in. In

case she believed them. 'What you are,' she whispered shakily, 'is overdressed.'

He laughed, low and deep, that way he did, and her nipples peaked with pleasure. 'Don't they say patience is a virtue?'

'Virtue is overrated.'

He growled and she felt the jolt at her core. 'Is this what you want?' he asked, rolling her nipple between thumb and forefinger, teasing it mercilessly before he curled his fingers around her breast and squeezed tight.

She whimpered, her eyelids fluttering closed, and he took her hand before she knew what was happening. 'Or is this what you want?'

She gasped when she realised what he had planned. Gasped again at what she felt, the size of him, the strength, and it was her turn to be awed.

Awed, and grateful too, because she knew she could not have been so bold and he had given her licence.

He shrugged off his shirt as she tested his length in her fingers. He was so big. Long. Thick. She felt a growing dampness between her thighs. Inner muscles clenched and unclenched in anticipation.

'Is that what you want?'

'Oh, yes,' she confessed, a germ of fear that he would be too large for her no contest for her willingness to try. She licked her lips, hungry at the prospect, already sliding down his zip to slip her hand inside. She squeezed them gently through his silk underwear, so sheer the fabric hid nothing of him, before gliding the back of her nails up his length. 'Yes, please.'

He groaned and grabbed her wrist in a hand made of steel. 'Then you will have me,' he said, his voice thick around the edges, 'but not like this. When I come, I want to be inside you.'

He wasn't slow after that. He wasted no time lifting her from the circle of her fallen dress and spinning her onto the cloud-soft bed, laying her down almost reverentially upon the coverlet. His trousers lasted no longer than a second after that. His underwear but a blink.

She caught her breath. Before her stood a god, broad-shouldered and hard chested and sculpted from flesh that had been fired in the kiln of burning need. A flame still flickered in his dark eyes, while his thick erection swayed proudly before him. Hungry. Seeking.

Magnificent.

No mere boy like that other one whose name had suddenly vanished from her mind, but a man, fully— no—*perfectly* formed.

And she knew what he was seeking and her mouth went dry as he knelt with one knee on the bed and every drop of moisture in her body headed south.

He leaned over her, smoothing the tangle of her hair. 'Suddenly I'm not the one who's overdressed,' he murmured and remedied that inequality with a smooth sweep of his hands that bared her totally to him. She revelled at his swift intake of air, before his mouth fell upon hers, his tongue plundering her mouth while his hands plundered her body, seeking treasure, giving pleasure. Spreading heat.

Every touch, every kiss, every stroke of skin against skin building the heat, so that she thought she would self-combust.

'Alesander,' she gasped when his fingers circled that tightly wound bud that seemed right now to be the centre of her existence.

'I know,' he said, lifting his mouth from her nipple, simultaneously soothing her with his words, only to build on her distress with his clever fingers and heated mouth.

But he didn't know. He couldn't, or surely he would *do* something. 'Please!' she begged, breathless and burning up in a firestorm that threatened to overwhelm her.

And he left her for a moment, a moment where air rushed in against her heated skin and she could catch her breath. A moment before he was back, his body poised over hers.

'Tell me what you want,' he said, stroking her sex more purposefully now, the tips of his fingers venturing inside, teasing her, driving her inner muscles wild.

Oh God, she thought, as momentarily relief evaporated in another heated surge. 'I want you.'

He smiled. 'Then you shall have me.' He dipped his mouth to hers as their bodies touched in the most intimate of connections.

He was big. She had known that from her first touch. When his tip nudged her entrance and lingered there, she feared he was too big. She was determined he wouldn't be. She was determined…

'Open your eyes,' he ordered, withdrawing from the kiss, 'and look at me.'

She blinked her eyes open, confused. 'Relax,' he said, dipping his head to kiss her lightly on the mouth. 'Relax and breathe.'

'You're so big. I don't know if I can—'

'Of course you can,' he whispered on another light-as-air kiss to one hard nipple this time, as his fingers joined the gentle assault, working their magic again around that tiny bud of nerves.

She moaned at the sudden spike of pleasure and felt

the pressure shift and deepen and closed her eyes, rolling her head back on the pillow.

'No,' he commanded. 'Keep your eyes open.'

'I can't.' Her protest was little more than a breath, the fever inside her mounting, the feeling of fullness inside her building as he edged inside her another delicious fraction. She gasped.

'Open them! I want to see your eyes when you come.'

She fought the compulsion to close her eyes and go with the sensation and did as he commanded, panting hard, opening her eyes to his darkly intent gaze. His brow was slick with sweat, his features achingly tight, and the need she saw so clearly etched upon his straining face only magnified the pressure of what he was doing to her and how he felt inside her and she knew she was on the very cusp of losing herself.

'Alesander,' she gasped, her fingers curled into his muscled flesh before she tipped over the edge and with one final thrust he drove himself home.

Dios, she was tight! She exploded around him like fireworks, muscles contracting in the most intimate of massages, and it was all he could do to grit his teeth and hang on. He wasn't ready for this to be over just yet.

He waited for her to wind down, whispering kisses over slick skin that glowed like satin in the moonlight. 'Better now?' he asked, his lips gliding over the shell-like curves of her ear. 'Feeling more relaxed?'

She nodded. 'Mmm,' she murmured. 'Lovely.'

'Excellent,' he said, slowly pulling back, waiting at the brink before powering back in. Her eyes opened—wide.

'What are you doing?' she asked as he drew back again.

'Giving you more of what you want.'

'Oh,' she said, surprise and a little wonder turning to delight in her eyes. 'Oh!' she cried, as he plunged to the hilt inside her, groaning at the feel of her hot body, a tight sheath around him as he pumped. He would not last long like this. There was no way...

He heard her cry out, a wild sound of release, before his own was rent from him, the note raw and savage and wrenched from a place deep inside—some place he'd never known existed.

CHAPTER ELEVEN

'I BROUGHT YOU COFFEE.'

Simone blinked, still half asleep and only half understanding what she'd heard. Something about coffee? And sure enough, the scent of freshly brewed coffee seemed to flavour air that was otherwise heavily laden with sex. Hardly surprising given they'd spent more time making love last night than sleeping.

But really, coffee? The man was built like a god, made love as if he actually cared that his partner climaxed, *and* he made coffee for her instead of demanding a beer?

She snuggled back into her pillow. She really must be dreaming.

'How are you feeling?'

Her eyes snapped open. *How am I what?* He was freshly showered and wearing crisp, fresh clothes— another of those tops that skimmed the surface of his skin and made you want to peel it off, and trousers that accentuated the long lean contours of his legs— and he really was pouring her a cup of coffee. She sat up, snagging the bedding over her breasts, and pushed hair gone wild back from her face.

Outside, the windows the bay sparkled under a

warm sun, a perfect autumn day. Inside her barometer wasn't anywhere near as controlled.

'I'm—' shattered '—okay,' she said, knowing she must look closer to the word she'd left unsaid. After the night they'd just spent, she couldn't imagine what kind of mess she looked.

'I thought you might be feeling tender. It was wrong of me to make love to you again this morning,' he said, as easily as he might have asked her if she wanted milk in her coffee. 'I should have given you some time.'

'I'm not…I wasn't…'

'A virgin? No, I know, but it's clear you haven't had much experience.'

'I have had sex before, you know. Several times. *A lot* of times, actually.' She'd even had the odd orgasm before, although admittedly she'd had to assist, so hadn't last night been a revelation? 'I told you I'd been in a relationship.'

He smiled at that. 'Oh yes. The boyfriend. I remember.' He sipped his coffee as he looked out over the view of the bay. 'Perhaps he wasn't as experienced.'

God, he wasn't as well endowed, more like it! She stared at her coffee rather than at him, so she wouldn't be forced to make any more comparisons, beyond the width of their shoulders, or the muscled firmness of their flesh, for instance. She shrugged and slanted her eyes up, feeling his eyes on her, knowing she was expected to say something. 'He wasn't put together quite the same as you, that's all.'

He smiled at her over his shoulder. 'They say size isn't important.'

Oh, they're so very wrong.

And then she made the mistake of looking at the clock and saw it was almost noon and didn't even have to feign surprise. Her cup rattled against the saucer as she sat up urgently, still clutching the bedclothes to her. 'I need to call the hospital and check on Felipe.'

'I already have. He is resting comfortably.' He tossed her a robe—his robe, she realised, and it was all she could do not to lift it to her face and breathe in his scent. 'I thought you'd want to visit so I said we'd be in to see him before lunch.'

She shrugged the robe around her shoulders, strangely touched, finding the armholes. 'You didn't have to do that.'

'You don't want to see your grandfather?'

'No, I mean you didn't have to call. I didn't expect you to.'

He shrugged, looking out of the window at the view. 'You were asleep. I thought you would want to know. Do you have a problem with that?'

'Aren't you worried I might think you were actually capable of being nice?'

She was half joking, but he didn't seem to take it that way. He blinked. Slowly. 'Whatever you think of me, I am not a beast. I am certainly capable of extending common courtesy where it is merited. Besides, don't you think it would look odd if I did not ask after my new grandfather-in-law?'

He turned and stared at her for a moment, one wholly unsettling moment under an intensely dark gaze, that had her putting a hand to her unruly hair and imagining he must be wondering what he'd done to be stuck with her.

Then he crossed to the bed, lifted her chin and kissed her briefly on the lips. A peck, nothing more.

'Besides,' he said, her chin still in his hand, his eyes

still searching her face, 'you know better than to read too much into it.'

He left her then to get up, leaving her utterly bewildered and baffled, and yes, sore when she made a move to get out of bed. So it was all part of the act of being a dutiful husband to his granddaughter? Nothing more than common courtesy?

Still, he hadn't had to call. He didn't need to impress anyone now. The deal had been made and they were married. There was no getting out of it for her. He didn't have to be thoughtful. And yet he had been.

She padded barefoot to the bathroom and wondered anew about the man she had married. The man who was now not only her husband, but her husband in every sense of the word.

Their deal was temporary, their marriage fated to last a few months, no more. But after a night like last night, when Alesander had blown her world apart and then bothered to kiss it back together again, he seemed almost the perfect package. And at times, almost a man she might even think about choosing for her husband—in some parallel universe where they had met under different circumstances without the history of deal-making and blackmail that lay festering between them.

Damn, damn and damn!

What was he doing to her, that she could even think of wanting him for her husband? Was she so blinded by his lovemaking that she had forgotten that this was nothing more than a business arrangement? Was she so blindsided that she had forgotten the sheer terror of a missed period?

She should never forget that feeling, not if she wasn't to be taken in again by someone who didn't care for her—who had never loved her—who she never wanted to see again.

Still cursing, she slipped out of the voluminous robe and stepped into the shower, lifting her face up into the spray.

Why had Alesander insisted on having sex? Why had he had to complicate things when their arrangement had been fail-safe? She'd known sex would complicate things. Sex always did.

But the land hadn't been enough for him and sex was the price he'd exacted from her.

A price she'd agreed to.

And no matter how mind-blowing the sex and the redemptive power of a potent kiss, was it a price worth paying?

The hospital let Felipe go home the next day, but only, they said, because Alesander had arranged a nurse to be there around the clock for him. But, they warned, it would not be for ever.

Still, Felipe seemed positive after the wedding. At least for a few weeks.

Winter was closing in around the vineyard, the leaves falling from the vines when she found him sitting in his usual chair, looking out over the near barren vineyard, his eyes half shuttered. He seemed not to notice her presence, even after she'd spoken to him, and so she assumed he was asleep, when she picked up his coffee cup and a gnarled limb reached out, a bony set of fingers grabbed her wrist. *'Mi nieta!'*

She jumped, and then laughed at her reaction. *'Sí.* What is it, Abuelo?'

'I have something to tell you,' he whispered. 'Something I have been meaning to tell you.' He craned his head around. 'Is Alesander here?'

She shook her head. 'He's out in the vineyard somewhere. Do you want me to get him?'

'No. What I want to say is for you, and you alone. Sit down here next to me.'

She pulled over a chair. 'What is it?'

He sighed, his breath sounding like a wheeze. 'I want to tell you. There is not much time left to me. I must tell you…'

'No, Abuelo, you mustn't think that way.'

He patted her hand as if she was the one who needed compassion and understanding. 'Listen to me, there is nothing the doctors can do for me now, but I can still tell you this, that since you came here, since your marriage, I have never been happier. I have you to thank for making the sun shine in my life again.'

'Please, Abuelo, there is no need.'

'There is every need. Don't you see what you have done? You have given me hope. You have reunited two families who have barely spoken to each other for more than a century.'

She dipped her head. If he only knew, he would not be proud at all. But still she managed a smile and patted his hand. 'I am glad that you are happy, Abuelo.'

'More than happy. The rift between our families goes back many years. I never thought to see it end. But Alesander, he is a fine man. He is like the son I never had.'

He stopped on a sigh and his head nodded down, and she thought that he had finished then, already drifting back into his memories and his regrets, when he suddenly looked up, glassy eyes seeking hers. 'Do you know what happened?'

'Alesander told me. One of your ancestors—your grandfather, was it?—he ran off and married the bride meant for an Esquivel groom.'

The old man nodded. 'Ah, *sí*, he did.' He laughed then, a cackle of delight, before his face grew serious again. 'But did he tell you what happened afterwards?'

'Only that it has resulted in a century of simmering rivalry and a cause of resentment between the two families ever since.'

'And the rest? Did he tell you the rest?'

She reeled back through her memories of her conversation with Alesander. 'No, I don't seem to recall anything else.'

He nodded. 'Ah, he didn't tell you, then—probably for the best. Anyway, it doesn't matter now.'

'What is it, Abuelo?' she asked, the skin at the back of her neck crawling. 'What doesn't matter now?'

'Only that when it was too late—when he discovered his bride was married to another, Xalbeder Esquivel vowed revenge and that the Esquivel family would drive the Otxoas from their land once and for all. That has always been their goal. That is why we have had to fight them ever since.'

Felipe peered at her, his watery eyes glistening, his crooked mouth smiling in a way she had never seen before. 'Don't you see what you have achieved by your marriage to Alesander? The curse is lifted. The Esquivels can never drive us from our land because the Otxoas will be ones with this estate for ever. I am so proud of you, *mi nieta*, so very proud.'

She let him pull her to him and hug her, feeling wiry arms around her, feeling bony shoulder blades stripped of flesh through his thick shirt, feeling the earth fall beneath her feet. If he only knew what she had done.

Oh God, what had she done?

By her own hand she had signed away the Otxoas' last links to this land. And she hadn't just let it happen—she had made it happen. 'Please don't be proud, Abuelo,' she pleaded, feeling sick. 'I don't deserve it.'

'Bah.' He waved her objections away with a sweep of one gnarled wrist. 'You have made an old man with no hope very happy. I am only sorry I did not trust Alesander at first. I thought he was only interested in the land. But he loves you, I can tell. And the way you look at him, with such love in your eyes…'

'Abuelo…' she chided with tears in her eyes, trying to gently cut him off. She could not bear to hear more, least of all to hear him talk of a love that had no place in her marriage. 'Please don't.'

But Felipe was equally determined to finish. 'Please, hear me out. There is not much time left to me now, and it is selfish of me to hope for anything beyond a death that lets me slip away quietly in my sleep and rejoin my Maria, that should be all I wish. Yet still I wish for more. I wish with all my heart that there might be news of a child before I go.'

'You're not going anywhere, Abuelo!' she cried, holding his knotted fingers in hers, knowing that his wishes were for nothing, knowing there could never be a child.

'You will tell me,' he insisted, 'if there is news. Promise me you will tell me and put a smile on an old man's face before he dies.'

'I will tell you,' she said as the tears streamed down her face, 'I promise.'

'Don't cry for me,' he said, misinterpreting her tears. 'I am not worth crying over. I did not mean to make you sad.'

'I'm sorry,' she told him, with one final brief, desperate hug, 'I am so very sorry.' And she fled from the cottage in tears.

What had she done?

She ran on and on through the vineyard, her emotions in turmoil, oblivious to the magnificent view and uncaring of the vines snatching on her hair and tugging at her clothes, totally gutted at what she had done.

She'd lied to her grandfather. Yes, to make his last days happy, it was true, but what consolation was that when she'd lost him everything he'd ever held precious in the process? The last of his vines and she'd as good as given them away.

And she'd piled lie upon lie upon lie until he believed so much in this fiction she'd created, that he was building an entire future based on this perfect marriage.

This perfect lie.

And he'd told her he was proud of her and he'd thanked her for saving the family, for breaking a vow of revenge and a curse on them for generations.

When she was the curse.

She'd betrayed Felipe and his trust in her. Betrayed his love for his only remaining relative, the only person he could put his faith and hope for the future in.

Lied to him and betrayed him by giving away all that he had left and held precious.

But seeping up through all the welter of emotions, through the tangle of her despair and her self-recrimination, there was a slow, simmering anger bubbling away inside the guilt and remorse.

For she too had been betrayed.

Because Alesander must have known!

All along, Alesander would have known about the vow to drive the Otxoas from their land. She might as well have offered it to him on a silver platter.

And then the land hadn't been enough and he'd wanted her too.

Was that part of the revenge? Was he laughing at her the whole time?

She felt sick. He'd played her for a fool.

She'd even imagined he cared.

Oh God.

She came to the edge of the property and the new fence where once she'd come in despair when she'd learned that Felipe was dying, and where she'd come up with a plan to make his last days happy.

A stupid plan.

A stupid woman to ever think it could ever work. A stupid woman to think she could pile lie upon lie and get off scot-free, with no consequences and no price to pay.

And she'd imagined that sex with Alesander was the price she'd had to pay.

No.

Knowing she'd betrayed the love and trust of the only family member she had left, the family member who was relying on her to save the family name from obliteration—this was the price she had to pay.

With a cry of anguish, she sagged, tear-streaked and heaving for air, against a trellis upright, ancient and thick. She clung to it, panting, looking out over the view that had once seemed so magical to her—the spectacular shoreline that curled jaggedly around in both directions, framing a brilliant blue sea, with the red-roofed town of Getaria nestled in behind the rocky headland—and she would swap it in a heartbeat to be back in a cramped student flat with noisy neighbours and lousy weather.

The whole time he would have known. The whole time he would have been laughing at her behind her back, thinking that she had achieved singlehandedly what his family had been unable to achieve in generations.

They would all laugh when she was gone. They were probably all laughing at her now, all in on the joke, just waiting for the old man to die.

And she'd gone to Alesander for help.

How could she ever face Felipe again?

'Simone!'

Oh God, she thought as his voice rang out again, closer this time. Not him. Anyone but him. She tried to disappear into the tangle of vines but in a blue and yellow sundress she was too easy to spot.

'Simone!' he said. 'At last.'

She turned her back to him, swiping at her tear-streaked face with her hands.

'Simone, Felipe said he'd upset you.'

'Go away,' she said without turning around.

'What's wrong?'

'Just leave me alone.'

He took no notice. He came up behind her and put a hand to her shoulder. A touch she'd become so used to. A touch that had warmed her in places she daren't confess. A touch that now left her cold. 'Simone, what's going on?'

'Don't touch me!' she cried, spinning around and shoving away his hand. 'Don't you ever touch me again!'

'What the hell is going on? What's happened to make you this way?'

'What do you think is wrong? Why didn't you tell me the whole story?'

'What story?'

'Your potted history of the troubles between the Esquivels and the Otxoas.'

He frowned. 'What about it? What am I supposed to have missed?'

'The bit you so conveniently left out. The bit about the Esquivels vowing to drive the Otxoas from their land!'

He shrugged his shoulders, his hands palm up in the air. 'What about it? I didn't think it was important.'

'*What about it?* Are you kidding me? Do you think I would have ever married you if I had known that your agenda the entire time was to run Felipe—to run us—off our land?'

'*Dios!* This marriage was all your idea. Don't you forget that. You were the one who came up with it. You were the one who so desperately needed it!'

'And you were the one who insisted on the land being part of the deal! Because you knew, didn't you? You knew all along that your family wanted us off. And because you saw a way of getting rid of my family from this land for ever!'

'Listen to yourself! Do you really think I care about something that happened more than a hundred years ago? Do you honestly believe I set out with the intention of banishing the Otxoas from their land?'

'What am I supposed to think, when the land is the one thing you expressly demanded? And now my grandfather thinks I've saved this family from some kind of curse and all I know is that I've made it happen. I've brought it down upon us. How do you think I feel about that? How do you think I feel?'

She broke down, her knees collapsing beneath her, sending her limp and sagging into the ground.

His hands caught her at her shoulders, pulling her up, pulling her towards him. 'What do you care about the land anyway? You're going home. You said yourself you don't belong here.'

She pushed with all her might against him. 'And that makes it okay? That's your defence?' She lashed at him with her fists, pounding at his unyielding chest, but he did not let her go and so she punched harder. 'Don't touch me!'

He held her at arm's length and still she managed to lash out at him. He grabbed her wrists, locking them within the iron circle of his own and pulled her in close. 'What the hell is wrong with you?'

'You knew,' she said, angling her face and her accusations higher. 'You knew all the time about the land and the curse. That land means everything to him and now you've taken it.'

His dark eyes gleamed dangerously down at her, his hot breath fanning her face, the cords on his neck standing out in rigid lines. 'And you made a deal, remember! You were the one who turned up on my doorstep begging.'

Fruitlessly she wrenched against the prison of his hands. 'But you knew! All the time you knew!'

'So what? The damned curse means nothing to me!'

'But it does to him!' She was so rigid she felt she might snap. She glared up at him. 'It does to him and I hate you for what you've done!'

He growled and shook his head slowly from side to side, his dark eyes like magnets, their pull insistent and strong. 'Oh no, you don't. You don't hate me at all.'

His slow words and his rich accent stroked her like

a slow velvet hand, and she felt the first unmistakable frisson of fear.

And the first unmistakable frisson of excitement.

No! That would be to let him win. She tugged desperately at her wrists. 'Let me go.'

He tugged her back so she ended up even closer to the hard wall of his chest, his mouth turned up at the corners, his eyes never deviating from hers, and she knew what he intended and there was no way…

'Let me go!'

He stepped closer. She stepped back. He took another step and this time her step was more of a stumble, until she found the old support she'd been clinging to before against her back. She'd welcomed it for its solidity then. Now she cursed it for preventing her escape, leaving her sandwiched between it and him.

He let her hands go then, to frame her face in his hands, his fingers deep in her hair, and she reached back, clinging to the support, keeping her hungry fingers away from him.

'What are you doing?' she asked, her heart beating too fast, too frantically, already knowing the answer.

So that when his mouth crashed down on hers it came as no surprise. His vehemence did. There was no remaining unaffected—his hot mouth and tongue seemed to want to plunder her very soul.

What had he done to her? she wondered as his tongue licked like a trail of flames across her throat. What had he reduced her to?

Feelings, the answer came back, as she gave herself up into his kiss and gave him back all he was offering her.

Feelings.

He had awoken her to feeling and she was a slave to it. *Slave to him.*

Her hands abandoned the support behind her. She was pulling at his clothes as fast as he was pulling at hers. The zip of her dress was undone, the tail of his shirt was tugged free. Her breasts exposed to his mouth, his chest was bared to her seeking fingers.

And his hands were at the hem of her dress, sliding the fabric up her legs, sliding down again once he'd hooked his fingers into her underwear and swept them away.

Air brushed the sensitive folds of her flesh. Cool air against hot torrid flesh.

'Alesander,' she cried, half plea, half protest as she battled to release him, a battle made harder because he was so hard.

'I know,' he muttered against her throat, her jaw, her mouth as he helped her. 'I know.'

And then he lifted her and he was right there, at her entrance, and she thought her world could end and she wouldn't care so long as he was inside her first.

She cried out when he pulled her down onto him. She cried out when he pulled back, knowing she'd been wrong. Because she didn't ever want her world to end. Not when her world made it possible to feel like this.

He pounded into her, angry and insistent, and angrily, insistently she clenched her muscles and hung onto him, only to welcome him back, her need building with each desperate thrust.

'Do you hate me now?' he asked, thrusting again, his voice barely a grunt. 'Do you still hate me?'

Her body was alive with sensation, her senses dancing wildly along a dangerous line that any moment they might teeter off into an abyss, and there was no way she could not answer honestly.

'I hate you,' she said, *but not because of Felipe or the land or a vow of revenge that was made more than a century ago, but because of what you do to me.* 'I will always hate you.'

He answered with a thrust that threw her head crashing back against the beam. He followed it with another and then another, each one deeper than the first. Each one more desperate, more insistent. Each one building on that screaming tension building inexorably inside her.

He won't make me come, she told herself, knowing the assault he was capable of, clamping down on that eventuality with all her muscles and all her might. Knowing what was in store if she just let him. *I won't let him. I won't give him the satisfaction.*

And so she fought and resisted and battled against the torrent of sensations he subjected her to and tried to imagine herself back in her tiny flat in Melbourne, where this man and these feelings would be just a distant memory.

But it was too hard a task, too much to ask, with his mouth at her throat and on her lips, his hands hot on her breasts and fingers tight against her nipples and his hard cock thrusting deep inside her. It was all…impossible.

And like a cough suppressed because you were in polite company, but that refused to be suppressed, so that when it was unleashed it was ten times greater than the original would have ever been, her release came upon her with the relentless force of a tornado, picking her up and spinning her effortlessly into its whirling spout, drawing her higher, ever higher in its never ending spiral until she came in a flash of colour and heated sensation and felt herself spat out of the tornado's spout. She drifted down to the earth, or maybe that was just her legs as he let them down, her fight gone as she rested limply under the weight of his body against hers.

And she hated that he could do this to her—turn argument into a storm, turn anger into passion.

She hated him because he could reduce her to a whimpering mess of nerve endings.

She hated him because she loved him.

Oh God, where had that come from?

She tried to wish the unwanted thought away. She tried to deny it. But the truth of it refused to be wished away or denied. It floated like a balloon let loose, flying high, freed of the shackles that could pull it down.

She loved him.

The concept was so foreign. So unexpected. And yet it explained so much of why she wanted to be with him and why at the same time she feared it so.

She loved him because of what he could do to her and how he made her feel.

She loved him and she hated him because at any moment he would look at her smugly and declare himself the victor of this particular encounter.

Except not this time, it seemed. *'Mierda!'* he cursed, and pulled himself free, pulling himself away as if she was poison. 'You're not on the Pill.'

She blinked, still in recovery mode, not sure why it was an issue. 'You know I'm not.'

'I didn't use protection.'

CHAPTER TWELVE

'OH MY GOD!' She was still reeling from her discovery. The last thing she needed was *that*. She put a hand to her head, recovery mode short-circuited by a panic that unfurled with a vengeance as she remembered another time, another fear that things had come unstuck, even after protection had been used.

But this time there had been no protection. No defence.

Oh God, was she destined to live her life making love to the wrong men, narrowly escaping disaster with one, only to hurtle headlong into catastrophe with the next?

She'd known from the very beginning that having sex with Alesander was a bad idea. Why had he not realised the complications that could result? Had he not realised how serious they could be?

Her panicked brain morphed to anger. 'How could you do that?' she cried. 'How could you be so stupid?'

Her answer was the thwack of the flat of his hand high above her head against the beam supporting her. 'Did you ask me to put on a condom?'

'And so it's my fault—?' even though she hadn't given protection a thought, and she knew she hadn't, but damned if she was going to accept the blame '—because you can't control yourself?'

'And you didn't want it?'

'Did I ask for it? Did I ever ask for sex from you, or did you simply demand it, as you always did?'

'You enjoyed it. You know you did.'

'That's not the same thing and you know it.'

He turned away from her then, his shoulders heaving, and she sensed the loss of him even as she celebrated the relief that came from the distance between them, and she wondered at the tangle of those conflicting emotions and wondered if love made sense of it all.

Ever since that first day in his apartment it had been the same, the relentless push and pull confusing her thoughts and tangling her intentions.

But now there was something else to confuse her thoughts and add to the tangle in her mind.

What if she were pregnant?

She'd lived this nightmare once before—the overwhelming fear of being pregnant to a man who didn't want her—the fear, the terror of thinking that she was, the utter helplessness at not knowing.

But beyond that, the endless soul-searching at being tempted to do something she knew she could never do. She wasn't a religious woman, her parents had brought her up with no particular belief systems that told her she should act one way or another and she had grown up believing she could do anything she wanted in the world. But, when push came to shove, she had learned that there were some places she could not go, some lines she could not cross.

What were the chances?

Luck had been with her that time, sending her a belated period that had been accompanied by a torrent of tears—grateful tears. As it was, she had held herself together these last few months by a tenuous thread. She could not have coped if she'd been pregnant with Damon's child.

And now the nightmare was happening all over again. Again the fear. Again the hoping. Again the anxious, endless wait and the anguished sleepless nights until she knew, one way or the other.

She couldn't be pregnant. She was leaving when this was over. She had to leave. She had to get away before he discovered the truth.

Because falling in love with Alesander had never been part of the deal.

'It was wrong of me,' he admitted suddenly, completely blindsiding her. 'I should never have made love to you. Not here. Not like this.'

She channelled shock into rational thought and turned her panicked mind to calculating dates, needing to be able to hope. 'It might be okay,' she said, needing to believe it. 'It's early in my cycle. It would be unlucky.' But then she'd been lucky last time. Did this kind of luck get balanced out? Was it her turn to be unlucky?

He had his back to her, refusing to look at her.

Two facts that didn't escape her. 'Luck does not come into it. It shouldn't have happened!'

She swiped up her knickers from the ground with as much dignity as she could muster, balling them in her fist, not bothering to further humiliate herself by stopping to tug them on now. 'You're so right,' she said. 'Maybe you might try remembering that next time.'

Alesander swung around. There wouldn't be a next time. Damn her, there shouldn't have been a *this time*!

He was a man of needs, it was true. He always had

been. But never since his first wild encounter with a woman, when he'd barely been a teenager and she was a wanton who'd let his night time fantasies play out in her hot hands and hot mouth and who'd given him a gold-plated initiation to the pleasures of the flesh, had he been so unprepared and made such a mistake. He'd used up all the luck he was planning on ever needing that time.

Because he wasn't a teenager any more.

There were no excuses.

Except to blame her.

That was the one thing he could do.

Because she did this to him. She was the one who reduced him to his basest level and his basest needs. She was the one who drove him crazy and made him blind with lust when he needed to be thinking straight.

'There can be no child!'

'My God, do you actually think I want one?'

'Why not? When you're the one who stands to gain the most by prolonging this relationship.'

'You think? Why the hell would I want to prolong spending time with you? No, I'm going home when this is over. A child of yours is hardly the kind of souvenir I want or need to take with me.'

'And if it's already happened? You can't just wish it away.'

'Damn you, Alesander. And whose fault would it be if there was? I *told* you I didn't want to have sex with you. I told you it was the only way to guarantee there could be no complications. But did you listen to me? No. Because Mr Can't-Live-Without-Sex couldn't exercise a bit of self-control.'

'And you haven't enjoyed it? You didn't cry out

in pleasure every time you came? Every time I took you there?'

'And that's relevant, because? You know damned well that I didn't want to have sex with you. You were the one who changed the terms.'

'Terms you agreed to!'

'Only because you threatened to tell Felipe our marriage was a sham if I didn't!'

How else was he supposed to get her to agree? 'You wanted it. You wanted me from that first time in my apartment. Do you think I couldn't smell your need? Do you think I didn't know then and there that you were gagging for it?'

The crack of her palm against his cheek punctuated the argument. For a long moment he said nothing, his nostrils flaring, his eyes like dark—*angry*—pits. 'You never were very good at dealing with the truth.'

She squeezed her eyes shut. Oh God, the truth. What was the truth any more? She'd told so many lies she was beginning to forget where truth ended and the lies began. She'd lied to Felipe every time she saw him and pretended to be happy in her marriage. She'd lied to herself pretending that she didn't want Alesander and then burning up with him at night. And now she was slapping a man she'd only just finished convincing herself that she loved. But there was one indisputable truth that he could not argue with. 'If we are talking truths, then I know of one truth you cannot deny—that if we had kept to the original terms of the contract, if we had never had sex, then we wouldn't be having this conversation now, because the chances of conceiving a baby would never have been an issue.'

Silence reigned between them, letting in the sounds of the vineyard, the rustle of leaves in the breeze and

the cry of seabirds amid the heavy weighted silence
of blame and regret.

'So when will you know?'

She shook her head, dragging in air. 'Three weeks?
Most likely less.' *Hopefully less.* She swallowed, a sick
feeling roiling in her gut. Would he ask her to make
sure? He was a man of the world. He would know
there were options. At least there were in Australia…

'I won't…' she started. 'I can't…'

'That is not our way!' he simply said, putting a full
stop on that particular conversation. 'Three weeks,
you say?'

'It's early in my cycle, which is good…well…it's
better. Safer.'

'*Sí.*' He frowned. 'I can wait that long. And meanwhile I will show you that you are wrong, that I can
exercise control and live without sex.'

She laughed, the sound bitter. 'Don't you think it's
a little late for that?'

Maybe it was, but he could do with the time away
from her. He'd enjoyed her in his bed these past few
weeks, and perhaps he'd enjoyed her too much. Perhaps that was the problem.

Putting distance between them, putting up barriers,
might be the best thing for them. Felipe was growing
weaker—the march of his disease relentless, the damage wrought becoming more apparent by the day. Soon
she'd be going home and there was no point getting
used to having her around.

And he didn't want her getting used to being
around. His women were supposed to be temporary.
That was the way he liked it.

That was the way he'd always liked it.

They were almost back at the cottage when they heard it, a crash followed by a muffled cry.

'Felipe!' she screamed alongside him, suddenly bolting for the door.

'They won't let him come home,' she sniffed, sitting in a hospital waiting room chair, repeating the words the doctor had just delivered. 'I should have been there. I should never have left him.'

'It wouldn't have made any difference. Felipe is ill. His bones are weak. If it didn't happen today, it could have been tomorrow or the next day.'

'But I should have been there.'

He pulled her closer, his arm around her shoulders. 'It's not your fault.'

'Felipe hates hospitals. It will kill him being away from his vines.'

'Simone, he's dying. He's too sick now to be at home. You can't look after him. You can't watch him twenty-four hours a day.'

And she sniffed again and knew that there was nothing he could say or do that would make her feel better. Felipe had needed her and she hadn't been there.

And where she had been and what she'd been doing—oh God—was Felipe to get his wish for a baby after all? Was that to be yet another price she would pay for her lies?

She buried her face in her hands and cried, 'I should have been there.'

Felipe's condition steadily deteriorated after that, the break in his hip ensuring he would stay bed-ridden. Simone spent as much time with him as possible. He had moments of great lucidity, where he would talk about Maria and how they had met and the fiestas where he had courted her.

He had moments of rambling confusion, where he would tumble words in Spanish and Basque and English all together and make no sense at all.

At night Alesander would collect her from the hospital and take her back to the apartment and make sure she ate something before she fell into bed and woke up to do it all over again.

He watched her withdraw into herself, watched the shadows grow under her eyes, watched the haunted look on her features and he marvelled at her strength.

And he ached for her.

God, how he ached for her.

He wanted her so much. He wanted to hold her and hug her and soothe away her pain. He wanted to make love to her and put life and light back into her beautiful blue eyes.

But, true to his word, he did not make a move on her.

He doubted she even noticed, and that made him feel no better.

At night he watched her sleeping, watching the steady rise and fall of her chest, her beautiful face at peace for a few short hours until she woke and the pain of grief and imminent loss returned.

'You don't have to go in every day,' he'd said to her after the first week. 'Have a day to yourself. Relax.'

But she'd shaken her head. 'I have to go,' she'd said. 'I'm all he has. He's all I have.'

And he'd ached for her that she had lost so much in her short life.

And what she hadn't lost, he'd taken.

They'd made a deal, he told himself, a contract, and that made him feel no better at all.

'He's all I have,' she'd said.

And it twisted in his gut that he didn't figure in her deliberations at all. Was there no place for him? Did he mean nothing to her after the months they'd spent together? After the nights when she'd lain so slick with sweat and satisfied in his arms?

Sure, they'd always planned to part and go their separate ways when Felipe died and their contract came to an end. But why should knowing that he meant so little sit so uncomfortably with him?

An ambulance brought Felipe home to die, the two nurses setting up his bed near the window of the cottage where he'd been born so he could look out over the vineyard where he'd lived his entire life. A day, they warned her, she'd have with him. Maybe two at the most.

She spent the first day sitting by his side, talking to him when he was awake enough to listen, about what was going on in the vineyard or about what life was like in Australia. Every now and then she was certain he had taken his last breath, and she would hold her own as he would grow absolutely still, only for the next breath to shudder from the depths of his sunken chest and make her jump. Sometimes his breathing came so fast he could have been running a race. And other times he fidgeted and shifted restlessly, muttering words she couldn't understand.

On the second day she grew more used to the breathing. Or maybe she just grew used to not knowing which might be his final breath. Still she expected his death to come that day.

On the third day she sat alongside the bed, feeling exhausted. He was eating nothing, drinking less, and still he held on. It was killing her watching him—listening to his stop–start breathing and hearing the bubbling gurgle in his chest. She held his hand, talking to him when it seemed he might be awake, sponging his brow when he seemed upset or agitated.

The fidgeting grew worse. Felipe fidgeted with the blanket again, murmuring words she couldn't understand. She touched her hand to his to calm him and chided him gently, 'You're cold, Abuelo. You should put your hands under the blanket.'

One of the nurses took her aside when he had calmed into a sleep and she had risen to stretch her legs. 'It's a sign,' the nurse said. 'His circulation is slowing. His whole body is closing down.'

'But why is it taking so long?' she cried. She didn't want her grandfather to die, but neither did she want to see him suffer. 'And he's so restless at times. He wanted to go quietly in his sleep. Why does he fidget so much?'

The nurse smiled and took her hands. 'Sometimes the living can't let them go. And other times people can't let themselves go. Sometimes there are loose ends or plans left unfinished. Is there anything you know of that he is worried about? Are there loose ends he wanted tied up?'

Simone shook her head. 'I thought he wanted to be reunited with Maria.'

'And there's nothing else he might feel has been left undone?'

She closed her eyes and sighed. Because there was one thing Felipe had wished for.

But there was no chance of that now. Her period had

come the week before. The much anticipated period
that would tell her if her passionate encounter with
Alesander amidst the vines had resulted in a child.

It had not.

She hadn't bothered to tell Alesander and he hadn't
bothered to ask, whether because he'd lost count of the
days or merely lost interest she didn't know. Maybe
because he'd believed her when she'd assured him it
would be okay. Maybe because all he'd ever cared
about was the land and any day now it would be his—
every day brought him closer to his goal.

Whatever, Alesander had stopped caring. He didn't
want to know.

And then, when it all came down to it, Felipe didn't
need to know either.

She looked over at him, shrunken and tormented on
the bed, biting her lip. Would it matter to tell one more
tiny lie? One more on top of all the others?

No, she decided, watching his busy fingers worry
the bedding again.

One more tiny lie would make no difference at all
now.

She sat down beside him, took his cold fingers in
her own and squeezed them gently. 'Abuelo, it's Simone.'

One of the nurses called him, warning him it was
close, and for a while he wondered whether he should
even be there. He'd kept his distance the last few days
she'd been living at the cottage again. Felipe was her
grandfather and after the month they'd had, he wondered if she even wanted him there.

But he couldn't stay away.

She would be leaving soon. Once Felipe died, there

would be no reason for her to stay. She would pack
her things and return to her home and her studies in
Melbourne.

He would probably never see her again.

He needed to see her again before that happened.

Besides, she was about to lose the only person she
cared about in the world. She needed someone to be
there for her.

He wanted that person to be him.

He wanted her to know he was there for her, even
if she didn't care.

He stepped into the tiny cottage, his eyes taking
a few seconds to adjust to the gloom after being outside, and saw Simone sit down next to the bed where
her wizened grandfather lay.

'Abuelo, it's Simone.' She took his cold fingers in
hers, wishing him her warmth.

He muttered something low and hard to understand,
but he was awake and still listening.

'Abuelo, I have some good news.' Tears squeezed
from her eyes at the lie she was about to tell. One more
lie to follow all the others, but maybe this would be the
end of it, she told herself. And if it let him go, maybe
this lie was the most important of all of them. 'You got
your wish, Abuelo. I…I am expecting a baby. And I am
hoping with all my heart it will be a boy because then
we will call him after you. We will name him Felipe.'

'Ah,' the old man said on a gasp, his hand jerking,
tugging her closer as his jaw worked up and down.
'Ah!'

She leaned over him. 'What is it?' she asked.

'Happy,' he gasped. *'Gracias, mi nieta, gracias.'*

The effort almost seemed too much as he sagged
back into the pillows, and she thought he was finished

until she heard his thready voice. 'Maria…Maria is here. I must go to her.'

'*Sí*,' she said, nodding as tears filled her eyes and spilled onto the bedding. 'She has been waiting for you. She will be so happy to see you again.'

How long it was after that she couldn't tell. She only knew that one of the nurses finally touched her on the shoulder. 'He's gone,' she said, and Simone nodded, because she had sensed the exact moment Felipe had gone to join his wife.

It was done.

CHAPTER THIRTEEN

SHE WAS PREGNANT.

Alesander reeled from the room, needing air, blind-sided by Simone's confession to a dying man. She was pregnant and she hadn't even bothered to tell him—*the child's father*—first.

He should be angry.

How long had she known? A few days? A week?

No, not just angry. He should be furious.

This was exactly what he had feared all along, and it was really happening. Their temporary arrangement had suddenly got a whole lot more complicated.

And she hadn't even bothered to tell him.

He turned his face to the sky, into air now as crisp and cool as the Txakolina wine produced from the grapes in these vineyards, searching for answers.

So why wasn't he furious?

Instead he felt almost…relieved.

He breathed out a breath he hadn't realised he'd been holding.

Because she couldn't go home now.

Strange how that idea suddenly seemed so right. He would not let her go. She was bearing their child.

She would have to stay now.

* * *

Felipe was dead.

Strange, how it still took so long to sink in, even when you knew it was true.

Desolate, exhausted, she gently placed her grandfather's hand over his chest and rose from her chair, kissing his snowy whiskered cheeks one final time. 'Goodbye, Abuelo,' she said. 'Sleep tight.'

Numb and bone-weary, she left the bedside chair that had been her home for the last three days. Her back ached, her head hurt and there was a hole where her heart had once been.

Abuelo was dead.

There was nothing for her here now.

Soon she would pack her things and return home. But not even that thought brought her comfort.

'Simone?'

She looked up to see Alesander standing in the doorway and he looked so familiar and strong that for a moment her heart kicked over, as if there was life left in it after all. And then she remembered that he was supposed to mean nothing to her and it died again.

'He's gone,' she said, finally accepting it, and with acceptance came a torrent of tears.

She would have fallen if he hadn't been there to catch her. 'I know,' he said, wrapping his arms around her and pulling her against his chest and he felt both a friend and a stranger. How long since he had held her in his arms like this?

And he felt so good, so solid and warm. He smelled so good. She drank in his scent in greedy heaving gasps, relishing the masculine scent of him while she could, knowing she would miss it when she was gone. He stroked her back until the crying jag finished. 'Come on. I'll take you home.'

Home.

Where was that?

Once upon a time she had been desperate to leave Spain and get back to Melbourne.

But now?

Now she'd fallen in love with a craggy coastline and cerulean sea and with vines that tangled above her head and gave the grapes a view of the sea.

Now she'd fallen in love with a man she had to say goodbye to.

Now she wasn't sure where home really was.

He led her to the car, drove her back to the apartment as day turned to night. He didn't talk while the lift carried them upstairs, he just stood with his arm around her shoulders and never before had she appreciated anyone's silence or support more.

She let him lead her through the darkened apartment to the bedroom with its big wide bed and strip her down to her underwear. There was nothing sexual about the way he touched her. It was like a parent undressing a child before putting them to bed. Gentle. Caring. But with purpose.

She clambered in, almost crying out in pleasure at the bed's welcoming embrace. She'd imagined he'd leave her then to sleep, but a moment later he surprised her by joining her, pulling her into his arms and just holding her close to him. She wasn't worried, he hadn't touched her for the best part of a month.

She felt him press his lips to her head.

She felt…*safe.*

Empty and numb, but safe in this man's embrace. And right now, that meant more than anything.

'Thank you,' she whispered against his chest, the wiry hairs of his chest tickling her lips.

'What for?' he said, his mouth in her hair.

'For just being here.'

He lifted her chin with one hand. In the darkened room she sensed rather than saw his eyes on her, she felt the fan of his breath on her cheek, before he dipped his head and pressed his lips to hers.

No more than a touch of flesh against flesh, and then another, just as brief, but she sighed at the contact, sighing at the memories it stirred inside her, whispers of past kisses like the tendrils on the vines, catching and tugging at her senses.

Oh, how she'd missed his mouth.

How she would miss it when she was gone.

How she would miss him.

She blinked into the darkness, and the darkness didn't matter because it was as if she could see. Suddenly she was aware of the press of her body against his, aware of every place their bodies touched, aware of the stroke of his long-fingered hand over her skin.

Suddenly she was aware of the tension in his body, as if he was holding himself rigid to protect her, so that he could comfort her.

And numbness turned to life as comfort turned to need.

Tomorrow she would have to make plans. There was a funeral to be arranged. There would have to be papers signed and transferred. She would have to make arrangements to return home.

But that was tomorrow.

First, there was tonight.

Maybe their last night?

'Alesander?' she whispered, her toes brushing his

shin, her breasts tight and aching in her bra and a pooling heat growing in her belly.

'Yes?'

She tilted her head higher, found his lips with hers and whispered over them the words, 'Kiss me again.'

He made a sound, strangled and thick in the back of his throat, even as he pulled her closer to him. 'If I do—'

'I know,' she said, smoothing her hand down the long gentle slide of his back, to the small of his back and the curve of his behind, memorizing him through her skin. 'I need it. I need to feel alive.'

She didn't have to ask him twice. His mouth took hers, warm and real and alive, and she drank in his taste and his heat, as welcoming as the mattress beneath her, while his hands tangled in her hair or swept down the length of her, his touch so sweet—so missed—it made her cry into his mouth.

Then he lifted his head. 'Are you sure it's all right?' he asked, and she thought how sweet he was to ask, as if finally she mattered, not just the sex.

'It's perfect.'

He did not rush. It was not like that heated encounter in the vineyard. He took his time reacquainting himself with her body, noticing the places where her flesh dipped lower or her hip bones jutted higher. She'd lost weight while she'd looked after Felipe, he could tell. He would see that she ate from now on. She would have to eat.

He slipped off her bra and her sigh sounded like thanks. He cupped her perfect breast in his hand and she whimpered with need.

'You're beautiful,' he told her as he lifted himself over her, not knowing how he could have let her alone for so long; promising himself he never would again, knowing he would never have to.

She opened herself to him and his fingers found her slick and wet for him. She cried out as his thumb teased her sensitive nub, arching on the bed. He should linger there, he knew. He should take his time and pleasure her properly and he would.

Next time.

This time he knew what she wanted.

He didn't reach for a condom. He didn't need one. She was pregnant already, with his child in her belly.

He stroked the flat of his hand over her mound, over that belly, over one perfect breast that would feed his child, while he steadied his swaying erection with the other, finding her centre, finding her hot and slick and oh, so sweet.

And, oh God, he thought as he entered her in one long thrust, and she angled her hips to meet him, so welcoming.

He kissed her then, in that exquisite moment of joining, making love to her mouth while buried to the hilt inside her.

It was mind-shattering.

And then he moved and it got better.

He groaned. He would not last. It had been a long time. Too long. And her needy cries and hungry fingers on his skin told him she needed this as much as he did.

Maybe more.

She moved both with him and against him, tight and hot around him, and so perfect he wanted to control it and stay this way for ever.

His traitorous body wouldn't let him, the slip and

slide of flesh against flesh compelling and urgent and unable to be withstood.

And when she came apart around him, any last shred of control was blown away in the fallout.

With a cry he unleashed himself inside her, pumping into her perfect body as her muscles tightened around him and urged him on.

Spent, he rolled off her, tucking her close against him as ragged breathing eased and their bodies calmed. He kissed her hair and she nestled into him.

'Thank you,' she whispered and he kissed her on the head again. He lay like that in the dark, listening as her breathing steadied and feeling her body relax as she slipped inexorably towards sleep.

How had they come to this place, he wondered, where he was so comfortable with her staying—where he was comfortable with the concept of her having his child?

Where he was happy with it?

When had the change occurred?

And why?

He had no answers as the woman beside him slumbered in his arms. Maybe tomorrow, with the cool clear light of a new day, it would make more sense.

Already he looked forward to the morning, but for more reasons than that alone. Because come the new day the woman beside him would awaken and they would have sex again. Come the new day she might be feeling better and more in the mood for talking.

Surely then she would remember to tell him about the baby.

CHAPTER FOURTEEN

SHE WOKE IN his arms feeling sad, but better than she had in weeks. Warm, cossetted and maybe even a little loved. For it would be nice to think Alesander loved her, just a little, after she was gone. Because last night had proved one thing to her, and that was that she loved him.

He'd helped her feel alive when all she'd felt was numb. He'd shown her that after death, life went on. He'd given her a gift of life-affirming sex gift-wrapped in his tenderness, and she loved him all the more for it.

Leaving him would kill her, but she would have the memory of their lovemaking to keep her warm at night.

She woke wanting to make love again, knowing there would not be many more times, but he gently put her away, kissing her on the forehead and telling her that he didn't want her to overdo it, and he would make breakfast for her. Confused and a little hurt, she wondered if already he was withdrawing, in preparation for her leaving.

Then, all during breakfast—while she sat and ate the omelette he'd insisted on making for her—he seemed to be watching her, almost as if he were waiting for something. Was it that she was leaving or did he worry she might suddenly collapse in a heap again? Was that the reason for his sudden care?

'Is something wrong?' she asked, putting down her knife and fork when she caught him looking sideways at her again.

'I don't know,' he said disingenuously. 'I just wondered if there's something you wanted to tell me.'

She blinked. 'Like what?'

'Oh, who can say?' he said, the corners of his mouth turning up. 'Can you think of anything you might be keeping from me that maybe you should share? That I might be interested in hearing? A secret, perhaps?'

A chill descended her spine.

Surely he couldn't know.

Not that. There was no way he could know that.

They'd barely spoken in the last month and she hadn't said anything last night in the depths of passion. *Had she?* 'I don't have any secrets.'

'None? Nothing at all to tell me?'

Nothing that you would want to hear.

'I can understand you might be nervous about telling me,' he said, and all the while she was thinking, *He knows.* 'I know I've warned you enough times, but I'd like to think our relationship has changed. I don't want you to think there is anything you can't share with me.'

She swallowed, both nervous and excited in case it meant he felt the same way. Could it be possible? Had Alesander fallen in love with her too? The way he had treated her last night made her want to believe it. And the way he was looking at her now made her think it might even be possible.

He took her hand in his and squeezed it gently. 'You don't have to be nervous,' he prompted. 'You can tell me.'

'Well,' she said, her heart hammering in her chest, trying to find the courage to tell him the truth. 'Maybe there is one thing.'

He smiled encouragingly. 'I thought so. What is it?'

His fingers were warm and reassuring around her hand, his eyes dark with promise and so she relaxed and smiled. 'Then I guess it's time you knew. Alesander, I love you.'

A blank stare met her confession. 'What?'

He shook his head. 'Isn't there something else? I thought you were going to tell me about the baby. When were you going to tell me about the baby?'

'The baby? There is no baby.'

He dropped her hand. 'But I heard you tell Felipe…'

Oh God. And she had just told him that she loved him. 'You were there?'

'Of course I was there. The nurses called me—told me it was close. And I heard you. You told Felipe you were pregnant, that we were having a child. You told him you were going to call it Felipe. I heard you!'

'Alesander…' she swallowed '…you have to understand—'

He spun out of his chair, strode away across the room, raking the fingers of one hand through his hair, his other on his hip. 'Damn it, you said it. Why the hell would you do that if it wasn't true?'

'Because it's what Felipe wanted to hear. It's what he needed to hear!'

'Felipe could barely hear you let alone understand that!'

'No, listen to me, that day in the vineyard, the day he fell—he told me that day that it was his greatest wish that there be news of a child before he died. He wanted to know his family would go on after he died.'

'But that was the day—'

'I know.'

'We had unprotected sex that day. And you said nothing since. And when you told Felipe that you were having a baby, I thought…I thought.'

'I'm sorry. My period came last week. I didn't tell you. We were barely talking and I didn't think you cared.'

No baby.

He strode aimlessly to the windows and stared blankly out of them.

She'd got her period.

She wasn't pregnant.

She'd thought he didn't care.

Why did he?

He'd tried not to. For the best part of a month he'd pretended he didn't care, but when he'd heard her tell Felipe that she was pregnant and realised that meant she would have to stay, he'd learned that he did care, more than he'd thought possible.

But no baby.

No child.

No son.

And that last grated more than the rest. He spun around. 'Do you ever tell the truth?'

'Alesander,' she appealed, 'please—'

'You've been spinning lies from the moment you arrived.'

'Yes, I've lied! All the time I've been here, I've been lying to Felipe and I hated myself for it, but there was a reason why I lied—good reason. Felipe was able to die happy because of those lies.'

'You probably don't even know how to tell the truth.'

'I told you the truth.'

'I don't think you're capable of it.'

'Alesander,' she said more firmly. 'I told you the truth.'

'But you said—'

'I said I love you.'

His eyes shuttered closed, his mind reeling back through their conversation. And she had said that, but he'd been blindsided by the words she hadn't said, by the words he'd been expecting, the words he'd grown used to since he'd first heard her utter them.

He hadn't had time to process these new ones.

'It was the truth. It is the truth. I'm only sorry it wasn't the truth you were wanting to hear.'

And they weren't the words he'd been expecting to hear, true.

But there was something in them, something that didn't bother him as much as he might have thought.

Something that resonated with him.

He didn't want her to go. He'd thought a baby would keep her here. He'd been devastated to know she wasn't pregnant, that she'd lied for Felipe when he'd wanted her words to be true.

There was no baby, but if she loved him, maybe there was a chance she still might stay.

'Do you have to go home to Australia?'

'What?'

'I know you have your studies to return to, but do you have to go? We have universities in Spain, after all. You could study here, finish your studies, improve your Spanish at the same time.'

Her heart leapt. What was he saying? She bit her lip, trying desperately not to read too much into his questions. There had been too many misunderstandings between them, too many times they had misunderstood each other and let each other down. 'Alesander?'

'Because if you do not need to leave, perhaps you could stay here, with me.'

'Even though I'm not pregnant?'

'Who says you're not? We had unprotected sex last night. I didn't think I needed to bother with a condom, under the circumstances. Only now I find the circumstances have changed and that perhaps you might be pregnant after all.'

'Oh.' Her heart sank. She'd been right not to get too excited. 'Oh, and you want me to wait. In case this time there's a baby.'

'Yes, of course I want any child of mine. But I want you too. I did not know that at first. I was determined to keep you here and when I heard that you were pregnant, it gave me a reason to make you stay. Because I want you here with me. Because I love you, Simone…'

She blinked.

'What did you say?'

'I said I love you. And I want you to stay. And we'll have unprotected sex as many times as it takes if it means you will.'

'Alesander…'

'I know I have not been easy to live with. I know I have treated you badly and that I have no right to ask for your love.'

Her heart was beating so fast it was all but tripping over itself, her smile was so wide it hurt and still she couldn't stop. 'You always told me not to make the mistake of thinking you were nice.'

'I am not nice. I am the first to admit it. But I will also admit that I am in love with you. Will you stay here in Spain with me, Simone? Will you stay and be my real wife and be the mother of my children? Will you stay and bear a son named Felipe and honour the memory of your grandfather? What do you say?'

'Oh yes,' she cried, her heart bursting with happiness. 'I say yes. I love you, Alesander, I love you so very much.'

And he smiled and took her into his arms and kissed her until she was giddy with joy.

'I love you too. I will always love you.'

EPILOGUE

SIMONE ESQUIVEL WENT into labour nine months later, on a warm autumn night where the vine leaves rustled on the breeze up the trellised slopes and where the wine grapes grew fat on the view over the spectacular coastline.

It was exactly one year since the day she'd arrived on Alesander's doorstep and delivered her crazy proposal, a year that had changed like the seasons, and been filled with despair and loss, and hope and renewal.

And like the vines themselves, ancient and strong and with roots eighty feet deep, love had featured through it all.

Alesander was more nervous than Simone, fussing and fretting as he tried to manoeuvre her into first the car, and then into the hospital, as if he were trying to herd the sheep that grazed between the vines.

And when Simone refused to be herded and told him to calm down, he tried to herd the staff instead, barking out orders and demands so that nobody was in any doubt that the Esquivel baby was arriving tonight.

He held her hand while she laboured and fretted, and barked orders some more. He sponged her brow and moistened her lips and rubbed her back when she needed him to. And when their baby was born he watched in wonder and awe at this strong woman who he loved deliver him a son.

'You didn't lie to him,' he said later, as he sat by her side, his finger given over to the clutches of their tiny child, clearly besotted by their new son.

She must have looked as if she didn't understand.

'To Felipe. That last time you spoke to him before he died. You told him the truth. You told him you were having a baby and that you would have a son and we would name him Felipe.

'Don't you see,' he said, 'our baby was conceived that night. You spoke the truth.'

She smiled at him, this man who was her husband, who she had married to make an old man happy but who had given her his heart and this child and who now was giving her yet another precious gift.

'Thank you,' she said. 'Did I ever tell you I loved you, Alesander Esquivel?'

'You did,' he told her, 'but I didn't believe you then.' He leaned over the child they had made and kissed her ever so preciously on the lips.

'But I'll never doubt you again.'

* * * * *

LET'S TALK
Romance

For exclusive extracts, competitions
and special offers, find us online:

f facebook.com/millsandboon

t @MillsandBoon

o @MillsandBoonUK

Get in touch on 01413 063232

For all the latest titles coming soon, visit
millsandboon.co.uk/nextmonth

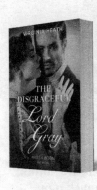  

MILLS & BOON

THE HEART OF ROMANCE

A ROMANCE FOR EVERY KIND OF READER

MODERN

Prepare to be swept off your feet by sophisticated, sexy and seductive heroes, in some of the world's most glamourous and romantic locations, where power and passion collide.
8 stories per month.

HISTORICAL

Escape with historical heroes from time gone by. Whether your passion is for wicked Regency Rakes, muscled Vikings or rugged Highlanders, awaken the romance of the past.
6 stories per month.

MEDICAL

Set your pulse racing with dedicated, delectable doctors in the high-pressure world of medicine, where emotions run high and passion, comfort and love are the best medicine.
6 stories per month.

True Love

Celebrate true love with tender stories of heartfelt romance, from the rush of falling in love to the joy a new baby can bring, and a focus on the emotional heart of a relationship.
8 stories per month.

Desire

Indulge in secrets and scandal, intense drama and plenty of sizzling hot action with powerful and passionate heroes who have it all: wealth, status, good looks…everything but the right woman.
6 stories per month.

HEROES

Experience all the excitement of a gripping thriller, with an intense romance at its heart. Resourceful, true-to-life women and strong, fearless men face danger and desire - a killer combination!
8 stories per month.

DARE

Sensual love stories featuring smart, sassy heroines you'd want as a best friend, and compelling intense heroes who are worthy of them.
4 stories per month.

To see which titles are coming soon, please visit

millsandboon.co.uk/nextmonth

JOIN US ON SOCIAL MEDIA!

Stay up to date with our latest releases, author news and gossip, special offers and discounts, and all the behind-the-scenes action from Mills & Boon...

 millsandboon

 millsandboonuk

 millsandboon

It might just be true love...

MILLS & BOON
MEDICAL
Pulse-Racing Passion

Set your pulse racing with dedicated, delectable doctors in the high-pressure world of medicine, where emotions run high and passion, comfort and love are the best medicine.

MILLS & BOON
True Love
Romance from the Heart

Celebrate true love with tender stories of heartfelt romance, from the rush of falling in love to the joy a new baby can bring, and a focus on the emotional heart of a relationship.

MILLS & BOON

MODERN

Power and Passion

Prepare to be swept off your feet by sophisticated, sexy and seductive heroes, in some of the world's most glamourous and romantic locations, where power and passion collide.